Praise for Tom Wilson

"Tom Wilson is every bit as good as Coonts, Brown, and Clancy." —Colonel Glenn Davis, USAF

"A knowledgeable writer and combat flier, [Tom Wilson] was there and tells the real story."
—Mark Berent, author of *Rolling Thunder*

"Leaves the reader filled with admiration for Tom Wilson's powers of description."
—Barrett Tillman, author of
Warriors and *The Sixth Battle*

"Gripping . . . grucsome . . . graphic . . . abounds with bullet-zinging action and narrow escapes. . . . Wilson writes with authority." —*Publishers Weekly*

Don't miss Tom Wilson's other novels featuring Link Anderson

Black Wolf . . . Introducing Link Anderson—Native American pilot, Gulf War veteran, and top-secret aviation operative . . .

Final Thunder . . . Anderson protects plane-crash survivors in the wilds of Utah from the worst of nature—and man . . .

Desert Fury . . . A rogue FBI agent becomes Anderson's target in a hunt-and-destroy face-off in the Nevada desert . . .

Black Canyon . . . Anderson tracks a criminal into the Colorado mountains—where a final act of vengeance is ready to explode . . .

Black Sky . . . The FBI is prevented from investigating a murder among the Manido-Ojibwe tribe. But it can't stop Link Anderson . . .

This is Tom Wilson's ninth novel, his sixth techno-adventure thriller featuring Link Anderson. His works include

Termite Hill

Lucky's Bridge

Tango Uniform

*Black Wolf**

*Final Thunder**

*Desert Fury**

*Black Canyon**

*Black Sky**

*Black Serpent**

* Published by New American Library

BLACK SERPENT

Tom Wilson

AN ONYX BOOK

ONYX
Published by New American Library, a division of
Penguin Group (USA) Inc., 375 Hudson Street,
New York, New York 10014, USA
Penguin Group (Canada), 10 Alcorn Avenue, Toronto,
Ontario M4V 3B2, Canada (a division of Pearson Penguin Canada Inc.)
Penguin Books Ltd., 80 Strand, London WC2R 0RL, England
Penguin Ireland, 25 St. Stephen's Green, Dublin 2,
Ireland (a division of Penguin Books Ltd.)
Penguin Group (Australia), 250 Camberwell Road, Camberwell, Victoria 3124,
Australia (a division of Pearson Australia Group Pty. Ltd.)
Penguin Books India Pvt. Ltd., 11 Community Centre, Panchsheel Park,
New Delhi - 110 017, India
Penguin Group (NZ), cnr Airborne and Rosedale Roads, Albany,
Auckland 1310, New Zealand (a division of Pearson New Zealand Ltd.)
Penguin Books (South Africa) (Pty.) Ltd., 24 Sturdee Avenue,
Rosebank, Johannesburg 2196, South Africa

Penguin Books Ltd., Registered Offices:
80 Strand, London WC2R 0RL, England

First published by Onyx, an imprint of New American Library,
a division of Penguin Group (USA) Inc.

First Printing, February 2005
10 9 8 7 6 5 4 3 2 1

This one's for the hardworking, often-maligned, and seldom-rewarded uniformed law enforcement officers. I thank you. Without your watchfulness and protection, chaos.

ACKNOWLEDGMENTS

There's probably a law of some kind that either Murphy or his wife wrote down that goes like this: "If something can go wrong, it will—and if given the chance, it will continue going wrong until something worse takes its place." If so, I have been that law's poster child.

A decade ago my son Chris (now a prosecuting attorney in Reno, then an undergrad student of history) became interested in a legend about a group of blood-thirsty pirates who had preyed on gold-laden vessels plying the redwood coast of Northern California. Since I'd lived there as a youth (and knew the secret handshake of being a local), I was drawn to the region like a moth. "What if those pirates still existed?"

In 2001, I submitted an outline of an adventure thriller about domestic terrorism to my agent (Ethan Ellenberg) and editor at New American Library (Ron Martirano), two professional bookmen whom I've learned to trust. The proposal opened with terrorists downing an airliner and attacking a New York City skyscraper. The hero's close friend was taken, and the terrorists left baffling, misleading clues.

Following the 9/11 disaster (and listening to hairy accounts by Ethan, who lived too close to Ground Zero for my liking, and Ron, who watched it all as he walked to work) I volunteered my services to a group of patriots offering suggestions to help secure the country while the Office of Homeland Security was pasted together. I studied Middle East terrorist groups, especially Al Qaeda ("the Base") and Hezbollah ("Party of God," or Islamic Jihad). Talk about wackos! Naturally the War Against

Terrorism and military action in Afghanistan dictated changes to the book's plot, so I started over from the beginning.

While visiting my son in Reno, I was rushed to the emergency room and spent ten days in isolation with two strains of pneumonia that attacked, one following the other. As I was on my back, I changed the plot—melding the original one with a new political reality—and met my lovely wife, Rebecca.

The following month, back at home in Texas, my dentist, Gayle Fletcher (an unrepentant USN submariner who has the look of a fireplug), was chiseling away on my bridgework as he discussed the physiology of deep diving, and a U.S. Deep Submergence Research Vessel called the *NR-1*. I almost let the anecdote go by—when, *bingo*, another of my problems with the plot was solved! I followed him into his office, my mouth still numbed, and we talked for an hour about the DSRV. Gayle even pulled up a couple of articles on the Internet and printed them for me.

The week that Operation Iraqi Freedom kicked off, my old practice of pulling 8 g's in air force fighters caught up with me, and a superb young neurosurgeon named Christian Fras replaced the C-4/C-5 disc in my neck with bone from a cadaver. As always, I was inquisitive. During each visit, he explained more about such medical procedures, as did my friend Dr. Phillip Steeves (whose life story is so incredible that I've included a sampling in this book). Unlike his counterpart's fate in these pages, Phil humors himself by visiting places like the North Pole. (He once wintered at the South Pole.)

Despite pain that was often intense, I continued working on the novel.

Warning to authors! Much of the storyline, written in a fog of painkillers, made absolutely no sense. What was I *thinking*?

Shielded from the outside world by Rebecca, I rewrote the novel from first to last. Finally I submitted this manuscript. Senior Editor Dan Slater at NAL took on the task of smoothing rough edges and making it better still. Production Editor Sally Franklin shepherded the manuscript through the publishing process, and copy editor Eliani Torres made sense of my sometimes puzzling prose *in two languages*. Finally the art, composition and layout artists spiffed it up so the book distributors and booksellers could offer this once-humble effort to you lucky readers.

Thanks to all of you who pitched in and made this book possible. Any deviations from fact are my own— some to misguide anyone foolish enough to attack us again, others for the sake of the story.

I like it. Once again, my world is good.

Prologue

Augustus P. Shepherd watched critically as the fore-and-aft coastwise schooner dropped anchor in ocean swells two hundred yards from shore. There was no harbor offering protection from the punishing elements of the Pacific, only the gently curved beach from which the coastal community a few miles south of the Oregon Territory border drew its name. While the townsmen contemplated building a pier that would extend well beyond the surf, present ships' captains simply gritted their teeth and ventured into the shallows as far as their gut told them could safely be done. Livestock were disembarked over the side, often with their owners, to wade ashore. Other passengers were given the option of waiting and being transported to the beach in rowboats along with freight and mail.

Augustus was reed thin and runty, and he appeared smaller yet due to his tendency to bow his head to peer over pince-nez eyeglasses. Since the lenses were improperly ground, wearing them presented a dilemma: When he looked through them for too long, he developed a headache. Without them, the world was indistinct. Regardless of task or situation, he wore a brown suit cut from sturdy upland wool, since that material was scientifically proved to be healthful. He carried a .30-caliber rotating-barrel pistol in a coat pocket, loaded with four paper cartridges and lead balls. At either side rested a sealed, heavy bag filled with gold dust and pea nuggets.

Transporting two identical bags of fortune was Mr.

John Grogan, a senior company's officer of stern demeanor, who was prepared for any trouble that might arise. Not only did he wear a brace of large-bore horse pistols in his belt, but the handle of a James Bowie fighting knife protruded from his coat front, and he cradled an 8-gauge blunderbuss, as well. Mr. Grogan had hardly slept since leaving their encampment on the Jedediah Smith River. There was warning that gangs of Australian thieves—called *owlhoots* because of their surreptitious night signals—had been chased northward from the High Sierra goldfields. There were also rumors of pirates who lured ships onto the rocks of the Northern California coast, and of bloodthirsty savage Indians who had learned the value of gold.

Still, their trip was of necessity. Wherever gold seekers discovered color, trading towns were hastily erected to offer everything from sail-cloth trousers to female companionship. Crescent City was such a place—vibrant, but without amenities such as a reliable banking facility. Any merchant worth his salt could heft and estimate a poke's weight within half an ounce, and the general store, two saloons, and the lone soiled dove readily accepted gold as currency. But if a miner sought fairness, he took his color down-coast to Eureka, San Francisco, or Monterey, where it could be properly assayed and banked.

"Ain't much to look at," growled Grogan, regarding the schooner and her captain, who displayed a slate board for the perusal of the group on the beach: San Frasisko, 5 days.

"It is already heavily laden," Augustus Shepherd commented, indicating the way the schooner wallowed and the number of people who were crowded aboard. The man was prone to bouts of mal de mer, and he wore an ashen pallor just at the thought of boarding the craft.

"We shall take it," Grogan decided. "It may be days before the next southbound ship stops here, and the weather may turn."

A storm was unlikely. Augustus had noted the atmospheric pressure with a weatherglass and found it was rising. Unfortunately, Mr. Grogan placed no faith in such devices. He raised his cap and waved it spiritedly at the schooner's captain. A moment later, a rowboat was

being prepared to retrieve them. Augustus did not argue,
for Mr. Grogan was second in command of their company of thirty-one miners, and he was only sixth in line.
As scientific officer, he determined how they'd channel
the hydraulics and where to set up the sluices and dig
for ore. Thus far, they'd encountered only casual deposits washed there by flooding, yet by following his coun-
sel, their take was more than that of most companies in
the region, and Augustus remained confident that he
would sniff out a proper concentration to make them
all wealthy.

He'd assured his wife of that prospect before leaving
her and their four children at her parents' farm near Sea
Ford, Virginia, on the York. Three years, he had told
her. No more. There were nineteen months remaining
in his bargain. With his knowledge of earth sciences, he
felt sure he'd return East with considerable riches, and
fame as well when he published the methods he used to
find gold. After claiming his own fortune, he did not see
why he should not share his secrets.

Upon arrival in San Francisco City, Mr. Grogan would
deposit their riches into the Bank of California, and forward a draft for half the sum to the bursar of the American Society of Exploration, in the city of New York,
whose wise members had provided their financial backing. Augustus would include his daily journal entries.
The pages would be received with enthusiasm and undoubtedly be included in their quarterly gazette. After
a look about the town of San Francisco, that had grown
into a metropolis since they'd last seen it, he would assist
Mr. Grogan in the purchase of supplies before they returned northward.

Augustus noted two other armed miners on the beach,
guarding their own sturdy bag. Undoubtedly they transported their winter's profit. He hoped there were not
many in their company to share such a meager amount.

A man ambled up, rotund as a pear and wearing a
worn mariner's peacoat. A hatchet nose thrust boldly
from his face, but the harshness of his appearance was
tempered by the sight of a well-thumbed Bible clutched
to his breast, and by the fact that he was unarmed.

"Not the finest vessel I have rested these eyes upon,"

the plump man said in cordial manner. His voice was sonorous, and he beamed as happily as a cherub.

"I, too, have seen more seaworthy craft," Augustus offered, wondering if they might convince Mr. Grogan to await a larger, better-equipped ship.

"Ye appear to be ill already, sir." The fat man rolled his eyes. "Stand to a rail handily once we board, and I shall give proper berth so I shan't be caught in the torrent."

Those standing nearby chuckled. Even Mr. Grogan was relaxing, since the threat from owlhoots and savage Indians would soon be past.

"Me name's Bull," said the plump newcomer. "Jack Bull."

When they'd introduced themselves, Mr. Grogan asked him, "You are a gold seeker?"

"Although I often be tempted to join that endeavor, I'm a humble man of the cloth, sent by me church to tend to heathen where I may find them. Are ye baptized, sir?"

Mr. John Grogan drew himself up. "Certainly. I am Episcopalian."

"Then God bless ye, for me toil is great just dealin' with Walking Elk's unholy kin." He nodded at a heavy-chested Indian whose face and body were covered with swirls of dark tattoos. They'd been warned that tattooing was a sign of murderous intent in the local savages; thus, his proximity was unsettling. As Mr. John Grogan's countenance clouded with suspicion, Jack Bull explained that Walking Elk had been converted from savagery to Christianity.

"Huzzah!" Walking Elk intoned at the mention of the word.

"Display yer piety!" Jack Bull demanded of the aborigine.

"My farter who'rt in heffen," Walking Elk began, and recited a semblance of the Lord's Prayer. When he finished, the men about him said their amens and went back to examining the rowboat that was plying toward them.

"We must hurry," called out the man at the oars. "The tide's about to turn."

The fare was thrice as dear as it should have been, an example of California's extravagant prices. Since the schooner was loaded to capacity, all but a few passengers would remain on deck for the voyage. Boarding was carefully done to allow for transfer of the gold, and half an hour had passed before a pair of seamen used the rowboat to tow the schooner to safer water. The captain shouted orders; then the sails were raised, and they were soon tacking seaward before a quartering wind.

As Mr. Grogan stood vigil near their gold, now secured in a padlocked bin, Augustus opened his journal to make the morning's entries. Jack Bull stared over his shoulder, seemingly interested. "And what might that be, Mr. Shepherd?"

Augustus explained how the events he recorded would appear in the American Society of Exploration's gazette, providing an eternal history of their expedition. Jack Bull seemed impressed—even Walking Elk appeared attentive—so Augustus related how his writing had been published in *Scientific American* magazine. His subject had been a clarification of Mariotte's law of gaseous behaviors. He'd described how pneumatics would soon revolutionize civilization, and that the editor had shared his enthusiasm.

"This will be known as the century of pneumatics," Augustus proclaimed happily, "and by that I do not mean merely steam power. Goods, even human passengers, will be placed in large cylinders and transported in great tubes. As vacuum pumps are improved, I foresee a transcontinental network of tubes. Eventually one shall cross under the Atlantic."

"I see," said Jack Bull, although he obviously did not. He walked on, followed by his tamed Indian. Augustus had hoped to forget his seasickness by engaging in a lively discussion of his theories. He felt the churning within his stomach and hurried to the rail.

A woman of uncommon beauty appeared from below, and two men nearby entered a discussion of the wealthy English newlyweds who had left their party in Victoria, capital of the Crown colony of Vancouver Island, to observe the California goldfields. Their side-wheeler had run aground at Astoria, and they'd transferred to this tub. A Jamaican manservant who stayed on deck with the miners had explained that thus far they were unimpressed.

The groom, a tall man with a royal British nose, came topside, noted the men gawking at his wife, and cursed them for their boorishness. When told that beautiful women were a rarity in California, he asked if American females were as ugly as the men were rude. If Augustus had but known what was to befall the fop, he might have been more charitable in his estimation.

He clutched the rail and forgot about all as he spewed forth. By afternoon he'd emptied his stomach, yet he remained just as ill when Mr. Jack Bull approached again, Walking Elk not far behind. "Ah, Mr. Shepherd. I see ye're workin' on yer journal despite yer sickness."

"I am an organized man, sir."

Jack Bull pointed out ocean swells off to their leeward. "Beyond be the entrance to Humboldt Bay. 'Tis fortunate for yer stomach we're not venturing there. The captain says there's no need, since we have a full load."

Augustus received the news with mixed feelings. He'd seriously been considering debarking in Eureka. On the other hand, the voyage would now be shortened.

When darkness descended, it brought Augustus little rest. Each time he curled up to sleep, the sickness threatened, and he'd rise and hurry to the rail. After several such trips, stumbling over prone passengers, he found a niche near the prow where his restlessness would bother no one. During the miserable night he slept fitfully, waking often.

As dawn approached, Augustus lay exhausted, staring at the shoreline with grainy vision. A few miles ahead, a fire flickered on the shore, and he wondered who had built it. He'd known of no one interested in the place where it constantly rained, where giant grizzled bears lurked, and earth tremors shook the giant cypress until they flung widow-makers large enough to crush a dozen men. Three years earlier, the Josiah Gregg expedition had tried to map that wilderness and perished almost to a man. Neither had there been any report of finding a single ounce of gold.

Too tired to concern himself further with the fire builders, he finally dropped off into slumber, and soon dreamt
of sinners crying out as they tumbled into fiery Hades.

A particularly shrill scream interrupted his sleep. Augustus shook his groggy head, then fumbled in his pockets for the eyeglasses and found them missing. He gained
his feet and squinted at a man's shadow approaching in
the meager dawn's light and discovered it was Mr. John
Grogan, staggering and clutching the hasp of his James
Bowie knife that skewered his own belly. He fell to the
deck only three feet distant, dead as a stone.

Augustus tried to walk but found the deck was awash
with blood. He stared with disbelief at indistinct images.
The Indian named Walking Elk held a man by the throat
as he swung a heavy hand-ax to lop off half his skull.
The savage then dragged the convulsing body to the
side, hoisted, and cast it overboard. A crewman painfully
pulled himself along the deck; the savage followed and
sank the ax blade so deeply into the sailor's spine that
he had trouble dislodging the blade. He lifted that victim
over the rail, as well, and went in search for more.

Augustus gaped about. The Englishwoman sat
spraddle-legged in a pond of blood, cradling her servant's head in the lap of her nightgown, trying to succor
him as he feebly waved the stubs of his arms, severed
at the elbows by Walking Elk's hatchet.

"Look lively," came Jack Bull's sonorous voice, "and
bring her about." He stood at the tiller bar, waving one
of Mr. John Grogan's horse pistols at the two remaining
crewmen who feverishly manned the sail lines.

As the schooner leaned into the turn, Walking Elk
pulled the servant from the woman's arms and dragged
him to the rail.

"But he's alive!" she cried.

"Not for long, I think," reasoned Jack Bull as the
Indian flung the man into the sea.

Walking Elk returned, bent over the young bride, and
thrust his tattooed face into hers. When she fainted away,
he laughed with obvious glee. Aside from the woman and
her husband, there were no other passengers. As Augustus
had slumbered in the arms of Morpheus, Jack Bull and his
"converted" Indian had slain them all. Their efficacy was

astounding, for there had been some twenty victims, most of them sturdy workingmen.

Augustus considered slipping overboard to strike out for the shore, perhaps taking a floating object, since it was three or four miles distant and the rocks so dangerous.

Beside the Englishwoman, the bridegroom cringed as Walking Elk pulled her sleeping gown up and knotted it above her head, exposing her white body. He lowered his trousers, his intent obvious, and Augustus was filled with loathing both for him and the cowardly husband. He tried to ignore what was happening a few feet away, where the woman came to and found her legs held wide, her arms and vision restricted. As the savage rutted, she cried out with each of his harsh grunts.

Augustus remembered then. The pistol. As he fumbled for it, first in one pocket and then the other, Walking Elk continued to labor. After a while he rose with a pleased expression, and as the bride thrashed to free herself, he motioned to Augustus.

"He's invitin' ye for a frolic," said Jack Bull. "Ye'll see, he treats his slaves well."

"May you both rot in hell!" Augustus cried, continuing to search his pockets.

Jack Bull roared with laughter. "Ah, Foolish Gus. We lifted yer pistol. Yer spectacles, as well, for Walking Elk did not wish them broke before we get ye home to the Weeping Tree."

The Indian motioned impatiently with the bloody hatchet, and Augustus could stand no more. Despite his sure death, he cried out and rushed forth to deal with the savage.

He was smote hard for his effort, and fell to the deck, stunned.

Morning, May 13, 1853—Area near Cape Mendocino

A light morning rain fell. Augustus awoke slowly, feeling a tender egg at the side of his temple. He managed to roll over, then to rise onto all fours. It would be impossible to stand, for the schooner was wallowing and proceeding ahead on light sails. The woman and her husband were no longer where they'd lain. Walking Elk stood near the tiller where he and Jack Bull looked into the mist as if expecting to see something.

Questions rushed through the aching head of Augustus P. Shepherd: *Why have I been spared? Where are we bound?*

He squinted through fuzzy vision as they passed near a towering stone formation that jutted from the water between the schooner and the dangerous shore. Jack Bull guided the small ship handily, tacking back and forth outside the stone as he and Walking Elk scanned the roiling sea, looking for something as if the water itself held the answer. Augustus heard the words *marea muerte*, and he recognized only the last one—*muerte* was Spanish for "death"!

Jack Bull called out casually: "If it were me own choice, ye'd be as dead as your partner, Foolish Gus. But Walking Elk is our *jefe*, and his word be our law or our death. Good for you that he admires your journal-keeping. Ye'll write about our past and what's happening today and what might happen tomorry, and ye'll tot up our treasures so none of our thievin' lot can cheat."

Walking Elk obviously understood English, for as Jack Bull spoke, he nodded his agreement, wiping his steel hatchet with a rag that had been the woman's gown.

Augustus waved at the deck where the couple had lain. "And what of them?"

Jack Bull shrugged. "I fancied the woman, but El Jefe had first choice, as is his right."

"You'd have taken her as your wife?"

"No, Foolish Gus. I'd've taken her as a slave for a while, and when I tired of her, traded her for a good cigar or sent her to the stone from which ye don't come back."

"Kill her, like he did?"

"Aye. That's in store for the crew there, as well, after they haul the gold to our home."

Augustus felt outraged. "You'll be tracked down and hanged."

Jack gave him a droll look. "We, Foolish Gus, *we!* Ye're one of us now. But they've not hanged us yet. We Serpientes have ruled this sea and our valley for longer than yer country has existed. We answer to no law but our own. That be your task for El Jefe, to record all of that."

The Indian interrupted with words that were at first incomprehensible, but which Augustus would remember for the remainder of his life: *marea de la muerte*.

Bull's response was immediate. "Aye, I see it, Jefe. Once more around?"

"Now," Walking Elk said firmly, studying the restless water.

"Aye, aye, Jefe," said Jack Bull, and called out to the doomed crewmates as he brought the craft half about and established a new course, bound directly for the stone formation. Walking Elk barked another order. Bull made a small correction and called out to Augustus, "And what sheriff will follow us here, Foolish Gus?"

Directly before them loomed a towering formation of craggy rock that in Augustus's indistinct vision took the form of a praying angel with furled wings. An increasingly deadly angel, though, for when they collided, the schooner would be reduced to splinters.

"For God's sake, turn!" Augustus cried, although it would no longer be possible to do so in time. The craft shot forward as if drawn by wild steeds, directly toward the angel of death.

PART I

Shepherd's Journal

1

May 17, 2005, 8:45 a.m.
Airborne over the Mediterranean, 70 miles NNE of
Benghazi, Libya

On sensitive operations, the pilot went by the code name
Black Wolf, taken from his Piegan Blackfoot great-
grandfather. He was equally proud of his adoptive white
parents and of the name they'd christened him with:
Abraham Lincoln Anderson. Among friends, he preferred Link.

Link Anderson was happiest when flying, such as he
presently was doing, shepherding the royal blue Learjet
60 D through a flawless sky with three souls on board—
himself and two copilots. The bird was pristine, with top-
to-bottom customizing and refurbishment having been
performed at the Wichita plant. Link Anderson had
begun the previous day with a test hop to check out
the whistles and bells such as integrated plasma cockpit
displays and modifications optimizing short field, desert,
and long-haul operations. Wider tires, air intakes rede-
signed to filter the blowing sand during *ghibli*s or siroc-
cos that tend to destroy fragile jet engines, and fuel
tanks that conformed to the aerodynamic shape of the
airplane, adding less "drag," were all part of the cus-
tomization. New PW turbofan engines increased the
cruising speed and range, and added thrust for climb and
maneuver. The fuselage was armored with sheaths of
ceramic and compressed polymer, and both seats and
bulkheads were reinforced with Kevlar. There was an
automated self-protection suite to tell the crew when

they were being targeted by radars, surface-to-air missiles (SAMs), or airborne interceptors, and select appropriate countermeasures, such as jammers, chaff, and flares. The cost of the retrofit was extravagant, but the result was a much more rugged, efficient, and survivable jet than the original 1993 model.

They'd made refueling stops at Teterboro, New Jersey, and Seville, Spain, and the navigation system showed that in an hour and thirty minutes they would arrive at Cairo, Egypt. Two pilots manned the cockpit while the third fetched coffee or then snoozed in the passengers' recliners. There was little to do while cruising at forty-seven thousand feet.

"I'm going to stretch my legs," Link told Squid. "You've got the airplane."

"I've got the airplane," Squid acknowledged, following the ritual to transfer control.

An Emmylou Harris CD was playing over the intercom when Link went back. As he returned to the cockpit fifteen minutes later, the copilots were shouting to one another over the ear-blasting noise of Good Charlotte. Link was about to turn over his personal odometer to forty-one, and he did not care that the copilots considered him ancient when he shut off the hard rock. His Blackfoot ancestors would have sought revenge for the discord in his ears.

Like others in Link's group at the Weyland Foundation, the copilots had military backgrounds. One had seen combat as an army M1A2 tank (heavy) reconnaissance platoon commander in what he called Desert Storm Two. The other, who presently occupied the right cockpit seat, had spent eight years as a submariner.

They'd come to work during the same week and had immediately begun arguing the merits of their services. Since both had difficult surnames (Worsczejius and Nyrzhinskiy), and one's given name was Stefan and the other Stephan, they were nicknamed Tanker and Squid. Due to the rivalry that continued through seven months of training to instrument, multijet, and commercial ratings, then factory checkouts, it was sometimes hard to tell they were friends.

Squid was talkative, and since Link had scuttled his music, he relieved the boredom of the flight by retelling submariner stories.

Squid had joined the navy at age seventeen and was still growing when he'd graduated from two years of nuclear submarine training. While he'd graduated with honors, he'd been too large to continue in regular sub operations. The navy brass's logic had been to send him to a smaller craft, crewing a thirty-five-year-old brainchild of Admiral Rickover called the *NR-1* that measured just 150 feet in length and twelve in diameter. He'd loved the job and the mission.

The deep submergence craft was used for research projects at depths of over two thousand feet. It was rugged, powered both by a nuclear reactor and turbo alternator. A five-man crew and two scientists could remain on the bottom—riding around on extendable wheels and examining objects using a mechanical claw— for long periods. The *NR-1* had recovered parts of the space shuttle *Challenger*, a Phoenix missile on a F-14 Tomcat that went down at sea, and a thermonuclear bomb jettisoned from a B-52 off Spain.

When Squid began to expound about his exchange tour with the Canadians, Tanker groaned. "We've heard it four times."

Link checked gauges and fiddled with the autopilot, while in the background Squid explained again how the Canadians had built a bare-bones version of the *NR-1* (sans reactor) and held dive tests off Vancouver Island. The craft worked, diving safely to fifteen hundred feet, but Ottawa politics took another shift to the left, and the antimilitary majority had it sold it off for salvage.

Squid had left the navy, gotten his pilot's ticket, and come to the Weyland Foundation. "It was an easy transition from subs to airplanes . . . ," Squid began anew.

"We've *heard* it." Tanker complained from the passengers' cabin.

Link said, "I've always believed the guys in subs are nuts. It's got to be claustrophobic."

"You *almost* get used to it. Anyway, we thought fighter pilots were crazy."

Tanker stirred around in the back. "You guys mind if I put on something a little less Hilfiger, like at least medium deck?"

Link was somewhat sure that in the Hipster dialect that Tanker and Squid used to irritate the codgers at the Weyland Foundation, *deck* meant "cool," and *Hilfiger* meant "mundane." Tanker wanted to put on his hard rock, which to Link was like listening to dying wolves.

"I mind," said Link. "Play the next CD in the stack."

"Aw, Boss, what the hell's a Waylon Jennings?"

Link bristled. "Just the best Western singer who ever lived."

"We heard him. He's downright fin, Boss," said Squid, from the copilot seat. "Left me wanting to boggle. You ever hear Smashing Pumpkins? Now *that* is deck!"

Link had no idea of what he was talking about. "Put Waylon on," he said ominously. The copilots were good aviators, as tough as they came, and Link was pleased they were on his side, but they sure had odd tastes in music.

A husky female voice came over the radio. "So how's the flight?" asked Erin, Link's technical assistant, who was calling from their office on the twenty-seventh floor of the Weyland Building. After Al Qaeda's 9/11 declaration of hate, it was the fourth largest structure in New York.

"CAVU," Link replied, an acronym meaning "clear and visibility unlimited."

"Still no word from Aozou," Erin said.

The mountain town lay 840 miles south of the Learjet, beyond Libya's southern border with Chad. The Weyland Foundation was contemplating a medical project at Aozou, and had sent a three-person evaluation team. For twenty days, everything had gone as planned, but for the past five days there'd been no contact. All three satellite phones had been silenced, likely meaning that they'd self-destructed when someone unauthorized had tried to use them. The protocol was for one of them to get to another means of communications and open the conversation with the flag words—in this case, "Wild Weasel"—identifying him or her as a team member. So far there'd been nothing, not even from the rudimentary telephone service available in parts of Aozou. Erin monitored with omnifrequency satellite receivers so sensitive, they would detect the slightest electronic murmur. Nothing.

Aozouans distrusted outsiders. Since ancient times, they'd drawn the wrong kinds of attention. For centuries, entrepreneurs from Tripoli, Algiers, and Tunis had passed through, and returned with slaves taken from the forests beyond the desert. Tribesmen from the south attacked Aozou to avenge their enslaved brethren, or because of the Aozouans' unholy Muslim beliefs, or simply because they felt the urge to spill the blood of their enemy. In 1880, a few Frenchmen had passed through and claimed the place as a part of French Equatorial Africa, then mostly left them alone until after World War I when they desperately needed money to pay war debts. They told Aozouans that they and their southern enemies were one country, part of a French world empire, and must levee taxes and follow unfathomable laws. They stripped the countryside, exploited mercilessly, and sent everything of remote value to the colonial revenue office in Paris.

When uranium deposits were discovered near Aozou in 1950, European spies and fortune-seekers abounded. In 1960, shamed by defeat in Indochina and preoccupied by bloody revolt in Algeria, the French legion abandoned Chad and left them to their devices, which was to return to their historical pattern of intertribal bickering and rebellion.

In 1973, four years after a comedy-act palace coup ousted the doddering king of Libya and installed a bumpkin tyrant unable to rise beyond lieutenant, the self-proclaimed Colonel Gadhafi decided to expand his empire. When Egypt threatened to clean his clock if he sent his military a step closer, he turned south, befriended a backward Chadian tribe, and announced that he was annexing that country. After fifteen years of battling with various war-loving tribes, including the one they'd befriended, Gadhafi's army withdrew up the country's length with the aplomb of the Keystone Kops, and occupied only the northernmost tip, called the Aozou Strip. In 1994, the UN ordered Libya out. Sick of the place and having found little uranium, they left.

Once again, Aozou was a place of no consequence, controlled by fundamentalists. During the past months, the place had exploded in violence. Four warlords fought for control. They'd killed reporters and UN representatives and were running wild.

An uneasy feeling welled in Link. His project leaders were good at extracting themselves from hot water, and Peter Phillip Steeves, M.D., was the best. He was resourceful and brazen. Doc Pete had served for six years as an air force flight surgeon, which was where Link had met him. He'd even talked his way into flying combat sorties in the First Gulf War in the backseat of an F-4G Wild Weasel—which was the name of the bird and the mission of aviators who destroyed SAM sites for a living—so he would better understand his patients. (That was also why he'd picked the flag words "Wild Weasel.") In the Air Force Reserve, Doc Pete had spent a winter at McMurdo Station in Antarctica. He'd come to the Weyland Foundation at Link's encouragement.

A good man, Doc Pete, whose talisman was a small tin canteen that he wore slung about his neck. It was marred by a bullet crease, put there by a Taliban fighter aiming for his heart.

Doc Pete's team included civil engineer, Ace Acree, and medical engineer, Gwen Svenson. They'd been guaranteed safe passage to explore building a hospital where researchers could study Central African diseases. People in the region needed such a facility. Few Chadians lived to see forty, and the primary causes of death were preventable. AIDS and sleeping sickness were pandemic. Chadian officials had lobbied to be picked for the honor of getting a hospital.

As Doc's team studied the feasibility, they'd gathered background information about the unstable region and answered requests from the CIA. The agency's HUMINT agents were spread tissue-paper thin, and Link had three trained operatives in place. Aozou's warlords constantly fought, and then despised Westerners. Pete's crew may have fallen.

Those concerns trekked through Anderson's mind. Otherwise he felt good. He loved to fly and enjoyed life best when he was away from the office.

"Link, this is Erin," sounded in his headset, a trill of excitement in her tone.

"Go ahead."

"I just picked up a VHF radio call from Pete. Very weak, maybe two by two, but I got a voiceprint match, and he used the proper flag words."

"Two by two" meant the call measured two on a scale of five for both volume and clarity and was barely understandable. But if the voiceprint matched . . .

"He's in trouble, Link. He's on foot, someone's chasing him in trucks, and his sat phone's disabled. This radio's batteries are also about done. Ready to hear his message?"

Link's mind had switched to emergency mode. "First, did you get his location?"

She recited coordinates as she simultaneously fed them into Dest 6 of his navigation system so there would be no transcription error. He pressed the NAV SYS function switch and viewed the position on the digital map. Doc Pete had traveled 150 miles north from Aozou and into southern Libya. Link zoomed in, examined the locale and a dry lakebed a few miles distant. A click on the lakebed's symbol showed the surface would support a five-ton vehicle. In its present configuration and fuel state, the Learjet weighed twenty-two thousand pounds.

"Where's our nearest help?" he asked Erin. "Helicopters or lightweight STOL."

"The CIA's closest air assets are in Iraq. That leaves Egyptian and Israeli military air."

Those would take too long—too many political sensitivities at work.

Link Anderson did not think further about outside help. A rule that he emphasized with his employees was that they always take care of their own.

He pushed the yoke forward and radioed Cairo Control on UHF, saying he was experiencing pressurization problems and had to descend. "This is *not* an emergency," he said, speaking clearly so they wouldn't misunderstand; then he switched the bird's transponder off so they couldn't easily monitor his position.

While satellite communications was secure, a combination of voice and message, each speaker using different portions of the electromagnetic spectrum, was more so. As the Learjet continued to descend, a message scrolled onto the screen before him:

E TO L. HERE IS DOC'S MESSAGE, RECEIVED 4 MINUTES AGO, WHEN ONE OF OUR WIDE-OPEN RECEIVERS PICKED UP A WEAK VHF BAND TRANSMISSION FROM THE COORDINATES I GAVE YOU. HE OPENED WITH THE FLAG WORDS "WILD WEASEL," SOUNDING TIRED & ANXIOUS, IDENTIFIED HIMSELF AS DOC PETE, AND SAID HE WAS TRANSMITTING IN THE BLIND, PRAYING SOMEONE WAS LISTENING. WHEN I ANSWERED, HE YELLED, "GREAT!", VERY EXCITED, AND "THIS RADIO IS PRETTY BATTERED, AND I DON'T HAVE MUCH BATTERY LEFT. THE BAD GUYS HAVE PICKUPS AND AN APC, & SOONER OR LATER THEY'LL GET LUCKY. THEY'RE UPSET BECAUSE—*GARBLED*—HAVE INFO ABOUT 2 HEZBOLLAH TERRORISTS. 5 DAYS AGO I— *GARBLED*—AHM—*GARBLED*—POLAH—*FADING*—SAJA— *GARBLED*—HAVE AUDIO AND PHOTOS—*FADING* & *GARBLED*.

DOC'S RADIO GAVE OUT. FOR 10 SECONDS THERE WAS A CARRIER WAVE HUM, LIKE HE WAS STILL TRYING TO TRANSMIT, THEN NOTHING.

Link thought, *She isn't wrong—Doc is definitely in deep trouble.* "Did Doc Pete mention the others on his team?"

NO. BUT HE WAS BROADCASTING IN THE CLEAR, AND HE WOULDN'T WANT BAD GUYS KNOWING IF THEY WERE WITH HIM. I SEE YOU'VE TURNED SOUTH, SO I'M GUESSING YOU'RE GOING TO HELP DOC. I'LL CHECK WITH THE NATIONAL RECON OFFICE TO GET CURRENT IMAGERY AND ELECTRONIC INTELL FOR THAT AREA. I'VE ALSO GOT HELGA MONITORING ALL RADIO FREQS, IN CASE DOC COMES BACK ON.

Helga was Erin's nickname for her heavyweight superfast computer.

"With that kind of low battery, Doc will wait to transmit again." Link leveled at five hundred feet above the desert floor and reset the throttles before explaining: "If it were me, I'd let the battery build up and periodically monitor the last frequency."

I AGREE. I'LL HAVE HELGA TRANSMIT A MESSAGE IN THE BLIND.

Link observed the electronic map. "Tell Pete to move to the dry lake bed seven miles to his northeast. I'll make a low pass and see if I can't land and pick him up."

THE DIGITAL MAP SHOWS YOU'RE TOO HEAVY. YOU COULD SINK IN THE SAND.

"We're a little overweight," he admitted.

A LITTLE? YOU'RE DOUBLE THE LIMIT.

"Let's hope there's a margin of error on the side of caution. Also we have new tires that are supposed to work better on packed sand."

HOPE YOU'RE RIGHT.

He thought about it. If he kept the airplane moving, it might not have time to settle.

Erin had another criticism:

I HAVE A PROBLEM WITH YOUR MESSAGE FOR DOC PETE. HIS TRANSMISSION WAS MADE OVER OPEN RADIO. PLAIN OLD VANILLA-FLAVORED VHF-FM, LIKE EVERY MILITARY IN THE WORLD USES. NOTHING SECURE ABOUT IT. IF THE BAD GUYS OVERHEAR US TELLING HIM TO GO TO A LAKE BED, THEY'LL BE THERE WAITING.

"Then just tell him to move northeast."

SEVEN MILES?

"Yeah."

YOU WANT HIM OUT IN THE MIDDLE OF THE LAKE
BED?

He groaned at her nitpicking. "Tell him to walk northeast and hide at the edge of a lake."

After a short delay she typed:

DOC'S FROM A TOWN CALLED POINT BLANK IN EAST
TEXAS. MESSAGE WILL READ: "WILD WEASEL. PRO-
CEED AS IF GOING FROM AUNT MARY'S TO UNCLE
DUKE'S. THEN STOP AND WAIT FOR BOSS."

A moment later, another of Erin's scrolling messages
appeared.

HELGA IS TRANSMITTING NOW. ANYTHING ELSE?

"Yeah. I'm betting Doc Pete's problems are because
of the two Hezbollah terrorists he mentioned, which
were part of the CIA's RFI."

RFI stood for request for information.

"Phone Lovelady, and tell him Doc has his information. If the agency wants it bad enough, maybe they'll
find a chopper."

THAT'S SMART. WILL DO.

That was all from Erin for a while.

The southerly course was down the border separating
Libya and Egypt, two not-so-friendly neighbors, both of
whom had jet fighters. The copilots talked it over. They
were for helping Doc Pete and crew. If it was them down
there, they'd want the cavalry to save the day.

Link watched the Dest counter roll down through 752
nautical miles, and did the math. They were flying at
low altitude at 480 knots ground speed, which was eight
nautical miles per minute (550 miles per hour). They'd
arrive at the lakebed in an hour and thirty-three minutes.

With one hour and seventeen minutes to go, Erin sent:

SPOKE TO STU AT CIA M-EAST DESK & RELAYED INFO.
HE CAN FIND NO US ASSISTANCE CLOSER THAN SEVEN
HOURS. IF YOU FAIL THEY'LL INVOLVE THE EAF, BUT
ESTIMATE 5 DAYS TO GET OUR PEOPLE OUT.

"Tell him to forget it. By then Doc and his people
would be toast."

Erin was quiet. So were Tanker and Squid, until
Tanker thought the situation called for a little heavy
metal. Link said he'd die first. Then how about some
Kool Keith? Link suggested a Willie Nelson album that
was in the stack after Waylon Jennings. Squid said he
may boggle, which Link knew meant "puke," but he put
Willie on anyway.

As Texas Willie rasped out "Georgia on My Mind,"
Link felt more twinges of trepidation. As he'd done in
combat, he gave himself a pep talk—boosted his
adrenaline—then tried to answer the hardest questions:

*Is Doc Pete getting the message? Will he be at the lake
bed? Are Ace and Gwen with him? Are any of them
wounded? How close are the technical pickups and the
APC? How can we get them aboard the Learjet as
quickly as possible?*

What will be our biggest threat?

He offered a primer on air combat to Tanker and
Squid: "Keep an eye on the threat warning system. If a
radar light comes on, we'll drop lower. Egyptian radar
may mean trouble. On the other hand, the Libyans have
the world's worst pilots and mechanics. To them, anvils
are high tech. When we get to the lake bed, look for
muzzle flashes. In the air, that means they're inaccurate.
On the ground it means the opposite."

Erin typed:

THREAT REPORT FROM NRO. ELECTRONIC ORDER OF
BATTLE SHOWS YOU'RE PRESENTLY IN RANGE OF 2
TALL KING GCI RADARS AND 2 SA-5 SAMS, AND WILL
PASS THRU COVERAGE OF ONE SA-4 IN 10 NM, AND TWO
SA-3 SAMS IN 40 NM. SUGGEST UNDERFLIGHT OF ALL
THE ABOVE THREATS. SO FAR NO RADAR CREWS ARE

ON ALERT STATUS. NRO IMAGERY NOW SHOWS 12 LT
AND MED VEH'S AT 4 TO 8 MILES S & SW OF LAKEBED.
ALL CARRY SMALL ARMS SHOOTERS. EXPECT A MA-
CHINE GUN ON THE APC. THE NUMBER OF VEHICLES IS
LARGER THAN NORMAL, SO EXPECT SA-7 SAMS. DONE
WITH REPORT.

"Understand, and thanks," Link radioed.

A threat warning lamp illuminated, beeped, and
blinked the word *RDR* in staccato. The screen showed
a winking radar signal at their three o'clock. Link descended to four hundred feet above ground level. The
light flickered. At three hundred feet it went out. For
good measure, he dropped to two hundred feet. "That's
a ground-controlled intercept radar, so watch for MiGs
and Mirages," Link told the copilots. Tanker and Squid
were vigilant. They'd shut off the music.

10:28 a.m.—Airborne over Southern Libya

They passed over a succession of blistering deserts, such
as the Sea of Sand and the Libyan Desert (in Egypt
called the Western Desert), all components of the vast
Sahara. The seven thousand-feet Tibesti Mountains were
a faint purple band on the horizon.

Squid still manned the right cockpit seat while Tanker
looked out windows in back, both confident that things
would go well. Link was not so sure. There was much
that could go wrong.

NEW NRO REPORT, typed Erin.
    YOU'RE PAST LIBYAN RADAR AND SAM COVERAGE.
NO THREATS EXCEPT FOR A PAIR OF LIBYAN FIGHTERS
ON ROUTINE PATROL. NRO NOW COUNTS SEVENTEEN
VEHICLES APPROACHING LAKEBED FROM THE SOUTH.
NSA IS MONITORING—THEY REPORT POOR RADIO DIS-
CIPLINE AND A LOT OF CHATTER ABOUT KILLING INFI-
DELS. THEIR LEADER'S SOMEONE IMPORTANT.

Erin paused.

SOUNDS LIKE A PICNIC FOR YOU GUYS.

She knew it would be no picnic. Pete Steeves did not cry wolf. His team was in trouble, caught up in something to do with the CIA requests.

At ten minutes to go, a message scrolled onto the screen:

E TO L. STU FROM CIA ASKS IF YOU'LL CONSIDER DROP-PING THEM A RADIO AND GETTING THEM TO TRANS-MIT THEIR INFORMATION BEFORE YOU ATTEMPT PICKUP.

The agency wanted the report now since odds were not good that Doc would get out. Regardless of how he felt about it, Link had to consider the idea.

"Negative," he finally answered. "It would draw too much attention to Doc."

The Threat Warning System emitted a rhythmic chatter of a radar sweeping them.

Squid was staring up and back, and he yelled, "Two bogeys at five o'clock high."

Link couldn't see them from his left seat. "Identify them and estimate their altitude."

"Mirage F1s, but I can't make out markings." Squid was breathing harshly over intercom. It was his first taste of air combat.

Libyans, thought Link, *and likely not their finest aviators. Those would be flying newer MiG-27s, despite the fact that they couldn't handle them.*

"Boss, I suggest we turn left," said Squid, his voice too high.

"Are they attacking?"

"Not yet, but . . ."

"We'll hold steady," said Link, purposefully keeping his voice steady.

Squid continued to peer up and back. "We're an *awfully* easy target."

"Not really. Now would you please estimate their altitude like I asked?"

"Sorry, sir. Nine or ten thousand feet."

"That means they're on routine patrol. We're down

at two hundred feet, over rocky terrain. They won't see us."

"But sir . . ."

"The Libyans have their hands full just flying straight and level. If we were to turn, they *might* notice us. Then they'd be forced into doing something that takes skill, like making an ID pass down here in the weeds, at which time one or both of them would undoubtedly run into the ground."

Squid gave him a dubious look.

"Trust me. And don't mention them again unless they attack."

The copilots waited, with bated breath as the dart-shaped F1 jets passed high overhead. The region was claimed by numerous nations, but it was so barren that none of them cared who else used it. Outlaw warlords operated with disdain for anyone's rules, vying for turf, possessing ramshackle Toyota pickups they called "technicals," loading them with militia and a hodgepodge of small arms. The most powerful warlord might have an armored personnel carrier, perhaps mounting a 50-caliber, seldom used since ammo was heavy and expensive.

The warlords were fiercely independent. It was odd that they were cooperating by massing so many vehicles to chase after three foreigners.

Squid read off the distance to the lake bed: "Fifteen miles." He periodically glanced northward where the bogeys disappeared.

"Something else to remember," Link said. "For the past fifty years, ninety-five percent of air combat losses have been to enemy SAMs and guns, not to fighters. Look for muzzle blasts and shoulder-mounted missile launches."

Erin typed:

JUST RECEIVED SHORT TRANSMISSION. DOC'S IN A THICKET OF STICKERS AT THE SIDE OF —.

The rest was too weak and garbled to understand.

Squid pointed at the lake bed, now only a mile ahead, and at the ants gathered at the far end.

Link pushed the throttles up to maximum power, and

as the engines squealed in complaint, he pressed the I/C button: "We'll make a fast pass to see how friendly they are and what kind of weapons we're facing. Keep your eyes out for the thicket of stickers Pete mentioned."

They flashed over the north end at five hundred knots ground speed.

Squid made an assessment. "The technicals are spread across the south end, moving toward us. Three more trucks off on the right side, and three to the left."

The warlords were sweeping the lake bed from one end to the other, looking for Doc.

"There's a thicket," said Tanker. "West side of the lake, and halfway down."

Once over the center of the oval lake bed, Link punched the WAYPOINT button so the GPS would store the precise position.

"I just saw a tube in back of a technical. Maybe an SA-7?" asked Tanker from the rear.

As they approached the trucks, Link rolled the bird over on its left wing and stared at an armored personnel carrier with twin barrels protruding from a camo net. Beside the APC stood a lone Arab in bright green desert robes, posed like Peter O'Toole in *Lawrence of Arabia*.

The remainder of the vehicles were pickups, each hauling a half-dozen shooters. What the hell had Doc Pete seen or done to get that kind of attention?

As they continued beyond the lake, the copilots gave reports of vehicle locations that roughly matched his own. "What's next?" asked Tanker.

"We do it again. Now that we've introduced ourselves, the fun begins."

When he thought they were out of vehicles' sight, Link turned in a lazy left-hand arc, wary of trucks they'd not seen. He rolled out and again accelerated toward the lake bed, so low they blew up a rooster tail of sand.

This time as they approached the trucks, there was a cloud of dust and streak of fire.

"SAM!" cried Squid.

Link continued ahead, throttles firewalled, counting seconds.

"Another SAM at three!" Tanker yelled from the passengers' compartment.

The threat warning receiver blinked I-R and squealed. Decoy flares were automatically ejected from ports on the rear fuselage.

Seconds later, Link eased off the throttle.

"They missed!" said Squid.

Link responded: "Going this fast, it's doubtful SA-7s could hit us even if we weren't using flares. Now they have two less missiles."

"We're also pissing them off," remarked Squid.

"And ain't it fun!" yelled Tanker, exuberant.

They continued to make the low-level, high-speed passes, varying headings. On each pass, two or three shoulder-fired SAMs were fired. The copilots got into the spirit of the game.

"When one's about to get us, it fizzles or goes chasing after a flare," whooped Tanker.

"Now *that's* scary!" yelled Squid, gesturing at the small arms fire winking at them.

Link came at the lake bed from the south, giving them another chance to use up rockets. A single SAM was fired, from dead ahead. When they were overhead, the missile went squirrelly, corkscrewing through the air in no particular direction.

On the next pass, no SAMs were expended, only small arms fire. As they approached, Link turned the bird on its wing as he'd done earlier, his eyes on the man in green who stood by the APC staring at the Learjet. Link had snapshot images of a tall, bearded man with angry features.

Link hoped he was so furious that he'd forgotten to conserve a missile. "Next time, we land."

2

Link hoped to get Doc Pete aboard quickly. Success would depend on their timing. He had confidence in his people but, try as he must, little esteem for the fighting moxie of Middle Easterners. Bring them to the States, and some became good warriors, but that was not so when they stayed in the desert.

He circled to land into the wind, to touch down at the opposite end from the vehicles, and warned Doc over VHF, opening with the flag words. "Wild Weasel." He paused, then said, "This is Black Wolf. We're on final. I'll try to get close, but then you'll have to come to us."

Hope he's listening, Link thought, *and the bad guys aren't.*

He racked the bird into the final turn, rolled out with wings level, and hovered over the earth.

"Flaps are full—landing gear is down and locked," Squid confirmed.

Link dragged the throttles back, and had started to bring up the nose for landing when Tanker yelled, "Boss, ahead about two hundred feet!"

There were ripples and waves as one might see in an ocean. Loose sand, not the hardpack they required. "Roger," was all Link said as he added a nudge of power. They passed over the edge of the lake bed at fifty feet, on the cusp, floating, holding a moderate angle of attack so Link could maintain speed and see the terrain ahead.

When the way ahead was smooth and without ripples, Link rotated the nose and sank earthward, feeling for the surface with the gear and praying it would bear their weight. The oversize tires kissed the hardpack. Link braked just enough to drop the nose wheel and began a high-speed rollout—realizing he'd been holding his breath.

They were half a mile from the low thicket—the trucks were half a mile beyond and had started fanning out into a vee that extended across the lake bed. The trucks drove into place and held, awaiting their leader in the APC to assume the position of honor in the middle. It was obvious that the drivers were communicating by radio.

Link reached out to the Self Protection Panel and enabled all switches by flipping up their red guards. He found the COM JAM switches, and as he activated them, a buzzing sound filled his headset, so annoying that he shut off the radio volume. The communications jammers were so powerful that their use was generally prohibited in peacetime.

Ahead, the technical pickups, bristling with ragtag shooters, held their places and awaited orders. None realized that they were only five hundred yards from the thicket where their quarry was hiding. It was also unlikely that they knew why their radios had become useless.

The APC pulled into their center and, after a lot of arm waving, led them forward.

"Boss," yelled Tanker, jabbing a forefinger at the APC. "That's a Zipper."

The APC's camouflage net was obscuring, but as Tanker had noted, it was a Russian-built armored vehicle. Rather than a .50-caliber, it sported two much larger 23 mm cannon barrels with excellent accuracy and a rate of fire approaching that of an American Gatling gun. Officially designated ZPU-23-2s, called Zippers because of the sound they made when they filled a sky with bullets. Link had faced them while flying over other battlefields, and he had not enjoyed the experience. Thankfully they were designed to destroy aircraft in the sky, not on the ground.

They were in the range envelope of small arms, yet the shooters in the technicals were holding fire. Link wondered if the man in green had told them to capture the airplane and crew intact. After another hundred feet and nothing hostile from the pickups, he decided that was the case. *Good*, he told himself. They'd await permission to open fire, and their radios were jammed.

"There!" yelled Tanker, pointing at three figures in desert robes trying to make their way through scrub brush and stickers, up to their ankles in loose sand at the lake's edge.

As the airplane raced past, they were close enough that Link recognized Doc Pete. He was supporting Ace, who dragged a useless leg. A woman, the agent named Gwen, was staggering like a drunk in the intense heat.

"All three of them!" Squid yelled exuberantly.

"Don't start partyin'," said Tanker, "until we have them inside."

Link continued toward the technicals and motioned both copilots aft. "Open the hatch."

The pickups were closing, their drivers surely wondering why the airplane hadn't slowed, none of them noticing the three figures on foot beyond the Learjet. Link continued directly toward the Zipper that carried the man in green. At a hundred feet of separation, he pushed the throttles up even more. On this course, the Learjet would slam into the Zipper and two pickups. He was betting on human nature and desire for survival.

At fifty feet, the outer vehicles darted right and left. The Zipper driver managed to clear the airplane's wing but smacked into the rear end of a technical. The truck fishtailed and shed a few shooters before overturning and tumbling wildly down the lakebed.

The Learjet was past the vehicles when Link rapidly slowed and stepped on the right brake as he pushed up the left throttle. The bird pirouetted like a football end faking out a tackler.

Link stroked both throttles forward. The engines thrust the airplane toward the technicals, now halted as if regaining their breaths. The drivers seemed content with the respite until they saw the Learjet bearing down once more, and again they scattered. Link sprinted past, toward the distant figures who were finally climbing onto the hardpack.

Link kept a wary eye on the surface; they didn't dare taxi into loose sand.

Should I stop a hundred yards from them? Do I dare get closer?

Although the trucks were behind and out of view, he envisioned each of them. As a fighter pilot, he'd developed a high degree of "situational awareness," keeping track of a sky full of friendlies and unfriendlies, and forecasting what each would do next. Not a simple task—which is why there were so few really good fighter jocks.

He knew the vehicles were scattered, the drivers pumping adrenaline, confused by signals from the man in green, who was frantically trying to rescind his command not to shoot. They were not at all eager. Their radios were screaming from the jamming, they were unsure about their orders, and twice now the crazy airplane pilot had tried to run them down.

Link decided that sheer confusion would buy Doc Pete twenty seconds of safe time. Their leader would continue to try to grant clearance to fire. Not easy without radios, he calculated, so add ten seconds because of the jamming. Unless Doc Pete's team had brought weapons, there were none available for the good guys. The drivers did not realize they could drive up within ten feet with impunity. Their nervousness made them gunshy. They'd seek cover and, if denied that, stay on the move. Due to those factors, Link thought, add ten more seconds.

Link was betting that Doc's crew would have forty seconds of safe time, from the moment he stopped, to get aboard. Forty seconds could be a long time. Or a very short one.

He heard the copilots opening the hatch. They were good men. Tough guys. He did not want them endangered more than was necessary.

He made a sharp zigzag, and looked behind. As he had forecasted the drivers had withdrawn to safe distances from the wild-assed pilot. Some were sprawled on the ground, where they'd fallen out of the rolling pickup.

Only two were standing, looking down the lakebed at the airplane.

Link continued taxiing until he was close enough to see Doc Pete's smile, one hundred yards from the lakebed's edge, sixty from the struggling fugitives. He dragged both throttles back and stepped on a single brake so aggressively that the jet swung ninety degrees, shuddering like a skier schussing to a stop.

Link glanced at his Rolex GMT-Master to begin timing. *Forty seconds to go.*

As the Learjet rocked to a halt between the vehicles and Doc's team, Link yelled aft to Tanker and Squid. "When they're close, pull them aboard, but don't go out and get trapped."

The threesome were forty yards distant, making poor time because of Ace's injury and Gwen's slow pace. Tanker and Squid were at the open hatch, yelling, *"Oorah! Go, go, go!"*

Doc Pete fell, dragged to earth by Ace, whose face reflected agony. Three seconds lost.

To Link's right, the Zipper appeared and stopped in view of the three Americans on foot. The man in green climbed out, motioning at the technicals, waving them on. Two drivers got the picture and started forward. They were out of effective range even if the pickups had been sitting still so the shooters could take aim. They posed no threat—yet.

Doc Pete saw the trucks. When Gwen caught up, he gave her a shove that propelled her in the direction of the Learjet, then turned his attention to his injured comrade. Gwen stumbled, recovered, and tried to run. Instead she fell again.

Come on! Link urged them, and examined his watch. Twenty seconds had passed. He pondered the unimaginable, leaving people behind, and hastily called toward the back: "One of you go after her! *Only* one."

Outside Doc Pete struggled with Ace, then looked at the airplane as Squid appeared in Link's view, running toward the fugitives.

Pete pulled his talisman canteen from around his neck and yelled something as he tossed it to Squid, who almost missed catching it. Squid shoved it into his shirt, then scooped up Gwen and hurried back toward the Learjet. She was sturdily built, but Squid carried her without effort.

Link's heart sped up as Tanker burst into his vision, racing toward the two who were progressing slowest, still twenty yards distant. He felt his hair crawl. "Come back!"

"Get the lead out, Tanker!" Squid yelled from the open hatch as he shoved Gwen inside.

Tanker ran hard, slid to a stop, and took Ace from Doc's grasp, hoisting him onto his back in a fireman's carry.

"Time's up," Link whispered hoarsely. He should have been yelling for Squid to close the hatch, but he couldn't speak the words with the three men still outside.

"Hurry, Tanker!" Squid shouted. A pickup slid to a halt between the aircraft and the three men. As shooters scrambled out of the truck bed, Link heard the hatch being slammed. The HATCH OPEN lamp remained on. The door was not secured!

Another technical arrived. The shooters in back were firing at the fuselage, the bullets thumping loudly as they struck the armored aluminum.

Link pushed up the throttles. The bird wanted to taxi, but was sluggish, then came to a stop as the gear became mired in loose sand. Link pulled back the throttles, firewalled them, backed them off, pushed them forward. The bird strained but went nowhere.

The Zipper arrived off their right wing, the man in green seated at an open hatch. He flattened a hand and held it palm down, a signal for the shooters to cease firing.

After a few more pops and bangs, they stopped.

Doc, Tanker, and Ace were dragged over to the Zipper, where the man in green observed them and then Link with a look of hatred and triumph. A gunshot sounded from a shooter in a technical, and he signaled once more. *He wants the entire crew alive.*

A smaller man beside the man in green was vaguely familiar, but Link had no time for a closer examination. He doggedly continued to alternately pull back and run

up the throttles. The bird responded by straining, relaxing, straining, rocking back and forth . . .

The man in green continued to stare at Link. He
smiled, placed his forefinger to his throat and made a
slow slicing motion. There was no humor in the act,
only promise.

The Learjet strained, shuddered, and—ever so
slowly—the oversize tires took purchase and crawled
forth, almost out of the rut.

The man in green became agitated, his mouth framing
words that were drowned out by the jet's squeal. He
motioned for drivers to block the Learjet's path, but they
acted as if they didn't notice him. They remembered the
game of chicken and weren't keen on doing it again.

The airplane continued to creep along, then began to
walk, and then, as if released by an invisible hand, it
gave a lurch and was freed from the sand's grip.

Link heard sounds of the hatch being slammed. "Can't
get the damned thing closed," Squid said over intercom.
"The canteen's wedged in the latch."

They taxied faster. There were new flurries of gunfire.

"We've got three pickups alongside, and every time I
crack the hatch they shoot." There was more gunfire,
another fit of cursing from Squid.

Some of the rounds were starting to punch through.
"Screw the hatch. Get away from it, and brace for takeoff," Link said over the intercom. "It's going to be
close."

"*There!* I pulled the canteen out." Squid's voice was
shrill with emotion. Link heard another slamming sound.
The HATCH OPEN lamp went out.

Link tried to suppress thoughts of leaving his men
behind. A new thought hammered at him: *Stay alive so
you can return for them.* A rifle round punched through
the cockpit and thumped into the bulkhead behind his
head.

One of the first things pilots learn is that takeoffs are
made *into* the wind. They were breaking that rule. They
needed twenty more knots, and the end of the lake bed
was looming.

"The technicals are falling back, Boss. They can't
keep up."

No, thought Link, *the drivers don't want to drive pell-mell into soft sand. Ten knots to liftoff, and the lake bed ends in another fifty yards.*

Link eased the nose up just a mini-tad—as his stepfather liked to say. He did not wish to apply weight on the main gear, but to magically "lift the bird off the surface."

In defiance of various laws of physics, he succeeded, and the wheels were skimming over the sand. If they encountered a swell, they would nose in. Link was concentrating so totally, so completely, that he failed to note the fiery arc of tracers that sliced and snaked through the sky just above the cockpit, although a vague neural reaction acknowledged that death was near.

Tracers were nominally loaded at a rate of one for each seven rounds, and they appeared as intermittent streaks, allowing a gunner to visually zero in on a target. In this instance, the loaders were ignorant of the fact that mixing in too many red-banded, phosphorous-tipped rounds causes Zipper cannon barrels to overheat. At some point, that barrel would warp and quit.

The rounds feeding the other barrel were all HEI, high-explosive incendiary, and they appeared as brown lines. Along the graceful arc of gunfire were occasional flashes marking the collisions of two rounds. The combination that spewed from the twin 23 mm barrels presented a spectacular and deadly show.

The airplane continued to skim the earth's surface, neither flying nor earthbound, but in a state somewhere between. Finally, when there was only soft sand left before them, Link felt that fathomless sensation sewn into the butt of every aviator's trousers. The bird was flying!

He pulled gently on the yoke to gain altitude and began a slow left turn toward Egyptian airspace, wondering whom to contact to set up the rescue of his people.

The bird climbed into the hot streams of 23 mm cannon fire. A brilliant light flashed, a sharp *crack* sounded, and the right copilot's glass cockpit erupted in a shower of plastic and metal shards. Link felt a stinging sensation in his forehead. There was another flash, that one from outside and left, and immediately following it, the corresponding engine stuttered.

He did not know the extent of the damage. The engines were fuselage mounted, impossible to see from the cockpit.

Annunciator lights for the left engine blinked on and off, warning him that something was very wrong, but he did not dare shut down an engine that was so critically needed.

His mind shifted to a hyperactive survival mode, as he'd done when piloting his A-10A Thunderbolt II "Warthog" in troubled skies. The Hog was so rugged, you could get into big trouble and survive, but you still wanted to do the smartest thing. Same with the Learjet. It was a good bird. All critical systems and controls had backup systems and controls. They'd been hit by at least two bullets, likely more, 23 mm HEI and tracer rounds from the Zipper.

Cockpit damage was limited to the copilot's instrument and radar displays. He felt no problem in the flight controls, the hydraulics, or electrical systems, although something was amiss with the left engine.

Link held the throttles full forward, praying the damaged turbofan jet wouldn't quit or fall off, and concentrated on the problem. *The Learjet 60 is designed to fly and even climb some with an engine down, but it's too much to ask that it ascend to normal cruising altitude of about thirty thousand feet and continue the thousand miles to Cairo on one engine.*

All those thoughts occurred in the two or three seconds following the bullets' impacts.

He allowed himself to feel the pain in his forehead. There was a pulsing sensation and a lot of blood running down his face, but he was rational, and obviously not too disabled to fly.

Something's changed. It took another second for Link to realize the gunfire from the Zipper had ceased. He immediately altered course.

"Boss," Squid said over intercom. "You're turning back toward the lake."

"Yes." There was a reason to continue the turn.

The ZPU is malfunctioning. If the man in green has his way, the gun will not be silent until I'm dead.

Gripping the yoke with his left hand, Link wiped

blood from his face with his right, grunting with pain as
he encountered a flap of skin. A gash extended from
right ear to midforehead. A dagger of plastic was embedded in bone, jutting from the center of his forehead like
a small horn. Link did not wish to bother with the injury yet.

"Squid, you'd better come up," he said over intercom.
They were flying low and slow—two hundred feet and
250 knots—in the direction of the gathered trucks. There
were no more bright bees, no sign that anyone was
shooting.

The man in green was inviting him back.

Squid came forward, yelling, "We're awfully low,
Boss!"

Link intended to rock the wings as they passed over,
let his men know they were not forgotten and that
he'd return.

He wiped more blood from his eyes as Squid slid into
the right seat and tried his controls. They were disconnected and useless. "Better turn and climb, Boss," said
Squid.

Link did not hear. He was staring out to his left, devoid of emotion.

From the back came a croaking cry. Gwen has seen
it, as well.

Link's eyes were transfixed on a scene that would remain with him forever.

Three men, all in his employ, had been pushed to their
knees. Now they were oddly asymmetric. The man in
green stood looking up at the Learjet, clutching a
curved sword.

The heads of the slain Americans had been tossed
aside like trash.

3

Upon arrival via an air force med-evac jet, they were met by a pair of U.S. Air Force couriers who took Doc Pete's canteen and disappeared by helicopter for the Weyland Building, where Erin Frechette waited. A security officer accompanied Gwen on a second chopper, bound for Saint Anthony's Hospital. Link had been given a broad-spectrum antibiotic shot and a tetanus booster, and his forehead had been repaired and sewn together by the flight surgeon on the med-evac bird. They'd rested during the long haul to the States.

At 5:30 a.m. Erin contacted Link, saying she had evidence of a terrorist threat. He asked her to notify Frank Dubois, chairman of the foundation, at home.

At 6:00 a.m. Frank called a senior official at the New York FBI field office and asked for an expanded debriefing. There was a threat of an attack on a target in New York City, although he did not yet consider the evidence firm enough to merit alerting the President.

Even after 9/11, government agencies continued to keep secrets from one another, a recipe for disaster that the president ordered stopped. Change came slowly, until the reluctant president finally allowed the removal of a few top people. They were not always the most guilty, but the warnings served their purpose, and agency wonks began tossing classified information at their brethren by the shovelful.

In January 2003, the FBI's Joint Terrorism Task
Group evaluated and shared information on a national
scale, yet the president wanted more, and he directed
the formation of the Terrorist Threat Integration Center
(TTIC, pronounced *tee-tick*) to operate under the stew-
ardship of the CIA, employer of the world's finest analysts. There, all terrorist data was to be received,
processed, dissected, analyzed, vetted, channeled, cata-
loged, compared, reanalyzed, fine-tuned, and hand-
somely packaged, then distributed by two hundred
resident (and ever more numerous) analysts. While the
accuracy of their conclusions was not disputed, at times
the analyses were reached so ponderously that they were
outdated before they were released.

There was also concern among regional agencies
about being overlooked and left unaware. After a few
late or wrongly distributed assessments—thankfully,
none involving disasters that were not averted—the simple act of holding short and timely debriefings to share
raw, unprocessed intelligence assuaged the critics.

For their meetings, New York's emergency actions organizations sent a single senior representative when a
threat of attack was uncovered. If the urgency was
deemed high enough, the President of the United States,
Secretary of Homeland Security, and National Security
Advisor were informed.

The chairmanship rotated among the members. Today
it was the FBI's turn in the barrel.

9:57 a.m.—FBI Field Office, Jacob Javits Federal Building, New York City

The debriefing was well attended despite the fact that
no eyewitnesses were present. Pete and Ace were dead.
Gwen Svenson was recovering from severe dehydration
and—hopefully temporary—traumatic memory loss.

There were two tables, a large oak one for the regional authorities and a smaller one for those invited to
speak. Link Anderson sat at the briefers' table wearing
a Western-cut suit and high-gloss Nocona dress boots.
His seven-star J. B. Stetson was at the hat rack, although

wearing it generated pain in his forehead where a one-inch-wide, flesh-tinted bandage masked his wound and a large number of stitches. Link showed little emotion; he was still coming to grips with the responsibility for the deaths of three good men.

Squid Worsczejius was at Link's side in blazer and blue tie. He studied his hands before himself, thinking of the death of his friend, who had once been decorated for charging into and defeating overwhelming numbers of Russian-built tanks while strapped into an Abrams.

Seated at the large table were eighteen executives from the New York offices of various agencies. CIA, DIA, NRO, DSS (Diplomatic Security Service), and NSA were responsible for U.S. interests worldwide. The rest were from the area's emergency services as organized under the Homeland Security Act. On March 1, 2003, they and 175,000 other government employees had reported to new management with orders to safety-seal the borders. Despite the harping of naysayers who felt it was the holy duty of journalists to criticize, most others agreed that major steps had been taken, and with every passing week America's security was better, tighter.

The one organization among them that was not connected to the government had supplied human intelligence (HUMINT) since its inception during World War II. The Weyland Foundation was the largest and by far the richest privately held benevolent organization in the world. Headquartered in the Weyland Building in Manhattan, its divisions were bastions of conservationism and human opportunity, champions of the arts and sciences.

Its least known division, Special Projects, quietly opposed tyranny and promoted democracy and capitalism in emerging nations, often in the guise of large-scale construction projects. Its deep pockets were normally welcomed virtually everywhere, and its project leaders used that access to make intelligence estimates where government agents found it difficult to tread. When possible the division shared the locations of despots and terrorists.

Its products were reliable. Link Anderson—VP of Special Projects—answered only to the handful of heirs of the Weyland Foundation's founders, all persons of wealth and patriotism, who had trust in their man. Like other details of his division, Link's functions were known only by a select few. Even some at the meeting were unsure of his position at the foundation.

After ten years, Link was familiar with the parks, bridges, traffic, the pedestrian swarm of New York, and he enjoyed the cultural treasures found nowhere else in the world, but he would never feel at home. He was a Westerner, drawn to the high country of Montana. When he died, he wished to be buried in a small cemetery that looked out onto the limitless prairie near his long-dead fiancée. While he did not understand them, he believed in spirits—as many men did—and hoped that his would not be caged or fettered.

There were problems at the foundation. For two months, there'd been a succession of outrageous charges raised against it. As of yet, none involved Link's division, yet Erin believed it was one of their projects driving the smear campaign. She felt the rhythm of events were building toward some dark crescendo, the first winds of a hurricane, and Erin's "guesses" were backed up by Helga, the power brute.

Frank Dubois was so swamped trying to respond to the false charges that he hardly listened to her predictions, and Link felt the grievances were made by an angry citizen because of some real or imagined wrong. Security had reported that queries were being made into Frank's and Erin's backgrounds. Helga had traced the inquiries to an Atlanta-based on-line "charity" that distributed funds and information to Al Qaeda and Hezbollah—when the charity's web site was erased.

Erin felt even more sure that organized terrorists were behind the libelous lies.

Regardless of the source, Frank was anxious to halt the lies.

Before his departure for the Middle East, Link had suggested that he temporarily sever all ties with the foundation and dedicate himself to searching for the answer.

Frank was beside himself, and inclined to accept Link's plan. Nothing else had worked.

Erin wanted them both to wait while she and Helga came up with more answers.

Now there was another reason for Link to leave the foundation—the deaths of his men in the Libyan Desert gnawed at him. He wanted to find and kill the man in green, and dance on the son of a bitch's grave. The Arab might think he knew about vengeance, but he would learn from one of the tribe that had invented the practice of "covering." When a Blackfoot was killed, five dead enemy would be laid atop his body to *cover* his death.

Three of Link's men had been killed. Many of the man in green's people would pay.

A more civilized portion of his brain suggested restraint, but he settled for postponement. It was not a question of *if* he would act, for that was sure. It was only a matter of *when*. He couldn't do so while in the employ of the Weyland Foundation. He could not bring any form of dishonor to the foundation or to Frank Dubois, his closest friend since Desert Storm I, when they'd flown A-10 Warthogs on combat missions into Iraq.

His retribution must also wait until after he'd stopped the slanderous attacks.

Those things coursed through Link's mind as the room filled with people.

The debriefing was held in a conference room at the FBI's enormous New York field office, their host a senior agent Link had known for several years. He considered Assistant Director in Charge Gordon Hightower a sometimes friend, regardless if the large and immaculately dressed black man had become so ambitious that he'd do anything for another promotion. He was not above elbowing, brownnosing or playing the race card, although it was common knowledge that he had climbed as high as he'd ever go. Link wondered if Gordon would give him the time of day if he were not a vice president at the Weyland Foundation.

Gordon had noted that most senior directors were personable, so in order to heighten his popularity, Gordon's meetings had become friendly tête-à-têtes.

He started to tell the joke about the CIA undercover bear at the Baghdad Zoo, and ignored the groans. "Bear gets thirsty and sneaks across the street to a kiosk," he started.

Stu Lovelady, a PhD fast burner at the CIA's all-important Middle East desk and maybe the next DDO, interrupted: "I don't have time, Gordon."

Hightower laughed anyway. "You knew the joke?"

Stu had relied on the Weyland Foundation in the past. It was he who had made the requests for information for Doc Pete's team.

Frank Dubois limped in (his faltered step a memento of an aircraft accident) and took a seat at the big table, in front of Link and Squid. The chairman of the Weyland Foundation rested a hand on Link's shoulder, acknowledging the gravity of their loss the previous day.

The last person to arrive was Erin Frechette. While she was blessed with a technical mind, that was not the first thing to enter the mind of any straight male capable of registering the slightest blood pressure. She exuded sensuality.

Her priorities were family first, everything else next. She was the widowed mother of a fourteen-year-old boy named John, and after working all night, she'd dropped by her apartment long enough to rearrange her son's schedule. She took a seat by Link and pulled a leather case into her lap. Link inquired about Johnny; they were buddies. She said he was fine.

ADIC Hightower began by extolling the Weyland Foundation as a friend of America. Yesterday that steadfastness had cost them dearly when three employees made the ultimate sacrifice. Hightower paused for a moment of respectful silence, then suggested that they move on.

He began by reciting the rules for the meeting. No audio- or video-recording devices. Classified minutes would be forwarded so everyone could sing from the same sheet. Anyone who felt it necessary could elect to depart by FBI helicopter to maintain anonymity.

"The Weyland Foundation called for this debriefing. Mr. Dubois?"

Frank Dubois introduced Link and Squid, and then

Erin, technical guru for the Special Projects Division, as well as director of a new Applied Technologies branch, where her engineers wrote AI programs for DARPA and various university projects.

He nodded at Erin. "Ms. Frechette."

As Erin walked to the console, her audience focused on subtle movements beneath the fabric of a pale yellow summer dress. She slipped an unlabeled DVD from her briefcase into the media player and spoke in an easy Western drawl. "Make that *Miss* Frechette, would you? I'm single and need all the advertising I can get."

The room exploded with laughter.

"What you're about to see and hear may be a forecast of terrorist attacks on America. If Gwen Svenson recovers fully, we may learn more. For now, after you've seen what we have, you'll have to use your collective wisdom to decide.

"Part of my job at the Weyland Building is to stay in close contact with project leaders such as Doc Pete, and field agents like Gwen and Ace, and to maintain a mental picture of what they're experiencing. I try to know their thoughts and their secrets."

Erin described the Aozou team that had joined up in Casablanca the previous month. Doc Pete had been experienced at managing projects and dealing with Arabs. Ace Acree was a competent full-time foundation employee. Gwen Svenson was a contract hiree, a hospital-equipment consultant with CIA mission experience in Afghanistan. While they'd waited in the pro-U.S. Casablanca, they'd practiced their undercover personas by passing as Arabs.

Erin had telephone-coordinated their visit with Chadian officials at N'Djamena, the capital located in the south of Chad. The bureaucrats there had asked if they'd consider moving the planned hospital southward, where people were Christian and civilized, not Muslim and difficult. She'd responded with a healthy amount of baksheesh—bribe money that greased the political wheels—and was sent visas and letters of safe passage.

The team proceeded to Benghazi, Libya, took a BP-owned De Havilland Otter to a remote oil station at al-Waha in the Sahara, and then south to the Chad border.

There the Otter crew turned back, and the team proceeded by Land Rover. The news of their arrival had been spread, their safe passage assured, but they were repeatedly stopped by militia driving technicals and collecting tolls.

Twenty-six days ago, they'd arrived at Aozou, where hatred between four factions was so heavy, they'd felt it in the air. Battles were like skirmishes between urban L.A. gangs. Combatants marked their territory like big cats pissing on trees, filled technicals with shooters and cruised dirt streets, made senseless drive-by shootings to maintain respect.

Doc Pete set up shop in a fan-ventilated apartment near the prefecture, where the local authorities hid from the warlords. Their contact, a midlevel official named Youssef, showed them around for long enough to make it clear that he wanted the electrical contract when the hospital was constructed. Then like the others, he'd disappeared into the prefecture. Only when they'd hidden the Land Rover, changed their appearances, and blended in did the team relax.

After twenty days, they were finishing their report when Erin called with two RFIs from the CIA. Both were flagged as potentially dangerous, but Doc felt they were no worse than what they'd already been doing, and he agreed to extend their stay for a week. One RFI involved Ace and Gwen driving the hills outside the city. They would keep the vehicle ready and the jerry cans filled. At the first sign of trouble, they would join up with Doc and drive northeast to Egypt.

Two days later, their individual satellite phones had shut down one-by-one, as programmed to do if improper codes were entered, and the team disappeared from her screen.

Erin then explained how she'd monitored the spectrum and finally picked up Doc Pete's weak call over an old VHF French Army radio. He—it turned out that the three were together—was in the no-man's-land far northeast of Aozou, running for Egypt. Link and his crew, ferrying an unarmed Learjet, had been their only hope of salvation.

They'd been able to save only Gwen. Erin explained

how Doc had tossed the good-luck canteen to Squid, told about the danger-fraught takeoff, and described the men's horrible deaths.

Erin paused. "That's the before and after. Do any of you have questions before we discuss what we now know happened before the team's disappearance from Aozou?"

When there were none, she casually smoothed her dress—an act that did not go unnoticed—and used a mouse pointer to activate the DVD.

"Remember the mental picture I keep of our team members? One thing I knew was that Doc Pete carried a digital recorder in a pocket sewn into his robe, and that he kept the controller in another pocket in his sleeve. The lens and microphone were invisible to observers, and he could jettison the whole thing as he walked. The only difficulty was when he had to remove a memory stick, conceal it somewhere handy, and snap another in place. So where did he hide them?"

"The good-luck canteen," guessed the woman from NSA.

"Correct. The tin canteen that had saved his life in Afghanistan. He had it soldered so it held water, and kept it partially filled. Except for the crease, it looked like a million others. With water inside, the sticks didn't rattle, and being submerged didn't harm them. When he was running out of time, Doc Pete threw the canteen to Mr. Worsczejius." She regarded Squid. "Did he say anything?"

Squid nodded. "Yes, ma'am. He said, " 'Take good care of this.' "

"On your way to Cairo, while you and Link were fighting to keep the Learjet flying, I asked if you had the canteen. Next I called a major at the air force's Information Superiority Command, and she flew in a team of officers and NCOs, who met you at McGuire. When we opened the canteen at the Weyland Building, we found six damaged memory sticks. The air force worked their wonders, and we extracted what we could."

"How much?" Link asked.

"Twenty minutes of audio, eight of video, and nine-teen still shots."

He felt dismay. "That's all?" Surely Doc's life was worth more.

"Actually that's a lot. Enough to reconstruct Doc Pete's last day in Aozou."

Erin looked down the table to CIA's Stu Lovelady. "You forwarded the RFIs. Do you mind if I discuss them?"

"I'd rather not, until I—"

"Actually it's only the second request that I'd like to talk about."

As they waited for Stu's reply, a searing pain shot through Link's forehead. He considered taking another hydrocodone pill despite the fact that the medication fuzzied his thoughts. When the pain subsided, he decided against the pill.

He was only beginning to accept the reality that the three men were forever gone. He could go back and wreak havoc, yet men who had relied upon him would still not return.

Link wanted to deny the disaster was his fault, but he could not. He'd seen people die. In combat he'd killed more than his share, but this was different. Needless. The countdown of seconds had been precisely as he'd predicted. Had he played it too close? He decided that timing had been the error, but he was not certain how he should change things if the situation arose again.

"Go ahead," Stu finally said, telling Erin she could discuss the RFI.

"Thank you. Could you provide background for the second request?"

Stu looked about. "Our sources had intercepted telephone conversations mentioning the phrase, 'Six and twenty from Aozou.' We felt it was a trigger—a code that turns an action on or off—or a measurement, like something's twenty-six klicks from Aozou—or just a filler phrase to fake us out. Since your team was in place, we sent the RFI."

"To learn if the phrase meant anything to terrorists in Aozou?"

"We'd not heard of any organized group there, but the phrase mentioned Aozou, and two of the people who spoke the words were Hezbollah."

"What was your internal priority?"

"Quite high considering the two Hezbollah."

Hezbollah—or Hizballah—literally the "Party of God," also called Islamic Jihad, was formed to drive invading Israelis from Lebanon more than thirty years ago. When the Americans and French intervened, the group had kidnapped their citizens and hanged a CIA head of station, but the terrorists preferred using bombs. Hezbollah had blown up a U.S. Marine barracks and embassy. When the Amis and the French withdrew, they'd attacked targets in Spain and Argentina. Nineteen American airmen had died at the Khobar Towers. The terrorists had strapped explosives to Palestinian children to kill Israeli children. The organization was arguably the worst of a despicable lot.

Hezbollah was headquartered in, and supported by, Tehran and Damascus, funded by Saudi charity groups and Saddam Hussein to provide weapons, explosives, and training, and to dole out rewards to the families of child martyrs. Following Saddam's ignominious defeat, Hezbollah had sent suicide bombers and builders of bombs to Baghdad. After the Hussein boys had been Swissed and Saddam was found cowering in a filthy rat-hole, Hezbollah turned from killing American soldiers to blowing up members of the Iraqi council. Al Qaeda had taken credit, yet the ten bombs that brought Spain to its knees had come from Hezbollah's textbook.

Recently the Hezbollah had been infiltrating cells and suicide teams into the United States.

Erin explained that Doc Pete had left the first RFI to Ace and Gwen and taken the second one for himself, using a disguise as a gossipy livestock trader. He spoke slang, mutilated French, pidgin, and Arabic just as poorly as the local rednecks. Add a trader's robe and skullcap, three missing teeth earned playing hockey in college, and his MD when it came to knowledge of donkey husbandry, and Pete seemed perfect for the role.

He'd heard the "six and twenty from Aozou" phrase from travelers, then heard it when it was changed to, "Six and twenty *days* from Aozou."

Stu Lovelady frowned. "Did Doc find out what they meant?"

"Before he got your RFIs, there'd been an inordinate number of visitors to town. Mostly from North Africa, but a few from faraway places like Yemen and Pakistan. Periodically they'd mention that phrase and the name Mullah Sajacento. Doc Pete's merchant buddies thought they were promoting a tent show, maybe a dervish or a magician. They were into gossip, but the travelers were closemouthed fundamentalists, and they didn't want to appear inquisitive.

"I ran Sajacento's name and came up with nothing, so I called on the CIA."

Stu Lovelady gave her a "so that's what it was about" look. "Our North Africa desk had never heard of him."

"Well, now we have his photo, and this morning air force Information people ran a facial-features ID and got a hit. Twenty years ago, a Chechnyan burglar named Muhammad Sazh was charged with murdering a Russian family. He next showed up in a Muslim community in Paris, a holy man using several aliases, preaching hatred for America and Israel. Then it was as if he got a PR agent. He began wearing green robes and claiming to be the judge of men for Allah. He was noticed by the eldest son of an extremely wealthy Saudi family from Riyadh named bin Polah.

"As a result, he may have a few billion dollars to spend killing Americans."

There were murmurs from the room. They'd heard of bin Polah.

"That kind of money is true power. Osama bin Laden had it, and look what he did. Now we have a new contender with another big bag of money."

4

Erin began the multimedia presentation. "During the next forty-five minutes, using videos, stills, and audio from Doc Pete's recorder, we'll find out what happened. There'll be a test. Someone's got to determine if it's a fake or real. Should we be punching a panic button—or putting this one in line with all the others?

"The morning they disappeared, Pete was more concerned about Ace and Gwen being caught than he was about himself. He was just another trader going to work."

Doc's voice came over the speakers describing the weather: "There's a minor *ghibli* blowing. Not a bad one, but enough to turn the air yellow and annoy us with grit in our eyes and noses. I told Ace and Gwen to remain close to the city."

Audio: A muezzin's call to morning prayer. Voices speaking Arabic and French, with interpretations in English at the bottom of the screen. Sounds of Doc Pete whispering, placing his prayer mat and kneeling. He'd had great respect for traditional Islam.

Still photos: Groups of meandering people. "The main bazaar," Pete muttered in Arabic.

"The center of this Allah-forsaken pesthole of a town," added his trader buddy, who had no clue that he was being recorded. The two discussed the various markets, important people, friends, and the many travelers. At the leather bazaar, Pete recorded the words of visitors from Morocco. They were giddy in anticipation of seeing Mullah Sajacento, God's judge of men, who would arrive very soon.

"Is this man a judge, magician, or dervish?" Doc wondered aloud in pidgin, and his trader friend admitted that he, too, was interested in finding out.

There was more audio, interspersed with photos and video clips. An idle period. Chatter about donkey and camel breeds, the diminished price of leather. Complaints about business.

The midday prayer arrived, and out came the mats.

As the faithful were putting those away, new voices were raised. A clip of video showed shouters with megaphones at the edges of the crowd, calling for men of the faith to proceed to the leather bazaar. Another fragmented cry: ". . . the time we have awaited. Great Sajacento, judge of men . . . reveal how . . . destroy America's . . . in six and twenty days."

"There it is," commented Stu Lovelady. "It's definitely a threat."

"Note the distinctive high and mellow voice," said Erin. "That's Mullah Sajacento."

A video showed the mob—males only, some glassy-eyed and supercharged from chewing the *kak* passed out by guards with AKs—pressing around a large, low tent as shouters warned them to "be watchful for pig-eating Americans and British, and despicable Zionists who would sell their daughters to harm great Sajacento."

Another audio clip reminded them of the "sentence for traitors—to be denounced and beaten. Their tongues removed. *To be beheaded.*"

Link's eyes were hard. Had all those things been done to his men?

"Death to traitors!" the crowd responded.

Video clip: Three men in robes and turbans climbed onto a platform. They were blurred; then there was a gap in the video. When they reappeared, the third person was leaving, almost off the platform. Then there were two men left, and it was still difficult to make out their features.

The camera steadied. A shouter pointed at the platform: "Great Sajacento! Right hand of Muhammad."

Link's heart beat faster. Although the image was not good, Mullah Sajacento was graceful, his movements fluid in his familiar emerald green headdress and robe.

Sajacento called out in a voice that was high and sweet: "Honor Allah. Listen to Muhammad the messenger for the true word as I pass judgment on men."

"Blasphemy," snorted a senior officer from the Transportation Security Administration, a Muslim. "The final prophet, the fifth messenger of God and the interpreter of the word and the law, was Muhammad alone."

The images became stills, and the men's features were discernible. As Link stared at the man he despised, the pain from his facial wound became harsh. He swallowed another pill and chased it with water, watching and listening.

Still photo: Sajacento reached skyward, his eyes filled with emotion. The same position Link had seen him assume at the lakebed.

Words flashed across the photo: RECORD FEATURES/ TRACK LOCATION.

Erin explained, "Here Doc was telling us, 'This guy's important. Follow him. Store his features in your memory.'"

Audio: A cheer erupted while Sajacento maintained his messianic pose. "From this place, and on this day, I renew our holy jihad for victory over those who defile our lands. Go home, Americans! Protect your children, or we shall slay them all!"

There was more cheering, more chanting.

Sajacento pronounced a name: Ahmed bin Polah.

Photo: A man dwarfs Sajacento and those around them. Bin Polah is tall, with an immense belly and torso. His nose is bobbed, his features a misshapen jumble of dark and light flesh, with tufts of whiskers where the skin is not ruined. Michael Jackson on a bad day.

Sajacento: "Faithful Ahmed has offered all his worldly possessions so we may fight on. Hasten, dear friend, to the greatest and most evil city of the Great Satan. Six days hence, warn them in the language we know they understand."

"Six days?" said someone at the conference table. "Today?"

Ahmed's voice was grating and harsh. "I will deliver your warning, Great Sajacento."

Sajacento grasped skyward. "Twenty days from this time in Aozou, an army of *jahid* [pronounced *shaheed*, meaning 'martyrs'] more plentiful than bees will follow me into the land of the Great Satan to destroy their future. Then we will do it again, and again."

The roar of the crowd was loud as Sajacento swept his gaze to the four warlords of Aozou, who had joined in the audience's chant: "Great Sajacento. Judge of man."

"Our cause is just. Allah is with us. No army can stop us."

Audio only: "I'll be damned," Pete whispered in Arabic. "He's united the warlords."

"Look. That guard is pointing at us." The frightened voice of Doc Pete's trader buddy. "What can he want? We must leave."

"It's Youssef, an official from the prefecture," Pete stated very clearly. There was rustling, sounds of hurrying. "Youssef is coming after us, bringing others. I'm compromised."

"What?" his buddy asked, but Pete's message was intended for the listeners in the conference room.

There were sounds of the chase: cries for him to stop, of heavy breathing as he ran. Then there were scratching sounds from the audio speakers, and nothing more.

"Doc was able to place the last memory stick in his canteen," said Erin. "He ditched the recorder and disabled his sat phone, thinking he'd be caught, but then he somehow escaped."

"How did Pete connect with his agents?" asked Stu Lovelady.

"Hopefully Ms. Gwen Svenson will fill that in," said Gordon Hightower.

"When she recovers her memory," Erin said pointedly. "Now you know what I know. I've burned a copy of the DVD for each of you so you can take it to your offices. My question is, does it constitute a valid threat?"

"Damned right it's a threat," said the representative from the NYPD.

"But is it valid?" asked the NSA agent. "The an-

nouncement was made in a poverty-stricken town in the
middle of nowhere. The only thing they've ever been
known for is their slave trade and a few uranium deposits. Why would they pick such a godforsaken place?"

The TSA agent was doubtful, unable to believe that
anyone as conspicuous as Ahmed bin Polah could penetrate U.S. safeguards and carry out an attack in such a
short period. "America's on guard. To pull it off would
take a miracle."

Others argued that money buys miracles. While none
had heard of the Chechnyan-born Mullah Sajacento,
whom they would hurry back to their offices to check
further, that was not the case for Ahmed bin Polah, a
Saudi citizen who had openly admired bin Laden and
been a frequent visitor to Saddam's Iraq, and who really
did possess several billion dollars in assets.

"Regardless, six days is impossible," a senior DHS
officer argued.

"*Impossible* is too absolute," said a quiet but often
accurate army general with the DIA.

The chatter continued, some believing, some dubious.

FBI ADIC Gordon Hightower, who had been talking
on intercom with his staff, gained the room's attention.
"That same day Ahmed bin Polah was seen in Tripoli,
Libya. Then he disappeared off everyone's scopes, in-
cluding ours, and those of the British, Egyptians, and
Israelis."

"Perhaps not impossible after all," muttered the
DIA general.

"There's no way he can get into the country in six
days," the DHS officer said doggedly. He reminded
them that the coast guard kept an eye on water approaches, the air guard on the air approaches, and the
border patrol on the ground. The President of Mexico
and PM of Canada were at long last supportive. Joint
patrols worked both sides of the borders in marked no-
enter zones. All who entered the U.S. underwent a thorough questioning and undignified search of their
persons.

Those in the room were professionals, America's best.
They were weary of warnings, of draining the citizens'
hard-earned money, of being reminded of great buildings

falling and shoe bombs and hat bombs and strap-on bombs, and anthrax and smallpox. American and alliance soldiers and agents were being lost in the line of duty. Retired generals in pancake makeup debated new tactics and spoke of weapons that emitted radioactivity, or spewed poisons or disease, all alien to the military they'd known.

Those in the room wanted to stop every threat—it was their sworn duty to try—but for a long time that proved to be a Sisyphean task. Recently they'd believed they were closing in on success, making America a truly secure land.

The big man on the screen had definitely been Ahmed bin Polah, who until five years ago had been cursed with a comically large nose and prominent ears. Following a procedure by a Swiss surgeon to reshape his features, post-op infection had left him with a countenance that looked like pale, rotten hamburger. The surgical team, doctor, nurses, technicians, and anesthesiologist had disappeared, and there'd been talk of horrible deaths.

Ahmed was six feet six, weighed 290, and seemed eternally angry. If he had turned his fortune over to a terrorist, it did not bode well. Although the attendees of the debriefing were split, they agreed that the NSC must be alerted, as well as everyone in the New York disaster preparedness, security, and law enforcement loops. To each they'd fax a synopsis of the meeting and photos of Sajacento and bin Polah.

They were in a hurry to get back to their offices and protect the city, and never, ever again be caught with their pants down.

Before they left, Frank Dubois made the disclaimer that he did at all their debriefings: "The information is yours. The Weyland Foundation can no longer be involved."

As they filed from the room, ADIC Gordon Hightower intercepted Link. "How's the wound?"

It hurts like hell. "It'll do," he said.

"How about I make my phone call to the Washington office, get us a ride to an Italian place I know, and drop you at your building after?" When Link started to beg out, Gordon lowered his voice. "There's a security problem."

Link agreed. They'd meet outside the front entrance in ten minutes.

The group from the Weyland Foundation gathered in the waiting area outside, near the express elevators. "Thanks for taking the briefing," he told Erin.

"You needed help." She stood on tiptoes and appraised him. "You still do."

They were allies and friends.

Erin smiled. "Look at it positively. You're getting a free face-lift."

Link tried to chuckle, but he was stopped by a new jolt of pain.

"Are we on standby for more briefings?" Squid asked Link.

"We gave them what we had. The rest is up to them."

"You're saying it's over for us?"

"I'm saying we're finished with these people."

"What about Tanker and the others?"

"We're done here."

"Bullshit!" Squid glared at him and stomped off toward the nearest stairs.

Link raised his voice: "Mr. Worsczejius!"

Squid halted. Link could see that he was still seething.

"I don't forget either," Link said softly. "I'm just telling you that we've finished with the group inside."

Frank Dubois joined them and pressed a button to summon the elevator to the roof, where a Weyland Foundation helicopter waited.

"Gordon wants me to hang around," Link told him.

Frank was not the prying sort. "Will I see you at the building?"

Link's face ached from all the talking. He held up two fingers, indicating he'd be in Frank's office at two o'clock.

"Coming?" Frank asked Squid as the elevator arrived.

"Yes, sir." Squid gave Link a look. "When you go after them, I want my part of it," he said as he passed by.

*   *   *

As his own elevator descended, Link thought of what Gordon had said. *There's a security problem.* Surely not with his employees. Special Projects was built upon a bedrock of trust. Employees held top-secret clearances, with access to sensitive information, following Level 3 FBI background checks. They were accustomed to speaking freely among themselves.

Link had a not-so-nice thought. *None of the scandals have been directed at Special Projects. Will this be the first?*

He stepped out into the mezzanine, visualizing the murderer in green and the billionaire who wore hamburger for a face. Those two were clear in his mind's eye, but not the third man, who had been on the platform only long enough to decide he didn't like it.

Then there was the unlikely timing. If bin Polah could get in in that short period, what target could he choose with so little preparation? Would another airliner be flown into another building? What had Sajacento meant by saying they would destroy America's future?

Despite hard work and determination, a single factor can impact the most sophisticated scheme. The superstitious call it luck, the ironic call it Murphy's Law, optimists a challenge. *We Muslims call it the will of Allah.*

That was what the large man was thinking as the midsize dark sedan approached the target. He prided himself that he was able to focus and push his fears aside as he estimated how many the explosion might kill. Quite a number, he decided, but it would be better if he could get beyond the entrance so the blast effect would include those in the lobby as well as some of the weight-bearing shell of the structure. Collapse of the immense building was too much to ask, even with the large bomb he was carrying, but he prayed that many of the infidels would die.

He was pleased that it would be caught on video. Tonight his family would watch his last moment on earth. He thought of their pride, how there would be no more averted eyes at the sight of his face.

Once again, the worries descended and he wondered if he shouldn't wait a little longer.

He was trembling so obviously that he was sure the female driver was aware of it. He wanted to stop for a moment to think it through again. The tasks that had seemed so simple—get out of the vehicle, arm the bomb, walk toward the building with the detonating switch in his hand—were impossible to get straight in his mind.

The harness was too heavy. Why had he insisted on carrying so much?

Perhaps he should get the woman to go on past and around the block so he could think it through again. Get everything clearer in his mind.

She was pulling to the curb now. He must not offend great Sajacento.

Link stepped farther away from the entrance to distance himself from a television camera crew setting up in the busy plaza, likely preparing to interview an executive from one of the government organizations in the building. When satisfied that he was out of their view, he pushed his Stetson back so it pressed more lightly on the bandage, glanced at his Rolex, and settled to wait, wondering what Gordon wanted to discuss about security.

He did not want to spend much time at lunch. There were a hundred things to do back at the building, dealing not with terrorists but with the scandals. Sajacento and the specter of his swarms of suicide bombers were now in the hands of the professionals. If they did not find the Green Mullah, it would become his own task, but that would be later, after the Weyland Foundation was removed from the barrage of constant attack.

A black Suburban pulled into the passenger pickup area, where concrete forms prevented vehicles from venturing too close. A neatly dressed female driver and male passenger emerged and looked about, serious as only junior FBI agents could be. Despite the fact that they showed the subtlety of a pair of neon signs, Link decided that this was Gordon's ride.

The television cameras were up and working; the reporter, practicing earnest expressions.

"Our ride's here," said Gordon Hightower as he walked up beside him.

Link maintained his silence as they headed for the Suburban. Some attributed his stoicism to his Blackfoot blood, which he found amusing. Many American Indians were chatterboxes. The facts were—one, he was not loquacious, and two, it hurt like hell to talk.

As they approached the SUV, an agent opened the rear curbside door.

"What's the security problem?" Link asked Gordon before they got in.

"We need to speak with Gwen Svenson to put the rest of the picture together. We know she checked into Saint Anthony's, but when we tried to find her, the nurse said someone had checked her out. Your security office doesn't know anything about it. Did you move her?"

"Of course not."

The last time Link had seen Gwen had been at McGuire Air Force Base, where they were loading her aboard a med-evac chopper. A plain-clothed security officer had said he'd make sure she got to the hospital, and got into the chopper behind her.

He took a sat phone call from Erin, who was on the rooftop waiting to board the helicopter, and listened. "I suggest they find her right away," he said, and when he terminated, he was faced with yet another puzzle.

"That was Erin. Frank wanted to drop in on Gwen. When she tried to arrange it, she was told the same thing as you. I'm guessing security moved her."

"You're guessing?"

"Erin will find her, but I still doubt she'll feel like being questioned."

The FBI ADIC wasn't pleased. "Link, I make my guys stay off your backs regardless if they think you should butt out of our business. But *this* sort of BS makes me wonder."

Link decided to end it and not add to his problems. "Let's go to lunch. Erin will find out where they moved Gwen, and her doctor will let us know when she can respond to questions."

A wash of apprehension swept over Link, as if he were being observed by someone who exuded malevolence. The sensation grew intense and remained as he

scanned the crowd. It was someone familiar and dangerous, someone he had known.

Gordon said something as he started to take his seat,
but Link's attention was fixed on a blue sedan two cars
behind—the woman driver and then the man who awkwardly emerged. Very large, heavily built, wearing sunglasses, a porkpie hat, and a raincoat, a phone held to
his ear.

"He's here!" the woman called Sydney whispered to
herself, and as the vision of Lincoln Anderson was processed in her analytical mind, she realized that in just
seconds the man she hated more than any other would
be blasted into a thousand scraps of flesh. Her fervent
prayers to any deities who might have listened were
being answered.

When she had last seen him, she'd been standing behind Mullah Sajacento, telling the Arab to stand proud
after the majestic thing he had done, his bloody sword
lifted high as Link Anderson flew past and looked down
on his slain employees.

Anderson's death had eluded her then. Now it was his
time, with the atrocities done to his loyal men fresh in
his mind. No vengeance could be sweeter.

Dead, dead, dead.

Link wanted to look away, knowing it was impossible
that there could be a coincidence such as the one his
mind was trying to convince him was happening.

"He's here," Link muttered, marveling at the improb-
ability as he stared at Ahmed bin Polah and his bulk—
as if he were carrying something large and heavy.

5

Gordon Hightower turned in the seat. *"Who's* here?"

There are differences, Link was thinking. The wispy beard was gone. Instead of a robe and turban, he wore a porkpie hat and Burberry raincoat.

On a cloudless and warm day? Hey, pal—this is New York. People wear odd clothes. *He is massive. His face is a patty of bad hamburger like that of Ahmed bin Polah.*

Link's doubts evaporated as bin Polah faltered under his heavy load, grasped the sedan's door until he was upright, and gave himself a shove, heading for the entrance to the Javits Building, holding the cell phone. Link glanced at the sedan that was pulling into the traffic flow. A Chevy? The driver was female, holding something to her own ear. She, too, was familiar.

He broke into a fast gait to intercept the man.

"Where are you going?" Gordon Hightower called from the Suburban.

Link was focused, still unseen by the terrorist, so he walked faster, thinking about the man's bulk. He was wired, and either he or the accomplice would trigger the explosives strapped to his torso. Americans were endangered by another mad-dog terrorist.

Ahmed bin Polah still held the cell phone to his ear, although he had not yet spoken.

Link walked faster, dogging Ahmed as he trudged past the television crew, pointed at the door with the cell phone, and called in an accented rasp: "Look, the vice president!"

The ruse worked. The TV crew switched on their cameras as bin Polah continued staggering under his load, staring ahead at the armed guards at the main entrance who were observing faces, looking for trouble. Ahmed would know about the metal and explosives detectors inside the entrance. He was already close enough to do significant damage. . . .

Link increased his pace, knowing he must get to the killer before the bomb was detonated. The giant had the cell phone to his ear, and reacted as if hearing a voice. He jerked his head about, mouth open with surprise as he stared at the man who had broken into a run.

Time slowed. Mere milliseconds passed as bin Polah dropped the phone and moved his hand to his chest, yet they seemed an eternity.

Link slammed into the terrorist and swept his arms downward, a tackler trying to strip a football from an immense fullback. His heart skipped as a wire was pulled from the raincoat's front, a button-switch dangling from its end.

Ahmed bin Polah twisted in his grasp, reaching for the switch when they came face-to-face, then tripped and fell toward the concrete. The terrorist impacted first and released a grunt as he took the brunt of their combined weight.

Two hats, one narrow-brimmed, the other wider, rolled in opposite directions.

Link felt bin Polah's massive arms moving in his grasp and held on desperately, knowing he couldn't allow him to locate the switch.

"Both of you, stop!" yelled a security guard who was tugging at his pistol.

"Have everyone move back!" Link shouted. His words were hurried, and there was no time for explanation. He tensed his right hand and jabbed the heel toward the base of the terrorist's nose, hoping to propel cartilage into his brain. Ahmed jerked away, and the rock-hard knuckles thumped into pavement. The pain was intense and immobilizing.

Before Link could pull back, the big man butted his head sharply forward, into the wound on his forehead. Pain and giddiness swept over Link, and blood drained from the reopened wound and onto the terrorist's face.

Bin Polah was fast regaining strength, and he knew Link's vulnerability. *Wham!* Again the massive head smashed into Link's face.

Link released a high, involuntary whimper as his vision faded. *Do something!* he told himself, but he was wafting in and out of lucidity, having trouble trying to think. If he was butted again, he'd lose consciousness, and if he couldn't restrain bin Polah's grasping hands . . .

As the terrorist drew back his head, Link tightened his hold to keep him in place. Again Ahmed tried to ram him, but this time Link's head was tucked in tightly. He had trouble keeping a grip on Ahmed's left arm, and twice his hand slipped, but he managed to hold on to the elusive wrist. Again the terrorist tried to butt him, but Link's head was so firmly held into Ahmed's bull's neck that the terrorist could not strike. Ahmed was powerful, and Link had been so intent on his own maneuvers that he did not notice that bin Polah's right hand was moving between them, grasping at his face. There was nothing Link could do to stop clawlike fingers and manicured nails from digging into his cheek. Furrows formed in ragged rows as the talons were drawn downward.

"Damn you, get *off* him!" cried the hovering security guard.

"Bomb. Move . . . everyone . . . back!"

Link mentally girded himself, telling himself that his motivation was more compelling than Ahmed's, that his tolerance exceeded that of this terrorist who would kill innocent humans.

It will boil down to which of us can tolerate the pain.

"Die, Satan's filth!" hissed bin Polah.

Do whatever it takes. Just don't let him get to the button.

Again bin Polah worked his football-size hand upward on Link's face, dug into the bandage, and began to drag his fingernails through Link's wound, snapping stitches and pulling loose the flap of skin.

Link used all his strength to hold the arm in place. Agony pulsated from his wound like penetrating lightning bolts, so intense that it was difficult to think, yet he remained fixed upon the only answer: *Create pain so intense . . . that he cannot . . . function. . . .*

The terrorist's fingers were tearing at stitches, trying to skin Link's face like he might a rabbit. As his wound fired with agony, Link released the terrorist's left hand.

He heard the droning of a reporter: "vicious attack taking place here before us. . . ."

I've got to hurt him so badly he cannot function!

Bin Polah hesitated, for a moment unable to digest the fact that his hand was actually *freed*! He then searched for the switch as he dug his talons deeper into Link's wound.

Link was trembling from agony, yet he continued exploring with his free hand until he found softness: Ahmed's eye. The terrorist shook his massive head and squinted to keep out the intrusion, but by then Link had ground his thumb into the clenched lid and was pressing into the quick of the eyeball, then deeper. . . .

The terrorist released Link's face, and his scream resounded throughout the plaza.

Link continued twisting the thumb, delving, gauging success by the loudness of the shrieks he elicited, wishing he could press the thumb all the way into the son of a bitch's brain.

The reporter's voice raised so she could be heard over Ahmed's screams, describing how "the second man is ignoring orders from security guards, who have now drawn their weapons. Both men's faces are covered with horrible masks of blood."

The terrorist was flailing, trying to twist away, hardly breathing between shrieks.

The solution is to . . . render pain so intense that he . . . can think only of . . .

Link extracted his thumb, eliciting a sucking sound, and placed his full weight onto the bulky explosives so Ahmed was pinned by the combination of man and bomb—and drove a knee into his groin. Another shriek.

The reporter's high voice repeated: "He's trying to kill him!" and was drowned out by the terrorist, whose shrieks were interspersed with grunts each time the knee struck home.

Yet the bomb's trigger was still loose somewhere, and Link had no choice but to continue.

"Damn you, stop," bellowed a hovering security guard, "or by God I'll shoot."

"Back off," ADIC Gordon Hightower said as he arrived through the crowd, ID in hand and pushing his way past the guards, yelling for his agents to control the crowd.

"Move 'em all back!" he told the guards.

The reporter's voice was high with excitement: ". . . we continue to witness the confrontation in front of the Javits Building. Here is the largest concentration of federal lawmen in our nation, yet they appear unwilling or unable to stop this brutal attack. . . ."

Ahmed's eye was useless gore; his testicles jellied. He was blubbering and drained of fight, yet he still posed a menace. Link gripped both the terrorist's hands, leaning on them with all his weight so that searching for the switch was an impossibility.

Later, when the video of the fight was timed, it was learned that the confrontation, from first body contact until Ahmed was a whipped and crying puppy, had taken forty-eight seconds. Part of the reason for the giant's defeat was the tremendous weight of the bomb, part because Link had indeed endured more pain.

Gordon knelt. "What the hell, Link?" Spoken curtly.

"It's bin Polah. He's carrying a bomb, and trying to get to the switch."

"Aw, shit!" Hightower added his considerable weight to the terrorist's hands, despite the fact that Ahmed's struggles had been reduced to shuddering.

"I oughta shoot him," Gordon said.

Link, who was not against the idea, explained another problem: "He was on a cell phone, with his driver I think. She may have a remote detonator, or dial a code through his cell phone."

Hightower yelled to the female agent, the driver of the Suburban, who located the cell phone on the sidewalk, removed the battery, and stomped the remainder into small pieces.

"Get NYPD to locate the vehicle," Gordon told her.

"A blue Chevy four-door," said Link. "With this traffic, she'll still be within a block."

"Tell 'em we're dealing with terrorists and to stop her any way they gotta."

The agent called over her radio. Her partner was using the authoritarian voice learned at the FBI academy to control the crowd, which pretty much ignored him.

"Tell the bomb detail to get the lead out!" yelled Gordon. "We need them here, *now*."

The people who were closest heard his words and finally backed away. "Bomb?" someone cried, and the word was picked up by others.

"The asshole's trying to talk," offered one of the security guards.

Link didn't dare relax his grip, despite the fact that Ahmed had ceased to struggle.

Bin Polah managed a smile that might have been beatific if his face had not been ravaged.

The speech that followed was spoken with a heavy accent: "I bring warning from great Sajacento, Allah's judge of men. Remove your armies from our lands. Nothing else can stop what is to come. Your future will die, and your people will mourn forever."

He hawked as if to spit but instead mouthed something.

"It is Allah's will." He bit down. There was a snap, the sweet odor of almonds.

Link realized what the terrorist had done, and he leaned close to bin Polah's ear: "Take my words to hell, Ahmed. Sajacento killed my men, and you are only the first to pay."

"What did you tell him?" Gordon asked, but Link did not answer.

"He popped a cyanide ampoule," Link said without charity.

Bin Polah convulsed so mightily that he almost tossed Link off. The giant trembled and shook, and was still.

Gordon checked for a pulse. "Nothing."

A dozen sheets of letter-size paper were scattered around, and others peeked from the pockets of the raincoat. Link picked one up.

LEAVE OUR LANDS OR NOTHING YOU DO CAN STOP THE TERROR TO COME. YOUR FUTURE WILL DIE AND YOU WILL BE IN MOURNING. PRAISE ALLAH! HONOR THE PROPHET! SA-JACENTO IS GREAT!

From the looks of horror reflected in the faces about him, Link realized that his own countenance was as hideous as Ahmed's. His forehead was a mass of blood, bone, and ragged patches of skin, deep furrows made by Polah's fingernails.

The crowd had observed a battle between monsters.

As he tried to hold the skin in place, his wound burned like the devil's breath.

Gordon stood, wearing an angry look. "Why the hell didn't you wait for me?"

Link did not answer the most idiotic question of the year.

"You'd better get inside." Hightower turned and cursed. "Aw, *hell*!"

The television crew was panning, focusing on the dead man, on Link's bloody countenance, and on Gordon's grim expressions. The female reporter spoke of the horror, that there was talk of a bomb, that the explosives ordnance detail had been called.

"Damn it, *clear* the area!" ADIC Gordon Hightower yelled at the security guards, and ordered the FBI agents to confiscate the reporter's cameras and tapes in the interest of homeland security. That might have flown if it weren't for the relay van, which had two transmitter dishes and several yagi radio antennas folded out for use.

They were shooting live. The reporter told her audience that they'd been following a tip called in by a person claiming to be an FBI agent, telling them that the vice president would show up to talk to a gathering of agents.

There was no vice president, but what they were getting was better.

Pandora's box, Link thought, *is wide open.*

6

There is, within the Building, a small medical station where employees can get rudimentary first aid. Link was hurried into a back room, where a nurse measured his vitals as the PA applied direct pressure. He withstood the wicked witch of pain and recited that he was up to date on his shots: tetanus, typhoid, typhus, plague, cholera, you name it. The PA had Link move his hand and concluded that he must be treated at a hospital.

"For now just put some kind of a patch on it and kill the pain."

Erin will insist that it be done again by a doctor of her choosing.

The PA asked him to lie back. He'd give him something to relax him and do something to hold the wound together.

Yeah, right. I'll relax.

The PA was right. After a heavy hit of morphine, Link hardly felt the repairs. As the skin was stapled and bandaged, he wafted about the room and read and re-read a flyer on the wall:

Emergency Preparedness Procedures
Be Prepared for No-Notice EP Drills
Know Your Evacuation Route
Know Your Role & Your Duty Station
Report Suspicious Persons & Abandoned Packages

He'd closed his eyes to rest for a couple of minutes, when someone stomped into the room sounding like a squad of jackbooted thugs. In the background was a cacophony of heehaw sirens.

"He's still sleeping," the nurse said, but Link managed to crack an eye.

"It's a circus outside," Gordon grumbled happily. "I didn't know there were this many news crews in the city. I briefed the mayor, and he went on the air, but now they're out there demanding more meat. More specifically, they want more about you."

He helped Link to sit up. ".'No statements," Link croaked.

Gordon snorted. "That wasn't so hard when the world's ugliest dead man was lying out there, coat open and showing off explosives like they were dirty photos. Now Ahmed and the bang box are gone, and the newsies are going nuts for more."

The wall clock showed that Link's couple of minutes of sleep had turned into an hour.

He gracelessly swung his feet over the side of the gurney, groaning because the morphine was wearing off. Along with the burning face, he had scrapes and bruises all over.

Gordon brandished a sheet of paper. "The TV crew got their damn video, so we needed an explanation. My guys wrote this so we'll be using the same hymnals."

"Just keep my name and the Weyland Foundation out of it."

"We'll try. Your face was bloody and your back was to the cameras. If we *have* to say something, you're a rancher from one of those large rectangular states out West."

Gordon sometimes joked about Link's acreage and cattle in Montana.

"What are you telling them about the fight?" he asked.

Gordon read from the paper: "While departing the NYC Federal Building via the plaza courtyard entrance, FBI ADIC Gordon Hightower determined that a person there, later identified as Saudi Arabian national Ahmed bin Polah, was wearing a torso bomb. Agent Hightower took control of the situation, ordering an unidentified male U.S. citizen to temporarily subdue the bomber while he secured the area and located the detonating device. A moment later, when the male citizen called for help, Hightower summoned his FBI training to vanquish the suspect, who took his own life before the senior agent could stop him. Further statements may be obtained by contacting the FBI's regional field office located in the Jacob Javits Federal Building."

Gordon looked up at Link. "Okay?"

Link retained little of it, but a word stuck in his mind. *"Vanquished?"*

"Too strong?" Gordon made a correction. "How about *controlled*?"

Link sighed. "Just keep my name out of it."

"We want you out of the picture as badly as you do."

Gordon was giving him the bum's rush out of the limelight—which, as well as Link could think through in his muddled state, was a superb idea.

He was handed a Macy's bag containing a Rolex watch with a broken band and a soiled Stetson. "We'll take you out in a bureau chopper. I'd advise you to get out of the city for a while and let us handle it."

Link managed to stand, and to walk out under his own power, ignoring the PA's insistence that he use a wheelchair. He didn't need it with an agent fore and aft and Gordon at his side. As they waited for the roof-bound express elevator car, Gordon repeated that Link had not been recognized, but the video was being broadcast to the world and it might happen. He'd pass any instructions through Erin—and gain access to Gwen Svenson as soon as she could talk.

The elevator car arrived, and they stepped inside.

"Something you should know. When the crime scene guys opened Ahmed's coat for a DNA swab, the ATF took a look and almost peed their pants. The forty-kilo bomb was the biggest known to ever be hidden on a human, and written on the harness were the blessings of the master bomb maker at Alpha-Nine."

Even in his fuzzy state Link was surprised.

Gordon shook his head. "Last anyone knew A-9 was in a van located somewhere between Palestine and Syria, working for the Hezbollah. In that business I don't think you can change employers."

According to the CIA and the Israelis, the A-9 professional and his assistant were the best. They measured a *jahid*'s torso, tailored a harness that fit snugly, packed it with preformed plastic explosives, and planted a fixed-impedance booby trap to foil any attempt to disarm it. All of that *before* the *jahid* bomber and the one who would set it off departed for the target.

Had bin Polah slept, eaten, and relieved himself with the bomb attached, all the way from wherever the hell A-9 was currently located until he'd arrived at the Javits Building?

How had he gotten into the country with all that shit hanging on him?

And why hadn't a second person set off the bomb with a remote, as was Hezbollah's normal routine? Alpha-Nine had never had a mechanical bomb failure—until this one.

Gordon said the ATF had not attempted to disarm the bomb with all the people around, just let the crime scene guys take a DNA swab, then dropped Ahmed and the shebang into the boom box, hoping to make it across the city to the blast site. A lot of things were different about this one. But the A-9 chemists had not forgone their booby trap. They'd made it ten feet before the explosion had warped the twelve-inch-thick steel walls of the box.

Link was strapping into the helicopter, trying to think it all over, when Gordon stepped back a pace and eyed him. "You should have told me Ahmed was there, and let me take the guy."

Gordon was actually serious, and was becoming a pain in the butt.

"Maybe next time," said Link.

As they lifted off, Link could see the mob of reporters at the entrance far below. He wondered how long it would take Gordon Hightower to be back down there among them.

1:00 p.m.—Weyland Building Rooftop

Erin waited at the superstructure atop the building, accompanied by a man and woman in white smocks. As Link emerged from the downdraft, she hurried over and went up on her toes, examining his bandage-swathed face, just as she'd done when he'd last seen her.

"You look like a mummy. What the hell have they done to you?" She took the Macy's bag from his hand.

Erin was not trusting when it involved the care of her men. She preferred to bring in the best medical specialists, and to look on critically as they worked.

The effects of the morphine was wearing off, allowing unwanted sensations to creep back into the various areas of Link's body.

"Frank wants to see you, but it'll be *after* you've been seen by the doctors."

"Just saw a doctor," he muttered.

"You were seen by a PA, and who knows what infections you picked up when bin Polah was trying to pull your face off."

"You saw the fight?"

"Along with everyone else in the country." She waved the doctors over. Erin was insistent. She was also methodical, thorough, extremely intelligent, pretty, and unconcerned with her looks. When one of the males assigned to her care was threatened, she displayed mothering instincts so strong that no one dared get in her way.

Link would undergo another inspection, willingly or not. As they followed Erin toward the elevators, he had a disturbing thought about coming out of this looking like hamburger-faced Ahmed.

"Have you located Gwen?" he asked.

"The hospital admin said her sister signed her out, and the officer with Gwen said it was okay. Problem one, Gwen's sister isn't shown on our records, and two, the officer showed identification, but he wasn't ours. Security's running all over the city looking for both of them."

"Call Gordon's people. They can help."

Erin accompanied him to the fifth floor medical clinic,

where the doctors unbandaged and prodded at his wounds, took blood, then conversed as if they were alone and he was not in pain. A female plastic surgeon poked various gashes with avid interest. He asked for a painkiller, and she finally gave him a shot.

"Just don't take alcohol," she warned him, "unless you want to pass out on the spot."

As the doctors worked, Erin phoned Gordon Hightower. Link could hear his vent of anger about them losing Gwen, then a lament about the prying media and how he'd had to agree to appear on national television.

Erin pressed OFF and immediately received a cell phone call.

As he waited for the shot to take effect, Link read a poster much like the one he'd seen at the FBI Building.

Emergency Preparedness Procedures
Be Prepared for No-Notice EP Drills
Know your Role, Duty Station, and Evacuation Route
Report Abandoned Packages & Suspicious Persons

The emergency preparedness people of the different buildings were organized similarly, which was a good thing. Today's bomb attempt would add even more motivation.

Again Erin punched her phone OFF. "There've been three new scandals. All minor and deniable, but they're just that much more harm. Even old friends of the foundation are starting to say where there's *that* much smoke, there's got to be a helluva fire."

Things had been building. According to the "reliable" information sent to journalists and e-mail group discussion leaders, the foundation had been established by rich Jewish dissidents to assist world communism in the overthrow of America. Information from the old USSR's KGB files confirmed plots involving the Weyland Foundation, Secret Police Boss Lavrenti Beria, and the worst mass murderer of the twentieth century, Joseph Stalin.

Upon examination, the accusation was proved to be false, planted misinformation, but some citizens believed all scandals, and now the foundation was dodging new revelations.

The Cultural Earth division promoted artistic endeavors. An article in the *Post* cited sources that accused them of purchasing stolen old master art.

Mankind Earth initiated charitable causes. An article in the *Times* suggested that Mankind Earth cheated its own personnel out of hard-earned retirement funds.

Habitat Earth's wildlife and flora councils purchased vast tracts of ecologically ruined lands around the world and returned them to nature. Yet another "reliable" source had just exposed a sell-off of historical properties to convert to shopping malls.

All would be proved erroneous, but that process took time. The attacks continued, and while investigators and lawyers refuted them, they could not determine who was behind them and the why.

"Anything directed at Special Projects," Link asked as his pain diminished.

"Not yet, but it's coming, and we'll need you here running things. I don't seem to be able to get you to understand how serious it's going to be."

In her eyes he was about to do something rash, and she thought he was being pigheaded.

"I can operate better independently. Frank's anxious to learn who's behind it all."

Erin glared at Link. "You just want an excuse to go back to Montana."

"If Frank goes along with my idea, I'll go there first. It makes sense. I've been away for a year, and Gordon just advised me to leave town."

She repeated that the smear campaign was about to turn nastier, and that it would involve Special Projects. Someone might be hurt.

"Physically?"

"It could happen," she said, although that seemed improbable. They had a security office that was efficient at protecting their people and stopping violence.

"Not many people even know about us, Erin. Those who do, think we kick clods in third world countries and do good deeds."

"Don't we?"

Erin was convinced the attacks were meant to sully their reputation and accustom the public to charges of corruption. A number of congressional representatives already demanded an investigation. The president, who had been supportive in the past, was increasingly quiet.

Erin felt they were being put on the defensive so they'd miss seeing the big one that was to come. She said she was getting echoes of the future. Something big and bad was in the wind.

Special Projects was vulnerable. While they'd toppled despots, one man's despot was another's hero. While they'd encouraged democracy in emerging nations, might another form of government have been better for those peoples, and shouldn't they have found their own way?

Or so the arguments would be made.

Erin was sure that the attack would come soon. If their reputation was sufficiently tarnished, few would hurry to help. The Weyland Foundation would be viewed as another Enron, its image irrevocably damaged.

Link brought up the question that stumped them all. "Why?"

"Please, Mr. Anderson," chided a doctor. "I'm measuring."

Erin had an idea. "One of our projects is a thorn in *someone's* side. They do not want it opened to scrutiny, so they are attacking on all sides to drag us down and stop the project."

Link mulled over her thorny project idea.

"I traced the dates of the attacks back to their beginning, then added and subtracted a few weeks, and came up with a time window. We started only two projects during the period. If I'm right, one of those is the thorn."

The doctors, who also held security clearances, were photographing Link's forehead wound and measuring his face, preparing for surgery. He was considering putting either the doctor's examination or the conversation on hold—when a thought surfaced about the thorny project. "Aozou?" he blurted.

"Timing's wrong. The hospital project was initiated after the slander began. Doc Pete stumbled onto something that we still haven't figured out, but it's not the thorn behind the attacks."

She said one of the projects that fit the timeline concerned Bulgaria. The country's rail system would be upgraded while the city of Burgas received a new terminal and warehousing facility and became the country's industrial shipping center. No one had raised opposition.

Link mused on it for a moment. "What's the other project?" he asked.

"A joint project with the University of California at Berkeley to recover an old document called Shepherd's Journal."

Erin's new Applied Technologies branch used pixel-by-pixel imaging and an artificial intelligence program to decipher indistinct letters and words, and repair such old writings.

"The organization they're learning about was downright sinister hundreds of years ago."

"It sounds unlikely that it's involved," he said.

"Maybe, but I still think one of those projects is the thorn."

They glanced at one another. With the new attacks on the foundation, it seemed even more certain that Link would soon leave the organization to discover who was behind the vilification.

Erin pleaded, "Don't do it, Link. We need you here."

At three thirty, Link left the clinic aesthetically improved (the only obvious sign of his wound was a narrow bandage that crossed his forehead), having been administered more antibiotics and anti-inflammatories, and given a larger bottle of painkiller. The plastic surgeon would operate in two or three days, when the swelling was reduced.

Link promised to return to see Erin later, and he took the elevator up to where Frank Dubois maintained a soccer-field-size office.

Frank met him at the door, congratulating him on stopping bin Polah. He pointed at a stuffed chair and sat in another. "I've had phone calls from about everyone who's aware of what happened, including the vice president and the Director of the FBI, asking me to shake your hand. Same with the members of the financial board."

The latter congratulators, scions of "old money" and among the wealthiest individuals in the nation, controlled expenditures for the Weyland Foundation. Link respected them for their contributions. On the other hand, he doubted that he was known by the vice president, whom he admired, or by the Director of the FBI, about whom he had mixed feelings, so he simply nodded.

"The guy in the cowboy boots is the media's new hero."

Link's stepfather, who had flown two tours of heavy-duty combat in Vietnam, had told him that the news media felt that human nature was as selfish as they were, and pronounced few lasting heroes who were not reporters, actors, or enemies of the bully U.S.

He changed the subject. "They're saying the bomb was made by Alpha-Nine."

"So I was told. This failure was their first big mistake, which makes you damned lucky along with being damned good. Care for a Scotch?" Frank asked.

"The doc said I shouldn't."

"I'd better not either. Another late meeting. We're holding a large-scale disaster-preparedness exercise tomorrow, and I have to approve the scenario."

"I saw the flyers. The DP people are getting serious."

"We hired a high-powered consulting firm to make sure we get it right. Our safety committee will look on and take notes."

Frank's secretary spoke over the intercom. "I know you didn't wish to be interrupted, sir, but the caller says it's important. Mr. Biddell of the *New York Times*." Lawrence C. Biddell was the *Times*'s newest editor in chief.

Frank went to his desk, grumbling that it had damned well better be important.

"What can I do for you, Lawrence?" Frank said pleasantly, partly because the foundation could use all the good PR they could get.

Frank listened much and said little. He ended with a single word, "No," then thanked him and hung up muttering a mild curse.

He pinned Link with a sour look. "We just found Gwen. She contacted their city desk, and identified you as the guy who stopped the attack, and us as your employer."

Link was taken by surprise. *Gwen?* He couldn't see her in the role of whistle-blower.

"She claimed you were the VP of a secret division here, and that you had just returned from the Middle East, where you were involved in international espionage, causing the deaths of three employees."

After a moment of reflection, Link nodded. "Everything she said was true."

"Bullshit. You didn't *cause* anyone's death. You were doing your damnedest to rescue your people. It's more slanderous lies, mixed in with just enough fact to make it dangerous. When Biddell asked her to come in and tell her story, or even meet him somewhere, she said she was afraid we'd harm her. She'll send him a signed letter giving names and places."

"Is the *Times* running the story?"

"Lawrence wants second source verification, which I did not provide. They've been stung, even humiliated, for going to print without second sources." He paused. "If they can authenticate the letter, they'll print it."

"It's getting worse, Frank, just like Erin thought. It's time for me to leave and go to work on it."

Frank looked troubled. "Perhaps we should think it through again."

"The foundation can't afford more revelations *or* to wait."

Frank limped to the window that overlooked the city and stared for a while.

Link followed. "Erin's convinced that the charges are made by someone trying to stop one of our projects. Maybe something that appears minor on the surface. I have trouble with that, but she's not often wrong."

"No, she's not."

"While I'm gone, I'd like to continue working with her."

"Of course. I'll let the handful know what you're up to at our next board meeting."

"But no one else, Frank. I trust them, you, and Erin.

Everyone else I'm paranoid about because their agenda doesn't include helping us. Gordon Hightower's gone Hollywood, fighting for scraps of publicity and a shot at deputy director at the bureau." Link's face had been racked with stinging sensations as he'd spoken, yet the pain hardly registered. His adrenaline was flowing.

"When do you want to go?" asked his friend.

"Right after we have that Scotch you offered."

If he passed out as the doctor had predicted, at least he'd have a good sleep.

7

Link took the restricted elevator down to the twenty-seventh floor, accompanied by two healthy-sized security officers who watched his every move as if expecting him to bolt and run. There was no longer a TOP SECRET pass clipped to his lapel. When he emerged from the elevator car flanked by the wary officers, he was stopped at the security desk, logged in to the custody of the officers, issued a white V badge to show that he held no "need to know," and was allowed to proceed "to your office only." The security guard appeared sheepish. Link had approved her for the job.

At 5:20, Link was ushered into suite 2775, which he'd occupied for the past decade. Erin's mouth was drawn. Frank had telephoned her in the security officers' presence, to tell her that Link was being terminated. He had no further need to know classified information, and he was to take nothing that belonged to the foundation.

Erin asked the security officers to remain in the outer office, saying they'd be finished in a few minutes, closed the door between them, and turned a look on Lincoln Anderson that was well beyond simply being upset.

"Why, for God's sake, are you doing this tonight? You're about to collapse with exhaustion, and you're scheduled for surgery in two days. Would you just *once* listen."

When he told her about Gwen Svenson's statement to the *Times*, she was as shocked as he had been. "I can't believe it!" Erin said. "*I'm* the one who brought her

over from the CIA to work with Doc. I interviewed her
and liked her, and I hired her."

"Don't take all the blame. Stu Lovelady recom-
mended her, and her performance reports were
outstanding."

"I still feel awful. And now this? Why are you rushing things?"

"Because I can afford to. I have the best replacement
we could possibly find."

"If you're talking about me, not yet, and not if I can
talk you out of this madness."

"Frank will call you at home to make it official and
speak to the division managers in the morning. I recom-
mend Squid Worsczejius as your number two. He's still
upset about what happened at the lakebed, but he'll
work through it. He's determined, his head's on right,
and he'll have time to learn the basics because there'll
be no covert projects. While I'm gone, none are to be
proposed, and none approved."

Erin raised an eyebrow. "Does the handful know of
this?"

"Frank used his prerogative as chairman. For now he's
notifying them that my contract is voided by mutual
agreement. He'll explain more at their meeting on
Monday."

"I hope they chew his butt off. Neither one of you
listened to anything I said."

"I'll be in touch, and then I'll listen all you want."

She continued to glare. "Take your sat phone, charger, and plenty of batteries."

"I can't. Security has orders not to let me remove
anything belonging to the foundation."

He examined his in-basket and desktop. Aside from
a flyer telling the employees to expect an emergency-
preparedness drill sometime in the next two days, it
was clean.

She sighed. "If you're leaving tonight, I'll call flight
scheduling."

"I'd rather not use a foundation jet."

She gave him a look like he was being a pain in the
butt.

"I'll take a charter flight to Washington—*not* one operated by my father's company because of his contracts with the foundation—and see my stepparents." He wanted them to know he was okay, and not to listen to what they might hear.

"Well, at least I can set up *that* flight." She tapped keys on his desktop PC. They settled on an eight-o'clock showtime at Teterboro. He'd spend the night at Falls Church, get a hop on one of his father's jets to Kalispell, where he'd left his pickup, and drive to Boudie Creek.

"I'll be there by afternoon," he told Erin.

"Stay in touch. I've got a bad feeling about all this." Erin handed over his repaired Rolex and freshly cleaned Stetson.

"I promise." He snapped the familiar watch onto his wrist.

She shook her head and sighed again, as if he still didn't get it. "First they put us on the defensive, now they've forced us to change our corporate structure and cease all covert actions, which was the primary reason the foundation was created."

He tried to make her smile. "Think of it as adjusting to meet a problem head-on."

"You're trying to make ice cream out of cow patties. Think of who Gwen's statement benefits, and you come up with the people behind the smear campaign. They're finally striking at Special Projects just like I predicted, and it's going to get worse."

"I thought you said there's no connection between the slander and Aozou?"

"Listen harder, Link. Aozou wasn't the thorny project, but they're all connected. Everything that's happening to us all at one time is not by coincidence. When the media hears Gwen's version of what happened at Aozou, they'll rub our faces in the dirt again. Today, *right now*, the Internet's buzzing with predictions that top officials of the foundation are about to run like rabbits. And guess what? We've got employees who read it and are scrambling to be first to put their paper on the street.

"We've got to find Gwen and learn why she turned."

"Now that's *really* smart. Gwen's telling them she's scared of us and she's all but accused you of murder.

What do you think the media will say if we continue looking for her?"

"Yeah. Bad idea." He looked around the office, trying to find enough personal items to fill his briefcase.

"Quit that—you're making me nervous. I'll UPS your sat phone and anything else you'll need. Then we'll go to work trying to get to the bottom of what's going on. Who knows, maybe you're right and Helga and I are wrong?"

He knew better than to join that argument.

"How's your forehead?"

"The painkillers are working." He did not mention the glass of good Scotch whisky.

"Good. There are a couple of things I want you to take with you."

Erin handed him an expensive zip-up folder that exuded a new leather smell. "Inside is everything we have on the Shepherd's Journal project: a six-page executive summary and our translation of the first eleven pages. Don't worry about security. It's marked unclassified."

"You honestly think it's the thorn you talked about?"

"Not at all. It's more like the only remaining suspect. Perhaps it's not the culprit, but I'm convinced it has something to do with our problems. You'll find it interesting—it's about California treasure, a weeping tree, and a band of murdering pirates and terrorists."

Link wondered. "I still don't see the connection."

"I'm not at all sure either."

He took the folder. "You said you had two things for me to take with me?"

She gave him a sly look. "So I'm now the VP, and you're on the outside?"

"That's the truth."

Erin walked over before him, reached up to grasp his lapels and pull his face down, and kissed him softly on the lips, dwelling for too long for it to be called friendly.

She released him. "Be damned careful, Lincoln Anderson."

Erin Frechette opened the office door and walked out without a backwards look. When the two security officers peered in, Link stood where she'd left him, heart thumping like a fifteen-year-old's.

The guards led the way out, and Link followed.

3:55 p.m.—San Francisco, California

Although only forty-two years old, Judge Lyle Bull wore his thin, mouse-brown hair swept forward to conceal baldness. A constant frown and amber-tinted mirror glasses gave him a cold, reptilian look. He was of average height, but was thick waisted and barrell chested, with a bull's neck and muscular arms and legs that bulged against the material of his custom-made suit. Years ago he'd played noseguard on the Eureka Loggers high school football team, and also for another three years at Stanford. There'd been an offer to go professional, but he'd elected to stay and attend the School of Law.

The judge arranged the next day's meeting, knowing that when you want to do something right, you do it yourself. He began by sending a one-line e-mail message to five addressees:

Meeting tomorrow. 10 o'clock at the Odd Fellows
Hall. Be there, E. J.

He telephoned their restricted numbers in the order that they had been accepted into the society, leaving a similar message in each of their voice mails. He was surprised when Wendell Welk, who was third on the list, answered, for all were busy men.

"Did you see the mess on television?" he asked Welk.

"Yes." His voice was rasping. The man could wear a tuxedo and still, because of his terribly pocked face and cruel expression, look like a street thug. He was chief of a small-town police force, and ran a tight ship. "Dumb shit rag-heads," he said. "If they didn't have all that oil money, they'd be shoveling camel shit."

"Yes, but we mustn't bite the hand that provides the feast."

They both chuckled. None of the others dared to be so personal or chatty, but he and Welk had known and relied on one another since childhood. Their fathers had relied on one another, and their fathers before them. They both had a line of ancestors in the book dating back even before an Indian member's name had been shortened to Welk.

In his youth Wendell Welk had also been muscular and tough, and had played fullback on the same high school team as Bull. He'd possessed a quick wit, yet the girls shunned him after a popular sophomore cheerleader made a snotty joke that he should get a job as the "before model for an acne ad." Try as he might, he'd been unable to get her to stop the gibes, or to halt the unsightly rash of pimples that flourished on his face and neck. Welk still had the residual scars.

One day the sophomore had disappeared on her walk home from school. She was taken to a lonely beach and beaten, her limbs were broken, and she suffocated on her own foot, which Welk had forced into her mouth. El Jefe, then sixteen, had provided the car and helped his friend dispose of the body, chopping it into pieces and hauling it out in a boat, dropping off the bigger portions tied to the rusty disks of an old set of Weider weights.

"I'd guess you're calling to set up a meeting," said the police chief.

"Tomorrow morning at ten," responded the Honorable Judge Bull.

"Dinner afterwards with the wives?"

"Send her out of town. It's going to last for a few days. Good-bye, Wendell."

The judge continued calling and leaving voice messages. Members checked voice and e-mail daily. There was no excuse for missing a meeting. None. He'd once absented himself from proceedings of the Ninth Circuit Court of Appeals, of which he was a sitting justice, rather than miss a meeting.

When he finished calling the members, he put some thought into his next phone calls, for those—trusted friends and relatives all—were candidates for membership.

8:00 p.m.—Teterboro International, New Jersey

Link boarded a Gulfstream bound for Reagan International along with three other executives who wanted to avoid the hassle of scheduled flights. He'd taken his belongings from a leased, fully furnished condominium, all of which had fit into a hang-up and two duffel bags, along with two boxes containing his good Stetsons and two more containing dress boots.

As they settled into their seats, Link's attention was drawn to a nearby Learjet, painted royal blue and marked with the Weyland Foundation logo, barely discernible in the airport's lights. He felt a pang of nostalgia, for he had piloted the craft several times.

The crew had boarded when he'd been standing outside. Surprisingly, he'd known only one of the members.

He casually wondered where they were going, watching as two women and two men climbed aboard. One woman appeared unsteady, and for a moment he was certain it was Gwen Svenson. But that was too unlikely. When after a few seconds the boarding steps were raised and the hatch closed, he looked away. She'd been on his mind, and he was weary.

Still . . . He fought an impulse to telephone Frank Dubois and ask if there'd been new developments. But there could be no more calls to Frank for a while.

The Gulfstream was first to taxi. He forgot about the Learjet and turned to his reading.

After opening the leather folder and extracting the first of two documents—pausing to critique the takeoff, as pilots tend to do—he focused his concentration and started reading from the top.

The summary opened with an explanation of the organization. The newest branch in the Special Projects Division was Applied Technologies, formed by Erin Frechette, who had taken on the role of branch chief in addition to her other tasks. For AT she employed a video expert and a number of software engineers who were adept at designing expert systems driven by artificial intelligence. They'd devised one called the Document Recovery System, consisting of detailed scanning hardware, and a complex AI word-processing program powered by Helga, the foundation's brute force server (operating at fifty teraflops—meaning fifty trillion, or one million million, floating-point operations per second) to decipher words, sentences, paragraphs, and entire documents.

A stunning number of historically important papers were lost to posterity because they'd become faded and unreadable after exposure to light, moisture, insects, bacteria, mold, mildew, and more. The new branch worked with ultrasensitive cameras and scanners, and it used formulae that considered context, subject, writing styles of authors, and even the placements of individual alphabetical letters. With as few as three appropriately spaced letters per paragraph, the system postulated which of the trillion or so different answers were most correct. With each calculated guess, earlier passages were changed, as would be the ones to come.

The Document Recovery System was proved on a packet of moisture-ruined letters from Benjamin Franklin to the Congress. While purists were horrified at liberties taken with Franklin's flourished wording, all agreed that his intent had been faithfully reproduced.

That was all that Link knew of the expert system devised in Erin's "spare time."

He turned the page and read about their second experiment of the year.

EXECUTIVE SUMMARY

Joint Project: 05-02

Short Title: Shepherd's Journal

Subtitle: Sociedad Serpiente ("Snake Society")

Legend: Entered January 23, 1885, California State History Reference

Before the first arrivals of Europeans, a vicious group of renegade Indians were said to prey on the tribes of Northern California by use of intimidation. By the time of the Spanish and Russian settlements, they knew the tumultuous Pacific coastline and its wayward currents well, and soon began to wreak their havoc by both land and sea. From that time through the transference of California to the United States and then until the end of the American Civil War, they were feared as ruthless killers (variously called Snake People, Serpents of the Seas, Serpent Society, Serpientes Obscuro, and Sociedad Serpiente) who would lie in wait for shipping commerce along the rugged Northern California coast. They were said to be as "elusive as phantoms, to know every ebb and flow, sea swell and craggy rock, and to be as ruthless as hell's demons." Believers in their legend wrote that the Serpent People were responsible for the frequent disappearances of vessels with all hands, often listed as lost to "unknown causes." There were tales of fishing boat crews and coastwise schooner crews sailing through fields of floating human torsos. Although the waters near Cape Mendocino teem with dangerous rocks and shoals, sharks and carnivorous fishes, believers insist that these remains were of seamen and passengers killed and mutilated by the pirates. While no one reported actually seeing the Serpent People, believers attributed that to the fact that all witnesses were eliminated.

In August 1864, various California newspapers reported that a man calling himself Shepherd, with a severe limp and withered right arm, emerged from the giant sequoia forests near Eureka, on Humboldt Bay, three hundred miles north of San Francisco. He was scarecrow thin and, despite the heat, clutched a ragged woolen coat to himself, crying out his praise to the Lord for his deliverance. Shepherd said, "Hurrah, for I have recently escaped the Snake People after a decade of miserable bondage" and for proof showed his many terrible scars. He further stated that he had taken with him one of the two journals he had maintained for his captors. In it were descriptions of the pirates, their past, their bloody crimes, locations of camps, watercraft, and caches of gold and treasure. The Sociedad Serpiente (as they called themselves) were only six in number, yet had their gruesome ways with larger groups by instilling fear.

Hovering near death, Shepherd warned his listeners to beware when they ventured south, for the Sociedad was merciless. Some they killed ceremoniously, using a red stone as their altar, daubing victims' blood onto a misshapen redwood called the Weeping Tree, which periodically made sounds as if mourning the misery that surrounded it. The society dominated nearby tribes, who were not allowed to view their members, and have through the years murdered most of those tribesmen. Like mythical creatures, they moved effortlessly between shore and sea, knowing every tide, current, and swell of the tumultuous waters, and steering craft of all sizes into the Death Tide at Angel Rock (about which Shepherd did not elaborate).

For the dubious, he recited names of prominent Californians lost at sea in their luxurious yachts during the decade, and explained that he'd met them. They were driven aground, their ships plundered, the men used as beasts of burden until they starved or were worked to death, the women accommodating their captors' whims. Slaves all, kept in the cavern beneath the Weeping Tree, where Shepherd had been chained until he'd fashioned a key of ironwood and awaited the next violent earthquake to escape. His listeners remembered that quake well, for it had broken window glass in Eureka and rattled San Francisco.

During the tumult, he had opened the lock and crept past the "sentinel," a prisoner the Serpientes had tortured and starved into madness until he did their every bidding for a morsel. Shepherd escaped, and no nectar was so sweet.

The story told by Shepherd was so bizarre that listeners demanded proof in the form of the journal. He replied that he'd been hindered by its weight, so he'd covered it with stones and left it on a ledge high over a stream teeming with river eels and salmon. Inside are secrets of great riches, but beware the wrath of the Serpientes.

In spite of Shepherd's warnings, at least two parties were formed to locate the journal. One group tried to backtrack Shepherd's journey, but they soon found the wilderness was too vast and the task formidable—there were thousands of hillsides overlooking streams with abundances of river eels and salmon. When three of their number disappeared, a search party found no sign of them, and soon became lost themselves in the dense forest, swearing that their compasses would not function. They returned empty-handed and discouraged.

Another party proceeded down the coast in three hardy craft, looking for Angel Rock, where Shepherd said a deadly current, *marea muerta*, was used by the pirates to propel themselves safely ashore. When one of the crews tried the maneuver at a rock projection near Cape Mendocino, their boat was lost along with the three souls aboard. The others returned to Eureka insisting that Shepherd lied, since the maneuver could not be duplicated without being dashed on the rocks.

As Shepherd's health improved, he became taciturn. He permitted no more visitors into his hospital room, nor did he allow his ragged coat to be moved beyond his reach. The reporters replaced his revelations with reports from the War of Secession.

The matter might have been forgotten had a reporter not learned that Shepherd had opened accounts at both Eureka banks with nuggets from the lining of the coat he guarded so earnestly. To fuel speculation, Shepherd moved into the richly furbished Inn of Eureka and purchased two woolen suits made in London. A new storm brewed at the Northern Californian newspaper in Uniontown, just across the bay, where a past editor, Mr. Bret Harte, opined that if Mr. Shepherd's nuggets were stolen goods, shouldn't he try to locate the rightful owners in order to return them?

In October, the matter was resolved when Shepherd suddenly disappeared. The sheriff reported that blood and ugly matter were splattered about his second-story hotel room, and a gout of it led to the window, where something "about as large as Mr. Shepherd was cast out." A "gorie trail" showed that the crippled man was dragged behind a wagon or buggy for the mile to the waterfront, but nothing more was found.

Added August 11, 1893, California State Historical Department Reference

In June of 1892, a discolored rectangular package was discovered by a state survey crew near Leggett's Valley on the Eel River. None of the crew were aware either of the existence of Shepherd's Journal or the legends of the Sociedad Serpiente. Upon cutting through a thick covering of congealed sap that had protected the document for twenty-eight years, the foreman noted that neatly scripted on the outer page were the words: AUGUSTUS P. SHEPHERD, JOURNAL: 1854 to 1864.

The foreman placed the document in a bin in a mule-drawn supplies cart, and four months passed before the survey team returned to Sacramento, during which time the pages were subjected to various elements and twice submerged in rainwater. In March 1893, the Western History Department of the University of California at Berkeley was given possession of the document. Unfortunately, when the pages were spread to dry, they were found to be ruined and unreadable.

Added February 9, 1907, California State Historical Dept. Reference

In this millennium, most California scholars consider the stories attributed to Mr. Augustus Shepherd, as well as more vague accounts of the Serpent People, to be—like those of highwayman Joaquín Murietta—folklore that is only tenuously based on fact. Yet while the legends of Shepherd and the Serpiente are not believed to be authentic, they remain as important myths of early California folklore.

Added June 24, 1979, Univ of California Historical Department Ref. Note

Attempts to interpret portions of the document have been made in 1921, 1948, 1962, and 1979. All, despite advances in modern technologies, have been unsuccessful. The document is in an advanced state of deterioration, and several pages are irretrievably destroyed by experimentation. There must be no further efforts to renew translation efforts until new technologies make success feasible.

Link placed the summary back into the folder, and thought about what he had read for the final ten minutes of flight. While the tale was entertaining, he could see no connection with the current world, and less of a link to the problems besetting the Weyland Foundation. Perhaps there would be something more useful in the eleven translated pages.

At the present, he had more pressing tasks. Find the source of the problem for the foundation, and when Frank had that one in hand, Link vowed to locate Mullah Sajacento and do what must be done. If the two were interrelated, as Erin believed, that would make things easier.

As they entered the intricate landing approach that had become mandatory after the tragedies of 9/11, he phoned ahead so he'd be met by an employee of his father's flying service. He'd try to get on tomorrow's schedule, then take a cab to Falls Church.

Link felt the pleasantness of returning to the place of his childhood. His stepmother kept his room just as he'd left it. He wanted to talk with his stepfather, Paul "Lucky" Anderson, who offered good advice but never pressed it on anyone.

As the Gulfstream's tires touched the tarmac—he gave the pilot a rating of six—he thought again about Erin's kiss and decided once and for all that she'd not meant it as a promise of more to come.

8

10:00 a.m.—Old IOOF Hall Building, Lennville, California

The Northern California town of Lennville was founded in the decade before the Civil War by families who settled, farmed, and ran cattle on the fertile land that stretched to the Pacific Ocean, several miles distant. While little could be done to protect the townsfolk from frequent earth tremors, they did construct sturdy buildings and plotted their town so it was protected from the blustery ocean winds by a series of rolling hills. A score of immaculately preserved Victorian homes, all listed in the state's registry of historical buildings, remained. Once several homes in a nearby town had been carefully torn down and reassembled in San Francisco, replacing those that had burned in the Great Fire of 1906, or had been toppled by earthquake. Unlike many homes in San Francisco, those in Ferndale and Lennville were constructed of brick and durable redwood.

The owners frowned on those who would sell their town's soul. Lennville was a jewel in the middle of nowhere. Thirty-five marshy miles to the north was Humboldt Bay and the city of Eureka, rowdy from its inception five years before peaceful Lennville—a fact that ate at local pride—by gamblers, gold seekers, merchants, seamen, lumbermen, and a fort filled with unenthusiastic soldiers, including Capt. Ulysses Simpson Grant.

The redwood forests south of Lennville were so thick and wild that much of them would still be poorly charted were it not for overhead satellites. A sprinkling of communities along the only highway catered to tourists, pot farmers, and various brands of invading tree-huggers, all the way to Santa Rosa, 250 miles distant, the first city of substance in that direction.

The IOOF Hall, where the Society was meeting, had been built in 1871, and like the attached offices and the long-closed businesses, it was owned and maintained by the men in the room, whose organization had nothing at all to do with the Independent Order of Odd Fellows. Six of Lennville's finest Victorian homes were owned by men in the room, but only three—the mayor, chief of police, and the owner of the largest fishing boat fleet on the West Coast—actually lived there more than part-time. The remainder commuted by private airplane whenever a meeting was called.

Theirs was a very exclusive rich men's club.

"Call to order," said the judge, the Honorable Lyle Bull, called El Jefe by all who were present. "I name the members: Bull, Lilac, Welk, Deaton, Fuentes, Zerbini."

On the bench, Judge Bull could frighten zealous attorneys and unruly defendants into silence just by staring. The members within this room did not become unruly. Their rituals were simple and easily comprehended, like those of other brotherhoods, such as Masons, Moose, or the Odd Fellows, whose lodge number in Lennville had been declared inactive in 1948.

While individual offices in the building next door were furnished with state-of-the art computers connected by wide band from an array of satellite dishes to worldwide stock markets and a host of organizations, the old IOOF chamber was more reflective of the nineteenth century. There were no telephones. Five oaken chairs were arrayed in a fan before the larger, central one that was occupied by El Jefe. One chair, closest and to his right, was vacant.

"Five are present," El Jefe growled in his guttural voice. "Julius Lilac is missing."

According to the book, from the beginning their number was six, never more or less. Unless all were present for meetings, their decisions might be less than wise. Julius Lilac, their scribe and keeper of the book, a member of the Society for far longer than anyone here, was also the founder of California's best known winery and, perhaps as a result, suffered from acute diabetes. Once he'd flown to Lennville meetings in his Gulfstream—which he'd piloted, as El Jefe did with his Cessna Citation—landing at their private strip east of town. This was the third consecutive meeting Lilac had missed, so El Jefe would have to decide whether he should be "sent to the stone" (a ritual that cancelled one's membership), or wait for the illness to improve.

Beyond the door, in an anteroom, were two nonmembers, trusted friends, or close relatives of Sociedad members, each hoping to be called on to help and earn membership. Like members, any determined to be untrustworthy by El Jefe were sent to the stone.

No two relatives could be members at one time, although when a member died, El Jefe might appoint a relative in his place. If a member fell from his favor, there was a single consequence: "expulsion to the stone." Those chosen to be sent to the stone knew nothing of the decision until they were taken. According to the rule a Jefe could send the fallen member's relatives and friends, as well, so they could not conspire. With the passage of time, many secret organizations mellowed. Masons no longer drew and quartered those members with loose lips.

It was left to El Jefe to ensure that the same did not happen to the Sociedad Serpiente. The rules were written in the book. Memorized by new members. Safeguarded by the scribe. Studied by members who visit Julius Lilac wishing to brush up on their history and rituals.

Save for a single slave of the Sociedad who lived one and a half centuries ago, no one had survived a trip to the stone. That slave's name was Augustus Shepherd, first compiler of the book, and he'd done them harm. Since that time, there had been no slaves, and trusted friends and close relatives were thoroughly scrutinized.

"Is our fortune great?" El Jefe asked in their age-old meeting opening. Greed was their sole motivation. All were obscenely wealthy, and they all wanted more.

"It is great," said treasurer Harry Deaton, who was

mayor of Lennville. "Since last we met, we've received two million in interest, three million from normal business operations, two million for smuggling various persons, and three million for importation of drugs. This morning twenty million more was transferred to us for the safe passage, preparation, and transportation of Mr. bin Polah. The cost of doing business has been nine million. We have increased our fortune by some twenty-one million since our last meeting, Jefe."

El Jefe insisted that he round to the nearest million, an odious act to the fastidious Deaton. Much of the sum would be distributed to the members, and El Jefe would receive twice that of the others, yet he did not smile. Instead he asked a second question. "Are there troubles?"

"There is a trouble," says Deaton, whose response was no surprise. They'd all watched the coverage on CNN and Fox News.

"Our contract with Sajacento was to receive ten million dollars for getting each *jahid* into the country, ten more to prepare and deliver him to their specified site, and ten more for success. This time there was no success. We got only twenty million."

"Only?" Like El Jefe and Welk, Peter Zerbini was a large man. He was the youngest in the room, with eyes that constantly shifted. His family had owned fishing boats and restaurants in San Francisco and Eureka for the past century and a half. The eldest son of the Zerbini family had been made a Serpiente since 1872. Of Italian extraction, the Zerbinis made annual pilgrimages, and ordered suits tailored in Rome and hand-crafted shoes from Florence. They knew the coastal waters better than any others, had a large number of boatmen in their employ, and frequently whisked people and contraband ashore underneath the coast guard's nose.

The family was immensely wealthy from its years of involvement with the Sociedad. Zerbinis controlled West Coast fishing and much of its commerce. Subsidiaries in Canada and Mexico brought in more riches yet.

Peter argued often with Harry Deaton, whose family had not been so distinguished. "We did damned well, Deaton. We smuggled Ahmed bin Polah ashore, imported the explosives, and brought in their chemists. We flew the idiot to New York, and El Jefe's half sister drove him to the building's doorstep. We can't carry their bombs for them. Or at least *I'm* not carrying one."

The treasurer puffed up like an angry toad. "Zerbini, despite your family's ties, you yourself are our newest member. Let me remind you that we're all here to make profit. I just spoke of ten million dollars! Why get that close and throw it away?"

"If we're *too* greedy, we risk losing it all. You just read the accounts. We have other business and more yet coming from this Sajacento. How many suicidal fools will he send?"

Peter Zerbini was critical to their marine operations, but El Jefe knew that Deaton was right. Even a Zerbini must learn.

"There will be ten *jahid* this next time," said Deaton, "and if those succeed, there will be even more."

"*Jahid* meaning idiotic suicide bombers?"

"Literally," sniffed stodgy Mayor Deaton, "it means warriors of the holy jihad."

"They're idiots. How much will that be at twenty million each?"

El Jefe interrupted with a growl. "Do not even *think* of the lower number."

Deaton's mouth was still open to respond to Zerbini. He closed it, and a smile worked at his lips. Deaton despised their newest member and hoped he was in trouble with El Jefe.

El Jefe stared hard at Peter Zerbini. "If we consider failure to be acceptable this time, next we'll become satisfied with it, and after a while, that's all we'll expect. We do not accept failure, Mr. Zerbini. It is not a word in the book, which you should obviously study more closely." He looked at Deaton. "How much will we get at thirty million dollars each?"

Deaton smirked. "Six hundred million. Point six billion dollars, U.S. currency. Minus costs of doing business, of course."

"Then that is the number we will achieve. You were correct, Deaton. We had trouble. Our customer failed, and in this case that means we failed. There will be no more of those."

Zerbini pushed his luck. "How can we be sure? What if there's another cowboy?"

"In the future, Sajacento will send a second person with a remote detonating device. If the idiot won't press the button, the other will. They would have done that this time if the rag-head bomb makers hadn't been so fearful of bin Polah."

El Jefe looked about. Other members were nodding their agreement. Deaton was pleased that Zerbini had been corrected. Zerbini studied his manicured nails, also nodding at the wisdom of El Jefe. He knew when to back off, and was succored by the fact that El Jefe had referred to the bombers as rag-heads and idiots.

"Are there other troubles?"

Joe Fuentes was a prissy professor of English. "I've spoken about this at our last two meetings. Our Western History Department is working to interpret the Shepherd journal. Two months ago, the decision was made to bring down the Weyland Foundation, who provide the document recovery system and computer, but *not* the university. They've deciphered eleven pages now. I've read them, and they're dangerous. We mustn't allow them to go further."

"I'm aware of that," El Jefe said. "But they're in New York, and your university is next door in Berkeley. I don't like to work that close to home on something this important." El Jefe had made that determination when he'd taken on the task. They all knew the importance of stopping the exposure of the journal that had, after additions and amendments, become the book—explaining their past, their present, and guidance for their future.

Shepherd's Journal betrayed the locations of the Valley of the Weeping Tree and the Hidden Lagoon, both critical to their operation from the beginning. It discussed secrets of currents and rip tides, and how to use the death tide to navigate between ship and shore. Should Shepherd's Journal be made public, it would cost them dearly and might even destroy them.

El Jefe had heard the displeasure in Fuentes's tone. While something must be done about the journal, he could not condone criticism directed at himself.

"We should stop them at this end, as well," said Fuentes. "Deal with our History Department as Sydney is doing with the Weyland Foundation."

El Jefe stared, unblinking. "You're aware that this is *my* task?"

Fuentes's tongue darted out to wet his lips. "Jefe, there's a Professor Shaw in our History Department who is not only convinced that the Sociedad existed, but that it may *still* exist. I'd like to eliminate him before he convinces others."

Fuentes was a psychopath, quite good at killing people. The problem was that once started, he was as difficult to stop as a terrier with the rage gene. While normally mild in disposition, once a mad terrier starts biting humans, you have to hit it in the head with a hammer. The last victims had been child prostitutes in San Francisco. This time it was to be professors in Berkeley.

"Not quite yet," he said. Not that El Jefe was against getting blood on their hands, but only after careful study, as the book said the Sociedad Serpiente had always done.

Zerbini spoke next. He had been reading the bad press releases for the Weyland Foundation. "Sydney is a true professional. She's turned public opinion against them. The world thinks they're just another huge corporation that doesn't give a shit about people."

El Jefe knew well of his half sister's successes. "Remember her warning about a man named Lincoln Anderson, and how we should look for him because he'd be trouble? She was right again. He's the cowboy who whipped bin Polah's ass in front of the world."

"And got his face ripped off doing it," said Wendell Welk.

"By stopping bin Polah, he cost us a great deal of money," Harry Deaton said dourly. "We should deal with him."

"Sydney wants Anderson for herself," said El Jefe,

"as she does the hostages. When we get our hands on them, we'll hand the three poor devils over to her."

"If Anderson knew about bin Polah," mused Chief Welk, "why was he alone when he stopped him? I would have had a dozen men there."

"Sydney saw it all. She believes Anderson just happened to be there. Now she's dealing with him in her own unique way," said El Jefe. "She took Anderson's employee out of the hospital and used her to leak his identity. It surprised even her that they fired him so quickly, but she's pleased he'll not be there for the fall of the Weyland Foundation."

"I'm curious how that will happen," said Deaton.

"Just be assured that it will." El Jefe suppressed a smile. "I suggest we watch the news this afternoon. Now let us proceed. Are there more troubles?" he asked, and when no one responded—"Then we shall proceed to new business."

He told Zerbini, for he was the newest member, having been with them for only eight years, to bring in Roberto, son of California winemaker and venerable member of the Sociedad Serpiente Julius Lilac, who had missed three meetings.

That was especially disturbing, for Julius was the keeper of the book.

As they waited for Zerbini and Roberto Lilac, El Jefe thought of his half sister. The last time they'd seen her, she'd appeared before them looking as plain as she'd been as a teenager, but of course, now Sydney was whatever she wished to be. Beautiful, coarse, educated, lustful—it did not matter. El Jefe was proud of her, although such emotion was kept buried. Others would probe his weakness, capitalize on it, and try to eliminate him. Such thoughts were ever on their minds. They were all rich, but a Jefe controlled an income many times that of other members.

But Sydney made him want to smile at the extent of her avarice.

After his Serpiente father was killed at sea, his mother had remarried a widower named Baumgartner, who was also a Serpiente. When Lyle Bull was seven years old, she'd spat out another child and named her after herself.

Little Irene had been gangling and unsure. But by age nineteen, when she returned with her baccalaureate degree from Santa Clara University, she'd become the most ruthless person Lyle had known—the natural who should rightfully have become El Jefe after the previous one had become unwatchful and let his car be forced off a highway precipice. Since membership was forever closed to women, she'd worked on behalf of her half brother, twisting truths so effectively that one of the most powerful Serpientes was sent to the stone by the others. Her brother had listened well, murdered the last rebellious member (as well as his family), and was named El Jefe.

She'd left for the East, gained her law degree at Georgetown by age twenty-one, and gone into government intelligence work, where she used pseudonyms and had a birthmark removed and her breast size reduced so she would not receive undue attention. She'd soon worked her way into a high position, training agents in the uses of disguise and deception, gaining influential contacts, and learning their secrets. She was poised to take the top job in her department when her boss was caught siphoning agency operating funds, and she was tarred with the same scandal. For a while she was pursued, although she had so complicated the evidence the case against her was weak.

She had so much dirt on so many elected and appointed officials that no one dared to look hard. A subpoena was found to be in error, and the matter was further clouded. A report was circulated that she had been killed in a mob hit. No one looked for her anymore, although there were certain ranking politicians from whom she quietly garnered favors.

Her private joke was that as they'd looked for her, she'd transferred another million from the agency's operating fund to her accounts in the Caymans.

Assumed identities came as naturally to Sydney as changing hats.

With the attacks of 9/11 had come opportunity. Recently she'd traveled the Middle East, expanding the

Serpientes' horizons and arranged lucrative deals. After the defeat of the Taliban, they had financed Afghani opium crops and reopened trafficking routes. As the Iraqi Army skedaddled before the Third Infantry and U.S. Marines, she'd arranged with Hussein's brother to haul cash by the truckload from the national bank to Syria. If it had not been for American warplanes, the Sociedad would have diverted entire truckloads for themselves. So close! Still their portion had been heady.

She'd secured the current deal with Mullah Sajacento and the Hezbollah.

Sydney had been pleased to add El Jefe's task of attacking the Weyland Foundation, since it fit so perfectly with their other plans.

Today would come their first reckoning.

When Roberto Lilac entered with Zerbini, the door behind him locked, closing all avenues of escape. The walls were thick, so soundproof that screams would not be heard on the other side. Those walls served a purpose: to intimidate all who entered. Yet Roberto, who was both patrician and handsome, the kind of educated, rich young man you hoped your daughter would meet, was confident as he approached the members. He'd known them since his youth. If he replaced his father as a Serpiente, they'd be able to trust him.

El Jefe motioned him closer. "Why is your father not here?"

"He's very ill, Jefe." Using complex medical terms to describe his condition, Roberto explained that his father would live no more than a month. His deathbed wish was that the honor of membership be bestowed on his son. "That is also my aspiration," Roberto said earnestly.

El Jefe shook his head. "I was at your christening, and you've grown up well, but that is not the way it is done. Go home now, and when you return, we'll talk about your father's successor." He told Roberto what must now be accomplished. Roberto sadly nodded.

"I will do as you say, Jefe. I promised my father to be ever faithful to you."

When the son was gone, El Jefe told Zerbini to accompany him. "When you return, take them and the book to the Weeping Tree. We will all participate in the ceremony."

As Zerbini left the room, he was told to send in Damon Lee.

A tall Asian man entered, looking sure of himself. He was another trusted friend, the son of a Serpiente who had drowned in the death tide at Angel Rock.

El Jefe had him approach, and handed him a note. "A chartered jet is waiting at the airport, and the pilot has instructions to fly you to Kalispell, Montana. When you get there, call that number. A woman named Sydney will provide instructions. The man she'll tell you about is dangerous. If she orders it, don't hesitate to kill him."

"Of course, Jefe." Lee acted as if it were a common task. There was more than a hint of arrogance. The best Serpientes had that spark, but Lee also possessed a dangerous temper. He'd disposed of two persons for them, and killed another that he thought had insulted him. His ambition since childhood had been to become a Serpiente, yet El Jefe knew his loyalty was to himself.

There was only one membership to be filled after Julius Lilac died, and he had narrowed his selection to either Roberto or Damon Lee, two very different young men.

When Damon Lee left the room, El Jefe explained that the members would recess and gather at his home at one o'clock to watch Sydney torment the Weyland Foundation. He knew part of it—enough to call it brilliant—but not all. Sydney insisted on her secrets.

The members would spend the night—out-of-towners would be guests at his Victorian home—be awakened early to observe an interesting event, and reconvene at 8 a.m.

Police Chief Wendell Welk stood and stretched. Then he headed for the back room, where they kept sandwich makings and ice-cold beer for the members' convenience.

Deaton came over, worrying as always. "The Weyland Foundation is massive. *Massive!* How much will it cost us just to nip at their heels?"

El Jefe shrugged. "As for size, no organization is

stronger than its weakest node. Cut off a giant's head, and it will die. As for cost, Sydney will provide an accounting."

Deaton wasn't pleased, but he set his lips and went on his way. El Jefe remained seated, looking idly about to study the other members. Only he could authorize an operation of such scope. If Sydney failed, they would lose time and a great deal of money, and the members might feel obligated to try to send him to the stone. But he was good at survival, and Sydney was even better at it.

But that was supposing Sydney would fail, which she would not do. This afternoon they'd watch the spectacle of smiting and destroying the giant. One more adventure among a lifetime of them.

Serpientes had never been known for their timidity.

9

The Learjet 35's captain taxied the bird to the small terminal, did a half-pirouette, and kept the engines running as he waited for the boss's son to remove his baggage. Five minutes later, the bags and boxes were all placed on a luggage dolly and moving toward the terminal.

As soon as the hatch was closed, the captain applied power, and they were taxiing back to the runway. It was an unscheduled stop, ordered by the seventy-something owner of the executive flight service, who could still fly rings around most of his pilots. The captain would lop off a couple of way points to make up the lost half hour and land at SFO on schedule.

11:40 a.m.

When the considerable parking fee was paid inside the terminal, Link and his baggage were dropped off in the back row of the long-term parking lot.

There stood a black Ramcharger 250 four-by-four pickup that was approximately Link's own age and, having survived several threats to remove it to various junkyards, was covered with an accumulation of Montana dust. It had undergone renewals over the years, including a prodigious amount of bodywork, but the holes were patched, the major dents were hammered out, and when Link had last been there, it had been drivable.

There was a new engine, or at least new when it replaced the blown one six years ago, a new and better transmission, and here and there along the drive train were other items of customized hardware—polished intake manifolds, fuel injectors, and exhaust manifolds connected to minimally restrictive mufflers had been added. The heavy-duty truck tires that were on all four wheels made a droning sound on the highway.

He unlocked the tool kit that occupied the bed behind the cab and stored his bags and boxes, then checked that the front hubs and four-wheel-drive lever were disengaged—which he might change when he reached the rough gravel road on the eastern side of Boudie Springs—and began his walk-around inspection, which he felt was important for aircraft or whatever else you were betting your butt would get you there safely. He went down a mental checklist. The custom adjustable shocks were set for an easy ride. The fluid levels were good. Next came a revelation that was not good—an alien but familiar flat rectangular box that was duct-taped in place, with a single wire taped along the right side of the frame.

The device was called a tattletale or bird dog and, along with the loose wire antenna, was used for electronic tracking. It was free of dust and newly attached, a self-contained battery rig, with a range of several miles, and not requiring power from the pickup's electrical system.

Link pulled work boots, a shirt, and worn Levi's out of a duffel bag, changed in the privacy of the cab, and slid under the truck on his back. He removed the tattletale, spent a few extra minutes underneath, and then crawled out to complete a thorough inspection, surveying for other unwanted accessories. He finished by wiping heavy layers of dust from the windows.

In the cockpit, he flipped a switch so electric power was supplied by dual batteries, turned on the ignition, and waited as a Bosch electric pump hummed and replenished the fuel lines. The gas tanks were full, just as he'd left them, so there would be no condensation. The oversize main held thirty gallons, and there were ten more gallons in the aux tank. Considering that the behemoth consumed fuel at an off-road average rate of six miles per gallon, he needed it all. He pumped the gas only once, and hit the starter.

Despite sitting for a year, the engine caught, ran roughly for a few rpm, and settled into a throatier rumble. After letting it warm for a couple of minutes, he eased forward and back a few times to get the kinks out and listen for U-joint surprises, then slowly set out.

The driver of a glistening, apple-red F-150 nervously watched him approach, the old Dodge lurching, dust falling away, dull coats of black paint obviously applied by brush and touched-up with hardware-store Rust-Oleum, a heavy slab of steel for a bumper and a winch on front, and prudently braked. As if embarrassed, he turned his head away as the rig went by.

Link dropped the tattletale into the immaculate bed of the F-150 just as the Ramcharger shuddered and almost quit. The engine was running more smoothly when he displayed a receipt showing the attendant that he'd paid the fee inside, but it responded with another wild lurch when he accelerated onto the feeder road.

He turned north on the highway toward Boudie Springs, glancing back at the F-150 and its cautious owner. Link hardly thought further of the tattletale. Such devices were as common as cell phones in his world, and he had more to worry about than guess who had placed it; whether Gordon Hightower's fibbers trying to keep tabs, or an overachieving local rookie who was suspicious that the vehicle had been left for so long that the registration was out of date.

Once the elderly Dodge was on the road, she gave no more trouble, having decided she was anxious to be home and that they were headed in the right direction. Link did not often think of objects as having human attributes, but the Ramcharger was family. At seventy-three miles per hour, there was a wheel shimmy that repeated alignments had been unable to cure. At eighty-two mph, a rattling sound resonated from somewhere near the behind-the-cab toolbox. Link kept the vehicle between the shimmy and the rattle, and as he passed clusters of upscale homes on lakes and golf courses, he pulled out the second document that Erin had given him.

He'd scanned the recovered portion of the Shepherd Journal during his flight from Washington, and was even beginning to believe in the existence of the pirates who had preyed on citizens and taken Shepherd's life, but he had trouble trying to think of a way they had anything to do with what was happening today to the Weyland Foundation. Or as Erin believed, with a mosaic of events that included both scandal and terrorism.

He raised the sheaf of papers and read it more closely as he drove.

May 8, 2005
The Shepherd Journal.

Note: The "Document Recovery Program" (DRP) mentioned herein refers to an expert system developed in 2003/2004 by Applied Technologies Branch/Special Projects Division, the Weyland Foundation, New York. DRP is proprietary, but is licensed to the University of California's Western History Department, Berkeley, for the term of this project without fee.

Note: Since words and phrases have evolved, and since we are working with fragments of letters and words, the output of the DRP are "estimates of meaning," rather than an attempt to reproduce the Journal precisely.

Milestones:
3/15/05: (Project Start) Total Pages of Document: 182; Pages damaged beyond recovery: 14; Pages Remaining to Recover: 157; Projected Completion date: 01/01/06.
5/08/05: Project is 6 percent complete; Number of pages recovered: 11;
Note: Pages 1 through 9 are damaged beyond recovery using current technology.
Begin program:

(p. 10) . . . years following the devastating wildfire, this valley appeared to be devoid of life. Only if one knelt and looked at a proper angle would he have detected the fragile growth that peeked through the crust. Most seedlings were of evergreen varieties with winglets, spread by breezes to hibernate until brought to life by new conflagration. They were vulnerable, yet after the annihilation of the fauna by the fire, few animals remained to devour them.

Of countless seedlings competing for sunlight and root space, three brethren came to be positioned forty feet apart in precise north-south alignment, and received liquid nourishment from a spring-fed pool at one side of a ruby-hued silica boulder, formed when a pocket of sand and another of red clay were fused by the fire's intense heat. In my scientific efforts to determine the birthdates of the brethren trees, I find that the great fire occurred some time before the birth of Christ, likely in the period of Hannibal Barca.

(p. 11) The red cypress (called *semper viren* by botanists, "redwood" by timbering men), are more stately than the shorter, squatter cypress found at the elevations of the Sierra. These tall redwoods are the most majestic of the earth's plants, so immense that the Pacific fog shrouding their heights condenses to run off each morning in brooklets. They grow only here in the world, suited to this arrangement of low-lying temperate climate, red clay, and plentiful drizzling rain of the north California coast.

During their first two centuries, the behemoths grew to 120 feet in height and 7 in diameter. Other wildfires reached the valley, but none fierce enough to penetrate the redwoods' thick, shaggy fur. The redwoods were dominant, a stand to themselves, and the brethren were the largest, most symmetrical of them all.

In Asia Minor, as a carpenter named Jesus challenged the wisdom of the elders of his faith, a cyclonic storm formed far across the Pacific Ocean and, after gathering strength for three or more weeks, swept into this valley.

(p. 12) Such phenomena are called *typhoo* by South Asians. That one brought a deluge and such wind that branches as large as ocean schooners were sent flying.

After three days, the storm abated, but as it left, another cataclysm struck. The earth shifted with a jolt, then began to sway back and forth, setting up a tempo that shifted the earth one way then the other, loosening the massive roots in their moorings. Fissures yawned, only to grind together. Animals ran about in mad fear as the forest shuddered. The northernmost brethren tree had been most exposed to the typhoo's soaking, and its massive roots and tentacles were wrenched from the earth, sounding like cannonfire as they were broken. The behemoth began to descend, and it seemed that surely nothing on earth could restrain it, when a great scraping noise was heard. After shearing off yet another hundred feet of branches, it became securely wedged into place, held on the west side by a brother and on the east by another.

Following a dozen years' pause due to suffering, the three brethren resumed growth. But the north tree, bent and disfigured, strained at its great stretched roots, and at times made eerie sounds not unlike a woman's crying. Human discoverers have, in their several languages, called it the Weeping Tree.

(p. 13) When Charlemagne was crowned King of the Roman Empire by conniving Pope Leo III, the redwood brethren were a thousand years old and eleven feet in diameter. The supporting brothers soared to three hundred feet. The twisted north tree still wept. It was shorter, its exposed roots strengthened by adversity, and a large cavern formed in its base, which housed generations of puma, wildcats, owls, rats, ground squirrels, bats, snakes, spiders, fleas, lice, and other flying, boring, and crawling creatures. There were grizzled bears, that according to legends of nearby tribes, spent their lives on their hind feet, and sows held their cublings to their teats to suckle. Who knows? They are gone forever, the pictographs carved into ancient sheets of bark thoughtlessly destroyed by the Serpent People.

Note: Here the writer changed writing style, from ornate script to print.

Dear reader, two hideous months have passed since I last wrote upon these pages. I hurt—oh, how I hurt. El Jefe was away on business and left no instructions regarding me, so my captors had me read these passages aloud while dancing a lively jig, then showed displeasure, saying that I danced too slowly. My captors competed to see how loud they could make me scream. The fingers of my right hand and the bones of that arm, then the bones of that leg were crushed and broken with clubs, leaving me with enough, they said, to perform my useless task. I would have ended my life, yet they did not allow it. Only when El Jefe returned and voiced his anger did they stop. Nor did I applaud when he slew my chief tormentor for damaging his property, for I realized that he would blame me for my inability to stop them. And he did so.

I lie in the cavern of the Weeping Tree and dare not whimper. But I am healing, and as El Jefe reminds me, I have many truths still to tell about the Serpent People. When I finish, the Weeping Tree will call me, and end my melancholy and agony.

One morning some four hundred years ago, not long before Christopher Columbus made his landfall, this redwood valley first received human visitors.

(p. 14) As I stand by the Weeping Tree facing south and down the row of brethren, my ruined right shoulder points to a clearing that extends alongside the trees. There, two score gentle-natured natives of the Pomo tribe halted to marvel at the red giants and the amazing way one was propped by the others. They rested here, drank cool water from the spring of the red stone, ate a meal of sun-dried lake fish, and as their children played, discussed their trek to the sea and how they would return with their finely woven baskets brimming with dried meats of sea lion, abalone, and great fish.

Unbeknownst even that they'd been followed, they ran about in terror as six savages rushed from the forest, howling and swinging heavy clubs, their faces and bodies covered with dark swirls. These criminals, banished from their tribes for the foulest crimes, slew the males, children, and difficult women.

As the Pomos' screams waned, the murderers gorged themselves with their food and sated themselves with the most desirable women. As they celebrated, the leader looked about, liking many things, and decided that they would stay for a while. When one argued, the leader flew into a rage and held him down on the red stone. One after another they clubbed the rebel's head, then daubed his blood onto the Weeping Tree. From that moment to this, the ritual for errant members is to send them to the stone.

There were few similarities in appearance or custom among the outcasts save that they were unafraid of man or beast, and any small act of charity was seen as weakness. They remained together only to ensure their survival. While other bands of outcasts have existed, few could have been as greedy and none so cruel.

Their leader was their strongest and least inhibited, who murdered all challengers until no one remained to question. Since they were outcast from different tribes, communicating was often done silently. The first leader called himself by hissing and gesturing with his fingers held at his mouth as if they were fangs. Soon the group identified themselves by the hiss, showing two fingers curved and extended. During their long trek, they came to communicate using portions of this language or that. To encourage fear, the Serpents left two parallel squiggles at sites of their carnage.

On their long journey from somewhere north and east, they'd established simple rules. Observe the prey, quietly and unseen. Share observations. Then be quiet, for only their leader could devise or change a plan. In battle, display cruelty. Disemboweling or dismembering women or children enraged the surviving men, making them easier to defeat. When a battle was finished and the leader gave his nod, they were free to loot those they'd slain, and use their women. Only their leader could approve the taking of slaves, who slowed them down. Finally, leave no sign of departing save for victims so mutilated that it is difficult to describe them as having been human. When the serpents departed, it was unlikely any sane person would come after them. Using those rules, they defeated many with their few, as they do today.

(p. 15) While none witnessed them and lived, rumors of their evil depravities abounded. Whispers of their coming spread before them, and entire villages fled from their path.

There were and are six of them, never more or less, for that is the mystical number. While they periodically kept slaves for temporary convenience, usually for lust or labor, the number of their members was never altered. Secret rituals, such as being sent to the tree and those for membership, developed.

Soon after their arrival at the valley, they captured a Kla

Mat outcast who had stolen a seagoing canoe from his oceanside village to the north. The leader was taken to sea by their newest member, and was so impressed that he ordered the canoe hidden at a small lagoon that lay over a high mountain and seaward from this camp. The lagoon is guarded from approach by sea by deadly currents, by land by two tall and impossible barriers of stone, one on either side. If invaded by great numbers of foe, there are escape routes, perilous hand and toe paths around the north tower, gouged into the layered stone by slaves, many who fell to their deaths.

The Serpent leader and the Kla Mat went to the lagoon often, and planned great things for the future. The following is taken from spoken stories of Serpents, slaves, and local tribes, and from figures on ancient mat paintings of the Pomo tribe who wove handsome baskets and waterproof boats from the reeds at their lake, and resided three days' walk from this valley.

The Kla Mat Serpent showed the craftsmen what he wanted, and supervised the building of two large boats, rugged and heavy, with sharply angled, well-reinforced bows. When the boats were completed, the Serpent picked thirty strong Pomo men, promised them peaceful lives of plenty, and in a feat that took many months, had them carry the heavy craft all the way to the sea.

They lifted the heavy vessels over obstacles and where no trail had existed, created paths through thick forests, up and down steep inclines. Any who faltered were slain. When they arrived at this valley, they delayed at the base of the high mountain for a year as slaves widened an earthquake's fissure to form a tunnel to the sea.

When the two boats were carried through the tunnel to the hidden lagoon by the sea, the Pomo males were taken to the stone so they could never reveal the location. The paths soon grew over, but to this time no Indian dares to go near them.

Within a decade, the Serpents were venturing up and down the coast. Where they came ashore, death followed. Early Spanish explorers reported silent and empty Indian villages found along the Mendocino-Humboldt coastlines.

Another puzzle that I have solved are words printed on

the bark of the Weeping Tree with the blood of victims, which I shall here attempt to replicate:

FIERE THE TRIE

Since these words are written in medieval English, they might present a paradox to less learned men, yet the solution is obvious.

One century after the outcasts' arrival, Sir Francis Drake scraped and repaired his galleon, *Golden Hind,* in a small bay well south of the hidden lagoon, yet too close for the liking of the Serpents.

It is recorded that as they waited, Drake had a sailboat constructed for the purpose of exploration, and that one of the men he sent out disappeared from the party. It seems sure to me that the Englishman was captured and enslaved, kept in the cavern beneath the Weeping Tree as I have been. Inscribed within the cave I have found other initials and names scratched into the massive roots. One is undoubtedly that of the unlucky explorer, who was kept as a tutor and taught some of the Serpientes to read. Surely other words were left for the future as well, but only those dyed into the Weeping Tree have survived: Fear the tree.

During the following two centuries, except to raid and discourage the fierce tribes to the north, or take slaves and finely woven goods from the lake people, the Serpents remained at the brethren trees and the hidden lagoon on the rugged coast. Slaves were kept in the great root cavern beneath the Weeping Tree.

The Serpents came to endure and then to enjoy the dampness, the storms, even the constant rumbles of the earth, for no others dared to venture here.

Never was more than one member of a family admitted to the Serpents at one time. Renegades from the Hupa, Kla Mat, Umpqua, Paiute, even fleeing Nez Percé and Shoshone murderers, were taken in. Some were enslaved. The few who were trusted filled the positions of members killed in battle or dispute.

(p. 16) When the Spanish built large rancheros and missions around San Francisco Bay, they were a curiosity to the Serpent People, who decided to kill a few to see how easily it could be done. Two Serpents fell to musket fire before they captured a soldier and his weapon, and tortured him until he explained its secrets. The Spanish, who had no idea who they faced, offered bounties for the ears of the murderous visitors the mission Indians fearfully called *Serpientes Oscuros* since they were dark and unseen. Before leaving for their redwood home, the mission records show that the *Sociedad de las Serpientes Oscuros* left the bodies of nine fallen Spanish soldiers, minus ears and muskets, at the gate.

Shortly later, a literate Mexican herdsman murdered a Spanish mission priest and was pursued into the redwood forest by militia. The soldiers were routed by the Serpents, and their firearms captured. The herdsman taught them Spanish and musketry. The leader felt the name, *Sociedad Serpientes*, had a strong sound to it, as did his own new title, El Jefe, but he eventually had the herdsman sent to the stone since he might be a spy.

Fifty years after, an Aleut sailor from Sitka named Booll, employed at a fur-trading fort and farming settlement that the Russians built too close to the Serpientes' sanctuary for their liking, stole a farmer's white whiskey and had his drunken way with his wife. When Russian soldiers went in pursuit, the Serpientes skinned one alive as the others fled. Booll, whose task had been to reap otter skins in a small sail craft, knew every crag and cranny of the treacherous rocks. Since his knowledge of the *marea muerta* was treasured, and he enjoyed their stock of women and Russian white whiskey and proved to be without conscience, Booll was inducted as a Serpiente. He fathered many children, but the only one not killed at birth was born of a Swiss woman who called the child Jack Bull.

(p. 17) As shipping along the tempestuous coast increased, it was natural progression for the Sociedad Serpientes to learn to seize and plunder any merchant's ship or rich man's yacht they found, and leave no trace. A favored method was to talk their way aboard, and at a proper time, perform such gruesome acts on the crew and passengers that they tossed down their weapons to beg for mercy. Victory was achieved in various ways, but always without quarter, always without mercy or survivors.

The Serpientes are first to describe themselves as evil. They revel in their malevolence. When one grows complacent, another will murder him for his women and spoils. Any small act of charity is viewed as cowardice or weakness.

Note: Here we arrived at the end of p. 17 of the document. While we attest to the age and authenticity of paper and ink, and to this computers' translation, we can make no determination of validity or authorship. Signed: Dr. Daniel Walsh, PhD, Weyland Foundation, and Dr. Bill Shaw, PhD, Professor of Western History, UCal–Berkeley.

Link slid the pages back into the leather folder. If there was a connection between the Sociedad—which the executive summary discounted as myth—and the present-day enemies of the foundation, it eluded him. Yet Erin thought the project might be a thorn in the side of whoever was responsible for the muckraking, so he would not ignore it. She was correct too often for that.

Since he had no sat phone, and other phones might be monitored, he would have to wait on the UPS package before he could call and gain more of Erin's insights.

He kept the old pickup between the shimmy and the rattle, and made good time.

10

Link tuned to the local station for the news, and heard his name. A CBS announcer ran an audio clip wherein an FBI spokesman gave a short background on ADIC Gordon Hightower, the official credited with detecting and stopping the terrorist bomber. The *New York Times* had identified the reluctant "cowboy citizen" who had assisted Hightower as Abraham L. Anderson, who until recently had been employed by the beleaguered Weyland Foundation.

An on-the-scene reporter graphically described the terrorist's attack at the FBI Building, including the bloodletting, and an ex-ATF agent concluded that if the terrorist had made it into the building's entrance to set off the Semtex, hundreds would have perished. The massive bomb could only have been carried by someone the size of Ahmed bin Polah, described as a Saudi businessman-billionaire-fundamentalist zealot and longtime critic of the West. In fact, the bomb had proved to be too heavy even for bin Polah. It apparently had been armed, and Anderson, half Polah's size, had been able to keep the detonating switch out of his grasp. The former agent concluded that Hightower and Anderson had both performed flawlessly and heroically.

When asked why the government had withheld Mr. Anderson's identity and his connection with the scandal-ridden Weyland Foundation, an FBI spokeswoman said they were being thorough and dotting all of the i's. Not only was national security involved, there were international ramifications. Bin Polah had been a Saudi. There was proof of involvement by an international terrorist group other than Al Qaeda. The matter was shuffled off to the State Department.

They shifted to the Weyland Building, where a foundation spokesman confirmed that Abraham L. Anderson had been employed as vice-president of their smallest division, which managed overseas construction projects. Mr. Anderson was a model executive, and had not been dismissed for anything concerning deaths of employees as reported by the *Times*. He had left for personal reasons, and they would respect his privacy. The spokesman showed reporters a file photograph of Mr. Anderson, taken several years earlier and somewhat indistinct.

The heat was being turned down some for Abraham L. Anderson, and it was unlikely anyone in Boudie Springs would connect him with the Link they knew. He came and went and owned property and ran a few head of cattle—like others who worked elsewhere because they couldn't make a decent living in Boudie Springs. Neighbors kept an eye on the cabin on the sparsely settled east side of town, and Joseph Spotted Horse, who had claimed to be seventy years old since Link had met him a decade before, looked after the livestock and horses. The latter included Ms. Stubborn—a muleheaded and not particularly fast mare with dogged endurance, a barrel chest, and good wind for the high country.

3:30 p.m.—The Weyland Building

The Weyland Building soared seventy-eight floors and took up a block of Manhattan real estate. There were tours given to the public to observe various points of interest. On the roof were clusters of varishaped antennas for its worldwide operations, and eight helipads, four of which were occupied by foundation-owned rotary wing aircraft. There were twenty-four restaurants in the building, and employees and guests could choose among everything from cafeterias to steak houses. Two solaria taking up portions of the twentieth and fortieth floors were maintained by the Habitat Earth division. One displayed the humid environment of a Brazilian rain forest, with appropriate plants, insects, birds, reptiles, and mammalians. The other showed an Arizona desert, with sand, sidewinders, cacti, horned toads, varieties of mice, and a coyote family.

No one was told about the side of the foundation that required Erin Frechette's skills on the twenty-seventh floor, to which no public elevators had access. She and Link had worked together well to provide balance to a post-USSR world. Their tasks became more critical after 9/11, when they'd obtained every possible scrap of information for use by American agents, airmen, seamen, and soldiers deployed to the Middle East. Four years later, after Afghanistan and Iraq, the crescendo of world hatred had not subsided. Terrorism fueled by fanaticism, religious fervor, and national jealousies was neither easily nor quickly overcome.

Despite the cessation of covert activities, Special Projects still had plenty to do. Its three floors housed banks of Helga's computer servers, a satellite positioning and control capability, a communications network, and a vast computerized library, which made the foundation's worldwide operations, as well as official U.S. clandestine agency activities, possible. While there were not great numbers of employees in the division, most of their personnel had advanced degrees and Top Secret SI/TK clearances.

Erin was now in charge, and while she could handle the job, she wished to hell that her hare-brained boss were still here, and that Frank Dubois had not let him go off playing cowboys, Indians, and fighter pilots, especially not in that order.

She'd confirmed something she'd known, being the widow of a combat pilot, which was that there is no trust more explicit than that between combat wingmen who have relied upon one another to survive—as Link and Frank had done.

While Link had kept Frank informed, he'd directed Special Projects with near autonomy. No one had looked over his shoulder or second-guessed him. He'd bent a few rules to get results, but not by much. He respected the foundation too much for that, and he hadn't wanted their reputation sullied. Now its name had been dragged into the gutter, and Erin understood why Frank and Link were anxious to slug it out with whoever was responsible. She just wished they'd done it differently, and listened to her inputs.

Recently, coming to work had not been boring. The big news of this morning was that one of their Learjets was missing from Teterboro Field, and so far it was nowhere to be found. One of their crew members, a pilot with impeccable credentials, had also disappeared. Erin had met him, and as with Gwen Svenson, it was difficult to understand how she could misjudge someone so badly, yet everything indicated that he'd taken the aircraft.

Which made Erin wonder if the two missing persons were part of the larger problem.

The fire alarm sounded, and an electronic voice boomed over the Emergency PA system: *"This is a CBR disaster preparedness exercise. We are simulating a chemical attack. All personnel will put on protective masks."*

If she hadn't been expecting it—the DP consultants had prebriefed essential personnel that it was coming—she would've jumped even higher. As the words were repeated over the PA, Erin searched through the lower drawers and located the mask that had been provided to her just that morning, still in its plastic wrapper and marked, VP, SPEC PROJECTS.

Instructions had been provided on how to slip the mask over their heads, make sure there was an airtight seal, and tighten the straps. She spent too much time just removing the wrapper. As she drew on the mask, the straps pulled sharply at her hair, and she made a face.

The interoffice phone buzzed, and she picked up, trying to remember the procedure.

That voice, too, was mechanical. *"Provide your name and status."*

"Erin Frechette! Status One," she responded as they'd been briefed, still adjusting the damned straps. Her response was muffled, so she repeated herself and hung up.

PA: *"Time is E plus thirty seconds. Remember that this is an exercise only. Proceed to your emergency station and prepare to perform your assigned duties."*

That one was easy. She was designated as essential personnel; her job was simply to identify herself and prepare for evacuation.

Erin remembered something else then, and pulled a green placard reading EP-10 from the bottom drawer, which she pulled over the mask and suspended about her neck, then looked to make sure there were no classified documents lying about (not in the procedures, but it should be), rose, and walked calmly (that one was in the procedures) out the door, through her old, now-empty office soon to be occupied by Squid Worsczejius, and into the hall.

Two dozen persons, all wearing gas masks, were moving in a somewhat orderly fashion.

PA: *"Proceed to your emergency station and perform your assigned duties."*

"Come on!" she yelled to two employees who emerged too slowly from an office. If they were going to have the damned exercise, she wanted her division to get it right.

PA: *"The simulated chemical attack is confined to the south entrance. Avoid that area and proceed outside. Remember, this is an exercise."*

The security guard at the elevators—which since the blackout of 2003 could be switched to operate on electricity provided by backup generators positioned about the building—was reading the placards hung about the employees' necks and comparing them with his guide. Blue-7s went to elevator three, Blue 4s to elevator six. Most placards were blue or white, no others green like Erin's. Most were boarding various DOWN elevators, some were being directed to the stairs. She was the only one pointed toward the express elevator car marked ROOFTOP.

From her perspective, it was going just as they'd been briefed by the consulting firm. Employees would evacuate to various lower levels, then, rather than flooding outside, be counted and tallied. They would simulate airlifting essential personnel, VPs and equivalents, from the rooftop. Frank thought it was a bad idea to show that kind of egalitarianism, and Erin was betting that he'd change it at the next Disaster Preparedness meeting.

She had to wait. According to the light, the car was making stops at the uppermost floors. Twice it started down, then returned to the roof. It was racing between floors, but time was passing and she didn't want to be the last one to report.

She also wanted it over with because when Link got to Boudie Springs and called, she'd tell him about the missing Learjet to get his ideas and listen to what he'd thought about Shepherd's Journal. If it weren't so far, she would take the stairs.

Finally the car made it down to the twenty-seventh floor, and the door whooshed open. She was the only occupant. As soon as she was inside, she pressed the ROOFTOP button.

In emergency mode, the elevator traveled even faster than its normal express speed. After a few seconds, the car slowed. As it stopped at the small superstructure high atop the Weyland Building, she heard a faint *bap-bap-bap* from outside, a sound she recognized. As the doors sprang open, she was still wondering. *Sounds of a silenced machine pistol?* Now that was true realism.

According to their briefing, all that remained was for her to check in with an official on the roof so her response time would be logged.

She was hardly out of the elevator when a slight man in close-cropped hair, wearing a gas mask, green T-shirt, dark slacks, and a red placard reading DP MONITOR, grasped her arm and led her out through the superstructure doors, then toward the helicopters.

"She's the other one," the slender man called out to another who was similarly dressed in a green uniform. "Close it down."

Up ahead were simulated casualties, lying about in unnatural but realistic poses.

"I believe I'm done," Erin said politely, but when she reached to remove her gas mask, the man rudely shoved her hand away.

"Not yet, you fool. Do you want to end up like them?"

Erin went along with the game. The man pushed her faster, and she was preparing to tell him that enough was enough when she noticed that like her, the casualties wore placards reading EP, for "essential personnel." She recognized vice presidents, managers, a top-level engineer—nine in all, their masks pulled askew, as if they'd been in the act of removing them. Their eyes bulged, and their tongues were grotesquely extended. Only one still wore his gas mask. The three gunshot wounds in his chest were draining too much fresh blood to be fake. *Too* realistic.

Erin realized what the muffled sounds had indeed been. She felt numbed.

The slight man continued to push her along, and when Erin tried to slow down as they passed that final bloody body, he became even more forceful. He was strong, and just as Erin was getting her courage together—as if he were a mind reader, he pulled a small pearl-handled automatic from an under-the-armpit holster.

"Keep walking." It was an order, not a request.

Erin was fortunate that she hadn't tried to run. Behind them were three others in gas masks, matching green shirts, and dark pants, carrying H&K submachine guns, like the ones Erin ordered for their own agents. Like the slight man, they wore red placards labeled DP MONITOR, and Erin realized that the drill had gone terribly wrong.

The man pushed her past four helicopters that were painted blue and showed the logo of the Weyland Foundation. The fifth was black and white, marked NYPD, its rotor blade clip-clopping in idle. Inside was Frank Dubois, wearing a green placard like Erin's, his printed with EP-1. Covering him was a policeman wearing a gas mask, flight suit, and a badge reading NYPD FLIGHT CREW. Observing from the front seat was another uniformed male.

"Inside," the slight man ordered. When Erin didn't respond quickly enough, he slapped the pistol against the side of her head. Erin staggered, almost collapsed. Spots were dancing in her vision.

"Do as you're told or you get hurt. Make sense? Now shut up, get in, and hold on."

Inside, Erin and Frank were handcuffed to a bulkhead in awkward positions. The four kidnappers from the rooftop belted up as the uniformed policeman took the left copilot's seat. An explosion sounded, and fire and smoke belched out of the superstructure door. The engine revved, and a minute later they were airborne and swooping away. Both side doors were left open for the first couple of miles, then were closed.

"Take off your masks," the slight man said in his nononsense voice. He revealed himself. Short, mousy brown hair, plain face, even features. Nothing notable. Easily forgettable.

Erin awkwardly removed her own mask with her free hand, pulling out hair in the process. Then she helped Frank, who seemed dazed. When his mask was off, she winced. He'd obviously fought them and received a bloody cheekbone and swollen nose for his trouble.

The right-seat pilot called back to the slight man. "To observers we look like a copmobile, but our identifier code says we're a transport chopper for a construction company."

Erin tried to get a look at faces. The copilot was pretty-boy handsome with finely chiseled features, and looked Iraqi or Palestinian. A familiar face that she knew from somewhere.

The slight man remained calm, glancing at a small watch and ignoring the hostages.

Erin got an eye on the compass. They were flying northwest, over the river.

Thirty five minutes later, they circled and landed between two abandoned hangars at a rural airstrip somewhere in New York State, but she was not at all sure where. They were uncuffed from the bulkhead, dragged out of the helicopter, and handcuffed together. Then they were marched along behind as the men pushed the helicopter into a hangar.

"How long?" asked the slight man, observing his watch again.

The pretty boy copilot replied, "Ten minutes."

Erin placed him. Muhammad al Badas, codename Kamil, was an active member of the *Hezbollah*. He'd attended flight school in Nancy, France, and had cockpit time in both fixed and rotary wing aircraft. Kamil despised Americans, was known to have stolen a Boeing 727 in West Africa to crash into a U.S. base in northern Italy. Thankfully an engine had failed and he'd been unable to take off. The CIA had information that he was trying to enter the U.S. His name and photo were shown in every post office, police, customs, and immigration office, yet he had somehow gotten into the country—just as Ahmed bin Polah had.

The slight man disappeared as the others stripped off police and disaster-preparedness uniforms in favor of street wear. Kamil did so slowly, staring at Erin as he stripped to shorts and socks. He cupped his privates and beckoned. Then he laughed and pulled on blue jeans.

Two men went to work pulling off plastic film that encased the helicopter. The black-and-white paint scheme disappeared, as well as the NYPD logo. Underneath the plastic, the words WILSON BROS. CONST. CO. were emblazoned in bright orange on white.

Frank and Erin were ushered into the second hangar, where overhead lights revealed a Learjet, freshly painted green and advertising an unknown charter air firm. They were rudely shoved up the steps, through the hatch, and into the back, where both were cuffed to the sturdy armrests of the plush leather seats. The hatch was then closed, and the lights in the hangar turned off. For a moment, their world was without light. Then klieg lamps glared, illuminating the compartment in bright white. Erin squinted and turned her head away.

Three persons, all wearing slip-on black hoods with eyeholes, were already inside, as was a man brandishing an amateur-grade video camcorder.

Erin heard a whimpering sound in back and turned, thinking nothing could surprise her. A woman lay sprawled by the bathroom door, so abused that she was hard to recognize. If she could hear them, Gwen Svenson would be unable to see them through her swollen eyes.

"Get on with it," said one of the hooded men to the cameraman.

The cameraman panned the compartment, dwelling on Frank, Erin, then Gwen.

Kamil came in, remaining out of the camera's view, and casually tossed four rolls of silver duct tape to one of the two hooded men at the back of the compartment.

The third pushed back the hood, revealing a plain-looking woman in a silk scarf, a sign of Muslim modesty and propriety. She narrated by speaking into a microphone with a voice scrambler that made her sound like Donald Duck.

Erin caught a flicker of resemblance to the slight man who had kidnapped her, and decided the two persons were the same. She watched closely, eyes narrowed as again she tried to remember. Finally she placed the woman, as well. Sydney was an American, a chameleon who could remake herself into anyone she wished. Reports of her death were clearly exaggerated.

Twenty-six minutes later, under the eye of the video camera, Gwen was shoved headlong out of the hatch, wrapped from head to toe in shiny duct tape and utterly unrecognizable. She landed with a thump on the concrete hangar floor, and released a muffled, painful groan.

The helicopter fired up outside and, a couple of minutes later they heard it taking off. As the clip-clop sounds of rotors faded, the hangar doors were opened, and one by one the Learjet's engines whined to life. Erin had been wrong. She was both surprised and terrified, for herself and Frank, and for Gwen, who she believed was in the helicopter.

Where are they taking Gwen?

Where are they taking Frank and me? Why?

The Hezbollah are obviously involved, but who does the woman called Sydney represent?

They taxied out of the hangar, and a moment later she heard Kamil radio for activation of his flight plan and ask to proceed westward at five thousand feet under visual flight rules. A moment later, the brakes were released and they rolled down the runway. Rather than climbing, they remained low, going God only knew where.

Erin thanked God that Link was not with them. As long as he was free, no matter where the terrorists took them, there would be at least one person searching to find them.

11

The familiar bar and grill was the "in" place with both
tourists and locals, and Link had trouble finding a parking place that was close to the entrance. Finally he located a space half a block away and hoofed it, thinking
it was good to be back and wondering why he stayed
away so much of the time. He stepped inside the pub
and, for the first time in a long while, felt at ease wearing
a Stetson and boots. Most of the others, tourists included, wore them, as well.

While he looked around for a seat, he heard, "About
damned time you came home."

Moira Bourne threw her arms around his neck and
pressed him to her bosom. Link felt uneasy but in-
wardly pleased.

"Where in hell's name have you been?" came another
voice, this one booming, followed—as soon as Moira
stepped back—by another bear hug. Jamie was not
nearly so buxom as his wife, but he was equally
enthusiastic.

"Here and there," Link said. "I never found anything
like Boudie Springs."

Link had once served on the north county search-and-
rescue team that Jamie still led.

"I saw Joseph Spotted Horse this morning," said
Jamie. "He said you were coming and he had to get
things ready."

Somehow the old Indian always knew, despite the fact
that he stayed in line shacks near the cattle without

phones or other trappings of civilization. To contact him, Link left messages with neighbors, which he had not done this time.

Moira sat him at the bar with a cold draft beer, a house phone, and a phone book. By the time he'd had his telephone line switched on and talked to the neighbor to ensure the cabin was standing, he had two fresh beers lined up from residents he knew. A corned beef sandwich and a garlicky kosher pickle, which—along with her blistering hot chili were Moira's trademarks—took the edge off his hunger.

By the time Link departed, an hour had passed, but he considered every minute at Jamie's Pub well spent. He dropped by Albertson's for groceries and headed home.

It felt good to pull into the long, looping gravel driveway, park, and get out in front of the cabin. A brown UPS van was there, and the same driver who had worked the route for the past ten years was about to leave. He stayed to chat and cast sly looks at the larger of the two packages he'd brought. He'd been mystified before when delivering parcels from Erin, for there was no originating address or tracking number.

The second package was the size of a legal folder, posted from Atlanta, Georgia. The sender had signed with a flourishing *S*.

Both Erin's package and the envelope were to be delivered upon receipt.

As the driver went on, Link unlocked the front door, switched on the circuit breakers, and placed groceries into cabinets and onto shelves and the wheezing and rattling refrigerator that he recalled was on its last legs. He then lugged bags and boxes from the truck, depositing them beside the bed in the large, open kitchen, living, and sleeping area. There was a second bedroom that Joseph occasionally used.

Link put away hats and boots, hung everything hangable, and placed the remainder of his things in the chest of drawers. He then sat at the table and sorted through a year's mail. The lady who had held the contract for his mail delivery route for the past twenty years had a house key. He'd asked her to toss anything that remotely resembled junk mail, pile important-looking mail in postal service bins beside the table, and forward the really important stuff, such as *American Rifleman* magazines.

Such courtesies were common here, unimaginable in the city without paying dearly.

He found an envelope with the registration sticker for the truck, and before going a step farther, went out and made the Dodge legal to drive on Montana roads.

Back inside, he sorted the rest of the mail, left those he'd answer in a single plastic bin, and methodically trashed the rest. As his mind grew idle with the task, he found himself imagining the horror again, as he had been trying not to do on this trip. Images of Doc Pete, Tanker, and Ace loomed into his consciousness. He wondered if they'd been tortured before being beheaded, and decided that it was likely.

"There's something to handle first," he said to Doc Pete's ghost. "But I won't forget."

He finished with the mail, took the DO NOT KEEP bin out and dumped it.

Link opened Erin's package with a large Buck pocket knife he retrieved from the bedside drawer, then placed it in his pocket. Here it was considered utilitarian to carry a knife on one's belt (or in a purse).

He drew out the satellite phone, then the extra batteries, which he immediately placed in the charger as Erin liked him to do. She'd included several electronic devices, most having to do with night vision, digital recording, GPS, or communications. Erin's life had much to do with computers and embedded processors, but she also had a sense of what would be useful and what would not. On the bottom was an ID kit—a small canvas bag containing birth certificates, drivers licenses, and credit cards, all showing his photo, good for four different aliases.

He found himself thinking about the kiss. Had he encouraged it? He did not believe in office relationships. Too easy to misinterpret. Dangerous because of all the sexual harassment rules. *What if she is no longer my subordinate?* He grew embarrassed with his thoughts and pushed them aside. *Call her like you promised.*

On the sat phone he punched in MEM 1—Erin's secure number then ENCODE/DECODE, and waited as the signal was encoded, bounced around between satellites, connected with the proper secure switch, and rang. Her voice mail came on, which surprised him.

When away from the office, Erin always carried a sat phone.

"I read both the executive summary and Shepherd's Journal," he said into her voice recorder. "I'll call about those later."

As he switched off, he heard sounds of a vehicle in the driveway, even noisier than his Ramcharger. He decided it was his neighbors bringing a welcome-home snack such as a deep-dish cobbler or carrot cake. He normally looked forward to an update on the local gossip, but this time his mind was far too busy for pleasantries.

A fierce rattling noise sounded at the front door, Joseph Spotted Horse announcing himself before coming inside. "You are finally here," the old Indian grumbled.

"Good to see you, Joseph." Beyond, he noted the 1940s' vintage stake-bed truck.

"In all my days, I have never seen someone who ignores his cattle and horses as much as you." Joseph seemed not to be aging. Which was not to say he did not look old, just in a sort of suspended animation.

"How is Ms. Stubborn?" Link asked.

"She missed you for a while." Joseph sat down, stared at the table for a few minutes, perhaps as many as five, and Link waited as a younger man of the People should. Joseph was the great-uncle of Marie LeBecque, Link's fiancée until she had died all too suddenly.

"Maybe you will call your friend and ask her to visit, and she will ride Ms. Stubborn while you ignore them both."

Link did not laugh. The old man was concerned about him and believed that Link needed a good woman after so long. Most of those whom Link had brought to visit had not met Joseph's standards. He was fondest of Maggie Tatro, who had made blueberry pies.

Link and Maggie, a short, pretty, explosive-tempered FBI agent, had been a hot match until their affair cooled down. They'd gone their own ways when she'd been promoted to a better job in San Francisco. He wondered if he shouldn't give her a call.

The telephone rang. He went into the living room portion of the cabin and answered.

John Dewey, a fire-and-brimstone preacher who also owned the local Sports Center, welcomed him home and told him about an obnoxious Asian man who had just left his store after trying to find Link's address. "The guy's trouble," Dewey told him.

Link thanked him and hung up. The townspeople were insular and often suspicious of outsiders. He'd receive more reports and learn the man's name soon enough.

Another phone call sounded. A woman's voice asked him to hold for Assistant Director Hightower.

"You're there." Gordon's voice sounded surprised.

"Just got in town a couple of hours ago."

"Where the hell have you been?" There was anger in his tone.

"I spent the night with my parents in Falls Church, got a hop to Kalispell first thing this morning, and drove straight here. Why?"

"You're in deeper shit than I ever imagined you could be, even though you go around like a cocked pistol."

"Deep shit with who, Gordon?"

"How about every law officer in the city? How about with *me?*"

Their friendship had its ups and downs. "What are you talking about?"

"Nine of the top vice presidents and senior engineers at the foundation were killed this afternoon. Frank and Erin are missing and presumed kidnapped."

Link was rocked. He closed his eyes and let the news wash over him. First the three men in the desert, now Frank and Erin?

"You still there?"

"Yeah." He paused, hardly believing. "They're really gone?"

"You don't sound surprised or sorry."

Link didn't argue. Gordon knew that he coped with emergencies by numbing himself. He quietly asked: "Do you have any idea where they took them?"

"I'm not sharing anything. Right now I just want to confirm where you've been."

"Call my parents. Call Executive Connections and the crew who flew me here." He paused. "I should return right away. I'll be—"

"If you budge from where you are without clearing it with me, I'll have you arrested." Gordon's voice trembled with emotion. "Damn it, you're a *suspect*."

"That's crazy. I wasn't anywhere near there this afternoon."

"That doesn't mean you weren't involved. You know the foundation and its vulnerabilities. What went on between you and Frank that made him fire you?"

"I wasn't fired. Frank and I—"

"Two foundation security officers say you were fired in front of them. They also say that Erin came out of your office crying. So stay right there, and don't try to run."

"At least try to listen, Gordon. Frank and Erin are my—"

"I'll have a team of agents sent from Boise or Great Falls. Until then, stay put!" Gordon broke off the connection, an unhappy man.

Link was stunned, both by the news and the treatment. He switched on the television. The terrorist attack and kidnappings were everywhere on the dial. They'd picked a good time, a disaster-preparedness drill, and had slain three consultant-contractors to take over the rooftop. They'd turned a mock chemical attack into the real thing, using a canister of chemical agent—which type the FBI was not yet saying—on the VPs who had shown up for the drill. When the chemical became dispersed and diluted by the breeze, they'd resorted to bullets. All four Weyland Foundation helicopters were still in place. No one was sure how the two known hostages, Frank Dubois and Erin Frechette, had been transported. No one on the lower floors, neither employees nor the consultants, had realized anything at the rooftop was amiss. None had heard gunfire.

The reporters were getting snippets of information and adding them to what they had. They interviewed employees. Few added anything of value, yet they continued to talk with them.

Thus far, and it was nighttime there, no one had taken credit or made demands.

Link turned the volume down, walked the floor and ruminated, trying to make sense of it all. He decided to wait for the agent from Boise as Gordon had ordered. He'd tell them what he knew to get them off his back and try to get something in return, although that was doubtful. Field agents liked information to flow in a single direction. They were gatherers, not givers.

Joseph had settled into the stuffed chair and watched the soundless television set without emotion. "There is a car with a Chinaman inside not far up the street. He drove by twice, and now he's watching the cabin."

"I'm not surprised," said Link. Gordon had been quick to move in surveillance.

A few minutes later, the closest neighbor delivered a deep-dish cherry pie. She wanted to chat, but picked up that his mind was elsewhere and that the distraction was important. "Before I go, there's a blue Camry with an Asian gentleman watching your house."

"Thank you."

The moment she left, Joseph got a plate and fork and silently helped himself to cherry pie.

Link went through Erin's package, hoping there'd be a clue. The package had likely been sent the previous evening, after he'd left the office, so it was unlikely to be illuminating. There was a note telling him to charge the sat-phone batteries. He dwelled on a memo she'd written to S. Worsczejius, asking him to see her at 8 a.m., saying she had something important to discuss.

She'd talked with Squid this morning about his new position. Which meant that in her absence, Squid was the acting VP of Special Projects.

He tried MEM 1 on his sat phone—Erin's secure number—as he'd done earlier. After a pause, a male voice answered. "Worsczejius."

"Squid, Link Anderson."

Another pause, then a flat tone saying: "Go ahead."

"I just got the news about what happened. Anything on Erin and Frank?"

"I'm not sure we should be talking. The word here is that you were fired and went off the deep end."

"Don't believe it."

"Where are you?"

"At my place in Montana. You can contact me by pressing MEM 1 on Erin's phone."

The line went dead. Squid had hung up on him.

Link walked a little more. Stood at the back door and looked out. When he turned around, he noticed the UPS envelope. Standard folder size.

He opened it, still in denial about Frank and Erin.

Inside were several sheets of onionskin separating two eight-by-ten color glossy photos.

The first photo showed three men in sprawled positions. Link's men, heads propped on their chests. Over them loomed Mullah Sajacento, staring into the camera, holding the bloodied sword, wearing the vivid green robes. Across the photo, hand-printed in permanent marker, was, *I AM THE JUDGE OF MEN. THIS IS HOW I DEAL WITH YOUR TRAITOROUS SPIES.*

Link remained stone-faced as he went to the second photo.

Gwen Svenson was curled into a fetal position. A man wearing a hood grasped her hair and turned her face to the camera. She was terribly beaten.

Bold letters were scrawled onto the photo: *THE FOURTH TRAITOR AWAITS DEATH.*

A final note was printed on a sheet of plain paper: *I HAVE DUBOIS AND FRECHETTE. SHOULD I ADD THEM TO MY LIST?*

At the bottom of the page was scrawled: *S.*

There was no doubt about the murderer's identity. *S* was for Sajacento, who claimed to be Allah's Judge of Men.

Sajacento had Erin and Frank.

12

Link had begun by digging out the laptop and diminutive
printer/scanner that Erin had included in her package,
hooking them up, and calling Assistant Director in
Charge Gordon Hightower.

Gordon's assistant said he was busy, which was fine
with Link, who would rather not waste his time listening
to another diatribe blaming him for what was happening
at the Weyland Foundation as well as the Lindbergh
abduction and passing nuclear secrets to the Russians.
Gordon would be like that until he got over his snit
about his next promotion, or whatever was bothering
him. He asked Gordon's assistant for their secure fax
number.

He'd still been numb when he'd faxed the photos and
the address on the envelope to Hightower's and Squid's
numbers. The laptop had completed the transmissions
in seconds, and one minute later, Gordon had phoned,
sounding just as shocked as Link.

Their conversation lasted for more than an hour.
There was little to be gleaned from the image of the
dead men other than it had obviously been included for
shock effect. When they'd examined the photo showing
a battered Gwen Svenson, Link recognized the interior
of a Learjet and the Weyland Foundation's distinctive
decor. Gordon just said, "Oh yeah?" as if he were surprised, and Link would remember those two words a
couple of hours hence.

"My guess," said Gordon, "is the Hezbollah were

after Frank Dubois, since he's as rich as Midas and owns his own golden goose."

"For ransom? If that's the case, why would they take Erin?"

"She got in the way."

"They killed the others who got in the way."

"Yeah. But you better bet this is being done for money."

"Erin thought everything's connected: Sajacento, Gwen, the bogus scandals, everything. She forecast that something big would occur. I just wasn't thinking big enough."

Link started to explain her "thorny project" theory, but Gordon was more interested in the fact that the photos had been sent from Atlanta.

NSA had been intercepting telephone and e-mail traffic discussing an expansion of terrorist cells in the Deep South. DHS knew of four groups of Al Qaeda–trained soldiers, and had recent confirmation that a Hezbollah cell had been established somewhere near Atlanta. Gordon felt the South was a likely place to start searching, and Link could not argue the point.

Before hanging up, Gordon issued a new ultimatum for Link to stay put.

"Aw, for God's sake. Do you think I'd harm my closest friends?"

"I don't, but there are some who feel you left at an awfully convenient time, and they have the statements that you were fired. I argue when I can, but I've got my hands full."

Gordon's words were too pious. "Who are these other *people?*"

"You know I can't tell you. Just cooperate and stay put, okay? It shouldn't be long before you're cleared."

Link brought up the Deputy Director (Terrorism), who had supported him in the past.

"He's too busy to eat. Leave it alone, Link. It'll work its way out." Gordon's voice dropped. "Know one reason I'm dragging my feet? I'd have to bring you in for questioning, and this is not a good time to be suspected of being involved with terrorists. We're at war with those guys, and we have a bag of weapons. One of those is if we pick you up on a terrorism charge, we lose the key for a while. You don't want that and neither do I, so please just stay put. I do *not* want you getting into this any deeper."

Link snorted. "*Deeper?* Sajacento knew I was here before the FBI did. He sent photos to my home when I was still en route. He's holding my friends and threatening to kill them."

"Dammit, I don't have time for this. If you want someone to argue with, I'll call the state cops and have them post a car out front and a trooper inside."

After a moment of thought Link replied unhappily. "I hear you." As he hung up, he swore that the minute he got an idea where Frank and Erin might be, he'd drop Gordon a third-class letter and forget the stamp, and go there himself.

Except for Joseph Spotted Horse's snoring in the second bedroom, which sounded like a four-way log-sawing contest, the house was quiet. Link went to bed with his mind filled with questions. He tried thinking through everything about the predicaments of Gwen, Erin, and Frank, but found no answers. Finally he mentally scanned through the Shepherd Journal and found no connections there either.

At 3 a.m. he nodded off to sleep.

5:20 a.m.

Link was standing in a small clearing near three giant redwoods. One was half-fallen, with hand-printed letters blood stained into the bark.

FIERE THE TRIE

Three headless men were arranged in a neat row, and a woman with swollen features lay beside them. Two others were faceless, and they struggled to crawl off a large red stone.

A bird sang shrilly.

A man in green robes walked toward the stone and

the two people there; a sword in his hand dripped dark
liquid. He turned and looked at Link.

The bird warbled again, and Link came slowly awake,
the images lingering.

"I am almost seventy years old, and I have never seen
such laziness."

Again the telephone rang.

Link switched on the bedside lamp and blinked into
its glare.

Joseph Spotted Horse stood in the kitchen in a faded
blue sweatsuit displaying the bull's-head insignia of the
Houston Texans. He appeared displeased. "Some young
men do not care if they awaken their elders who need
their rest."

The phone sounded once more before Link picked up.

"No respect," Joseph muttered as he pulled out a sack
of coffee beans.

"Anderson," he answered, noting the time: a little
after five o'clock.

"Worsczejius here." It was seven o'clock in New
York. Squid had obviously just gotten to work and read
Link's fax.

"Are we secure?" Link asked.

"Yes." Squid's voice was tentative, almost trusting.

"Frank didn't fire me, Squid. We had a plan. I was
going to sever my connections with the foundation and
independently find out who was doing the sabotage. Erin
didn't agree with what we were doing, but she knew
about it and she was going to work with me."

"I went through her classified memos. She wrote the
same thing you just said, plus how she thought you
weren't listening enough to her."

"We weren't. She said something big was about to
go down, and everything that's going on right now was
somehow connected. She was right on the first part, so
she probably was on the second."

"What's next?"

"How are you with computers?"

"Not nearly as good as Erin, but there are others here
who are wizards. The big problem will be trying to keep
them around. The engineers are starting to quit. Project
leaders, too."

The foundation's a sinking ship, Link thought. After a moment, he said, "Pick one of them that's staying. Someone resourceful." *Like Erin,* he thought.

"Mary Long knows how to use Helga. Last night when the PD couldn't tell us what kind of agent the terrorists had used, she asked for a couple of swipes from the rooftop and used a spectrograph hooked to Helga. It was old-style sarin nerve gas, probably sold to Saddam by the Russians when they were buddies. It was watered down—or it could have been a lot worse."

Link recalled Long as being competent but also remembered Squid's quipping about her great "set of lungs," which in navy jargon did not mean organs used for breathing.

"See if she'll take the job after what happened to Erin."

"She already said she'd like to help out any way she can."

"Just don't fool around with the staff."

"I won't, Boss." With the latter word, Squid reaffirmed his loyalty.

"We need to learn where the terrorists took our people, and how they did it."

"There's the Learjet." Squid told him about the airplane that was stolen from Teterboro.

Link frowned. *Why didn't Gordon tell me about that when we discussed the airplane in the video? He doesn't trust me an inch. Does he really think I'm guilty?*

He remembered observing the Weyland Learjet through the window of the charter flight, and recounted to Squid how he'd thought he'd seen Gwen.

Squid said, "There was a screwup by someone. The FAA never got a handoff from Teterboro and didn't assign a track to the Learjet. They were looking for wreckage, but it's been reclassified as a stolen aircraft."

"The pilot likely flew down low over the water with the IFF transponder shut off."

"Next question, Boss. How did they get Mr. Dubois and Erin off the rooftop here?"

"Either a chopper was involved or they're still in the building."

"We've heard those, plus one about parachutes. No one saw chutes, and we searched the building, so I'm going with the chopper idea. The problem with that is there were no strange helicopters, only the normal police, television, and passenger shuttles between airports."

"Have Mary bring up all aerial photos of the city's skyline taken yesterday. If we're lucky, she'll find one of the Weyland Building with an extra helicopter."

"Got it."

"One last thing. Erin was interested in a document recovery project called Shepherd's Journal, like it may be a connection with everything that's going on. I read it and couldn't see it."

"One moment, Boss." Squid paused. "Here it is. A Dr. Daniel Walsh is project leader. He's working it with a history professor from Cal–Berkeley: Dr. Bill Shaw."

"Take a look and see what you come up with. Also give Walsh a call and ask what he thinks about Erin's idea that it might possibly be connected with what's happening today."

"I won't have to call. According to this, he's on the red-eye and should be here in a couple of hours."

At six thirty Link awoke again, this time to a mug of Joseph's hundred-proof coffee and the morning television news. The disaster at the Weyland Building had captured the world's attention as the newest episode in the war against terror. A representative of the terrorist group Hezbollah had contacted the *New York Times*, giving information that only the perpetrators could know and taking sole credit for the attack:

"The corrupt Weyland Foundation executives deserved to die. Until coalition forces withdraw from the holy lands, there will be many more deaths. We will come to America like a swarm of bees. Your future shall perish."

There was no mention of Frank or Erin.

Lennville, California

The Serpientes had been stunned by what they'd observed and heard on television. The attack had been perfectly executed. They'd used horrific methods, killed leaders and potential witnesses, and escaped without a trace, taking with them one of the richest men in the world.

The Hezbollah had provided Sydney with trained guerrillas and a pilot, and taken full credit for the attack.

At four that morning, as the rest of the town slept, the quiet streets monitored by Welk's policemen, the members had been driven to the small, private runway, where Police Chief Welk had powered up the automated instrument landing system. El Jefe had spent seven million dollars of Sociedad money for the extravagance, and as always Mayor Deaton had been critical.

Drizzle and fog had blown in silent swirls as they'd huddled, miserable and sleepy, wondering what was in store. After twenty minutes, El Jefe had spoken the word, "On," over a handheld radio, and the transmission had automatically triggered two rows of white lights.

"What are we proving by standing here in the rain?" Deaton had grumbled.

El Jefe had switched channels and radioed, "The runway lights are now on."

An accented voice responded: "I am receiving the ILS. No runway lights are in sight."

"The visibility is obscured," El Jefe had answered into the radio.

"Who was that?" Fuentes had asked.

"The pilot of an executive jet," El Jefe had said.

"I suppose he's done this many times."

"Actually, this is Kamil's first time, although he did others in a simulator."

"He's *crazy*," Fuentes had said, staring at the fog.

The weather was so poor that they'd half expected to see a fireball in the distance. Or would they only hear an explosion?

"We are five miles out." The foreigner had paused. "We still cannot see runway."

Nor had the Serpientes seen the airplane's landing lights.

"Trust the ILS," El Jefe had cautioned him.

"Three miles out," the pilot had radioed, his voice somewhat higher, the first sign of betrayed emotion from Kamil. Still nothing had been in sight.

It was then that the members understood, and spoke among themselves in excited tones.

"They're coming here?" Deaton had asked.

Fuentes: *"Now?"*

"Where else would you want them?" El Jefe had asked.

At one mile, they'd still been unable to see or hear the airplane.

The jet had appeared suddenly out of the gloom, flared too late, and landed so hard, El Jefe wondered that the gear had not been driven through the wings. The airplane had veered right; then the pilot overcorrected by applying too much brake and almost went off the packed runway.

El Jefe had directed the pilot to taxi to the second hangar. His own airplane was parked in the first, larger one, as were two GM Hummer H2s and several Yamaha ATVs.

He had been anxious to see Sydney and the hostages she'd brought for them.

At eight o'clock, they reconvened in the Odd Fellows Hall, and El Jefe could not subdue a smile. He brought the meeting to order and slowly looked about.

"Does anyone think it could possibly have gone better?"

There were no takers. Only reflections of his good cheer.

El Jefe looked at Deaton. "You were concerned?"

The dour Deaton actually smiled. "No more, El Jefe."

El Jefe did not think that would last for long, and he did not further delay what they were all looking forward to. He sent Professor Fuentes to the outer room for his half sister.

Sydney made a triumphant entry, sweeping into the room with an enigmatic smile playing on her lips. Today she was a striking adventuress with piercing green eyes, wearing khaki clothing as if on safari.

El Jefe tried to hide his pride. "Are there problems?" he asked.

She looked directly at him. "There are none."

"Deaton was concerned about costs."

"Twelve million to the *Hezbollah*. Two million more for bribes. Two million five for operating costs."

"That last seems extravagant," said Deaton, unable to hold his tongue when funds were mentioned.

"The Learjet pilot's wage is included. Kamil didn't come cheap."

"Then he should stay until we finish," said Deaton. Frugality was his calling, and he saved the Sociedad many dollars, as his uncle had done before him. "I further suggest we discuss the ransom for Mr. Dubois. He's worth a fortune. Gates and Buffet are beggars in comparison."

Deaton looked at Sydney for her response.

"It must appear as both a terrorist attack *and* a kidnapping. But you do realize that Dubois has seen too much, and we can't let him live." Sydney's eyes glittered. She had her own plan for the hostages. They would suffer.

Deaton shrugged. "That's another matter. I'm talking about offsetting expenditures. We get what we can, even for a dead horse. How much can we milk out of his family? How much from the foundation?"

Sydney cast them a demure expression. "That will be up to the members, of course."

Deaton liked her response, and he leaned back in his chair, calculating.

"Where's the woman hostage?" asked Professor Fuentes.

"In the building next door. I hope to make her . . . amenable. I told her if she doesn't do precisely as told, I will have her son's throat cut. She knows that I can do it."

El Jefe took a call on his cell phone. Zerbini was ten minutes away. Everything had gone well. He was returning with the book as well as the Lilac father and son.

It was a good day for the Sociedad Serpiente.

"Bring Mr. Dubois in so we can all have a look," said El Jefe.

After they'd viewed Frank Dubois in prisoner's chains, the Serpientes would take him to the Weeping Tree, where there was work to be done.

Sydney would remain and continue to convince Erin Frechette that unquestioned compliance was in her—and her parents' and son's—best interests.

13

Weyland Foundation, Special Projects Division

Squid felt that he was an unlikely candidate for the job of VP in the organization. At twenty-eight, he was younger than the project leaders, and even younger than many of the engineers in the Applied Technologies branch. Except for himself, Mary Long, and two dozen diehards, and in spite of his arguments, the remainder had submitted their resignations.

He blamed himself. His size was so intimidating that few others argued for long. He was prone to reach judgments too abruptly.

Normally Squid was much more pleasant natured, and made friends easily, but Tanker's death had drained his pleasantness, and the attack on the Weyland Building left him bitter.

It mattered little. The exodus of employees was almost complete. If any more went, the foundation would lose critical capabilities and be unable to function.

Squid heard a series of strange squawks emanating from the multiline telephone, and punched various buttons until they went away. A moment later, Mary Long peeked in, saying she'd had trouble with the intercom. Dr. Daniel Walsh had just arrived from Kennedy.

Walsh, who was middle-aged yet lean and athletic looking, appeared surprisingly fresh after the red-eye flight. He carried a briefcase in one hand and a steaming mug of coffee in the other. Following a juggling act, they shook hands, and Squid offered him a seat on the couch.

The lean project leader settled, inhaled a gulp of coffee, and expressed sympathy about the terrorist attack.

"I'd like to kick someone's ass," Squid said, "but I don't know where to start."

Walsh surprised him. Rather than sitting sad-eyed, he released a string of curses, and stated that it was time to say enough to all terrorists. They deserved extermination.

Squid formed his humorless smile.

"Mr. Woshuski, er . . ."

"People here call me Squid."

Daniel Walsh was not one to mince his words. "I'm here to discuss Shepherd's Journal."

"I was about to call you on the subject when I learned you were on your way."

"My project falls under the Applied Technology branch. During our last conversation, Ms. Frechette said you'd assume her previous duties. That was the morning of the attack. Will the project be continued?"

"I believe so, but I'm only guessing," answered Squid. "The foundation has been struck hard. Without the chairman and the veeps, we're coasting—operating on last known guidance. As far as I know, there's still a Special Projects and an Applied Technology branch."

"Are you knowledgeable of my project?"

"Not the technical details of the document retrieval software." Squid nodded at his PC monitor. "But I've read over the summary and the recovered portion of the journal."

After a short discussion, Squid learned that Walsh preferred to be called Dan, and that the Shepherd's Journal project was at a standstill until they were granted fifteen more hours of computer time to recover more pages. Erin had promised that it would come soon. While they waited, Dan and Professor Bill Shaw were working out of a hotel in Eureka, California, making field trips to locate remnants of the ancient encampment mentioned in the journal. While they'd not found it, they were steadily narrowing down possibilities.

"Then you both think it existed?"

"Dr. Shaw is sure of it, and I find myself leaning that

way. After we recover the next batch of pages with Helga, there should be more light shed on it all."

Squid asked Link's question: "Could there be a connection between your project and what's going on today—either the scandals or even the terrorist attack. Could someone want it stopped so badly, they'd unleash terrorism?"

Walsh seemed not nearly so surprised as Squid had anticipated. He stared out the window at the panoramic view of the city for a moment, taking his time.

"First realize that this all sprang from an old, often discredited California legend. Yet Professor Shaw believes not only that Shepherd's Journal is historically accurate, but that vestiges of the Sociedad remain, and that they've grown in power and sophistication."

Squid stared. "For what purpose?"

"Something highly illegal, probably to do with smuggling." Walsh gave a small shrug. "I'm a doubter, but I can't discount it. Some of our forays are obviously unwelcome—we've had vandalism, tires slashed, things like that. On the other hand, there's simpler reasons to distrust outsiders. It's remote, and much of the marijuana and methamphetamines sold in the cities come from there. The locals blame the prohibitions on fishing and logging for taking their jobs, and don't give a damn about laws made by a government that doesn't give a damn about them.

"Professor Shaw believes the Sociedad is incredibly rich and has a powerful lobby. Even in my short period of observation, I've noticed a concerted effort to halt economic growth, done in the name of protecting the ecology. If anyone mentions new industry or a compromise on environmental restrictions, a new group of protesters blocks it. Shaw thinks the Sociedad's behind it to keep the area remote and depressed, and no one has studied them as thoroughly as he has. He feels the first step in proving it still exists is to locate the old encampment."

Squid tried not to show skepticism as they discussed areas where Dan and Professor Shaw had searched. On the walls were various glass-covered maps. Dan went to the largest one of North America and used a dry marker to draw a line down the coast from Cape Mendocino to Point Cabrillo, one hundred miles of the most rugged shoreline of North America.

"We've eliminated everything north and south. If it exists, it's within those boundaries."

Mary Long interrupted their conversation. "Mr. Worsczejius. We've received a FedEx package from Charleston, South Carolina, addressed to A. L. Anderson."

Squid's pulse quickened. "Has it been scanned by Security?"

"Everything goes through them now."

He asked Dan Walsh to wait in a lounge down the hall while they examined the package.

Boudie Springs, Montana

Squid called with a development. They'd received a FedEx package. The sender had signed with a simple *S.*

"Contents?" Link tried to prepare for the worst.

"A videotape with a Post-it note on front reading, *This traitor was Number 4.*"

"Have you viewed the tape?"

"Yeah." Squid's voice was gruff. "It opens with the interior shot of the Learjet, and shows Erin, Mr. Dubois, and then Gwen, who's been beaten even worse. Two guys wearing hoods wrap her in silver duct tape from her feet to her head."

Squid paused, as if he did not want to continue. "Gwen was still breathing when they pushed her out the hatch." He hissed, "Rotten bastards."

Link agreed. "Could you get any idea about where they were flying?"

"Too dark outside the windows to see anything. Give me your e-mail address, Boss. Mary's digitizing a copy to send to your laptop."

Link gave him the dot org address taped onto the laptop. "Have her send another to Gordon Hightower along with a message that you're standing by for their analysis."

But we're not holding our breaths, he told himself.

"She'll transmit in ten minutes."

Link hung up and powered up the laptop. He avoided the cyberworld, thinking it robbed a person of too much time, but he knew more about it than he let on to Erin. A *little* more, at any rate.

There were the sounds of hooves at a canter. Through the kitchen window, he watched Joseph Spotted Horse trying to rein in Ms. Stubborn, who insisted on continuing to a tasty growth of alfalfa. There she nonchalantly grazed as Joseph crawled off, lecturing her on the natural hierarchy of humans over beasts.

Link heard a beep declaring the arrival of e-mail. He stared reluctantly at the screen, thinking there'd been enough horrors, opened the message, and clicked on the symbol of the attached video. It was as bad as he'd guessed. Several times he paused the action, trying to see what was outside the aircraft window and ignore all the rest.

A computerized voice sounded like that of a cartoon character: *"I take pleasure in killing your friends, knowing you cannot protect them. You will be contacted with terms to keep the others alive after our mutual friend Gwen is encouraged to fly."*

A mummified Gwen was dragged forth and cast out into the air stream.

"The Weyland Foundation must meet all demands precisely. From this moment, neither Mr. Dubois nor Ms. Frechette will receive food. Tomorrow they will be hungry, and each day thereafter, their craving will be worse. In five days, the hunger will diminish, for they will have begun the process of dying. If the ransom is not received as specified, they will perish slowly, knowing you refused to help."

Once more Link had the feeling that the words were meant for him personally, that the speaker was someone he had once known. Someone evil. Someone filled with hatred. He quelled his emotions and played the footage again, looking for a clue or mistake.

For a full half hour he'd watched when he began to wonder about something that he should have noted earlier.

Like a discrepancy when the terrorists dragged the

silver mummy to the open hatch—which was not shown: the wind effect seemed less than it should have been. If they'd been in a Learjet blasting along at four or five hundred miles per, the wind would have been more extreme.

Only one who had been exposed to the elements at the hatch of a jet aircraft would know.

Conclusion—the video had been taken on the ground, either at night or in a dark hangar, with a powerful fan or something similar providing the wind effect.

Gwen still had a chance of survival. He reached for the sat phone to tell Squid of his discovery. It buzzed in his hand before he could enter the memory number.

"Anderson."

Squid's voice caught as he blurted, "We just received a report from the Georgia State Troopers. A duct-taped body hit the pavement on I-20, not far from Augusta." Squid paused for a breath. "Some of her was still taped together. Most of her—" His voice cracked, and he stopped and cursed *them*. "They attached photos. Enough of Gwen was intact to recognize her features."

"Did the trucker see the impact?"

"Yeah. He was motoring along since there wasn't much traffic. Then something large and silver fell and sort of exploded on the concrete. He swerved to miss it. If you're asking if she was actually dropped from an airplane, the answer is yes."

But from what aircraft? Link wondered.

"It was dark. Five fifteen. I figure they were flying down low, and then landed before there was light enough to see them. If the pilot continued in a straight line—"

"Why assume that?"

"I'm not, but listen, Boss. If we know when and where they threw her out, and how far they could fly before dawn, which was at five forty there, we can come up with a minimum and maximum radius, inside of which they probably landed."

Despite Link's undefined suspicions, it made sense. "Keep going."

"Just like the last time the FAA didn't have a track

on the Lear, so they had to be low. If they threw her out at five fifteen, and it was light at five forty, they'd have only twenty-five minutes before they could be seen. Less ten minutes to taxi and hide the airplane, and they're down to fifteen minutes, meaning they most likely landed within a hundred miles of Augusta."

Squid was thinking properly, analytically. "It's worth looking at," said Link.

"They're probably using one of the drug-runner airfields."

"Erin keeps the classified list of those stored in Helga."

"Good. I'll chase that one." Squid sounded happy to be contributing.

"Run it past the DEA and Gordon. Try to get satellite coverage of the air traffic during that period. And look for *all* types of aircraft. I'm not sold it was the Learjet."

"Aye, aye, Boss."

"Did Mary locate any aerial photos taken during the terrorist attack?"

"She thought she did. One image shows a police chopper on helipad five, and a few consultants wearing green. The date-timer was wrong, though. NYPD air ops doesn't show a copper chopper on the building until six minutes after the call went out."

Link thought on it. "Let's keep it simple. Assume the date-timer was accurate and the helo belonged to the bad guys. Have Mary blow it up and try to get close-ups of the people."

He remembered something else. "Did you get to talk with Dr. Walsh?"

"Yeah. He goes by Dan, by the way." Squid told him about the discussion, and how the two doctors had been searching for the Serpiente encampment site. Squid explained where they'd searched, and how the professor believed that the Serpientes still existed. "I've gotta tell you, Boss, it's damned unlikely. They want fifteen hours of dedicated time on Helga to process the next batch of pages of the journal, but—"

"Give it to them," Link said.

Squid argued, "Boss, *everyone* wants time on Helga."

Erin feels the project is connected with our troubles.
"Work it into the schedule. In the meantime, tell Dan
to continue looking for the encampment."

10:40 a.m.—The Weeping Tree

El Jefe rode all the way to the walking trail seated by
Frank Dubois in the Hummer. For the first hour, Dubois
refused to chat, but after stopping twice for Welk to
apply his metal baton to the sensitive and ruined calf of
his crippled leg, the billionaire had become loquacious.
From that point, it was pleasant for El Jefe, for Dubois
was intelligent and informed, and able to discuss recent
trends in the American judicial system. They agreed on
some points, differed on others, but the scope of Dubois's knowledge was impressive.

Julius and Roberto Lilac were in the rearmost seat,
and except for an occasional unanswered plea from the
father for El Jefe to end it swiftly, they were quiet. Julius
knew what lay before him. He'd done to others as would
be done to himself. The Sociedad could not allow him
to continue to miss meetings, even for the month it
would take him to die, or else others might think it was
acceptable to bend the rules, as well.

Roberto could have only a notion of the secret ceremony, but he knew the finality of it and had sworn his
loyalty to El Jefe. He was distraught, a devoted son.
Julius was scared and would likely have already killed
himself to avoid the stone, but he knew the horrors the
Sociedad would have brought upon his family. If he'd
turned to the authorities, they'd have suffered worse.

Twice they turned into blind places, where they waited
as Welk and Zerbini moved bushes and saplings that
appeared like the real thing, but were mounted on sliding rails.

As soon as they arrived at the walking trail, they all
dismounted. Due to the beatings, Dubois could hardly
hobble. Julius Lilac was too frail to walk at all, so he
was supported by his son. Zerbini was up front with El
Jefe, carrying the heavy book that he had removed from
Julius Lilac's safe. They took a main trail for a hundred

yards, then veered left past another false blind and continued through the dense redwood forest.

El Jefe remained watchful for the sentinel. That, too, was an ancient custom, to keep a madman roving the area in search of strangers. For a long while, they'd gone without a sentinel, before Welk had resurrected the tradition. The procedure for creating a sentinel was an interesting chapter in the book. Human vulnerability had not changed over the years.

El Jefe slowed and halted. Ahead was a small cabin, crude in appearance, built at one side of a clearing in the midst of giant redwoods. The sentinel stood before the cabin with his hunting rifle and blank expression, as he'd done the last time they were here.

Police Chief Welk had tried twice before, but the candidates had not survived. This one had been a hunter, caught when he'd ventured into their valley. Welk had brought him to the cabin, where he'd castrated him and then stripped and staked him out in the rain and weather for the four months of winter, precisely as directed in the book. He'd fed him little and beaten him into insensible raw meat at the slightest disobedience; when he failed to grovel at his approach, could not lift incredible weights, or later, ventured a single foot past small red flags—the kind used to train pets—planted beyond the perimeter of the clearing.

As the book had described, Welk was left with a human beast that would do anything to please him. One day he'd given him back his own rifle and told him to shoot a human target that he'd brought, and the sentinel had done so without question. Now the sentinel patrolled the clearing with his rifle, as crazy and as dangerous as a rabid Doberman. His stare was that of a dumb animal without the power of reasoning, focused only on protecting the clearing.

If they continued forward, he would not shoot them, for they wore policemen's stars that Welk issued years before. Still, they judiciously waited as Welk came forth.

When the sentinel saw Welk, he cringed, eyes frightened and averted.

Welk snapped out an order, "Up!" and the sentinel rose slowly, as would a dog that might be beaten. He

had the rifle, but Welk said he'd die before breaking a
rule or threatening his master.

El Jefe observed the horrified reaction from Frank
Dubois. That was what the Serpientes wanted from outsiders. It was their way, to instill disgust and terror.

"Inside!" Welk said. The sentinel hurried into the
cabin and shut the door.

Welk brought him food, old clothing, and runaways.
Like a keen-nosed bloodhound, the sentinel had tracked
down and killed them, and dragged the bodies back to
the clearing for later disposal. Welk had lost count of
their numbers. There were many runaways hitchhiking the
highways north of San Francisco.

The sentinel had been at the clearing for nine years,
and so far had shot and killed a pair of intruding wilderness campers and three marijuana growers in search of
new fields.

"It's safe," Welk told them, and El Jefe led the way
to the massive brethren trees, where they all paused to
observe their splendor.

On the side away from the clearing, a low bungalow
blended with the forest. At its far end was a bunkhouse
large enough to sleep fifteen, ready for use by Sajacento
and his *jahid* when they arrived. Two men of the Middle
East—a master chemist and his assistant—stayed there
to manufacture Mullah Sajacento's bombs. The vest-
bomb tailored for Ahmed bin Polah had either malfunctioned or he had changed his mind about martyrdom. El
Jefe bet on the latter. Despite what they'd seen, A. L.
Anderson couldn't be *that* good.

Bin Polah had insisted that his hatred was so enormous that he must be fitted with the largest bomb ever
strapped to a man. The A-9 bomb maker had been
afraid to refuse him, even when he'd insisted that they
not use a remotely operated detonating switch.

Frigging idiot coward. If there were more like Ahmed
bin Polah, it would mean more failures, and less money
for the Sociedad.

The chemists, who were understandably scared shitless
of the sentinel, had been taken into Lennville to spend
two days relaxing in a small hotel owned by the

Sociedad—so that they would not be around for the ceremony now at hand. They'd return before Sajacento arrived with his *jahid* martyrs.

El Jefe walked around the Weeping Tree, the others following, and stopped at its side where the words "Fiere the Trie" were written in twenty-four-inch letters. They were legible, although it had been a long time since the tree's last replenishment. The dark bloodstain went deep. Through the years, there'd been many ceremonies for those deemed untrustworthy in the eyes of past El Jefes. According to the book, there'd been an early period when a bloody *X* had sufficed, but that was changed when Snake People had enslaved an Englishman from Sir Francis Drake's crew and they'd learned to read and write.

Ten yards farther was the blood stone, although it appeared more like a rust-colored lump. Beneath accumulations of earth and the stains of blood and other liquids was a boulder of ruby-colored quartz. As beautiful as the valley itself, and just as deadly.

El Jefe motioned to Zerbini, who carefully placed the book beside the tree, then opened it and found the page that described the ceremony of the stone. El Jefe motioned for Julius Lilac to be brought forward.

When Roberto tried to accompany his father, El Jefe shook his head. "Not you."

Welk roughly grasped the old man by the collar and dragged him forward.

"Please be gentle," Roberto called with obvious concern.

The scholar Fuentes observed Roberto with a frown, then turned and kicked the old man in the butt. Zerbini laughed and kicked him in the same spot, making Julius stumble.

Roberto clenched his eyes, unable to watch as Welk shoved the old man face forward onto the stone and planted a heavy brogan on his back.

"I bring you new blood," Welk said, as the book described.

El Jefe held out his hand, and Fuentes opened the sack carried from the vehicles. He laid a scarred aluminum bat in the leader's palm. "A wooden one," El Jefe muttered, and Fuentes exchanged the aluminum bat with a heavy Louisville Slugger.

He distributed a bat to each of the other members.

Julius Lilac was crying, his son Roberto still clenching his eyes and shaking his head.

El Jefe raised the bat and clubbed Julius—*whap*—but not so harshly that he was rendered unconscious. Julius let out a screech and tried to rise, but he was held in place by Welk's boot. The others stepped forward and were not so restrained. *Whap. Whap. Whap.* Welk laughed, raised his own bat, and swung it down so hard, it broke a gaping crack in Julius's skull.

Roberto screamed for them to stop. He hurried forward and shielded his father, protecting him from more, and the members swiveled their heads to see El Jefe's reaction.

El Jefe raised his bat again, and this time swung much harder. *Whap!* The bat smashed into Roberto's upheld arm, breaking it so it angled askew. Roberto's next screams were not for his father. El Jefe struck him again, this time in the head, and the younger man flopped around like a dying chicken. Welk raised his hand to stop them, dragged the son back onto the father and held him in position with the same brogan. They all began to pound with their bats. *Whap. Whap. Whap.* For more than a minute they continued, until both men's heads were cracked open, and brain matter and blood were flying. Still, there were signs of life.

El Jefe stepped back, nostrils flared with bloodlust, his clothing spattered.

"Honor the tree," he said in a strained voice, and they started with Roberto, lifting and holding him firmly as—for the thousandth time using the fresh blood of a dying or freshly killed human—the words were repainted into the bark of the living giant.

FIERE THE TRIE

When they finished and both human husks were emptied, the members' bloodlust satisfied so they stood mutely staring at what they've done, El Jefe motioned at Roberto's body. "He was a young man to be trusted."

"Yet we killed him?" questioned Deaton.

"If Damon Lee succeeds in his task, I'll name him to replace Julius Lilac. Then we must watch our backs. It's better like that, staying alert and knowing whom not to trust. With Roberto Lilac, there would never have been a question, and we would grown complacent."

He turned to Frank Dubois, who looked on in horror. "Did you think we'd forget you?"

They would deal with Dubois quickly. El Jefe was anxious to return to Lennville, to see what had developed with Erin Frechette.

After all, the billionaire had not been their target.

PART II

Fíere the Tríe

14

Weyland Foundation, Special Projects

Stefan Worsczejius had told Dan Walsh that he would get the fifteen hours of computer time as soon as it came available, then shook his hand to wish him luck before he headed for Teterboro Airport to board a Gulfstream IV that Mary arranged. While waiting for the newly deciphered pages, Dan and Professor Shaw would continue to search for the encampment.

Federal agents and officers still swarmed through the building, measuring and double-checking on floors that the terrorists had not visited during their deadly attack, stringing CRIME SCENE—DO NOT ENTER tape in the Special Projects secure areas. When Squid objected, they ignored him or flashed new subpoenas demanding access to everything imaginable.

After passing on Link's observation that the wind blast in the video of Gwen was too meager, and the photo of the rooftop taken during the attack showing an early-arrival NYPD chopper bearing the wrong tail number to Gordon Hightower's office—receiving not a hint of a thank-you, only a suggestion that he and his people were getting in the way and not to call unless there was something new about the Hezbollah—there was very little left for Squid to do.

Two more Special Projects personnel announced they were leaving. On their three floors, in all of the twelve managerial suites and ninety-odd offices and work areas that made up Special Projects, fewer than forty persons remained. They were down to treading water, unable to do anything more than hopefully keep the organization alive.

When Squid returned to studying the documents of the Shepherd's Journal project, he regarded them with fresh eyes. It did not take much to make the jump to the fact that the Serpientes had once existed, much as Shepherd had written. After all, outlaws and pirates had been around since there were fortunes to be stolen. But at some time that morning, he'd become convinced that they were still around, doing their bloody work.

What they were doing, beside some vague notion of working with Hezbollah and smuggling them into the country was impossibly vague, yet knowing the Serpientes were associated with the Hezbollah and the Green Mullah made them guilty of Tanker's death.

The friend of my enemy is also my enemy.

Like Dan Walsh, he was anxious to learn what the next pages of Shepherd's Journal might hold, what modern secrets it might solve.

In the meantime, he dwelled on those parts of the deciphered pages that dealt with his specialty, the sea, and the phenomenon that had made the Serpientes' seafaring capabilities unique: their ability to be transported from sea to shore and return to the sea at their whim.

Squid had known of riptides and surface currents that moved watercraft along swiftly, but at certain times it seemed the Serpientes had been ferried both to and from the shore at their whim. Shepherd had called the intense current at Angel Rock, *marea muerte.* In English it translated to "dead tide." One implication was that many had died trying to master it.

What had been the original descriptive words for the Serpientes given by the Spanish?

Sociedad de las Serpientes Oscuros. Dark and obscure serpents—deadly pirates who were able to disappear at their bidding, using something they called the dead tide.

He was left with two critical questions. One, what was unique about that particular coastal area to create the *marea muerte* current? If he could learn those ingredients, such as the undersurface terrain, currents, and other variables, he might be able to find the place.

Two, the Serpientes' original seacraft had been made

of reeds woven into thatch. What kind of sturdy and *oscuro* craft would modern Serpientes require to transport high-value cargo?

There were advantages to working in the twenty-first century, such as the ability to build precise computer models. He had an edge—the conglomerate of computers called Helga.

Squid was pleased with his reasoning, and was thinking about his first step—to learn everything possible about this particular hundred miles of coastline and the dead tide—when a curious thing happened to the computer.

11:45 a.m.—Boudie Springs

Damon Lee was keeping A. L. Anderson—or at least his cabin—in sight, waiting for permission from Sydney to shoot him.

After being dropped off in Kalispell the previous day, he'd tried to contact her, as El Jefe had ordered. Eight times he had called before she'd answered, then claiming she was too busy to talk for long. After reading off an address—speaking over the quiet rumble of jet engines—she'd told him to pick up a package, then to locate and keep an eye on Lincoln Anderson, and wait until she called with instructions. Then the line had gone dead.

Damon had had enough problems trying to convince El Jefe that he should become a Serpiente as his father had been, which meant he'd make a shit-pot full of money. Now he was taking orders from a woman who treated him like the freaking hired help.

Upon renting a dark blue Camry from Avis, Lee had loaded his gear, which included a heavy, oblong metal case, then stopped by a Mailboxes USA to pick up a canvas satchel per instructions from the person who had left it there.

Having already put in a long day, he had then driven a hundred miles to a cornball tourist town named Boudie Springs, surrounded by mountains, grass, and large cows. There he had taken a device from the satchel and tried to use it to locate the pickup truck, which Sydney had said had an electronic tracking device attached to the undercarriage. Nothing worked.

After looking for an hour, he'd obtained a tourist map from the Visitor Information Center, and again tried to find the target's address. Following another hour, he'd stopped at Dewey's Sports Center, picked up a warm Hudson Bay blanket, a box of chocolate power bars, and a box of .300 WSM ammo, placed it all on the counter in front of a dumb-shit, smiling-for-no-reason clerk, dropped a platinum Visa on top, and asked where he'd find the target's address.

The clerk had called him *brother*, which he'd found irritating, and explained that RR 1 box numbers were east of town. North and west was Rural Route 2. Route 3 was south. . . .

Lee, who was irritated with the general situation, had broken in. "I don't need a freaking geography lesson. Just tell me where the asshole lives."

"Like I said, brother, RR One means it's east of town. Who're you looking for?"

Finally. "Guy named A. L. Anderson."

The clerk's smile had widened. "I didn't know Link was in town. You a friend?"

Lee had noticed crucifixes on the walls and racks of I LOVE JESUS and similar window and bumper stickers.

In order to establish the pecking order of the asker and the askee, and to speed things along, Damon Lee had turned so the butt of his 9 mm pressed the fabric of his jacket, making it obvious even to the cretin that he was carrying iron. He had visualized sticking the Beretta up the redneck's right nostril as he spoke in a mean-as-hell tone: "Listen up, dumb shit, where—does—he—live?"

The clerk had continued to smile, which Lee took as a sign of gross stupidity. With his palms up in what looked like a peaceful gesture, he lowered his hands behind the counter.

"Why are you looking for him?"

"Try again," Lee had snarled, moving his hand so it rested on the Beretta's custom grip. He was out of patience. Even the smooth feel of rosewood was not calming. People where he came from knew to move back when Damon Lee was about to explode. To be fair, the clerk hadn't known what Lee was capable of. The three men he'd killed had not spread the word.

He'd spoken through gritted teeth. "Okay Jesus freak, let's start the goddanm conversation over. One question. Where the *fuck* does he live?"

The clerk had turned just enough that Lee could see the .40 S&W Glock riding high in a worn belt holster for quick access; and with his eyes on Lee's, he had raised his hands from under the counter so Lee could observe the yawning muzzle of a well-used 12-gauge shotgun.

Mossberg model 590, pump-action, flat finish with scratches from use, circa 1980, once called a riot gun.

Lee had frozen, and only too late noted the uncontrollable spasm in his sphincter.

The clerk had spoken in an amiable tone. "Let me give you some advice, brother. Never threaten a gun-store owner, and never, *ever* curse in this preacher's store. I want you to memorize those two things. Gun store, don't threaten—preacher's store, don't curse."

Lee had stared at the black muzzle and managed to whisper, "I understand."

"Drop your hands to your sides. No, *wayyy* down, like you're trying to touch the floor. That's good. Now turn around and get out. If you come back, I'll assume you've decided to rob me, and the *second* thing I'll do is say a prayer for your tormented departed soul."

Lee had felt giddy with fear as another spasm shuddered in his sphincter, and he knew that he must find a bathroom. He'd turned and hurried for the door. Outside, he'd glanced back once, saw that the owner still held the black shotgun, and sprinted all the way to the Toyota.

The store owner replaced the Mossberg into its under-the-counter rack, and dialed the number for Link Anderson. After welcoming him home, he described the visitor.

Damon Lee had driven three blocks before he'd parked and sat for a half hour, engine running and hands clenched on the wheel as he'd calmed himself. The smell in the car was atrocious. After a pit stop at a gas station, where he had washed up and changed shorts and pants in a phone-booth-size restroom, he had asked a courteous question of the attendant, and was given directions to Anderson's home.

He'd still been rattled as he'd driven into the boonies, went past the cabin twice for an eyeball, then parked and observed through binoculars from a distance, which was easy because the only thing between the home and the Camry was a scraggly collection of sagebrush.

In front had been a battered old black pickup and an even more ancient stake-bed truck.

He tried using the tattletale tracking receiver again, to no avail, stuffed it back into the satchel, and threw the useless thing into the back. His hands trembled. Try as he must, Lee had been unable to stop thinking of the Jesus freak, and how he'd been disgraced.

To reassure himself, he'd pulled a case from the trunk and carefully assembled a very special rifle. When he was done with Anderson, he'd stop outside Dewey's store. He wouldn't have to get close to use what he'd bring to the party. With it, Damon was deadly at half a mile. As the vestiges of fear left him, he'd begun to seethe.

A white Blazer had pulled into the drive, and the woman who emerged with a covered dish had been met at the door by a tall man in jeans and a dark shirt. He looked athletic, perhaps an inch taller than Lee. Soon afterwards, the woman had left, peering as she passed the Camry.

Lee had spent the night in the car, angry that he'd left the blanket on the counter, starting the engine now and then for warmth. A few times he'd dropped off, but invariably a freaking light would come on in the cabin. Since he hadn't wished to miss Anderson if he left during the night, he'd rested little, and by the time the sun rose above the distant mountain—so raw and bright, it gave him a headache—he was grainy-eyed and weary. More hours had passed. He'd become ravenous, remembered the chocolate power bars he'd left on the counter, and blamed one more thing on the store owner.

He'd been about to make a run to town for food when an old Indian man, dark and weathered and moving slowly, came out of the cabin, gave the Toyota a stare, and started the stake-bed truck. Lee decided that the other, younger man was Anderson, and wished that Sydney would call with the order to shoot him while there was only one person inside.

More than two hours later, the old Indian had returned on a barrel-chested brown horse and, after tying it up, went back into the cabin.

When the cell phone jingled, Lee was so wound up that he jumped and cried out. He felt sheepish as he answered. It was the woman, Sydney.

After hearing his description of the situation, she warned him, as El Jefe had done, that Anderson was extremely dangerous. Was he aware that Lee was watching him?

Damon Lee thought of the neighbor and the store clerk, but decided not to go there. "No."

As he spoke the word, Link emerged from the cabin.

"He just came out," Lee told Sydney, and watched the tall man check the horse's halter and saddle, then mount up and ride off at a brisk pace, heading toward the plain and the towering mountains beyond.

"He'll be coming back in a couple of hours," she said confidently. "Too much is going on for him to ignore." She gave instructions, and he listened.

Lee carefully examined the terrain. There were dirt roads that were good enough for him to follow in the car and set up an ambush. "I may have to hurt him," he told her.

"I don't care what condition he's in, as long as he's alive when you get him here."

Lee liked that part. He was in the mood to hurt someone.

Aozou Plus Eight
12:30 p.m.—Boudie Springs, Montana

Link kept Ms. Stubborn at a leisurely trot for a half hour, keeping her reined in and minding her manners all the way to the foothills at the base of the big mountains.

Although he preferred to be light-handed, guiding her with knees and subtle pressures, they were getting to know one another all over again. Joseph Spotted Horse had known what he'd needed, and fetched the mare for that purpose—to let Link sink into his own mind without all the baggage that was accumulated at the fringes. A man could not think clearly with the weight of the world on his shoulders.

The Blackfeet had been horse people, their warriors as tough as any light cavalry in the history of man. The thrill that had run through them as they'd bonded with horses was part of what made Link homesick. But it wasn't only horses that instilled the Blackfeet's love for the high country. Once there had been no horses, and dogs had been their companions, strapped down with heavy loads as they moved their homes from one hunting ground to another. Dogs had guarded the encampments, ever ready to be a friend. Although horses came to carry the heavy load, the Blackfeet continued to befriend dogs. At the worst time of Starvation Winter, when the U.S. government had succeeded in destroying all the wild buffalo and promised them beeves to replace them, and watched them die as they waited, they had been reluctant to eat their canine friends. Many of the People had starved to death first. Half the People had perished.

How many others would do that? There are no faster companions than the Blackfeet. No prouder people. None who remember a pledge of friendship longer. That is my heritage.

Link bypassed the east canyon, and let Ms. Stubborn run some as they rode around to the bluff that overlooked it.

As he came closer to the rim, he slowed the mare to a walk and let her blow a little.

So what am I doing here when my friends are dying elsewhere?

As he approached the lookout, the mare protested by pulling at her bit and shaking her head. He gave her a nudge of boot, and she edged forward just a little, then no more, saying, in effect, "Listen to me, man. This place is dangerous."

Link remained astride, looking down the precipice at the canyon road that twisted its way down one small sagebrush-covered mountain and up another. When he'd lived here, he'd negotiated it daily to cut firewood and bring it back to sell. When it was dry like this, it was a dangerous drive. When the snow came, it was more treacherous still and best avoided.

Erin pleaded for me to listen, but I did not. Am I so wise that my ears are closed? Now they have taken her and Frank.

Ms. Stubborn remained stock-still, as if afraid to become restless.

Who had taken her? From all indications, they consisted of Sajacento, the mullah who dressed in green, and the American-hating Hezbollah with whom he was allied.

Why am I so reluctant to accept that at face value?

Because from everything he had learned about Middle Eastern terrorists, the things that were happening were too *different*. The Hezbollah leaders that he'd studied would have used more bludgeon and less refinement. The attack on the Weyland Building, for instance. The Hezbollah he knew would have tried to move a big bomb into place. If they'd gotten onto the roof, they'd have stayed and killed more people. They liked to dip their hands in your blood and laugh at your helplessness, and disdained the kinds of finesse exhibited in this operation, like badmouthing the Weyland Foundation until it was demonized by the public. Like killing the Weyland Foundation VPs with nerve gas so the press would jump on that, as if it were worse to die by exposure to sarin or cholera or plutonium than by a gunshot—or beheading.

Whoever had planned the attack on the Weyland Building was cagier, smarter than Hezbollah. Those differences had bothered him from the first, but had been lost in the logjam of horrific acts that continued to pile up. The smart person who had planned the attack had ruined the foundation's reputation, undermined the infrastructure, *then* attacked and murdered the decision makers. The organization called the Weyland Foundation was as surely destroyed as if the building had been leveled.

He carefully reined the mare straight back, turned and nudged her into a trot, and shared her happiness at being taken away from the steep place.

The sat phone buzzed, and Miss Stubborn took a two-step skitter. When it buzzed again, she remembered and ignored it. On the fourth ring, he reined in and answered, "Anderson."

"Boss, it's Worsczejius. We got more news."

He steeled himself. "Go ahead."

"I was building a computer model of how the Serpientes might use currents to smuggle the Hezbollah, when Helga went crazy on us. Mary's trying to determine the extent, but she thinks it's fatal. Some kind of worm invaded the active archives and data banks, then took out the operating system and the computer hard drives. I'm talking about *everything*."

Another critical function of the Weyland Foundation destroyed.

Erin had said such an outage was impossible because of safeguards she'd installed. The computer's loss would affect not only the Weyland Foundation but also the operations of every U.S. clandestine agency that relied on Helga, which consisted of hundreds of powerful computer servers strung in parallel. The amount of information involved was gargantuan.

"We're informing everyone on all networks," said Squid.

"Is it widespread? Are other major mainframes affected?"

"Mary says it was specifically intended for Helga. She's scrambling to find out what's retrievable and what's not, but she's not hopeful. She also needs more help."

A thought wheedled at Link. "The Shepherd Journal?"

"I had it on the monitor when everything crashed, and got to watch the Document Recovery Program cannibalize itself. All we have left are the hard copies."

"Contact the Air Force Information Superiority Command. Erin worked with a Maj. Jana Stradley. She knows the Helga system, and even more about worms and viruses."

"I'll call her now." Squid disconnected.

Link then telephoned Gordon Hightower and, after a wait, was connected. The FBI supervisor was uninterested in Helga or the photo of the fake NYPD helicopter on the Weyland Building rooftop, or the possibility that Gwen had not been at the open hatch of a jet in flight. Instead he told Link about *his* idea to locate the Learjet.

He had taken Squid's plan as his own. He had an army of agents head to Georgia to search every foot of the hundred-mile radius for the aircraft and hostages. FBI media relations specialists were transmitting a plea for assistance from Georgians who might have seen the low-flying Learjet. Citizens were calling in. Several sightings already fit with the track and timing model.

There was other supportive information, but Gordon would not discuss it. He asked if Link could think of anything he'd missed.

Link queried about other possible locations, and Gordon said he was being flexible.

Meaning he was hardly considering other locations.

Again Link told him about the computer crash and Helga's importance.

Gordon was not surprised. That sort of thing happened when every hacker on the block was gunning for you. Despite the terrorist attack, the Weyland Foundation was not beloved. There was a fringe that felt the Weyland Foundation executives had it coming, just as some thought that American foreign policy had brought on the disaster at the WTC.

Link explained his idea that someone savvier than Sajacento or the Hezbollah was involved in the planning and attack on the Weyland Foundation, and perhaps would coordinate future attacks.

"I doubt it."

"Gordon, I need to be closer to the action so I can look for myself."

"The heat on your burner's too high. The word's out about Frank firing you. You say it was a con job? Well, it was a hell of a *bad* one. What were you thinking?"

"Gordon, if I'd known this would happen, I would've stayed and called you, and we'd have stopped the terrorists. No one had a clue."

The senior agent did not respond. He was fishing for anything new that Link might have. Something was exciting him. A promotion?

Link recalled something. "Gordon, did your people hang a tattletale on my truck?"

"Sounds like a good idea, but I didn't authorize it."

Link was about to ask him about the Asian in the Toyota down the street, but Gordon announced that he had a meeting. "Like I said, stay put. At some point I'll pull you in for a long talk. Once you're cleared, you can join me in Atlanta for the endgame. Gotta go now."

As Gordon hung up, Link thought of how he remained focused on the South. He was sure that there was more than he knew that was causing him to think that way.

While Link respected the bureau's people and capabilities, Gordon had a degree of blindness and ambition that he'd never yet seen before.

He recalled his troublesome dream about the giant red trees and his friends being threatened with bloody death. Erin had believed that everything was interrelated. That could include the slander, the attempt to silence Doc Pete, the Hezbollah's plan to destroy America's future, the attack at the Weyland Building, and now the problem with Helga. If Erin was right, one common denominator was Shepherd's Journal.

A lightbulb flickered at the back of his mind. *Erin built safeguards into Helga that no one could have gotten past. Her fail-safe approach would have shut down the portals and isolated the worm at the first hint of intrusion. There'd been traps and multiple firewalls built between the world and Helga, and more between Helga and her dominions, such as the archives. She spent years ensuring that no person could disable the supercomputer.*

What about Erin herself!

A smile formed at his lips. *Erin had been alive this morning when the system went down. The bad guys needed her to erase every trace of Shepherd's Journal. The University of California had a supercomputer like Helga. They'd want Erin to clean that one out, as well, and it would take longer since she was not as familiar with it.*

Why did the smart person plan an overt attack on Weyland Building?

To get Erin.

Why Erin?

To destroy Helga and the effort to resurrect Shepherd's Journal.

In some form, the Serpientes still existed, and one of them was the smart person who was helping Sajacento and the Hezbollah. Someone very canny was liaising between the terrorists of the East and the ancient ones from America. Someone vain and sure.

Perhaps it was the indistinct person Doc Pete had photographed on the platform in Aozou, the robed and turbaned man he had seen at the dry lake beside Sajacento.

He considered Shepherd's Journal and moved what he'd read about the Serpientes into the modern world. If the organization was as secretive and rich today as it had once been, it would want to stop the journal from being resurrected.

New thought. Squid had been working on how the Serpientes were smuggling the Hezbollah into America. He, too, believed the Serpientes were around.

Three miles distant, a rooster tail of dust traversed the high land. A cattle owner checking his beeves? As Link urged Miss Stubborn into an easy canter—which she could do all day without tiring—he began to ask himself the hard questions, and reality raised its nasty head.

Everything I just concluded is improbable. Gordon's a professional, and he's sending his resources to Atlanta. Why am I so sure that he's wrong? An old, likely bogus, manuscript?

Doubts popped up like prairie dogs rearing their heads. If he left Boudic Springs, Gordon promised to have him arrested. It was a dismal thought, to be jailed as a supporter of terrorism.

I have no choice but to go west. Erin's alive there, and Frank may be, as well.

The rooster tail was slowing, negotiating onto various

roads but continuing in his general direction. Finally the vehicle slowed and pulled to a stop. He could not make it out clearly, but it did not appear to be a pickup, as most local residents drove in the countryside.

Link caught a glint. Binoculars? A rifle scope?

More likely a chrome bumper or an outside mirror.

15

Damon Lee set up on the hood of the Toyota. Since the metal was unbearably hot to the touch, he draped his jacket on the dusty hood, set out the Leica range finder, then spread the rifle's built-in forearm tripod, with its metal hinges and rubber feet, and crouched on the jacket, taking aim. The weapon, an FN Herstal Police Rifle, boasted a futuristic black polymer stock, a chrome-lined barrel and a Winchester pre-1964 style action, meaning it was smooth as silk and as indestructible as a ballpeen hammer. The weapon was topped with a three-by-fifteen Leupold premium scope. The drill would be to look through the range finder to get the yardage to target, set that number into the scope to solve the bullet-drop problem, put the post on the target, and go bang.

Lee was not good up close—his flashpoint temperament was too volatile, which made his confrontation with Dewey all the dumber—although he still planned to kill him—and neither did he have the endless patience required to be a truly expert long-distance shot. But he had learned that having the right equipment and the willingness to use it made all the difference.

Three neat yellow stars on the cheek plate attested to that fact. One star for each kill.

He slowly swung the muzzle in an arc around the prairie, using the rifle scope, and noted a single row of trees that angled across the land. There was likely a stream there, but nothing on this side of it to block his view of the man and his horse. Between them there was only sagebrush and an occasional small rise or depression. A perfect place for a shooting. He joked to himself about maybe moving here, since the openness was suited to his profession.

Lee thought of himself as a professional gunman and assassin. His prey could not see as far as he could with the Leupold, and if they were armed, and more than likely they were not, they'd be unable to shoot back and hit anything at the distances he preferred.

He opened the breech and pressed in three .300 WSM rounds, sufficient for his purpose, and adjusted his stance so he was comfortable. He flipped up the scope covers, carefully wrapped his hand about the pistol grip, and pressed the butt of the stock to his shoulder. The stock was customized with a mercury shock absorber, which reduced the recoil to nil.

The range finder showed the target was 1,330 yards out. He next viewed the target, rider and horse, from over the scope, crouched and looked through the lens at three power, and zoomed in to ten power for a close look. The man he knew as A. L. Anderson was staring back at him as if he could see details without magnification. Damon Lee was sure he could not, but there was something unnerving about the determined expression. He decided to get it over with when Anderson closed to twelve hundred yards, where he knew he was deadly accurate. He dialed in 1,200, then moved back, and worked the bolt, enjoying the smooth-as-velvet feel as a short magnum round slid into the chamber and, with a light snick, was locked in place.

The rider continued ahead, toward Damon Lee.

He breathed in, touched the trigger with the meaty part of his forefinger, exhaled, and began to take up the minuscule amount of slack.

Link could not see the vehicle distinctly, but he thought it was the same one that had been parked near the cabin. As he drew closer, he verified that an individual was propped across the hood, as if aiming a camera's telescopic lens or sighting a rifle—*at Link*.

Link reined Ms. Stubborn hard left, crouched into a low profile, and gouged her with his heels. He had not guessed wrong. The first round whistled just behind the mare, a miss but not a bad shot at that distance.

The barrel-chested mare ran full out, but she was not the swiftest of creatures, and Link decided they would not make it to the row of trees flanking Boudie Creek— still a hundred yards distant—if the shooter fired a second round. He reined sharply right, toward the shooter, then hard left again. In fighters they called it jinking, flying unpredictably to make it difficult for ground gunners. In the air, he'd had the added advantage of a third dimension; here he did not. Ms. Stubborn's footwork was sure, but she squealed from the sting of the graze at the top of her neck, causing a spatter of blood and mane hair to spray onto Link.

He continued to lean low across the pommel, kicking the mare steadily as she ran, hoping to save both their lives. As they passed behind the first small cottonwood, another round whipped by, so close, he felt the fan of air.

He slowed and let Ms. Stubborn blow and resume the canter. Boudie Creek traversed the prairie all the way to Canyon Road, and they'd have cover. In order to intercept them, the persistent hunter—or whatever he proved to be—would have to drive to the Canyon Road bridge and lie in wait.

Ms. Stubborn tried to reach back to the source of the sting, but he kept her moving in a distance-consuming line.

The intersection of Boudie Creek and Canyon Road was around a bend a hundred yards distant when he reached back and pulled out a vintage Smith & Wesson .357 magnum revolver—a model 27, heavy-frame—that he placed in his saddle pack before a ride.

They approached the road, and Link urged Ms. Stubborn up the embankment. There, at the side of the road, he stopped and carefully listened and looked about, holding the .357's muzzle upward. At the first sign of ambush, he was ready to level and fire.

The mare was first to hear the engine sound. The driver had driven on past the creek, but was not far. He reined the mare to the right, and urged her into an easy gallop. When her gait was established, he stood in the stirrups and turned, and found the car was still out of sight.

Link turned the mare into the corral in back of the cabin and called for Joseph Spotted Horse. Ms. Stubborn still bled and needed care, and the old Indian was as good with large animals as any veterinarian. He doted on the barrel-chested mare that could run for five miles, blow out for ten minutes, and run another five, even though she was as cantankerous as Joseph himself.

The Indian emerged from the cabin with a grumble. "You are already back? This old man was about to take a small rest." When Joseph saw the wound, he let Link have a measure of his sternest glare.

"She was shot," was all that Link told him as he went inside for his truck keys.

He emerged and headed for the Ramcharger, revolver still in hand, noting that the Toyota that had been parked through the night was indeed missing. He fired up the pickup, let it warm for no more than a few seconds, and eased out of the driveway and onto the road.

Another left and he was on Canyon Road. Five minutes later, he approached the bridge, slowing and noting the parked Camry, and the Asian standing before it brandishing a dull-finished rifle like those carried by SWAT teams. As soon as he realized he had company, he hastily put away the rifle.

Link yanked on the parking brake lever. He left the revolver on the seat and dismounted. As he stalked forward, he fought to suppress his anger, knowing part of it was overflow from the disastrous past three days. Those solutions remained out of his reach. This one was not.

"What do you want?" the man called out.

"You've been staking me out since I got here, and now you've shot my mare." Link continued toward the man and the idling Camry, deciding to turn the idiot in to the deputy in town.

"Stay back," the man said shrilly, edging his hand into his jacket.

Link slowed, realizing he might not be doing the smartest thing in the world by confronting an armed man. "We're taking a drive into town," he snapped.

"I said stay back!" The Asian's voice was rising higher, laced with panic.

Link was too far away to take him before he pulled a weapon, so he judiciously turned on his heel and strode back toward the pickup. It was time for the deputy to intercede.

Bam!

The shot was unexpected, and although the pistol round kicked up dirt ten feet in front of Link, it was slow sinking in. *The idiot just shot at me—again!*

Link sprinted, then dived around the front of his pickup.

Bam! Spanggg!

He'd shot his truck. Was the fool crazy?

Link darted to the still-open door, reached in, and grasped his revolver.

Bam!

Glass shattered. The quarter-panel window was half gone.

Link rolled away, crouched, and brought up the big revolver in a two-hand grip as the other man fired again. *Bam!*

The Asian man clambered into his car and slid across to the driver's seat.

Link sighted on the shooter's head. "Stop!" he cried.

Without closing the door, the man shoved the gearshift into DRIVE and shot forward, headed toward the canyon.

Link's anger mounted as he climbed back into the pickup to follow.

The Ramcharger seemed to sense his outrage, and while the Toyota was faster, it remained in his view as they headed for the canyon. The driver of the Camry was accustomed to high speed and handled the turns deftly, slowing and accelerating, holding his lead, but Link stayed with him, still in four-wheel, high range, tires sticking to the road as if they were glued.

The Asian crested the hill and disappeared, now on the steep winding grade down the side of the canyon.

The Ramcharger went over the top going fast, left the ground momentarily, and crashed to earth. There was a sharp bend ahead, so he let off the gas. Before him, the Camry fishtailed, slowed and leaned, and almost lost it, then came out of the turn accelerating.

No way I can catch up.

The man before him took the next turn in even better stride, speeding up as he entered a mile-long straightaway, easily outpacing the pickup and widening the gap.

What's next on the road? Link thought, trying to remember as he skittered around the harsh turn. As he entered the straightaway, he recalled twists and hairpins, but those were far below, and by then he would be outdistanced.

He looked out over what appeared to be a precipice, trying to recall . . . then Link slowed, remembering a connecting road that was just ahead.

He slowed more, watching as the Camry continued toward the distant turn. He tried to visualize the turnout. It would be a steep ride, but his memory's eye recalled that it was not far down to the next level of roadway.

He slowed to a crawl, and twisted the wheel hard to the left. For a moment there was only endless space before him; then the pickup nosed over and down the rocky hillside.

Link held the brakes, corrected, then held them again, sliding, staring at the roadway below. If he overshot, the Ramcharger would continue across and off the side, and impact a hundred yards below. He corrected, braked again, gaining purchase as he continued to slide on the loose rock.

The Ramcharger bounced as it impacted the roadway, slid sideward for a short distance, and halted. Link sat perfectly still, heart pounding. The pickup blocked the roadway from side to side, even better than he had hoped. No way a vehicle could get by. Finally he looked toward the curve seventy yards distant, where the Camry would appear.

Link got out on shaky legs, then leaned back inside to collect the revolver.

The Toyota appeared as it exited the turn, which the driver negotiated with skill. He'd started to accelerate— when he saw the black pickup filling his vision. The

Asian leaned on the brakes and slid for fifty feet before coming to a halt an arm's length from the Ramcharger.

Link stepped out from the side and walked forward, the big revolver in his hand.

A California driver's license showed his name as Damon R. Lee, born in 1976, 157 pounds, and five feet eleven inches, his residence an apartment address in Fortuna, California. Link decided he was a mixed blood, like himself—probably American Indian and Chinese. He appeared so frightened that Link might have felt sorry for him if Ms. Stubborn were not suffering from the gunshot.

Damon Lee stood in front of his vehicle, staring woefully at the SWAT rifle and the Beretta in the dirt at his feet. Lee rushed his words, claiming to be a tourist who was camping in the car. He'd shot the rifle that was lent to him by a friend, aiming for various sagebrush, certainly not at a horse and rider. Later at the bridge, he'd thought that Link was threatening and fired the pistol to scare him off. Not to hit him or anyone else, just to defend himself. It would certainly not happen again.

The explanations were obvious lies, yet the sound of his own voice seemed to bolster Lee. He was increasingly calculating as he realized Link wasn't going to kill him out of hand.

"I'm a tourist. Never been in Montana before. I'll move down the road tonight."

"Throw both weapons over the side," Link said.

When he hesitated, Link did it for him. "Hey, that's expensive," Lee complained as the rifle sailed into the canyon.

The Beretta and range finder followed.

"Now look down there," Link told him, and after a moment of dubious hesitation, Lee edged closer to the precipice. He was peering down as Link tossed his billfold—from which currency fluttered—and cell phone, which smashed onto roadside rocks far below.

Lee was almost belligerent. "You can't *do* this."

"Lodge a complaint. Who sent you? Gordon Hightower? A newspaper?"

Lee looked genuinely confounded.

"How about the Serpientes?"

A flicker of recognition on Lee's face made Link wonder.

He tired of the game, went to the Camry, and raised the Smith & Wesson from his side. "Who sent you?"

Lee answered warily. "I'm on vacation."

Link fired a round into the engine compartment. The roar echoed through the canyon. There was a hiss of steam from under the hood.

"Jesus. How the fuck am I supposed to get back?"

"I don't really care, but when you get there, don't come near my town again."

Link still did not know who Lee was or what he was after. Lawmen didn't do what he had done, and most were better pistol shots. He was unconvinced that the Sociedad still existed. Maybe a reporter or a mistaken bounty hunter.

He started toward the truck.

"Damn it—," Lee began.

"Aw, to hell with it," Link muttered. He pivoted and swung his fist, hard. With the impact, Lee backpedaled for a dozen feet before collapsing in a limp heap.

"That's for shooting my mare."

On the drive to the cabin, Link dropped Lee down on his priority list to a par with the tattletale.

For the first time that day his facial wounds throbbed, but he knew that his friends were suffering worse than he was. Yet Erin was almost certainly alive. Perhaps Frank as well, since they would likely use him to collect a ransom.

He wondered about the foundation. Who was in control with Frank gone? Would Squid remain in charge of Special Projects? Mostly he considered what should be his smartest next step. Regardless of how foolhardy it might be to believe in Shepherd's journal, Link kept coming back to the belief that he should be searching somewhere out west in the big trees.

If he went there, one of his first acts would be to look up Dr. Dan Walsh, the foundation's project manager who was returning to Eureka to search for the old encampment.

On a whim, Link called the San Francisco FBI office and asked for Assistant Special Agent in Charge Margaret Tatro, hoping Maggie might have information about an organization that matched what he'd imagined about the Sociedad Serpiente. She was out of the office. Link hung up, surprised at himself that he'd called. It had been a long time since they'd spoken, yet he'd felt a once-familiar warmth in anticipation of talking with the woman he'd been so close to.

It was four o'clock. He decided to take Joseph Spotted Horse to dinner at Jamie's, where the talkative old Indian was sure to spread the word about what the "Chinaman" had done to the mare. Damon Lee would find little cooperation from the people of Boudie Springs.

Tomorrow morning, Link would drop back in on Jamie Bourne and ask for his help.

16

The rumor mill at Jamie's Pub had done its job once the old Indian had informed everyone within listening distance about what the Chinaman *tourist* had done to Ms. Stubborn. Lee had stumbled into the edge of town at seven thirty that morning, haggard and dirty and asking everyone he encountered if he could use their phone. Doors were shut in his face. Lee had walked into the new Sheraton Hotel at eight o'clock. The manager, a recent newcomer from New Jersey, told him that their phones were out of order and he'd have to find one elsewhere. When Lee skulked on up the street, he was passed by three black Ford Expeditions carrying nononsense out-of-towners wearing partially zipped jackets and military hairstyles. Those who were watching—with raised curtains and phone in hand—said that neither they nor Damon Lee seemed to know one another. Speculation was rife about their identity and purpose.

Jamie Bourne, owner of Jamie's Pub, was as angry about Ms. Stubborn as anyone. After breakfast, when Link asked if they could go somewhere to talk, the publican led the way to his spectacular home north of town, then out behind a spacious horse barn where Jamie's animals were kept at the far end to make room for rescue gear and his collections of "old bikes."

The rescue equipment was for the North County Search and Rescue Team. The motorcycles were Jamie's hobby and passion.

"This should be private enough," Jamie said. He

pulled the dust cover off a gleaming, meticulously restored motorcycle, picked up a lightly oiled rag, and began to wipe it down.

"A 1950 Triumph. I rode it in last month's rally. There are a few other biker fanatics in the county, including a number from the rescue team, and we get together and ride."

Link remembered, although he'd never participated.

Jamie pointed at three other neatly covered shapes. "There's also a 1955 Indian Chieftain, a 1958 Harley Highway Patrol Special, and a 1975 thousand cc Goldwing, which is the newest of the lot, but the first year Honda made 'em. They all run like the day they were built."

Link let him ramble on about his hobby.

"Last time you were here, I'd just received a crate filled with parts from a guy in Iowa. That's become the Indian there." Jamie explained how he'd worked the restoration with a new Indian manufacturer in Gilroy, California for as long as they'd remained in business.

"And they all run you say?" Link said, loping an idea about riding a motorcycle out of the state through his mind—which was abandoned since he knew nothing about them.

"When I finish with a bike, it's better than new, because I seal up the rims and put on a pair of new Metzlers. Modern tire technology is the biggest advance in biking in the past fifty years. You can turn on a dime, lean a bike all the way down to the pegs and not worry, while the old ones might've slipped out from under you."

"I have a problem, Jamie."

Jamie quietly tinkered with the Triumph's chain drive.

"I've been ordered not to leave town."

"FBI?" When Link nodded, Jamie said, "Everyone figured the guys in the Expeditions were Feds. How about the idiot that shot Ms. Stubborn?"

"He's too poorly organized and not disciplined enough to be any kind of a lawman."

"So the FBI's watching, and you want to get out of town without them knowing."

"I have two close friends who are in deep trouble and need help."

"They're in trouble with the law?"

"With kidnappers."

Jamie's eyes lit up. He watched the national news. "You're a suspect in *that?*"

"Not like you think. An FBI supervisor doesn't want me interfering in his investigation. If I were guilty of anything, I wouldn't be involving you, Jamie."

"You didn't have to say that." Jamie mused for a moment. "When you leave, they'll immediately think you took an airplane, you being a pilot, and check at Kalispell, and the smaller strips. They may even have agents watching them."

"If I take the pickup, I won't make it ten miles."

Jamie nodded, then looked up. "Where are you going? Not specifically, just a direction?"

"Last night I asked about your brother in Susanville. I'd like to drop by for a visit."

Susanville was in Northern California, not far from Mount Lassen. Jamie's brother owned an auto dealership there.

Jamie pulled the cover back over the gleaming Triumph. "When do you want to leave?"

"Just as soon as I can. Got any ideas?"

12:45 p.m.—Boudie Springs

Squid called to tell Link they'd received another videotape. Link asked him to e-mail a copy.

Fifteen minutes later, Link had the video downloaded. The opening scene showed Frank and Erin weighted down with rusty logging chains, gaunt and staring at something to the left of the lens. Erin's hair was shorn close to her scalp.

They're alive!

The garbled voice said, "Greetings from S. We're having such fun watching your friends starve! But alas, it is time to open the bargaining."

The backdrop was a wall of rough-hewn lumber. The camera zoomed in so only the faces of the captives were visible.

Frank flinched as if an insect had flown into his eye,

and blinked to get it out. The audio was turned low, yet his lips formed the words that something was in his eye. A gloved hand slapped him viciously. *A work glove,* noted Link. *The rough-out kind sold in hardware stores.*

"Be quiet until I tell you differently," said the Donald Duck voice.

Frank nodded, and again began to twitch and blink to dislodge the insect.

"Now we shall establish ownership."

The camera shifted to a table and a lit blowtorch, like those used in construction projects to heat rivets, its flame focused on the end of a half-inch diameter rod of steel rebar.

Link's hard eyes narrowed.

"Watch closely," chided the altered voice, as if speaking to children.

The rod was lifted from the flame, now superheated to a bright orange-red color. The camera returned to the faces of the hostages, and the glowing rod that was lifted slowly to pause at a point two inches from Erin's face. Her eyes widened. A large hand reached out to grasp her shorn head and roughly hold her in place. The hot iron moved slowly forward. Her scream was shrill and awful as the iron moved very slowly, tracing the curve of a snake.

Link was frozen into place, his face stony, unable to move his eyes from the slow course of the cherry-red steel rod, unable to block out the screams. Finally the branding iron lifted, yet the flesh still sizzled and curled. Blisters were already forming.

The still-glowing iron was shifted to Frank, who was still rapidly blinking, and the fist grasped his neck. The iron was pressed into the skin, tracing a path and forming the same *S* as had been done on Erin. Frank gritted his teeth in stoic silence, then began to whimper aloud as any brave human would have done, his eyes fluttering in pain. When the iron and the fist around Frank's throat were withdrawn, Frank's head lolled as if he were near unconsciousness.

Erin was jerking her head from side to side and crying, more pitiful because of the stubble that replaced her golden locks. Frank made a whimpering sound through clenched teeth, and blinked even more, as if it were something he could not stop. The camera pulled back, showing their miserable conditions.

"Their new status is apparent," said the voice. "Their pain shouldn't last for too long. They've not eaten in three days, and I promise you they will not until you've met our terms. Thirty million dollars for Dubois and the once-pretty woman. When you've paid and we've received, they will be fed and returned, not before. We will provide instructions."

The video, four minutes and twelve seconds' worth, ended.

Link regarded the screen with ice-cold eyes, his mind awhirl, thinking of what he'd watched and what he would have done if it were he who was the hostage. It did not take long for him to put it together.

As he grabbed for pen and paper, Link instructed Squid to send a copy of the video to Gordon Hightower and another to the Financial Committee—"the handful"—normally chaired by Frank Dubois.

The tap code that Link had learned from his father was conceived by jailmates in a New York prison, and in 1966 was purposely taught to a select few U.S. military pilots whose mission was to strike targets in North Vietnam, and thus had the highest probability of becoming POWs. Since prisoners were prohibited from talking, the tap code had become their means of communications, and had not been suspected by their guards. A cryptology expert had once told Link that a simple linear code was best if the opponents were overly sure of themselves. The Vietnamese had never realized the POWs were using the tap code in front of their noses. Hopefully neither had these captors.

Link had passed the code on to his roommate during Desert Storm I. Fortunately neither man had been shot down, but he was sure Frank remembered.

On the pad, Link jotted down a matrix, starting with the five letters *A* through *E*, then a second row with *F* through *J*, and so forth, omitting only the *K*, for which *C* could be substituted.

He went through the video again, going slowly, watching for Frank's eyeblinks.

Pause, then blink-blink, then pause and a single blink. That was two dash one. On his matrix, he went to the second row of letters and picked the first one: *F*.

He started over, pausing often to watch his friend's blinks and wrote

2—1, 2—4, 1—5, 4—2.

The camera moved away from Frank, so Link inserted three slash marks to indicate a break. When the camera showed Frank again, Link resumed:

2—3, 1—5, [Space] 4—4, 4—2, 2—4, 1—5 [Space] 1—1, 9—

He used the matrix to decipher the letters that Frank was sending.

F—I—E—R /// H E (Space) T—R—I—E [Space] A—followed by a long succession of short blinks.

As Link wrote it out, it appeared like a garble.

FIER /// HE [Space] TRIE [Space] A—?????????

Something seemed wrong. Phonetic spelling? He wrote down? Fire? He? Try? A?

As he stared at the first three words, he saw something familiar, but at first it was not apparent. He tried other phonetic spellings, and when he tried *fear*, it came to him.

In Shepherd's Journal, the Weeping Tree was said to have a message stained into its trunk using the blood of victims: "Fiere the Trie." It fit.

Frank had seen the words at the entrance of the cavern, had been spelling out most of the first word before the camera had moved to the blowtorch. As Erin was branded, he'd blinked out part of the second and then the third words, then, as he was disfigured by the red-hot rod, he'd had the fortitude to go on, but was hurting when he'd blinked *A* followed by a series of dots.

They were held in the California redwoods. At the Weeping Tree. It was the stuff of fantasy and swashbuckling pirates but if stretched, it fit. They did not need to send a thousand fibbers to murky up the water and imperil his friends. What they needed was a damned capable Blackfoot Indian.

Squid Worsczejius called Link on the cabin's hard line. He'd forwarded copies of the video upstairs to the Financial Committee and to Gordon Hightower. The handful had just ordered him to report to them immediately.

Squid was nervous. "What should I do, Boss?"

In the corner of his eye, Link noted something that at first gave him pause, and then made his scalp crawl. The LEDs on top of the sat phone were flashing in sequence.

There was an electronic bug! The sat phone was designed to detect and help locate them via the lights. He blurted, "Is your end of this line secure?"

"Can't tell, Boss. Remember about Helga being down. Mary says—"

"I'll call you right back."

Link retrieved the sat phone and walked out into the sunlight, When he was fifteen yards from the cabin, the warning lights stopped flashing.

It's in the house.

He pressed MEM, then ENCODE to activate the sat-phone scrambler.

Mary answered on the first ring and transferred the call to Squid.

"Better use my sat phone from now on," Link told him. "My cabin's bugged."

"Will do, Boss. How much do you want me to tell the Financial Committee?"

"All of it. They own the place." Link wanted to tell him of his discovery that Frank and Erin were in California, but something about the bug made him hold his tongue.

"What if they ask me about you?"

"Tell them I'm doing what I can and I won't let either them or Frank and Erin down. Tell them that I advise against paying any ransom. If there's a question, have them contact me."

"What if they tell me not to talk with you again, Boss? Without you on the other end, I couldn't handle any of this."

"Yes, you can. That's why I wanted you there. Unless the handful order you to do otherwise, call me again after you've talked to them."

"Before I go, Mary's working on Helga with Major Stradley and her team from the AFISC. You were right, they're damned good, but they say it's going to take a while before Helga's back up."

"Just keep me advised. Now, go up and face the handful, Squid."

Link disconnected, thinking he'd just piled another load onto Squid's broad back. Frank had not had time to brief the handful, and Link had not even tried. They would likely have a hundred questions for Squid to explain.

He went back into the cabin and tried to use the sat phone as a bug detector, noting the number of lights that flashed in different locations. After half an hour of ignoring Joseph Spotted Horse's complaint that the last of the pie was gone—he'd discovered nothing.

The FBI agents, two of whom were staked out at the end of his driveway, had obviously tapped his phone. Should he disregard the bug and openly phone Gordon to tell him he was now sure that Frank was in Northern California?

Gordon's code breakers, or "encryption analysts," might decipher Frank's message, but without Shepherd's Journal, they would have no clue what "Fiere the Trie" was about.

For now he'd keep them in the dark. If Gordon sent another army of agents, there was a chance they'd endanger the hostages. He would tell Squid in case someone like Damon Lee got in a lucky shot. Still something was amiss. Not with Squid, but something else.

At two o'clock, the sat phone buzzed, and Link walked outside to join Ms. Stubborn at the corral. Two vehicles were parked across the road. An FBI agent stared at Link from a Ford Expedition, his partner outside chatting with the state troopers from a cruiser that was parked just behind. Two vehicles and four lawmen, openly surveilling the cabin.

"Anderson," he answered.

The caller identified himself as Mr. Scott Cerone.

Link had met the newest member of the Financial Committee only once, and had formed no opinion other than he seemed aggressive and self-assured.

"Yes, sir?"

"These are terrible times for the foundation, Mr. Anderson."

. There were background whispers—the handful often used a speakerphone.

"I agree, sir. Erin tried to warn both Frank and me that something big was coming. We simply couldn't connect the dots."

Cerone's voice raised angrily. "Then why, for heaven's sake, didn't you advise us?"

"Frank was going to explain everything at this week's meeting. My role was to discover who was slandering the foundation and stop them. I've been—"

Cerone interrupted in his unhappy tone. "I would say that goal has been overcome by events. At present, we need to learn who is killing and kidnapping our people."

"Yes, sir, and remove Frank and Erin from harm's way."

Cerone snorted. "So far it seems you've let us down on every front, Mr. Anderson."

A low voice, one of the two women on the handful, told Cerone that he was going too far.

Link was not one for excuses. "I should not have left New York."

Cerone barked, "Security tells us that Frank Dubois terminated you. Is that true?"

"That was for show. We decided that I could work better if I was temporarily separated from the foundation."

"The other members and I have been discussing that point, Mr. Anderson. Some feel it's best that you remain permanently 'separated,' as you call it."

"That, of course, is entirely up to you."

A quieter voice spoke up. "Link, Mr. Cerone's position is not universally held. It's presently a tie vote, with two abstaining. I have faith in your abilities and trustworthiness."

Mr. Scott Cerone spoke again: "I offer a compromise, Mr. Anderson. For the present, you may continue working with Mr. Worsczejius without any legal connection with the foundation—on the condition that you keep us informed of all findings *and* gain our approval before proceeding with future actions."

"You don't trust me?" he asked Cerone.

"All I'm telling you is that you must work within the limitations we provide."

Link's next words emerged matter-of-factly: "Mr. Cerone, Frank Dubois and I flew combat together. I went to work for him after he asked for my help. Miss Frechette and I have worked together for ten years. I'm sorry if I've let you down, but I will not seek anyone's approval when it comes to saving the lives of my friends."

"Then unfortunately, this discussion is terminated, Mr. Anderson."

"I understand." As Link started to press the OFF button, voices were raised.

"Lincoln, don't hang up," came the quiet voice. "Scott is being an ass. He came up with the ideas he just spoke about on his own. I was against them, and two others wanted to wait until we heard from you. We need you now more than ever."

He thought about what she'd said. The handful had been good to him, and to the country.

The octogenarian spoke next. "All of this is ridiculous. Of course we need Link."

"The vote just became two to one," said the woman.

"Make it three to one," said another voice.

A quiet argument ensued. Finally: "I'll acquiesce—*this* time," said Mr. Scott Cerone, but not happily.

"I'll try to keep you informed through Squid and Mary," Link told them. "I can't promise more. In the meanwhile, I'm advising you *again* not to pay a ransom."

As Link disconnected, he noted the surveillance team at the road. It was obviously boring business. An agent was showing the troopers the set of night-vision goggles they'd use later, in the darkness. Without a battery pack, the NVGs would be useless.

Link smiled at an audacious thought.

Squid called on the sat phone to tell him how a member of the financial committee had severely criticized him for following Link's instructions. He'd hardly had time to get to his office when they'd received a new directive from the handful to continue working with Link, and to get him whatever he needed.

"Here's something you should know," Link said, and started to explain Frank's message.

"Boss," Squid interrupted. "Major Stradley just came in saying . . ."

The connection went dead. A message in the sat phone's window flashed the words: SYS SHUTDOWN. There was a snapping sound as circuits self-destructed.

Fifteen minutes later the laptop beeped, announcing the arrival of a new e-mail. It was from Maj.JRStradley @AFISC.bs.gov.org, addressed to users of W. F. Satellites.

MESSAGE FOLLOWS:
The satellite network was invaded and is being controlled by unknown server. Review satellite phone calls made and/or received for past 25 hours & assume your locations & conversations were compromised. All satellite positioning and communication capabilities are inoperable, and instruments have been duly disabled.
SIGNED: J. R. STRADLEY, MAJ, USAF
END OF MESSAGE

Helga had controlled satellite positioning and communications, tracked sat phone locations, and provided encryption. The Serpientes, or whoever, had forced Erin to destroy Helga, and then had invaded and monitored the satellite network. It was possible that Al Qaeda and Hezbollah had benefited; the Weyland Foundation provided the majority of CIA sat phones.

If they'd been listening, they'd know he was working with Squid Worsczejius, Mary Long, and Major Stradley. None of that was certain, because it was a matter of timing and luck and having enough people to intercept useful conversations and cull out the rest. Although Major Stradley had acted prudently by shutting down the network and destroying sat phones, a feeling of isolation drifted over Link.

It was time to get on with things. He made a call from the hard-line phone to Gordon's office and left a single routine voice message.

17

Gordon Hightower was already up despite the fact that he had not left the office until well after midnight. Yesterday had marked a new chapter in his career and he was determined to succeed. If he did not, his countrymen would suffer, and despite his ambition, he was a patriot to the core.

As the scope of the disaster at the Weyland Building was unveiled, the Director of the Federal Bureau of Investigation had come under intense pressure from the president to stop the Hezbollah before they could do more harm. He needed someone new "out front," and considered the obscure ADIC at the New York office who had, seemingly single-handed according to the official report, stopped a suicide bomber at the Javits Building. The FBI Director queried the Deputy Director (Terrorism), who knew nothing bad about Hightower. They could select a worse candidate for the position.

The Deputy Director (Terrorism) had made the telephone call. Gordon would have access to funding and personnel. Since Hightower was certain that the Hezbollah had retreated into the Deep South, he would have freedom to operate in four target areas: Georgia, the Carolinas, and North Florida. If the Hezbollah were found elsewhere, Gordon would transfer his information, support, and assets to the new project director.

Gordon Hightower had readily agreed. The appointment had been released to the public overnight, along with the fact he was initially sending twelve hundred agents and as many state troopers to search for the terrorists and hostages.

He would shuttle between offices in New York and Atlanta. At 5:00 p.m. EST, he would be introduced by the director on national television and release a statement designed to reassure and gain the support of the public, and issue a warning to the Hezbollah.

As his army of lawmen descended, preparing to turn over every clod and stone, agents in place, NSA listeners, Homeland Security officers, and others continued to turn up clue after clue.

It was the challenge of Gordon's lifetime, and he hardly dared to think of the rewards that would come, yet he was admittedly paranoid about the potential fly in the ointment: his old friend and loose cannon on deck, Link Anderson.

If Link were at large, his high-ranking cohorts in the clandestine world would believe that he'd had a part in stopping the terrorists.

Montana was the obvious best place for Link while the game played out, yet there was a problem with that. The same Deputy Director (Terrorism) who had appointed Gordon had worked closely with Link Anderson in the past and thought highly of him. When he'd learned that he was cooling his heels in Montana, and that Gordon had ordered it, he'd arranged for an observation team to watch over him, and set up a question-and-answer session to clear him.

ADIC Gordon Hightower had visions of Link Anderson being freed to assist him.

He reached for the telephone, thinking the observation team might need closer supervision.

4:50 a.m.—Sheraton Hotel, Boudie Springs, Montana

The FBI agent in charge of the "observe and protect" operation, whose name was Norman Frith, was awakened by a telephone call well before daylight. Two of his agents were on duty at a simple rotational stakeout, ordered to openly watch a subject, ensure his safety, and follow the directions from higher headquarters that were to come. If they lost track of the "sub" or he was harmed, it would be Norm's ass. Or so the special agent in charge of the Great Falls FO said, although Frith could not understand what they might do to him other than assign him to another remote office where the winter snow was chin-high to a giraffe.

"Hello?" Norman answered, trying to stifle a yawn.

"Not too official this morning, are we?" commented the unpleasant SAC.

"It's different when you get out in the field once in a while. Makes you not want to give your name, rank, and serial number to every redneck psychopath who comes along."

Norman was testy. Recently he'd thought a lot about his twenty-four uneventful years in the bureau and the fact that he was still an Assistant SAC of a backwoods office. The SAC—whom Norman had once called a PPA, meaning a "politically perfect asshole," not realizing that he and a visiting assistant director were standing directly behind him—would soon be promoted and move to a larger field office in a warmer clime.

"Activity?" asked the SAC, who was eight years his junior, unforgiving, and vindictive, but normally did not awaken him at half past four in the morning.

Norman sighed, turned on the lamp, and read from his log: "Subject's domicile identified at 1545 hours, and two-agent stakeout established at 1600 hours, augmented by two uniformed Montana state patrolmen. Two occupants, one being the subject, Abraham L. Anderson, the other an elderly Native American male, first name Joseph—last name unknown since none of the neighbors proved to be helpful—were observed entering and leaving the domicile. At 1630 Joseph departed in a Dodge pickup, black, est. manufactured in 1964, pulling a horse trailer containing a brown mare with a bandaged neck. He returned at 1725, and with the assistance of the subject, removed a dappled gray horse from the trailer, placed it in a corral at the rear of the cabin, then disconnected and parked the trailer. At 1840, both men departed in the pickup. They were followed by the FBI team to Jamie's Pub, where they had dinner. At 2025, they returned to the domicile. Lights were extinguished at 2105."

"I assume the subject is sleeping in the cabin?"

"Possibly. If you want, I'll call the stakeout team and have them make a bed check."

"No need." The joke had gone over the SAC's head. Norman tried again. "How about a panty raid?" He grinned at his joke.

The SAC sighed. "I'm calling from home, Frith, trying to do you a favor. I was just awakened by a big kahuna from back East, who told me more about our visitors from Washington this afternoon. There'll be a polygraph guy and a couple of interrogators, and they'll be on the horn with a deputy director. They want Anderson here in Great Falls before two."

"You want to do me a favor? Send an airplane." It was a tedious drive to Great Falls.

"Like I told you before, none are available."

Then what the hell are we talking for at dark o'thirty in the morning.

"Minimum hassle?" Frith asked. Meaning should they walk up and politely knock on the door, since Anderson had not been described as anything other than a law-abiding citizen.

The SAC hedged his answer. "I'll fax the Warrant to Appear that we just got from the judge and leave the details to you. Just make sure there's no problem with the sub."

That was different. Norm's understanding was that it would be an informal, voluntary meeting.

"The kahuna on the phone advised me that the Deputy Director for Terrorism's involved, and the guy might not be all that easy to take down."

Take down? Norm came wide awake. "Anderson's a terrorist?"

"The guy didn't say that in so many words, but tell the guys to watch their asses."

The SAC hung up and left Norman wondering why they hadn't been told all of that before.

It became a no-brainer. They'd strike early, while Anderson was groggy, and use a show of force: one team of agents watching the back while the other went in the front and nailed Anderson down. The five men he'd brought were bored. Now he wished he'd brought twice that number. There'd be no state trooper participation. If a terrorist was to be apprehended, Norman Frith wanted every ounce of credit.

As he pulled on his clothing, he reviewed the words he'd use in his briefing to the agents. *Let's get him up, take him down, and take him in.* He repeated them, liked their sound, and was trying to decide whether to use the phone or knock on the agents' doors, when his UHF radio buzzed. "Agent in Charge Frith," Norman answered crisply, snapping his Kimber .45-caliber model 1911 into its inverted under-the-arm holster. If he pulled this off without a hitch, he just might get an attaboy and a ticket out of Great Falls.

The senior agent on stakeout duty spoke without haste. "One of them just came out of the cabin and started the pickup."

This early? "Is it Anderson?"

"I think so. Big hat and bulky coat. There's no porch light, and it's too dark to tell."

"Use your NVGs."

When the agent spoke, his voice was hardly audible. "They aren't working."

"Neither pair?"

"Someone removed the batteries from the pack."

"How the hell did someone get into your vehicle?"

"Uh— We were walking around earlier—you know—limbering up and talking with the state troopers. I'm guessing one of them decided to play a joke."

Another voice came over the frequency. "This is Trooper One, and that's bullshit. We were not in your vehicle, and we didn't play with your night-vision gear." He paused. "Anyway, I'd guess the guy in the pickup's just going to breakfast."

"At this time of morning?" Frith asked.

"Yeah. Farmers and ranchers get together at Jamie's to talk weather and do business."

The on-scene agent spoke: "The sub's driving off—heading toward town."

Norm Frith hastily considered the vehicles involved.

"Follow the pickup, Trooper One. Keep us informed of your location but do *not* apprehend the suspect until I arrive. Stakeout one, stay in place and watch for the second man."

"Aw, damn!" came his agent's voice. "Someone just rode a horse out of the corral."

He had guessed right! "You're in a four-wheeler. Go after him." Norm remembered something and added. "Be damned careful. We may be dealing with terrorists."

"You've gotta be shitting me!" said the state trooper.

5:20 a.m.—*Private Grass Airfield West of Boudie Springs*

A rancher who was also a member of the North County Search and Rescue Team pulled the chocks, climbed aboard, checked the controls, and then started the engine of his Cessna 150. After a suitable warm-up period, when the engine smoothed out, he lined up on a southerly heading on the well-mown grass strip, ran up the power, and released brakes.

The flight around the southern perimeter of the town took precisely fourteen minutes. When he flew over Link Anderson's cabin, there was just enough light to make out details of the grassland below, yet it was not sufficient to observe the airplane's identification numbers, or even its color from the ground.

He noted that a large SUV was bouncing along on the roughest, worst-rutted dirt road in the area, and continued ahead, eyes glued, until he saw a rider moving at a leisurely canter. After waggling the Cessna's wings in greeting, he turned. The rider below also turned in that direction, slowing as he maneuvered the horse across a series of steep, rocky arroyos.

The rancher circled once, lined up on a grassy stretch, cut power, and landed without incident. Three minutes later, as the Cessna's engine idled, the rider arrived and gave a wave.

He dismounted from the airplane as the rider did so from the horse. While both men wore denim jackets and jeans, riding boots, and light-colored hats, the rancher was older, taller, and wider. His name was Robert, but he was better known as Earthquake Titus.

"Good seeing you, Link." They shook hands, then turned and peered, but could only vaguely discern the distant vehicle as it bucked and bounced along.

"There weren't any vehicles near your place, except for Joseph's old stake-bed."

"That's good to know, Earthquake." Link thanked him, received a final hearty clap on the back that almost buckled his knees, then untied the duffel from the gray, loaded it into the small airplane's right seat, and climbed into the left seat of the Cessna's cockpit.

"I'd appreciate it if you'd cover her and tie her down good," called the rancher as he swung into the saddle.

"No problem." Link waited until Earthquake was trotting away, heading for a badlands area that would not be passable for any vehicle, and pulled back the throttle. In the crisp morning, the little 150 was as spry as the gray had been. He made the takeoff in a minimum of distance.

He flew east for a few miles, observing the beginning of sunrise and the soaring snow-clad mountains.

6:00 a.m.—Boudie Springs

The state troopers in the cruiser had had no problem following the aged pickup as it continued at a snail's pace around the perimeter of the town, slowing even more when they'd pass a field of cattle. The trooper on the passenger's side periodically reported their position to the FBI agent in charge, who had dispatched in a second vehicle to catch up. He still insisted that he be there for the takedown.

The driver of the vehicle chasing the gray horse was having trouble with terrain. A light airplane had flown overhead fifteen minutes before, and he suggested that the agent in charge contact the local airfields.

"I've got a bad feeling," said the Montana state trooper driving the cruiser.

"Not our problem," said the other. "I talked to Jamie Bourne yesterday, and he swears by Anderson. Couple days ago some asshole tourist shot his mare by mistake."

"That could piss *me* off," said the first trooper, who owned and liked horses.

Quite suddenly, the driver of the black pickup pulled into a parking place and shut off the engine. He'd emerged and started for the door of Jamie's Pub when a FBI vehicle swerved around the troopers and stopped in the middle of the street behind the pickup. Two agents piled out, drawing their pistols.

"FBI," announced Agent In Charge Frith. "Stop right there."

The troopers got out in time to see the old Indian turn, frown, and slowly shake his head. "I have never seen so many policemen this early in the morning."

The old man resumed walking.

"Damn it, stop!" yelled the second agent.

The Indian peered back. "Are you talking to this old man?" he asked.

Agent In Charge Frith told the second agent to holster his weapon.

"We're looking for Abraham L. Anderson."

"I am a Joseph, not an Abraham. Are you talking about my nephew?" When they didn't answer, he went on. "Lincoln was going to ride his gray horse, but sometimes young men are lazy and he may have gone back to bed."

"Anderson's on the gray," said the state trooper who liked horses.

"Or in the airplane," said the other.

The driver of the Expedition in pursuit of the horseman said they'd lost track of the rider and the airplane and had to turn back because of the terrain.

"This is Lincoln's truck," explained the Indian. "He lets me use it to go to breakfast, but in all of my days I have not seen a worse-driving truck. You would think that a young man would have a better truck."

6:15 a.m.—Private Grass Airfield, West of Boudie Springs

Jamie arrived at the parked Cessna riding the thirty-year-old Goldwing. It was large, boxy, painted silver, and

outfitted with a windshield and two luggage compartments. Jamie said any grandmother could ride it so long
as she had well-developed biceps.

"You've honestly never ridden a bike?" he asked Link.

"Not one with an engine."

"Get on back and act like a gunny sack of spuds, and
watch what I do."

They rode to the highway gate and back a few times,
Jamie calling out pointers; then Link moved to the front
and Jamie explained the controls. Link took it out and
back alone, and almost fell over on three occasions before remembering the part about keeping his eyes up,
looking where he was going and not where he could fall.
Much like riding a horse.

"Harley people talk like the Wing's a sissy bike, but
it's big, durable, and faster than most things on the
road." Jamie went over a few pointers and hints, and
turned him loose again.

He did better, and even found himself leaning
properly.

"Good," said Jamie. "Riding slow is a *lot* harder than
going fast. Now let's tie your duffel bag on back, and
you can take me to my house so we can pick up my
Triumph."

It was seven miles to the Bournes', and Link made it
alive, which made Jamie feel proud and also very lucky,
since he was on back. Five other riders were awaiting
them. Another rode up just as Link almost let the
Honda fall but then remembered to put down his kickstand. One thing he had already learned: there was nothing like a heavy motorcycle to make a person feel
humble.

Most of the machines were newer with only two other
vintage bikes like Jamie's. One of the lone riders was
female, and a couple—a dentist and his wife—rode a
dazzling new Harley-Davidson touring bike that looked
more like a living room on wheels.

Link shook hands around. They'd all served as volun-
teers on the search-and-rescue team, and no one asked
hard questions. When Jamie had called at the last moment to organize the ride and said that their friend
needed a favor, that had been enough.

Jamie looked him over with a critical eye. Link wore sunglasses, denims, and Western boots. The boots bothered Jamie, as he thought that the heel might catch on something, so he had Link stow them and provided a pair of clodhoppers. The denim jacket was replaced with a scuffed-up leather one with an array of pockets and zippers. Finally he handed him a battered white helmet with a visor, a pair of fingerless padded gloves, and a bandanna to sponge up sweat. When the helmet proved painful on Link's wounded forehead, Jamie pared out some of the padding with a knife.

Link was eager to be on his way.

After twenty miles, heading southwest on mountainous roadways, Link had the general knack of it, and was removed from the leader's position—which was easiest to maintain—back into their midst. Link managed to stay upright stopping and starting at the traffic lights in Kalispell.

After four hours, they stopped for food and gas and ate outside on picnic tables provided for biker travelers. Jamie took Link aside, showed him a cut down series of maps that fit on a small clipboard that was held in place by suction cups, and motioned at the highway.

"Three miles, and you'll come to I-90. Go on through the underpass and stay on the county road. Twenty miles, and you're in Idaho. I marked the maps so you can avoid major highways all the way to Winnemucca. That's six hundred miles. You'll be tired as hell because bikes are hard on a body. Don't tense up. Try to relax when you're riding, and stop every hour to walk around. At Winnemucca, you'll have to take Interstate 40 or spend forever getting across the desert on back roads that don't connect. It's not a dirt bike, so don't ride on sand. If the bike falls over, you can pull it upright, but I guarantee you can't pull it out of sand by yourself."

Link nodded.

Jamie attached the clipboard to the Goldwing. "We'll leave you here."

"I owe you."

"Yes, you do. In return, I'd like you to take care.

Truckers don't see motorcycles. They'll kill you if you give them the chance, so watch out for 'em."

The bikers prepared to go on.

"They don't know where you're heading, and I'll keep it like that." Jamie pulled on his skull-and-bones do-rag and was transformed from successful restaurateur into a scruffy biker.

He grinned. "Fun, ain't it?"

3:00 p.m.—J. Edgar Hoover Building, Washington, D.C.

Gordon had been angered by Link Anderson in the past, but he had never been lied to by Link so blatantly. Forget that he'd twisted the truth some himself.

Since he had left New York too early to do so, a subordinate back in New York had culled through his more important IMMEDIATE and PRIORITY voice mail. It was noon before the agent had trudged through those that had been coded ROUTINE, and called to Gordon's attention: "GORDON—SORRY, BUT I HAVE TO BREAK OUR AGREEMENT. REGARDS, LINK."

Gordon saved it since it proved beyond doubt that Lincoln Anderson was a loose cannon.

With a single call to Great Falls, he confirmed that Link had disappeared from Boudie Springs, and the grasp of the six agents who had surveilled him.

Next, Gordon called the Deputy Director (Terrorism). After spending a moment to reflect, the deputy director decided there was merit to Gordon's case that Link was at the very least an unreliable security risk. He agreed that they did not need him on the team.

Gordon then phoned the Assistant Special Agent In Charge (Criminal) in Denver, who had heard of his appointment. If Link showed up, Gordon wanted him detained for questioning. If necessary, Gordon would suggest charges to be brought. The important thing was to buy time until the terrorists had been dealt with.

In the event that Link traveled west, Gordon phoned Margaret Tatro, Assistant Special Agent In Charge (Industrial Espionage) at the San Francisco field office.

She'd known Link since childhood, and a few years earlier, they'd been much closer than mere friends.

When she volunteered to help, Gordon pulled out a folder that he'd relegated to a bottom drawer and told her of a place Link might go. She said it sounded crazy, and he agreed. Link was losing it. By the time he hung up, he had made an ally. Maggie Tatro had a score to settle with Link Anderson. Who was more vindictive than a woman scorned?

Gordon made two more telephone calls to block Anderson's passage in two other directions. Only when he was sure there could be no more surprises from his old friend did he turn back to his upcoming speech and the search for the Hezbollah terrorists.

18

The ride across the meaty part of the pork chop–shaped
state of Idaho, south through the Snake River canyon
and boundary with Eastern Oregon, and down the top
third of Nevada to Winnemucca—six hundred butt-
numbing miles of tertiary roads, switchbacks, and potholes the size of chasms—left Link dog tired. Jamie had
told him that the aging Goldwing rode like a dream and
made long trips seem much shorter. If that was true,
Link *never* wanted to try it on the bikes that Jamie was
comparing it with.

The good news was that he'd eaten up a lot of miles
and was that much closer to Northern California. The
bad news? When he'd raised the visor, the remainder of
the bandage had been blown askew, so he'd pulled his
bandana do-rag lower and let it suffice. He was also so
exhausted that he was starting to see things, like phantom animals wandering across the highway, and he knew
that only sleep would stop them.

A mileage sign read that Reno was 150 miles ahead,
but there was no way he could make even that relatively
short distance without replenishing his Z's. In the corner
of his eye he spotted another white cow grazing far
ahead on the other side of the interstate. When he
looked there a moment later, a semi rumbled past. He
decided that he could wait no longer.

An eight-by-thirty-inch, green highway sign announced that the next turnoff was to the DEBERRE RANCH—PRIVATE. Grateful for the anticipated respite, Link slowed, took the ramp off the interstate, idled onto a well-packed gravel road, and rode a quarter-mile to a fence line. An ornate wrought-iron gate blocked his path, adorned with two tastefully painted signs, one atop the other showing: PRIVATE PROPERTY, NO TRESPASSING, and a larger one reading, IF YOU ARE EXPECTED USE THE INTERCOM TO ANNOUNCE YOUR PRESENCE—OTHERWISE YOU WILL BE SHOT AND THEN PROSECUTED.

It did not matter, for Link didn't intend on going farther. He killed the Goldwing's engine, swung off, and remembered to drop the kickstand. Link picked a thermal blanket from a side bag, pulled off the biker boots lent to him by Jamie Bourne, rolled up in the blanket in a grassy stretch beside the fence, told his inner clock to wake him up in no more than three hours, and severely crashed.

6:15 a.m.—DeBerre Ranch Turnoff, I-80, Southwest of Winnemucca

He awakened to a *thumping* beat. Link pulled the blanket from over his eyes, squinted into the morning sun, and blinked until he spotted a small, side-by-side, two-place helicopter steadily working down the fence line. He was considering getting another hour's sleep when he realized that it would pass overhead at twenty-feet altitude, and that the windblast would not bode well for the heavy Goldwing that was precariously balanced on the kickstand, looming over the person curled up beneath it.

He threw off the blanket and tried to wave away the white and shaggy-bearded man of considerable age at the controls. The helicopter doggedly continued ahead, and Link had to hold on to the Goldwing until it had passed and was setting down a dozen yards distant.

Link pulled on boots, stuffed his blanket into a side bag and closed it, and was adjusting the sweat-stained do-rag on his head, the helmet held between his knees, by the time the helicopter's engine was shut down. The pilot who climbed out was in his sixties and wore a few extra pounds. He brandished a worn Marlin 30/30 lever action as if he would enjoy using it.

"Stay put for the law, boy. You knew you were on private property when you settled, so there shouldn't be any arguments. I don't care for your kind out of hand, and I—"

Link asked, "Who *do* you like, old man?"

The rancher flushed. "Impertinence won't help your case. Might as well settle for a while. I called the Pershing County sheriff's office before I—"

"When did you grow the beard? You look worse than Robert E. Lee after he got his tail whipped at Appomattox."

The rancher's eyes bulged, and he sputtered for five full seconds before finding his voice: "Move that motorcycle so much as an inch, and I'll shoot the damned noisy thing."

"Yeah, right. I remember enough of your war stories from when I was a kid. I don't suppose you recall visiting Paul Anderson, who you called Lucky. It's been only five years since I visited you in Colorado."

The rancher's jaw drooped. He peered closer. "Link?"

"Good to see you, sir."

Tom DeBerre had served in the air force twenty years before Link, a backseater in various fighters beginning with the F-105F Thunderchief and F-4 Phantom, ending with the F-15E Strike Eagle. Link's father, who had flown with DeBerre on various occasions, said he'd been a great GIB (guy in back) as well as the most cantankerous officer in the air force. Now he was the orneriest retiree, a title that he did not dispute, but at present he was appalled, for he also had the well-deserved reputation of being a superb host.

Tom unlocked the gate, muttering about getting so old he couldn't recognize friends.

"When *did* you grow the beard, Tom?" Link asked. "It changes you."

"When I decided to take a bride and found my face was filled up with wrinkles. The beard hides 'em so well, she was accused of robbing the cradle." He chuckled. "She's off visiting her people up in Boise. Next time make sure to tell us you're coming so she can be here."

On his visit home four days earlier, Link had been told that DeBerre had married a well-endowed (in all respects) widow, and exchanged his modest spread near Montrose, Colorado, for a much larger one in Nevada. Now he bred and ran several hundred Brangus—a Brahma and Angus mix—on a few sections of grazing land.

"When the bride hears you spent the night out on the ground when we have a perfectly good bed at the house, she'll likely yank out the beard plus my hair. Do it again, and I'll use this rifle on you in matrimonial defense. Just ring the buzzer on the gate, and we'll fetch you."

"I got here at two thirty in the morning."

"I don't care what time you get here—ring the buzzer. Now let's go up to the house so I can make up for some of it."

"I can't stay long, Tom," Link tried, although he had been debating how he might get a message to Squid for the last hundred miles of his ride.

Tom pushed the gate wide. "You're comin' to the house. Move that contraption over on this side where no one can steal it, and we'll take that ugly little helicopter.

Link decided to go along or DeBerre might use the Marlin 336 to defend his reputation as host. His frowns and grumbles were reminiscent of Joseph Spotted Horse. He'd wondered how the old Indian was faring under questioning by the FBI and decided that Joseph would hold his own. By now the agents had probably learned a great deal about an old man's sorry lot.

He parked the bike where Tom DeBerre pointed, retrieved a change of clothing and the laptop computer from the side bags, and locked up. As he climbed into the helicopter's left seat, Link asked when Tom had gotten his rotary-wing checkout and received an incredulous look.

Link held on, hoping they'd remain upright.

After making a radiophone call to call off the sheriff, telling him the incident had been a joke played by an old friend, Tom flew around the property to show it and his cattle off, then to a sprawling Spanish-style home situated on a hilltop with superb views in all directions. DeBerre explained that he ran the place with only four ranch hands because of modern conveniences, such as the helicopter and GPS tagging for certain of the cattle. Aside from the helicopter that Tom kept parked on a concrete helipad in the daytime, there was a dirt strip and a canvas-covered Piper Cherokee Six. During inclement weather, the aircraft were pulled into a small hangar.

At the house, Link met a middle-aged Mexican couple that Tom said his wife had hired a couple of years earlier to keep the place up and running. They were served pastries, juice, and mugs of steaming coffee to hold them until breakfast.

Tom asked about Link's recent life, which subject he avoided, and Tom was gracious enough not to pursue. Then he asked about Maggie Tatro, who had been Link's lady friend last time they'd seen one another, and received another abbreviated response. Instead they found common ground by discussing mutual acquaintances, ex-military friends of Tom's and Lucky's and Link's with whom they had flown in various combat aircraft.

It took no arm-twisting for Link to accept the offer of a shower, which felt so luxurious that he stayed under the pelting water long after he was clean. He wanted to shave, but did not. Instead he pulled on a bathing suit laid out by the Mexican man and joined DeBerre in an outdoor hot tub, where he listened to more war stories about Lucky Anderson, who had risen to lieutenant general yet retained his friendships and loyalties with those of all ranks.

By the time he'd changed into fresh clothing, the Mexican woman had his dirty ones washed and ironed and set out in a neat stack. He came out to a country breakfast of freshly made biscuits, chorizo, ham, steaks, eggs, and potatoes, served on the patio table. The temperature was hot and climbing, but the soft spray from a nearby fountain provided a cool breeze of relief. As they ate, DeBerre pointed out the vista of multihued chimney rocks and canyons.

"You have a good life here, Tom."

DeBerre slowly nodded. "All I need is one more adventure. Hard to be so active and in the middle of every big fight, then just stop and vegetate like this."

"I feel sorry for you, having it so good," Link told him.

8:45 a.m.

When Link asked to use a phone line to send an e-mail, DeBerre showed him his office and a telephone jack for a dedicated broadband Internet line.

"Use my computer or yours, whichever you wish." He closed the door and left him alone.

On the road, Link had decided that if anyone's computer was secure, it would be Major Stradley's, whose job required her to remain on the cutting edge of computer technology. He did not know if that would include her laptop, but the idea made sense.

He went online, prepared a message to be sent to Major Stradley, asking the major to pass a note to Mr. Worsczejius: *Squid. Ask the major about the "tap code" to learn where I'm going. Tell Dan that I'll contact him when I arrive. Brief handful about everything, but do not share with G-H yet. I will remain online for 15 minutes for your response. If none, I'll contact you later. Best. L-A.*

He pressed the SEND button. The transmission took two seconds flat.

"Dan" was Dr. Walsh, project leader for the Shepherd's Journal effort. He should be back in Eureka, California, looking for the old camp. Link was not willing to share anything more with G-H (Gordon Hightower) unless they got something in return.

Ten minutes had passed when the laptop beeped. The message, sent from the major's e-address, was short and to the point: *Aye aye. Another message follows. Check Six. Squid.*

Link was smiling at the brevity, a trademark of naval officers since the days of semaphore, when another beep sounded. This second message had come quickly on the heels of the first one—yet it showed the proper e-mail address: *L-A, message unclear. Major Stradley isn't familiar with "tap code" so he asks 2 please explain. Where R U going? When will U get there? Which Dan? I await U'r response. Squid.*

There was an unopened attachment, titled: MORE PHOTOS.

Link frowned at the screen. The message was too wordy, Jana Stradley was not a he, and it seemed odd that the air force's own spooks wouldn't know the prisoners' tap code. Finally, Erin preached that e-mail attachments were ripe for compromise, and if in doubt to can them.

Still, could someone send a message from another's address like that?

He poised the arrow over the paper-clip icon, MORE PHOTOS, wondering if finding out was worth disabling the laptop.

As he hesitated, a new message arrived from Major Stradley's address: *2nd message U received from Squid is bogus. Delete all and do NOT open attachment. I had already solved the puzzle & know where U'r going, & approx where U'r located. Our opponents do not have that capability. Here's Squid. //Dan will be advised. Same with U'r other instructions. As I said in first message, "Aye Aye—I will comply." Hard to determine friends from enemies, so watch U'r six. Best. Squid.*

That sounded a lot more like Squid. To simplify his problem, Link deleted all three messages plus all of those received earlier, emptied the trash can, and shut down the laptop. He had no time to try for more answers.

He went out to find Tom DeBerre and tell him he had to leave. The aging air warrior was looking for a final adventure, but Link was determined not to involve him in this one.

10:00 a.m.

Tom DeBerre drove him to the gate in a pickup, offering the use of everything from the Piper Cherokee to a four-by-four. Link declined them all and was quickly back on the road.

Once again, the old Goldwing ran like a precision clock, purring rather than roaring, presenting no mechanical challenges and letting Link concentrate on problems at hand, such as his inability to contact anyone at the Weyland Foundation without being compromised.

When Link pulled onto the interstate, a jet helicopter approached from the west. As he accelerated, he noted that it was descending to land at the DeBerre ranch.

He rode in the midst of a group of vehicles that were traveling in a cluster, settled back and thought about the e-mail messages.

Assuming the messages were being read by Erin, could he covertly pass a message to her? Then he wondered if she'd embedded something in the *bogus* one. There were obvious errors, like the major's sex and asking about "Dan." Had Erin purposefully done those to raise flags.

Major Stradley had said that *we* (Erin's people) could determine the locations of senders of e-mail. So did they know where the bogus e-mail had originated?

Could they tell if Erin and Frank were in California, or somewhere in Georgia?

Why would Major Stradley reveal that she could locate the senders, and that the bad guys could not. Had she done it so they would hesitate to listen in? It was convoluted but not unlikely; confusing an enemy was the thing Major Stradley's people did best.

On both his messages, Squid's advice was for Link to "check his six," the time-honored way that fighter pilots told one another to "watch your ass."

Link heard the squealing sounds of small jet engines at the same moment that his eyes were drawn to the shadow of something flying overhead. There were no wings on the shadow. A chopper?

Link pushed his right rearview mirror all the way up. The image of a helicopter slid into view, then slowly fell back to a position a quarter-mile behind. It was a Jet Ranger with black lettering on the sides and underbelly.

An official-use helicopter flying in formation, keeping the motorcycle in sight. Link felt his anger rise, first for allowing himself to be spotted, and then, remembering that it had landed at DeBerre's, for involving a friend.

He tried to convince himself that the helo could be tracking any of the vehicles in his cluster. A family-occupied maroon minivan was in the lead, likely on cruise control set at eighty-five miles per hour, using the state trooper guideline for ticketing at "speed limit plus ten percent." A tractor and semi-trailer rig had pulled into the passing lane when Link slowed to view the aircraft. A brown five-ton UPS truck was moving up on his rear.

The town of Lovelock was fifteen miles distant, where he'd have to refuel if he was to get past Reno without stopping again.

The next five minutes passed without change, the cluster traveling at co-speed, the helo maintaining its position behind and above.

Was the pilot cruising at eighty-five, as they were? Link thought.

Given the opportunity, most pilots followed major highways. It was possible that this one was not after anyone, just following I-80 to Reno. Perhaps he'd landed at Tom DeBerre's for some perfectly explainable rationale.

Dream on. Link recalled that the Jet Ranger's cruising speed was something in the order of 130 to 150 mph, and decided that one of the vehicles in his cluster was the target. Since he believed it was the Goldwing he rode, it was time for Link to disappear.

The helicopter remained locked in place as Link's cluster passed a turnoff onto the access road that, he noted from Jamie's detailed map, was the last one before Lovelock. Two miles ahead, the access road intersected with a paved county road that passed under the interstate, proceeded south for four miles, then passed a small thicket of cottonwood and willows and angled toward Lovelock's back door.

Link decided that with a little luck, what he was conjuring up was doable. It was certainly better to do *something* rather than let them capture him when he ran out of gas.

An inner voice cautioned him not to wreck Jamie's toy.

Link looked far ahead and measured. There was five feet of gravel shoulder, then hardpack earth that dropped ten feet at a steep angle to the road below. No drainage ditch on this side, which was good.

The big rig was passing on his left, the brown UPS five-ton was coming up behind, and so he accelerated just enough to allow the semi to continue by while discouraging the driver of the UPS truck not to pass. Or so he hoped.

In his tilted rearview mirror, the helicopter did as he'd hoped, slowly sliding forward until it was flying farther out to the right of the interstate. The pilot was getting a little sloppy with his flying, perhaps speaking to the crew about whatever was to come.

The semi continued to pass Link, who waited with mounting impatience since the gentler slope was now only a quarter-mile distant.

As soon as the rear of the big rig's trailer was by, Link abruptly pulled left into its wake. He encountered intense turbulence, wobbled a few times, then stabilized and slowed abruptly as he applied pressure to both front and rear brakes.

Another semi was coming on fast, moving up from behind, giving a long blast of air horn at the motorcycle rider who seemed intent on committing suicide.

The helicopter crew would not hear the horn over their own engine and rotor noises.

Link had slowed enough that the UPS truck was passing on his right. As soon as it was clear, Link swung right, almost into the truck's rear bumper. He braked harder yet, locking the wheels, letting off only when the bike threatened to skitter from under him.

He'd slowed to fifteen when he rode the bike onto the shoulder, then at ten miles per hour, he went over the side.

The ride down the steep incline was wild, his front tire pulling this way and that. The bottom came abruptly, and the front of the bike bounced and reared. He tried to correct back onto the access road, and despite all his efforts the motorcycle's rear began to slide. He steered

into the slide, and after a precarious moment, the bike
fell out from underneath him.

10:30 a.m.—Airborne Eight Miles Northeast of Lovelock, Nevada

None of the three in the helicopter were monitoring the
motorcycle rider below. The woman was conversing with
the pilots about the best place to stop and take Link
Anderson on the motorcycle beneath them.

"Five miles ahead—two miles this side of Lovelock,"
the pilot said, "there's a place to land. Of course, he
may just ignore us. Then it'll take a cruiser, if they can
catch him."

They were in contact with the NHP, who had vehicles ahead.

"Plan on using two cruisers. He's too stubborn to
make it easy." She went back to controlling the gimbal-
mounted television camera.

"Damn it, I've lost him," she said. The copilot took
back control and observed his screen, but there was no
sign of the motorcycle.

The pilot was grim-faced as he made a crisp 180
maneuver.

"He didn't look too steady. We'd better see if he was
in an accident."

Maggie prayed he was not.

10:35 a.m.

Link was at full throttle, the speedometer steady on 115
miles per hour. The velocity and openness to the elements were exhilarating. He also felt exposed. If he
struck a pothole or smacked into a wayward animal, he
could be launched like a stone from a slingshot. Flying
fighters provided a similar sensation, but that was a calculated risk, planned and executed with deliberation,
and with the comfort of knowing that there was always
the ejection seat.

He chanced to turn his head for a look. The helicopter

was a few miles distant, reversing course, finally giving away the crew's intent and telling Link that the search was definitely for him.

It seemed preposterous that Gordon's FBI agents could have tracked him down so quickly, but the Jet Ranger was definitely going back for a look, and it would not be much longer before they saw him.

He rocketed on until he arrived at the thicket of cottonwoods and willows masking the road, and let the bike coast to a more reasonable speed. One hundred seemed slow in comparison. Ninety miles per hour was downright pokey.

He considered his options. There was no way to change his appearance to the spotters above. The big, boxy motorcycle was unique, as was the battered white helmet, and regardless of what he took off or added, he would be recognized.

Still he could not abandon his quest to find Frank and Erin. If Link were caught, Gordon had promised to toss him in jail.

Link pulled off under a canopy of low-hanging willow branches, noting that the engine was running hot, reasonable with the hundred-degree desert heat and the fast ride. He shut down, and other than a few pops and crackles, there was quiet. As his ears adjusted, he heard the faint flutter of helicopter blades and rumbles of passing traffic five miles away on I-80.

He got off and walked around, favoring the bruised leg that the motorcycle had so ignominiously pinned down until he'd disgustedly pushed it off. He'd made the maneuver just fine until he'd bottomed out, forgot to keep up his speed, and fallen.

Jamie's meticulous old motorcycle was no longer a virgin. There were scrapes on the engine protective bars and the chrome pipes. The paint on the right saddlebag was abraded and badly scratched, but nothing was amiss with the vitals of the tough old bike.

He focused on the distant interstate and the helo hovering there. Finally his pursuers turned north from the intersection, taking the opposite direction.

When they'd finished searching there, they were sure to come back this way, and just as sure to discover him.

Link started the Goldwing and eased back onto the county road. A minute later, he negotiated the right turn toward Lovelock and twisted the throttle for more speed. He'd fuel up, hide until the copter was gone, and then get back onto the interstate and ride like the wind.

19

Squid settled in a chair before the nervous-acting VP of Habitat Earth, and her panel of "experts," who were tasked by Squid to find out everything they could about the *marea muerta*—the dead tide—and the natural conditions that would create such a phenomenon.

The VP opened by saying they'd approached the project as a multidisciplined problem, as they did all studies of major importance, since one environmental facet surely impacted another. As an example, she mentioned the endangered snail darter, and the multiple studies being initiated to study the animal.

Squid growled, "Let's move on and forget the sales pitch?"

"Yes, certainly," she said as she lowered a plasma screen showing a map of Northern California. She smiled. "Ninety percent of the world's most spectacular plants, named *Sequoia semperviren* by—"

Squid snapped, "I don't need a damned tourism pitch about flora and fauna."

She looked puzzled, glanced again at the map, and sat down in her chair, flustered.

"Who's next?" Squid rumbled.

An exuberant male began a dissertation about demographics and ecological challenges of this sparsely populated area, despite it being part of the nation's most populous state . . . how much of it was closed to settle-

ment by state and federal laws enacted to protect the
redwoods and various endangered . . . how Habitat
Earth division was instrumental in rescuing endangered
species . . .

Squid interrupted. "I'm interested in an area ten miles
inland from the coast to thirty miles out to sea. Tell me
about its uniqueness. How does the dead tide work?

The briefer nodded energetically. "Okay. *Unique*. Due
to the efforts of various protest groups, oil drilling is
prohibited along the entire coastline, despite known deposits of . . ."

Squid sighed and shook his head. So far he did not
even believe they understood the question. "Damn it,
tell me what *is* happening there, not a list of prohibitions."

"You don't understand, sir. This is what we do in
Habitat Earth. Our job is to improve or maintain the
ecological balances of nature."

"Hey, I gave at the office," Squid said. He looked at
his watch, wondering if he shouldn't explain what he was
after again.

A briefer who looked just as serious as the previous
three flashed his subject on the screen: SEISMIC ACTIVITY
WITHIN NORTHERN CALIFORNIA.

Squid huffed a sigh and had started to stand up as the
briefer switched to his next slide.

"Forget—" The complaint froze in Squid's throat as
he read the legends and defined what he was looking at.
Throughout Northern California, across land and
ocean—a web of orange fault lines were displayed in
various degrees of brightness, outlining current seismic
pressure, as well as the seams between large areas shown
in different colors, representing tectonic plates.

While he had seen seismic maps before, something
about this one seemed illogical. He stood and walked
closer to the drop-down plasma screen, and stared at a
confluence a few miles from Cape Mendocino, the westernmost point in the forty-eight contiguous states—the
"knee" in leg-shaped California. Three of the brightest
fault lines converged upon a centroid in the ocean only
seven miles west of Cape Mendocino.

To make the juxtaposition truly incredible, shown at that same location was the confluence of three major plates.

"What the hell is all that?" Squid asked, pointing at the gaudy maze.

"The Mendocino Triple Junction is one of the most unique places on the planet." The briefer explained the plates (the largest being the North American). To the north, one plate was actively "subducting," or sliding under, the continental landmass. Then he explained the brightly colored faults, the best known being the San Andreas.

"The area's extremely active. There are daily tremblers, ranging from nondetectable to major quakes. Periodically the plates become locked with one another and build up pressure, then let go with a granddaddy earthquake so violent it causes ruptures, lifts and lowers mountains, and sends tsunamis across the Pacific. Those occur on an average of one every five hundred years. The bad news is that it's been locked for a very long time and one is overdue right now."

"Could the seismic action cause the dead tide?"

"Cause it?" The briefer looked puzzled as a new briefer entered the room. She looked tired, but was able to form a curl of a smile as she came forward to join them.

"Dr. Miller!" said the acting VP, as if the cavalry had arrived.

"Virginia Miller," the new briefer said in introduction to Squid. "I do oceanic currents and trenches. The conditions required for the dead tide phenomenon were likely formed by the last massive earthquake at the Junction, and they'll undoubtedly be altered by the next one."

"Have those conditions existed for the past two centuries?"

"Actually it's been eight hundred years since the last big quake at the Junction."

"You know what might cause a phenomenon like the dead tide?"

"If it exists it has to do with sea currents and underwater terrain. The computer model showed more than a thousand possible combinations. I kept the computer crunching all last night, and narrowed it down to three."

Squid left the room convinced that Dr. Virginia Miller would discover the secrets of the *marea muerta*. He only hoped it could be done in time.

Back in his office, Squid scanned through Shepherd's Journal in search of clues to the dead tide's location. Even if Dr. Miller found precise conditions that caused the *marea muerta*, there would remain the problem of where it would be found along the rugged shoreline. He finally decided there was not enough information to make such a decision until they knew more.

But if what he believed might be true, that the Serpientes were somehow using the dead tide to smuggle terrorists into the country, what kind of watercraft were they using? What were their requirements, and, with those in mind, what was available?

He'd found an expert in Virginia Miller to provide answers about the dead tide. But whom could he turn to who knew of an appropriate watercraft? The previous night he had gone through his long list of naval contacts, when a name had jumped to the forefront: Ret. Com. Billy Hemby knew more about the dynamics of the ocean and the capabilities of the world's ships and boats than any man he had ever met.

He called out to Mary Long that he was leaving the building for a while. Despite reassurances, he still did not trust that the phone lines at the Weyland Building were secure.

1:20 p.m.—Sparks, Nevada

Link rode into Sparks on I-80 feeling better about his chances of eluding the helicopter. Reno was almost in sight, and the California state line was just beyond.

His first sign of trouble was his last, and it was professionally done—a white rail was to his right when a grimy pickup swerved in front of him and slowed; a plain sedan pulled in close behind; and a heavy van drew abreast in the passing lane, the passenger brandishing a badge and jabbing his finger toward the offramp. They left him no other choice when they eased him over.

Halfway around the right-hand half-loop, his escorts shepherded him right again, this time into a pullout where the same Jet Ranger he had seen earlier was parked.

As he halted, Link searched for a way out, but the sedan behind and the shabby pickup in front were pulled in too close to allow escape.

Officers climbed out doing high fives. The one who had waved him over wore a suit and had the look of a muscular bulldog. The badge and folder IDed him as Christian G. Wilson, a deputy district attorney for Washoe County.

Link nodded at the patrol cars. "I think they've done that before."

"All the time," Wilson said. "You were free practice. Another half an hour, and we'll be doing the real thing."

I'm not the real thing? Link pulled off the helmet and do-rag and scratched his scalp. The deputy DA had the sedan back off a couple of feet so he could read the motorcycle's license plate.

"The bike belongs to a friend."

"That's what I understand. Are you carrying, sir?"

"A revolver in the left side bag. I have a handgun permit." He wondered what they'd say about the ID kit and the half-dozen driver's licenses showing different names.

Wilson wasn't interested in looking. "The question's routine for fellow officers."

Link was intrigued. Fellow officer? *Why aren't they arresting me?*

Link observed the helicopter and two people in civvies beside it. Assistant Special Agent In Charge Maggie Tatro was with a youthful-looking man in a dark suit, undoubted another FBI agent, who had pulled up in a not-so-new Suburban.

"Special Agent Tatro wants to speak with you, sir," Wilson said.

Maggie thought he made a good biker, duded up in scruffy denims and boots and glistening with sweat. He was almost as lean as before, still in good physical condition. A fresh scar ran low across his forehead, drawing the skin so there was a new crispness to his features. He was unshaved, and looked tired and dusty. Considering all of that, he looked good, making her wish she'd avoided more carbs and shed a few more pounds.

She walked over and gave him a small greeting hug—which he of course did not know how to handle—pulled back, and asked, "So how are you, Link?"

"Gordon sicced you on me?"

"His verbal directive was to toss you into the nearest jail and have you transported East on the first plane so he could roast you alive."

"I'm lucky to have such friends."

"Yes, you are. Take Chris, there," she nodded at the departing deputy DA, "who offered to help as soon as I told him you'd flown fighters in Desert Storm One and needed assistance. Same with the elected DA, and the cops. They're all ex-military, and they really are logging this as a practice takedown."

"They're damned good."

"That's what I told them you'd say. Betcha thought you were pretty slick, getting away from us back in Lovelock. You oughta know you can't hide from us feds."

Link was not pleased with his circumstance. "How did you find me?"

She gave an impish grin. "Joseph likes me, remember?"

"Don't get Joseph involved. He had no idea where I was going or why."

"After Gordon asked me for help, I put in for a bureau jet to take me to Kalispell, where Joseph was giving the interrogator fits, talking about how hard it was for an old man with an uncaring nephew."

Link could not withhold a smile.

"The agent-in-charge felt Joseph had told them what he knew, mostly about the weather and how the livestock were doing in the heat. He especially enjoyed taking polygraph tests."

"But Joseph talked to you?"

"Joseph likes me," she said. "He also trusts me, which

you should try doing. I took him out and bought him a couple of desserts. Then I promised to visit and make him blueberry cobbler after I found you."

"That's evil."

"He said I'd better get you pretty quick, because you were going out west somewhere with a valley, huge trees, and bad people."

Maggie had guessed that he'd meant the Sierras and the giant sequoia. "That's when he said Jamie Bourne might have something to tell me about your trip."

"Joseph has a very big mouth."

"Maybe a little big, but he's sweet."

"You called Jamie Bourne next."

"Now that would have been dumb, getting Jamie in a testosterone test to see if he'd really die before ratting on a friend. I called Moira and told her you were being difficult, and I was trying to help. Not only are we friends, she thinks you missed out on the catch of your life, meaning me, which is true."

"Moira didn't know anything about it."

"Get real, Link. She called me back after half an hour to tell me when you left and what you were riding. A motorcycle? That freaked me, Link. You don't ride. I had this vision of you wobbling down the highway in front of big trucks. You could have been killed."

Link stared at her. "You got all that from my *friends*?"

"They were *our* friends, if you'll recall. Like Tom De-Berre, who we visited in Colorado. I looked up his new place on a map and figured you'd stop by on your way. We arrived at Tom's not five minutes after you'd left."

"And Tom told you about me?"

"Two years ago I took time off to go to his wedding. Tom has a lovely wife, by the way. He's your friend, but he's mine, too, and he knew you wouldn't keep anything from me."

As they talked, Maggie cast Link more than a few glances. Good thing it was over between them or she'd reach out, maybe get a hug in return after so long.

She pulled her hand back from where it had rested on his arm.

"So what now?" he asked.

"We talk. Gordon thought you'd be on your way to Georgia to look for Frank and Erin."

Link was not verbose, which she remembered was sometimes irritating. Around him she was always talking at sixty miles per hour, while he just nodded or grunted a couple of words.

She encouraged him: "But here you are heading west. How come?"

"Because I think they're here, not there. What's the latest on the search?"

"That's too official, Link. I still love you but—" She stopped herself, heat glowing in her cheeks. "Let me rephrase. I think you're the most capable person I know at a lot of things, but we can't talk about what's going on with the official world. That's a violation of FBI 101."

"Frank and Erin are my closest friends, Maggie."

They were her friends, as well, and she had been worrying since she'd first heard.

"Have you seen the videos?" he asked quietly.

"They were released to the field offices. The shots of that poor terrified girl in the airplane were horrible, and the brandings—" She shook her head, hoping she wouldn't tear up, which she might do with Link standing there.

He asked again. "Has there been anything new over the past two days?"

Maggie thought about it more. Officially Link still held his security clearances. "Gordon is convinced they're east of Augusta, north of Atlanta." She told him about Gordon's promotion, which did not surprise him at all.

"Is anyone working the case in California?" he asked.

He was so damnably earnest. He honestly cared for Frank and Erin. She told the truth. "Not very hard."

"Good," he muttered. She could see his intensity, knew his moods now as if they'd never been apart. He was on a trail and didn't want anyone interfering. Not her, Gordon, or anyone.

"I told our friends that I wouldn't use what they told me to harm you."

"Thanks," he said, meaning it.

"That carries an *if*, Link. I can't let you continue alone. Gordon's all wet about clapping you in jail, and he knows it, but you can't charge around on your own."

"Just one person. You and no more." He smiled as if he were recalling their good times.

Not so fast, Lincoln. Not with this *minion of the FBI, who fought her way up the ladder of relative success, regardless of how wonderful it sounds. Anyway, I didn't bring proper clothing.*

Maggie turned and nodded toward the young agent. "Stan will go along to look over your shoulder. If you need help, he'll call me."

She introduced Special Agent Stanley Goldstein, who wore a steely-eyed visage as he shook Link's hand.

As Link examined him, Stanley gave Maggie a nod, saying he could handle it.

Not unless Link lets you, she thought.

"You'll have to keep up. I won't coddle you."

Maggie felt relief. Link seldom gave in so quickly.

This morning she'd called Gordon as they'd closed in, and asked for the option of sending an agent to ensure that Link remained far away from the ongoing search. After an argument, Gordon had agreed, adding that if Link took off again, he would go behind bars.

Maggie wished it was herself tagging along. They'd once been a good team, professionally and otherwise, and she felt as if she were betraying him. If it came to having either Gordon or Link on her side when she was threatened with danger, the FBI ADIC would not stand a chance.

Link thought Maggie looked great—all five feet two of her, from her sensibly shod feet to her full-busted body on up to a shoulder-length mane of auburn hair. He wondered why they'd drifted apart, since they were like-minded on so many things. Perhaps that was the problem; they were similarly hardheaded to a fault. When she'd called with avid excitement in her tone about the promotion to ASAC if she moved to San Francisco, he had not tried to argue her out of it, even though he'd sensed that staying put was something she'd consider—for him.

Several times in his life Link had stone-faced his way

to a bachelor's fate. Once he'd been engaged, and if Marie had not died, they would be together in Montana. But she had passed away, and he'd grieved every day since. Maggie was the only woman who had made him forget. Marie had left a letter in such an event, encouraging him to move on with his life. But Link had dragged his feet and missed out again.

When it was over with Maggie, he'd told himself that it was for the best.

He measured Special Agent Stanley Goldstein. "Load your stuff on the bike."

"You're taking the Suburban, Link. You drive—he'll watch," Maggie said.

"It's a vintage Goldwing. I can't just leave it."

"No way Stan's getting on a motorcycle."

After more words they compromised, as they'd once learned to do. Stanley would follow in the Suburban until Link found a freight company to haul the bike to Boudie Springs.

She warned Link that if he made as much as a motion to try to lose Stanley, the agent would contact her and she'd arrange for the Reno FBI field office to pick Link up.

"This is Stan's first operation. Do not take advantage of him, Link. I'll expect him to call from Placerville. If he doesn't—" She shook her head, emphasizing her point.

He liked the way her hair shimmered. "You call that trust?" Link asked.

She tried to get him to confirm his destination, and he told her that wasn't part of the deal. Her lapdog would tell her where they were.

Maggie's voice rose, as he remembered it doing when she was upset. "Stan is a fully qualified special agent. He was third in his class at Quantico, and he's extremely reliable, which is more than I can say about you." She stopped herself from going further, but her jaw was set.

He'd forgotten about the way she became cuter as she grew angrier.

Link took I-80 into Reno, keeping his speed down and looking back to make sure that Stanley was not left behind. He pulled off at the first moving company's sign. After assuring himself that the special agent had made the turn, Link rode back on the frontage road, parked in front of the warehouse-office, and went over to the Suburban. The agent rolled down his window.

"I'll just be a minute," he told Stanley.

"I'd better go along."

"I may have to pee. Do you want to follow me there, too?"

"If necessary."

"Aw, hell." Link reached inside, deftly picked the cell phone from the agent's lap, and brandished it under Stanley's nose. "You just lost your lifeline to Mommy."

The agent's eyes bulged as he reached into his coat, but Link was ready. He clamped down on Stanley's shoulder with a harsh hand, numbing the arm, and removed the Glock .40 from his weakened grasp. He also took the keys from the ignition.

It was not a matter of training. Link had experience dealing with situations.

"Rule one," Link said. "Always carry a backup." He had studied Stanley back at the pullout and noted that there was no hint of a second pistol at either belt or calf.

He shucked out the Glock's clip, ratcheted out the chamber round, moved the weapon's caliber slide just one-tenth of an inch back, field-stripped the weapon, and dropped the parts into Special Agent Stanley's lap. "I'm going in, you'll stay here and play with your gun, they'll ship the bike, then we'll be on our merry way."

Link turned and went to the office door, Stanley's cell phone in hand.

At the desk, he told the woman that he had a Goldwing motorcycle outside and would she have one of her men wheel it into their warehouse. He gave her a twenty.

Outside he noted that Stanley was busily reconstructing the Glock, except for the recoil spring that rested in Link's pocket.

Two hefty moving men went out and got the bike, which Link had left in neutral. They pushed it through an open, garage-style door.

Stanley was still frantically searching the seat when

Link handed the woman the phone, spring, and the Suburban's keys. "The guy out there will need these," he said, and walked into the bay where the men had left the Goldwing. He leisurely got on, fastened the helmet, and started up. "Thanks," he said, and rode out the open back door, thankful for the relative quietness of the old Honda.

After four blocks of back streets, he returned to the access road. There Link rode onto I-80 and accelerated to traffic speed. Three miles farther, he turned onto US 395, heading north. He remained in heavy traffic for the next ten miles before he was finally able to boost the bike to cruising speed. He crossed the California state line, was waved through the agriculture inspection, as were most motorcycles, and noted the distance to Susanville: sixty-five miles.

By then he felt that Stanley was able to get in touch with Maggie, and that she would launch into her cursing and throwing mode. She'd once said that only Link could get her that upset.

Susanville was well to the north, in the same vicinity as Mount Lassen. The roads there were heavily canopied and difficult to observe from a helicopter flying above.

Jamie Bourne's brother owned the GMC dealership in Susanville and was waiting with a fully loaded new Yukon, the flagship of SUVs. Jamie's brother would ship the Goldwing back with the next load of used cars. He'd spend the night in the Yukon, and in the morning try out the new four-by-four by taking US 299 from Redding to Eureka, which was located three hundred miles from Yosemite.

20

10:00 a.m.—The Weeping Tree

Frank Dubois patiently waited on a beetle that was reluctant to venture close enough for him to grab. He lay in the musty cavern formed by the ancient roots of a redwood giant, constantly bearing the heavy weight of badly rusted logging chains that had been secured and padlocked by a man in policeman's garb called Chief Welk. The brand that had been burned into Frank's forehead on the second day no longer stung as severely. After five days without a meal, he was thin and weak. He was no longer hungry but periodically suffered from pangs of emptiness.

Condensation ran off the massive tree each morning in finger-size rivulets, and he knew he could survive if he consumed water and ate even small traces of food. He'd torn apart and devoured a few unsavory bats that had roosted in his reach, and twice had feasted on unwary mice. Chipmunks and squirrels were too smart to be so easily caught. Spiders were bitter. Beetles and large ants actually tasted good.

Frank was not one to give up, despite the brutality. He had faith in God and America, and knew he would either be rescued (although he did not know how) or find a way to escape. When they'd videotaped them for the branding, he'd repeatedly blinked the words "Fiere the Trie"—the words stained into the bark at the entrance to the cave—using the tap code. Since the chemists had returned to the bungalow, and he had recognized the Palestinian master from Alpha-Nine from past photos, he had added, "A-9." It had seemed too much to hope that his captors wouldn't detect it, but so far there'd been no reaction.

Frank had always been a target for kidnappers, but there seemed to be no reason for the brutal treatment. And why had they taken Erin? He'd not seen her since they'd dragged her into the cage three days ago, done their taping, and taken her away. He prayed that she was alive.

A tremor made the earth quiver beneath him. He'd become accustomed to them.

He sensed that his captors were coming and scrambled over to an opening that faced the clearing and the walking trail on its far side. Behind him, on the opposite side of the Weeping Tree, was a long bungalow, where the Palestinian master bomb maker fashioned intricate firing circuits and shaped and dried RDX and Semtex building blocks. His helper used a pedal-operated Singer to fashion prefit halters of various sizes. On occasion the helper brought his handiwork outside for examination by the Alpha-Nine master. They did not stay long, not with the sentinel looking on with his blank, hungry stare.

The sentinel had also heard others coming down the walking trail, for he emerged from his hut and stood silently, gripping his well-used hunting rifle. Several times Frank had tried to converse with him, but he'd elicited no response other than a blank stare.

The sentinel gripped his rifle tightly as the woman named Sydney appeared across the clearing, pulling Erin along. Though a cord was tied taut about Erin's neck, and her hands were secured before herself with steel bracelets from which a chain was attached to her ankles, Frank was elated to see she seemed relatively unhurt. Sydney yanked harshly on the chains, as if irritated, and turned so that her star badge was seen by the sentinel.

Behind came Chief Welk. "Inside," he barked at the sentinel, and the madman stared with his blank expression for a fraction of a moment before complying. Frank had noted that there was always a delay between the moment of cognition and his reaction, as if it took that long for the impulses in his brain to connect and be processed.

Was there a way to use that when he and Erin escaped?

Sydney wore a cotton shirt, khakis, and heavy hiking boots. Her hair was golden and curled naturally. As Chief Welk proceeded to the bungalow where the chemists worked, she shoved Erin—who stumbled headfirst into the cave enclosure—and ignored her groans as she padlocked her to the same impossibly heavy logging chain that Frank wore. Erin was badly bruised, with scabbed sores on her face and the exposed portions of her neck. While she appeared to be broken of spirit, Frank knew he did not look any better.

Sydney regarded Frank. "Hungry?" she asked, and when he croaked that he was, she smiled humorlessly. He'd learned not to remain silent when questioned. Chief Welk had beaten him severely, breaking his nose and reinjuring his crippled leg.

Sydney tossed her head. "Don't you think her hair looks much better on me?"

Frank stared, understanding now why Erin had been shorn. Her blond locks had been fashioned into Sydney's new wig. He wanted to vomit, but had nothing in his stomach to bring up. He managed a faint "yeah."

"It makes me look young, don't you think?" When he'd concurred, she offered a twisted smile. She was a monster without pity. Link had once briefed him about the woman who could change her appearance like a chameleon, but he had not realized the extent of her avarice.

Sydney regarded Erin. "The letter I burned into butch-cut's forehead. Can you guess what it stands for?"

"Slave?" he tried.

"No, darling. It's the initial of her new master. It shows ownership, the same as yours."

She stood over him, looking down, and lowered her voice. "Who is your master?"

"Mullah Sajacento?"

She sighed, as if in disgust.

"The Serpientes?"

"I said *ownership*, Frank. If you acted like a man, I'd squat down and make you give me the ride of my life. You are mine, darling. That's why you both wear my initial. Do I have to piss on you like a bitch marking her turf?"

"No." He'd known that the others lacked sanity when they'd killed the father and son in the frenzied rite, but he'd believed that Sydney might be capable of reason. He'd been wrong.

"Have you wondered why either of you are alive? Butch-cut there drained the world's most secure computers dry, and cracked into others so I could learn their secrets. If she hadn't, I would have had her darling son Johnny's throat cut and delighted in showing her the photos. Now that I have everything I need from you both, you are utterly useless to anyone."

She toyed with him, rubbing the toe of her hiking boot against his genitals.

"This morning your fools at the Weyland Foundation transferred thirty million dollars to an untraceable maze of accounts, which my greedy friends happily took off their hands. They asked us to react by showing mercy." She smiled and shook her head at their folly. "My friends prefer to kill you, darling. You saw the ritual of the stone. You and butch-cut will experience it, although you don't deserve the honor."

For no apparent reason, Sydney's face darkened and her voice rose. "How I *despise* you." She drew back and kicked him where she'd been rubbing. The pain was sharp, and Frank did not restrain a shriek. In the past, those had mollified her. Sure enough, Sydney calmed.

"My friends would kill you right way, but in return for all I've done, they're allowing me to keep you alive."

He managed to rasp out, "Thank—you."

"I intend to bring Lincoln Anderson here, too, you know."

Several times she'd mentioned Link's name during their ordeal. Whenever she did so, her eyes flashed with hatred.

"I will castrate him and cut out his tongue. Then I'll have him watch you on the stone while I dice you both up like potatoes, one small inch at a time."

"Why do you—hate us—so much?" He earnestly wanted to know.

"You know part of it, how I once taught American

agents to disappear among their enemies and became indispensable. Then there was a time when I was hunted by my employers because I dipped into certain operational accounts more than they felt was necessary. It took resources, *my* money, threats to expose scandals and secrets that I'd learned in my former job, but they finally stopped the search so long as I remained out of sight. I was pleased. I found a new position and even a lover."

Link had called her a murderous, man-hating chameleon.

Sydney smiled radiantly. "He was young and brilliant, and I became whomever he wanted me to be. Loving or demanding or sweet, or a perverted bitch."

She's a natural for the latter role, Frank thought.

Her face shadowed with anger. "Then Lincoln Anderson interfered. He exposed me and told the world what I had done, and I had to stage my own death for a second time."

She succeeded. Even the FBI believes she's dead.

Her voice trembled with emotion. "I *loathe* Lincoln Anderson."

Sydney's hatred was driven by limitless ego—she'd been beaten at her own game by a male. Egotism was her weakness. Frank wondered if there was a way to use it against her.

She hissed, "You are the dearest friends of my enemy. I *hate* you and butch-cut for that."

Sydney bore down on his groin with her full weight. Frank bellowed.

She bent close, whispering. "Did I tell you that Lincoln is missing? The fool I sent to bring him back says he's no longer at his cabin, and not even the FBI knows where he is. I sent Kamil to help find him, and he could do no better. Do *you* know where he is?"

"No."

"Do better, darling."

Frank had learned to scream more than he suffered and always appear weaker than he was, yet this time he rebelled. "He's—coming—to *destroy*—you."

"Coming *here*?" She put a fingernail to her lips as if she were thinking about it. "I do hope he comes. Chief

Welk knows every move of every new arrival, and he has Lincoln Anderson's description. Even if he came, it would be impossible that he'd find you. No outsider has discovered this place for the past five centuries."

"You are Sociedad . . . Serpiente?" he tried.

"They'd never allow a woman, although I've known them all my life." She smiled with a clever thought, looked around to see if anyone were near. "Once I was frightened, the kind of child they particularly enjoyed. First there was one Serpiente, and soon there were two, but each time they tried, I disappeared before they could do it to me." She pulled back conspiratorially. "You understand. It was *always* someone else they did it to."

"Yes," he said, although he did not understand. He wondered what horrors she had endured.

"Now they're dead, dead, dead." She twisted her mouth and nodded as if he were her confidant.

An Arabic voice was raised inside the bungalow. Sydney's voice returned to its normal pitch. "*Where* is Lincoln Anderson?" she murmured.

Frank remained silent, while Erin breathed shallowly. When Sydney left, he'd tend to her.

Sydney made up her mind. "No, he's not coming here. Kamil believes he flew to Georgia, and I agree. We've invested too much money and effort convincing everyone you're there."

"He'll find you," said Frank, trying to work at her superego.

"He'll have to hurry. In eight days, a swarm of martyrs will be loosened on this country like a pestilence, striking where none expects." She paused, and her voice took on an Arabic accent and a higher, sweeter note: "Twenty days from Aozou, an army of *jahid* more plentiful than bees will follow me into the midst of the Great Satan to destroy their future."

Frank had heard the words before, using that same tone. "Sajacento?" he whispered.

"Very good. But I wrote the words. The great Mullah Sajacento's a simpleton, but he has charisma and listens well. In Paris I convinced him he was the Judge of Man, as great as Muhammad. I introduced him to Ahmed bin Polah, who eagerly became Sajacento's benefactor. I

traveled to Iran and Syria as a man and spoke with leaders of both arms of the Hezbollah. We would smuggle
their soldiers into America to support Sajacento's jihad.
They would take credit for all we would do. When they
agreed, I went with Sajacento to Aozou to announce his
jihad. I was at the lakebed and told Sajacento how to
capture Lincoln Anderson's spies. Then I had him kill
the spies and display them so Lincoln Anderson would
see."

At first Frank doubted that she could have done those
things. No Arab would listen to a woman. But now, observing her as trickster and master of disguise, he believed that she could easily masquerade as a male—or
as anyone she wished.

"America will be transformed, Frank Dubois. Bin
Polah told you it would happen. As the FBI rush around
in Georgia following the clues we leave and think they
are trapping the Hezbollah, my friends will bring Sajacento and his martyrs ashore here. They will perform
their atrocities, and my friends will make their fortunes.
As the deaths mount up, no American will trust the
government."

"What are Sajacento's targets?" He did not expect
an answer.

"Didn't you listen? Sajacento told everyone at Aozou,
and Ahmed bin Polah told America. They'll take your
country's *future*, darling. The brightest of your *youths*.
When Lincoln Anderson tries to stop it, Damon Lee or
Kamil will bring him here. That will be the end for you
and another beginning for me. While Sajacento's martyrs
attack, I'll snack on your liver."

He watched her moods fluctuate. Sydney was as mad
as the sentinel. She was also brilliant and accustomed to
success. Again she entered a dark mood, and without
warning crushed her heel into his testicles, twisting her
foot as he screamed, this time in earnest.

She started out, but stopped and turned at the doorway. "Don't die on me, darlings. Continue drinking the
slime and eating rodents, and survive until my dream
comes true."

1:30 p.m.—Eureka, California

Link was trying to be vague, so he wouldn't stand out in any crowd. He'd even forgone wearing his Stetson.

He drove slowly, taking in the small city that had been founded on Humboldt Bay as a rowdy seaport for the shipping of lumber and gold. The sun was shining brightly, so it was hard to visualize a place so wet and dismal that Capt. Ulysses Grant had turned to whiskey and given up his officer's commission to return to Ohio.

He had spent the previous night in back of the new Yukon—paid for by Jamie Bourne, who owed that amount to Link for the lease of pastureland—rolled up snugly in his blanket. He'd been up at daylight, took a whore's bath in a public restroom, and drove on.

Link found himself thinking about Maggie Tatro, and how enjoyable it might have been if she'd come with him. He didn't like that he'd broken his word to her.

His denims were faded. The dusty "pewter" color of the vehicle was as neutral as he could ask for. Except for the fact that the Yukon was new, its appearance was unremarkable. The winch in front was recessed and hardly visible. For the third day, he had not shaved. Being half Blackfoot meant it came out more limp than stubbly, giving him a shady appearance. He'd noted the surprise reflected in Maggie's eyes when she'd examined him. As Erin had joked, he'd gotten a free, albeit unwanted, face-lift.

Link pressed FIND, then the LODGING button of the dash-mounted GPS. He found the listing for INN OF EUREKA, the same one—not considering the three times it had burned and been reconstructed—that Augustus Shepherd had been staying in when he was tossed out of the window by his killers, undoubtedly the Sociedad Serpiente.

According to his conversation with Squid, Dr. Dan Walsh was staying there, and he had been alerted that Link would drop by. There was also a professor of history from Berkeley who helped work on the document-recovery effort for Shepherd's Journal. Link was eager to join their search for the old encampment.

He turned right and followed the GPS's directions.

The Inn of Eureka rested on a knoll, surrounded by gardens. It appeared almost regal, painted a dark-yellow color with gargantuan cypress cross timbers. There were manicured lawns, shrubs, and blossoming rhododendrons, surrounding an ageless structure that put to shame the glitzy faux luxury chain hotels.

Link pulled in, idled past most of the vehicles, noting that the lot was almost empty, and parked. He was reaching into the canvas ID kit bag, picking the topmost packet, when a tall Asian man walked from the back of the hotel toward him, looking about and carrying a medium-size cardboard box. The Yukon's windows were dark-tinted. Damon Lee gave him not a glance before depositing his load in the rear of a Nissan Pathfinder parked in the adjacent space.

Lee started up and drove away, as if he had a reason to hurry. Link considered following him, then decided against it. Was Lee an FBI agent? It didn't match. Lee was impulsive, too much of an amateur—Link could tell just in the way he'd hustled out with the box and hastily left. Link's associates in the bureau were cool and capable, looking for long-term justice. Lee struck him as a sneak.

He got out of the Yukon and took along the duffel for appearance's sake.

The lobby was as impressive as the exterior, with redwood burl furnishings, thick carpeting, and piped, barely audible classical music. Link dropped his duffel before the desk and received a cool smile from a nicely dressed thirty-something woman who noted his worn denim clothing and weathered cowboy boots. A name tag identified her as the shift manager.

It was not a busy season. Aside from a couple of gentlemen who were seated in plush chairs reading their newspapers, the lavish vestibule was empty.

He pulled out a Montana driver's license, learned that his identity was George Washington Andrews, and remembered that Erin had a sense of humor. The shift manager asked if he had a reservation, and when he said he did not, she haughtily responded that they were full.

Yeah, right, he thought. He asked about a Dr. Daniel Walsh.

"He's no longer with us."

"Could you tell me when he checked out?"

"Are you a relative?"

"A business associate."

"Dr. Walsh and Dr. Shaw were involved in an automobile accident yesterday evening."

A bad feeling washed over Link.

"It happened on the coastal road north of Trinidad. The *Times-Standard* reported they went through a barrier and off a two-hundred-foot drop on the rocks below."

Another Weyland Foundation employee's death. While he did not remember meeting him (he'd worked for Erin in the Applied Technologies branch), Dan Walsh had been in Link's chain of employees, and his demise was altogether too convenient.

Who was behind their vehicle on the highway? Link wondered.

He told the manager that Daniel Walsh had a computer and some papers that belonged to their company. "Could they be in his room?"

"They should be. The police have it secured." She said a relative was driving up from Oakland to claim Dr. Shaw's belongings. The hotel management would like to clear the second room, as well, but they did not have a family contact.

"Maybe I can help." He jotted down his office phone number in New York, told her the vice president there was Walsh's employer. She could call collect.

"And you are?"

"Just tell them you're calling for the boss."

Wearing a dubious look, she entered the number. After ascertaining that the person on the other end of the line would accept the collect call from "the boss," she explained the sad news about Dr. Dan Walsh. After a moment she jotted down an address and phone number for Walsh's next of kin, and then, smiling for the very first time, handed the phone to Link.

"She'd like to speak with the boss." The manager walked away so he'd have privacy.

Mary Long was on the line. "This connection's clean on both ends. Sounds like you have bad news about Dan Walsh."

"I was looking forward to working with him. You know where I am?"

"The manager told me, and I've got you on caller ID. I also have a voiceprint match. We're paranoid as hell around here."

"That's a good way to stay." He glanced at the shift manager and decided she was out of earshot. "Could I speak with Squid?"

"Mr. Worsczejius is away. He said to tell you it has to do with his old occupation."

Away at a time like this? Something to do with his old occupation? It must be important.

"He checks in twice a day. Do you want me to give him a message?"

"Let me think on it. Is Helga getting better?"

"We're rebuilding her from the ground up. Major Stradley and her wizards helped us get started, but they had to return to D.C., and my people are doing a great job."

"Anything else?"

"Last night the terrorists contacted the financial board demanding money. Mr. Scott Cerone thought they should cooperate. The others tried to reach you first, but he convinced them it was the only way to save Frank and Erin's lives. At three a.m. they made a transfer of funds without letting anyone know, including us or the FBI."

Link's heart sank. "Tell me it didn't go through."

"After a dozen electronic shuffles, the money disappeared and the bad guys cut off all contact. Sort of like thumbing their noses."

The ransom had been their only remaining leverage. "How much?"

"Thirty million. The others have just unanimously asked Mr. Cerone to resign."

"The cows are already out of the barn." The Weyland Foundation was left with three on the financial committee. Less than a handful.

"Mary, I want you to check Cerone out all the way back to his baby roots. I doubt he's a spoiler, but odd things happen when big money's involved."

"I thought the handful were untouchables."

"Cerone's no longer one of them. See if Gordon Hightower will help."

"I doubt he'll talk to me. Hightower's high profile now. We see him on television, standing next to the attorney general. The handful tried to contact him about the kidnappings, and his office replied with a demand to know where you were."

"I'm pleased you're there, Mary." *Unlike Squid.*

"We keep plugging away, sir. Anything else?"

"Do you have Squid's location."

"All I can tell you is he bought an Air Canada ticket to Edmonton, and he was going to connect with another flight."

"So he's somewhere in Western Canada." It was an immense area. Link knew Squid had talked about a final exchange tour with the Canadian Navy back when he was a submariner.

"He said he contacted someone who may be able to provide answers, and he was excited about going, but he doesn't want him involved more than necessary. Mr. Worsczejius had some other good news. In a couple of days, one of the scientists in Habitat Earth may have answers on how the dead tide functions."

While it seems improbable, any progress is welcome.

"My name's George W. Andrews," he told Mary. "Could you talk the manager here into letting me into Dan Walsh's room?"

"Mmm. Can I tell her I'm an acting vice president?"

"Certainly. That's what you are."

"Then consider it done. Good talking with you, Boss."

Link called the manager over and handed her the telephone. He could hear Mary explaining her status as acting vice president and bullying the manager into granting permission for him to search Walsh's room for foundation's property. Her words rang the proper chimes; by the time she hung up, the manager was saying "yes, ma'am," and giving Link looks that indicated a turnaround in her perspective about his status.

"This way, Mr. Andrews." The manager acted like a private who had received an order from the first sergeant. She drew a key from the rack and led him upstairs to a well-appointed room. "Please feel free to take as long as you wish."

Walsh had been a tidy person, keeping his suits and hung-up clothing neatly arranged in the closet, his accessories in the proper drawers. There were no computers or professional papers—in fact, there was nothing at all either on or inside the desk.

Link picked up a page of bond paper from the trash can, a draft of a personal letter to Walsh's daughter that he'd edited by scratching through words. He'd obviously had a word processor and printer. Either he'd taken them or someone had removed them.

Someone like Damon Lee?

On their way back down, the manager remembered that she had rooms after all, and asked if he'd care to rent one. He declined. The place was not at all nondescript.

She said they had a wonderful lounge and dining room, perhaps he'd care to drop in after he was settled in wherever he was staying. She was obviously interested in persons that vice presidents of large foundations called boss.

"Maybe later," said Link.

"There's one more place to look for Mr. Walsh's possessions," she said. "We store valuables for guests at the desk."

She knelt behind the counter and dialed numbers into the safe there. When she opened it, she examined several different packets and compared the names and room numbers of guests. Finally she smiled, pulled out a plastic case containing a shiny DVD, and handed it over.

Link wondered if it was what he wanted: something that offered clues to where the old encampment might have been located. If he had gotten the clues right, his friends were being held there, in the Weeping Tree.

"Could I get your name for our safe log?"

"Certainly." George W. Andrews showed his driver's license and signed with a flourish.

21

Link let the Yukon idle through the streets, munching on a drive-through Big Mac, searching for charts of the area. He found a stationer and a maritime supply store and left with a dozen maps of differing scales, got back onto US 101, and drove south for twenty-five miles. There he turned onto a paved road, toward the smattering of towns on the north side of the rectangle that Walsh had drawn. If he was correct, somewhere in the hundred miles between here and Point Cabrillo lay whatever remained of the Serpientes' camp.

After a mile he came upon a Y. To his left was a nicely paved road bearing a tasteful sign: LENNVILLE—GATEWAY TO THE PAST. Three miles straight ahead was the community of FERNDALE, and its FINE RESTORED VICTORIAN HOMES. He remembered that twenty miles beyond Ferndale was the Pacific, where the road veered south to the coastal town of Capetown—at Cape Mendocino—and on to tiny Lisbon, which was on the Mateole River.

He continued toward Ferndale, hoping for a suitable, unobtrusive hotel or motel. A mile farther, he approached a homely two-story building that called out for paint, with a sign that declared it to be REBECCA'S BED & BREAKFAST RESORT. Another faded sign read VACANCY. He pulled in and parked between two pickups. The Yukon had attained a thick layer of fine, red dust, doing its part to be as unnoticeable a vehicle as those of lumbermen. His own appearance fit with those of the saw-mill workers and loggers who took rooms there.

The front door was locked, but inside a television was tuned to a soap opera. After five minutes of knocking, the volume was turned down and a middle-aged woman answered. She apologized, saying the guests usually went in the back way, and she hadn't expected him.

Rebecca's Resort was an old-fashioned boardinghouse that catered to the few remaining loggers and sawmill workers. In the common room were old sepia-tone photos of lumberjacks with two-man crosscut saws and sawmills with vast cold-decks—the yards where the logs were stored when first trucked in from woods operations. Her guests were a dying breed. The forests had receded, and environmentalists made the lumber businesses difficult and danger-ous by spiking trees with steel nails that could skewer a sawyer or edgerman, and restrictive. Only the massive con-glomerates prospered. Her boarders toiled in small, mostly failing sawmills that worked with fallen timber and culls.

When she realized he was interested in obtaining a room, Rebecca began her spiel. There were eight rooms; he had his choice of three that were empty. Overnight guests would be an additional twenty dollars. If a room lacked a necessity, take it from an empty one. Breakfast was provided if he signed up the day before. She'd pro-vide fresh linen on Thursdays, but no housekeeping. Link picked an upstairs room that was handy to the rear entrance, signed for a week's stay, and tried to pay using George W. Andrews's Visa. Rebecca did not take cards or checks. It was two hundred dollars cash up front.

Link hauled his two bags upstairs. He'd begin with the DVD and then prepare to search where Walsh and Shaw had left off. Time permitting, he'd take a drive around the area.

Following a shower, or whatever one called the experi-ence of a blistering hot trickle that periodically and with-out warning turned into a cold gusher, he pulled on jeans and a T-shirt and set up the laptop on the table. When he inserted the DVD, Link was pleased to find an index:

Executive Summary
Shepherd's Journal (11 pages)

Drake's Expedition (1583, British Admiralty)—S
California, Map of (1779, Spanish Expeditions)—S
Northern California, Map of (circa 1825, Mexican Republic)—S
California Coast, Charts of (1850)—S
Overland Expedition, Capt. Josiah Gregg (1850)—S
Northern California Goldfields, Map of (1852)—S
California, Shipping Losses, Unknown Causes, Map of (1840 to 1865)—?H
Northern California (circa 1855, State of California)—S / NH, A
Northern California, Survey Chart of (1880, State Geodetic Survey)—NH, A
Northern California, Survey Chart of (1900, U.S. Geodetic Survey)—NH, A
California Seismic Faults (2003, Univ. of California, Berkeley)—NH, A
Walking Surveys (Apr & May 2005, Drs. Walsh and Shaw)
(S: Serpiente)—(NH: Natural Hazard)—(??H: Unknown Hazard) (A: Avoid)

It was like wishing for a sip of water and being handed a fire hose. Link stared, wondering where to begin, and decided to do so from the top, as the doctors had undoubtedly intended.

He'd already perused through the first two documents. Shepherd's Journal and the summary provided insights into the past of the Sociedad Serpiente. He proceeded to the charts. Because of the varied years of their printing, they showed the expansion of human settlement. Link went through them all, trying to glean a sense of why those particular maps had been chosen. He noted yellow circles drawn by a highlighter pen.

Maps with an *S* suffix had yellow circles drawn about one or more warnings, such as: "Dangerous Outlaws," "Murderous Tribe," "Wild Savages," "Highwaymen," "Snake People," "Vishus Crimnals," "Serpientes," "Serpientes Negras," "Serpientes Oscuros," "Pirates," "Phantoms of the Sea," as well as skulls and crossbones, and squiggle symbols.

There'd surely been outlaw attacks nearer the goldfields, but Walsh and Shaw had picked only those shown north of San Francisco, most of them in the redwoods not far from the coast. Beside each annotation were the initials "DW" and "WS"—Dan Walsh and William (Bill) Shaw. Link assumed they had left their initials to vouch for the chart's authenticity.

The first chart, produced after Sir Francis Drake's return to England after terrorizing the Americas, showed an outline drawing of the chalk bluffs of Drake's Bay, and the position of the *Golden Hind* as it had been pulled onto the beach, the bottom scraped, the vessel retimbered and refurbished. To the north was a collection of squiggles, the early symbols used by the Snake People, and the printed words: "Fiere Ye Thees Fierse Men."

So similar to the admonishment to "Fiere the Trie."

The second map, printed after Father Serra's explorations, had been produced in Mexico City in 1779. In the uncharted region north and east of the Bay of San Francisco were the words "Sociedad de la Serpiente," symbols for six snakes, and the crossed bones of pirates.

The earliest explorers had known of the murderous Serpientes, just as Shepherd had written. On the remainder of the charts marked with an *S* were other estimated locations for the Serpientes, each differing from the last and the next.

Seismic and oceanic charts marked "NH-A" showed natural hazards to be avoided, such as treacherous waters, and confluences of fault lines, the most ominous lying only seven miles offshore. A few miles inland were annotations like the "Quaking Grounds," and "Liquid Earth." "Fracture Zone" and "Rifts" were shown on ocean floors. A maritime chart depicted coastal rock formations and shoals and eddies along the map's shoreline.

The nautical chart marked "??H" listed ships lost to unknown causes, and their last known positions. The most densely marked areas were off Point Arena, Point Cabrillo, and Cape Mendocino. Other dangers were a rock field and boiling water, located just south of Monterey Bay, but those were outside his rectangle.

Link decided that the maps collectively displayed the two doctors' best guesses as to where the Serpientes had lived and ruled the sea. Together they made a credible case that an organization (or organizations) called the Serpientes had existed.

Now came the bigger question—what had they become in the past 150 years?

Link then sorted through the current maps that he'd purchased. Several were of fine detail, showing such landmarks as buildings and minor trails, and he selected the best one to take along. Then he chose one of medium scale, on which he would lay out his routes of travel.

The redwood wilderness had stretched in a thick band from the Oregon state line down past Monterey to Big Sur. Urban sprawl had eliminated the southernmost portion as far north as Santa Rosa and Bodega Bay. The doctors had whittled it down farther yet.

On the medium-scale chart he outlined a fifty-by-one hundred-mile rectangle using a green marker. The encampment had likely been located within that five thousand square miles.

On the laptop he brought up the chart labeled *Walking Surveys (Apr & May 2005, Drs. Walsh and Shaw)*.

The doctors had started at a northernmost point near Trinidad and worked their way south, using a grid to cover every mile of observable territory, including improbable places as well as more likely ones.

Link did not have time to look everywhere. He had to forget the most improbable places. He began with the oldest charts on the DVD and moved forward in time to the modern ones, eliminating areas of human encroachment: settlements along roads and highways, sawmill towns, suburban sprawl creeping northward past San Rafael, Santa Rosa, Ukiah, and state parks and resorts.

The area left for him to search steadily diminished.

He wondered about the most hazardous area, the Quaking Grounds. There were no homes or communities, no access roads, and the latest maps warned of frequent tremors, falling branches, and uncharted chasms. Westward across Bull's Ridge there was no lagoon as Shepherd had described. Finally Link decided that if he finished without success and time remained, he'd pay a hasty visit to the place of quakes and liquefied earth.

He eliminated everything east of Highway 101—too far from the ocean.

In just twenty minutes, the area to search had been diminished by half.

He highlighted in red the zone that included the town of Leggett, once called Leggett's Valley, on the South Fork of the Eel River, where the survey crew had discovered Shepherd's Journal. Next came various uninhabited areas pocked with small valleys, places like Big Mountain, the southern portion of Bull's Ridge, Handy Woods, and King Mountain, until there were seven "hot" zones to explore, each about two hundred square miles.

In each hot zone he traced certain back roads and trails. Another man might feel cowed by the scope of his search. *Not me,* Link thought. *I'm just pigheaded.* He would have to hurry, drive what he could, and move along game trails at a brisk dogtrot.

He marked the hazardous zone in blue, denoting cold areas where he would look last.

Link folded the maps and stowed them in the canvas bag with the DVD. Tomorrow he'd be running, using routes that transected the hot zones to discover the Serpientes' old home.

Burnaby, British Columbia, Canada

Commander Billy was sixty-seven years of age, outspoken, and often angry, single all his life but periodically taking a female companion until she'd tire of his irritability and controlling nature. His card read William R. Hemby, Commander, Royal Canadian Navy, Ret., but the card was in error. There'd been no Royal Canadian Navy since 1968, when the Canadian Forces had been unified by act of Parliament. From then until 1985, when a less anti-military government was formed in Ottawa, the various services had endured the ignominy of wearing common green uniforms regardless of their branch. Like many who had served during that period, Billy would despise Prime Minister Pierre Trudeau—*that cow-*

*ard who fled the country in World War II so he wouldn't
have to serve!*—until he took his final breath.

Squid Worsczejius had spent an exchange tour with
the Canadian Maritime Command, stationed in
Nanaimo—directly across the sound and no more than
fifty miles from where he sat—working for Commander
Billy to construct a unique research vessel. Hemby was
the most intelligent naval officer Squid had known, a
walking encyclopedia of the sciences of watercraft design
and dynamics of the sea. He'd been denied further promotion because of his unwillingness to compromise with
desk-bound bureaucrats, which was why the two had tol-
erated one another, regardless if Commander Billy dis-
dainfully called Americans "you alls," and Squid
referred to Canada as America's "backward state."

Squid had described his problems in detail over the
telephone, keeping very little back from his old mentor.
He had expected incredulity, but not only had Commander Billy taken him seriously, he had also become
excited and ordered Squid to get his arse to Burnaby
without delay. When Squid had arrived the previous evening, Commander Billy had tersely called out for him to
enter his home office, walls covered with photos of ships
and boats that he had commanded or designed. Included
was the *CNR-2* research submarine, on which Squid had
spent three years of his life, the Canadian maple leaf
flying proudly from the bridge.

For the next hour the retired Canadian officer had
told Squid to go over it all again. After dragging out
every minor detail, Commander Billy demanded to
speak with the scientist who *thought* she could learn the
secrets of the *marea muerta*. After due hesitation, Squid
phoned Habitat Earth, introduced Dr. Virginia Miller,
and tried not to act as if he was listening to their conversation.

Commander Billy took command, chiding with Virginia that she was dealing with a long list of variables
to re-create even the simplest of two-way tidal phenomena, and a longer list if they were to flow in opposite
directions alongside one another.

Squid felt uneasy as the commander continued to
speak as if Dr. Miller were a third grader and not a

gifted scientist. *Do I do that?* he wondered as he listened.

The commander spoke rapidly, taking no brook and no questions: "The Pacific is particularly turbulent along that portion of the coast, where two major sea rivers run in their separate paths, colliding here and there. One sweeps past the glacial ice in southern Alaska and British Columbia. The median temperature of the Canadian current is ten degrees Celsius in the winter and only a few degrees warmer in the summer. The other river, erroneously called the Japanese Current, reaches—"

"I know all that," Virginia Miller finally interrupted. Squid was surprised at the strength in her voice. Following another rebuke by Billy, she claimed to have received an important call, and disconnected.

Billy's face grew cloudy. "The woman hung up on me!"

Squid waited until Billy's ranting was over. "What vessel would they choose," he said. "You have an idea. Otherwise, I'm wasting my time." When Commander Billy failed to respond, Squid went on. "That's why you've been making the phone calls, to see if one's been available that the terrorists could have gotten their hands on."

Commander Billy smiled. "One of what, may I ask?"

"Some sort of submarine? That's all I've been able to come up with, but—"

The doorbell rang. This time the commander hurried out to greet his visitor. He returned with a short, quick man he introduced as "a friend," although his guest did not act as such.

"Before we begin, get us all a Blue, Mr. Worsczejius?"

"None for me," said the newly arrived "friend."

Squid retrieved a single Molson, twisted off the cap, and handed it over. Commander Billy took a healthy drink and sighed happily. "Now tell us about the *Sinner*, Mr. Worsczejius. I'd like my friend to hear it in your words, how it began and what I built."

It seemed an odd request, but Squid saw no harm in it.

In the U.S. Navy he had been assigned to a very different kind of submarine, Squid explained. The *NR-1* was a deep diver: 150 feet long, weighed four hundred tons, carried five crew and two scientists, and could putt along forever at four knots, since it had both a nuke reactor and a battery-driven turbo-alternator. If the terrain allowed, it could crawl around the bottom ad nauseam on extendable wheels. For twenty-five years the *NR-1* was hauled by its tender vessel to sites of various crashes and disasters, submerged for as long as it took, and used a retriever claw to salvage critical—often classified—weapons and components.

In 1995, the Canadians needed the kind of marine research capability the *NR-1* offered, and even came up with the bucks to build one, as long as it was done on the cheap.

Petty Officer Squid had been sent, along with a lieutenant, on an exchange tour with the Canadian Forces, Maritime Command, to help the Canucks plan and build a deep submergence research craft for themselves. They called it the *CNR-2* project, but the worker bees called it the *Sinner Two*, which became just *Sinner*.

They'd started with the *NR-1* blueprint and reduced it by sixty tons and twenty feet by doing away with the nuke reactor. The *NR-1*'s mini-reactor had allowed them to stay down long enough to get the big jobs done. Nothing else in the world could do that. Commander Hemby had retained the extendable wheels and the retriever arm, and fattened it from twelve to thirteen feet so they could haul more research gear, which also meant the craft required more air handling and electrical demands.

The friend interrupted. "So the basic design was faulty?"

Commander Billy didn't respond, just took another swig of beer and waited.

The weight they'd saved by eliminating the mini-reactor had been added back on by the extra batteries required. Time on bottom became a crucial factor. The *NR-1* could stay down for days, but on paper the *Sinner* could only operate free of the tender vessel for three hours. Figure an hour going and another coming, and it got dicey.

"So it didn't work?" asked the friend, although Squid felt he knew the answer.

The *Sinner had* worked, because Commander Billy

knew how to build boats and how to compromise. He'd added a lightweight thirty-kilometer titanium-reinforced tether from the control vessel to augment air flow and electrical power. If it broke, which was unlikely, they'd have a full charge to immediately maneuver to the surface. Four years after the project started, they'd tested it in a trench off of Vancouver Island, and the *Sinner* operated better than they'd dreamed. It dived to 1,500 feet, first with a test crew, then with eight people aboard. Commander Billy had taken videos and recorder data and sent them to their headquarters at Halifax with a message that they were ready for operations. They'd cheered and celebrated, and awaited the answer.

Shortly after, when the commander was summarily relieved and the project canceled, Squid and the lieutenant had folded their tent and returned to the States.

"It was a real bummer," said Squid. "Six months later I got out of the navy."

Commander Hemby took over. "The *Sinner* worked superbly. It was rugged, safe, and inexpensive to operate, and we had requests from several universities for research projects. All expenses would be recovered within a couple of years."

"But you were relieved, and the project was canceled. Do you have any idea why?"

"Someone lobbied very persuasively against it and convinced the Minister of Defence that the project should be abandoned. It was obvious that they wanted the *Sinner* for another purpose. When Mr. Worsczejius called, asking me about a rugged underwater craft to be used by terrorists, I wondered if we had a match. Especially since it's disappeared."

The *Sinner* was missing, just as Squid had suspected. He almost missed seeing the "friend" remove a recorder from his pocket to check the battery level.

"When are you leaving?" the friend asked Squid.

"Tomorrow afternoon."

"I'd like to meet with both of you gentlemen at our Vancouver office at nine thirty in the morning." He doled out business cards, reading Solicitor General of Canada, RCMP, Chief Marine Investigator, Inspector Ray Cunningham.

"Ask for directions to my office, and *please* be on time."

"We will," grumbled Commander Billy. "I've waited for the past four years!"

Cunningham said, "I doubt very much that you'll be pleased with what we have to say."

4:30 p.m.—Lennville, California

Link drove through Lennville then Ferndale. Both towns featured a number of mid–nineteenth century Victorians, and he saw no residual damage from the seven-point-two earthquake they'd suffered fifteen years earlier. Lennville was the wealthier of the two, obvious from the way the communities' infrastructures were supported—rather than rely on county deputies in rattletrap Chevies, Lennville had its own police department and several late-model Crown Vick cruisers; its volunteer fire department had a new pumper-tanker and a ladder truck to handle the two-story homes. Other than those observations, there was nothing of note.

He continued past Ferndale toward the Pacific on a road that turned to gravel. After wending through a series of rolling hills, he passed a small herd of Herefords, then crested a rise. Blue stretched before him. The day was sunny, kept brisk by the gusty wind, and he wondered why Ulysses Grant had written to his wife that it was such a dismal place. A few miles farther, he passed a fenced government installation and a sign identifying the coast guard detachment. Two coastal radars were sited atop a promontory, one to keep track of aircraft, the other one surface vessels, and a pair of rescue helicopters rested on alert pads.

He pulled over to watch the spectacular sunset.

Tomorrow he would begin his search.

22

The previous evening Link had returned to the room, shucked off his clothing, rolled out in his blanket on top of the bed, and slept hard until the images of his dead employees came to haunt him. He was later awakened by nightmares of Frank Dubois and Erin wrapped in logging chains.

It was now almost daybreak. After pulling on sweats, running shoes, and headband, Link finished his warm-up exercises, then went downstairs and out, ran the uphill mile back to the road intersection, and coasted back down. His legs would get more mileage as the day wore on, but the morning ritual stretched the long muscles of his body and prepared him for the day.

Link showered under the icy trickle and toweled off, feeling grubby about not shaving. He put on fresh denims and the comfortable-as-glove-leather boots, and felt he was close to his goal of inconspicuousness.

From the moment he had awakened he'd been sure that he was doing the right thing. The puzzle pieces were falling together. The video from Aozou had forecast the attack by Ahmed bin Polah. Link's men and Gwen and now Dr. Dan Walsh had been murdered. Hateful warnings for Link Anderson.

Who could hate me so much? The smart person?

The Weyland Foundation had been smeared then attacked by the Hezbollah. They despised Americans.

They were Sajacento's and the Serpientes' kind of people. The attack at the Weyland Building had nothing to
do with the Foundation or Hezbollah. The smart person
had stopped the Shepherd's Journal project, and any
chance of getting more proof that the Serpientes existed.
Sajacento's swarms of martyr bees would try to destroy
America's future, and must be stopped.

An answer had come to him during the night. Frank
had blinked his code, signaling Link from the Weeping
Tree. Then he'd added the letter *A*, followed by nine
blinks. "A-9."

Anyone could say a prayer and blindly go to his death,
but it took more ingenuity to build a bomb. The chemists of Alpha Nine were there with Frank and Erin.

As Erin had said, it all fit together, but he would have
to find convincing proof.

If Gordon was right, Link was three thousand miles
off track. He had his agents deployed in Georgia, and
Link could do little to help. But Gordon was *not* right.
The Serpientes were here, and Sajacento and his Hezbollah *jahids* would be coming to be outfitted by the
bomb makers.

Still, the puzzle remained unsolved. A key piece was
still missing.

Link reexamined the seven critical "hot zones." He
placed the big revolver and its tie-down holster, charts,
and the devices Erin had sent into a small olive-drab
pack, and took it along.

He stopped at a service station in Fortuna, topped off
the tank and filled the five-gallon jugs. He loaded up on
snacks, with high sugar content, since he would be burning a lot of calories.

Link passed through Scotia, then Redcrest. At Garberville, he purchased a medium-size McCullough chain-
saw from a clerk who was just opening her store. Five
miles farther, he stopped for a quick breakfast at a resort
called Benbow Inn, not taking time to enjoy the scenic
drive. To him, the stately giant redwoods were obstacles,
keeping him from using an airplane to narrow his search.
He continued through stands of them, the sunlight flick-
ering like lamplights being switched off and on, as he

crossed into Mendocino County, and passed more road-side tourist stops. At Confusion Hill, large signs claimed that gravity failed.

He slowed and turned onto California State Highway 1 at Leggett, not far from where the Shepherd Journal had been discovered. He did not yet have a sense of how long his searches might take. The disastrous expedition led by Capt. Josiah Gregg in 1850 had been treacherous and slow, but he reasoned that there were old logging roads and trails, and he had both a vehicle-mounted and handheld GPS. Without them navigation would be impossible. The trees were nearer the road here and seemed more immense.

Four miles farther, he turned onto a long-unused dirt logging road shown on a topographical chart. After fifty yards, a steel gate blocked his path. A warning sign erected by a lumber conglomerate, proclaimed no trespassing. After ensuring he was alone, Link got out and examined the gate that was secured by chains and lock. He ran out the winch line and pulled the gate off its hinges.

Maggie Tatro once said that when Link was on a mission he was not going to be stopped by anything, including reason. She'd said it at a time when their relationship was disconnecting, and had not meant it as a compliment.

After securing the winch line and driving through, he propped the gate in place and went on.

Seven miles farther, he halted for a fallen tree that was not to be moved by anything he carried. He took the handheld Garmin GPS, pulled on pistol and backpack, and set out on foot.

Link had run for an hour and fifteen minutes when he approached a valley and heard a male voice. He slowed but went on, pleased at the way the forest giants soaked up sound like a sponge. He came upon a hut, remembering the insane sentinel mentioned by Shepherd. The voice began to chant, rapping out a song that Link did not know.

Link froze then as a wraith-thin woman came into the small clearing before him. "You've got a voice like a billy goat," she called out, still walking toward Link. She stopped and called again, but her voice was drowned out by louder singing. She turned and shouted. "You checked 'em. I'm ready to go back. This place is spooky, and I keep thinkin' of what happened to Augie."

The singing stopped. "We don't know what happened to Augie, except he wanted to go where nature never intended anyone to go and didn't come back."

It sounded as if the speaker was coming ever closer to Link.

"Think someone caught him?"

"Augie's too cool for that."

"How's the shit?" she asked.

"Growin' like weeds." He laughed at his words. "Two weeks, and it'll be ready. Then we'll stay until we're done. We'll have enough shit for four trips. That's the dangerous time. You get caught looking, no one can blame you for screw-all. Get caught haulin' and it's your ass."

A dog yapped, and Link fought the urge to stiffen. The girl was looking directly at him but not putting together the realization that a human being was six feet away, motionless as a statue.

Be a part of your surroundings. Be a fern or a stone or a tree.

The dog barked more shrilly. "Give Molly a treat," the girl called. "She's hungry."

"She ain't nothin' but a hound dog," he sang, complementing the dog's noisy yapping.

When the girl turned to yell again, Link disappeared. He circled them, smelled the cannabis they lit up. Heard Molly growling and then snacking on some treats. Heard that Augie might have ran into some wild animal, because it was not likely that a Fed could be slick enough to take him in. Maybe a bear. The girl was frightened. Molly yelped. The punk listened to an announcement over his two-way radio by someone named Craig that it was going to be a bad night at Big Daddy's. Feds were plannin' to be out, and they'd have night vision.

There were no big trees that leaned. No words stained into one of them. No bloodred stone. Link took a look at the GPS. One more waypoint on this loop. He went on, wary of more punks out to check on a crop. At noon he emerged at the Yukon, turned it around, and departed, wearily anticipating the next long run.

The second loop was as promising as the first, but was also in vain. There was no Weeping Tree, just more punks growing Mendocino gold. Enough were armed to make Link hope they knew how to use their weapons well enough not to be dangerous. He got his answer when a pot farmer fired shots at imagined sounds, wielding an Uzi knock-off set to AUTO-FULL, rattling off a dozen rounds before the Brazilian-built weapon jammed. When he left, the punk was spooked by other phantom noises, working frantically to clear the weapon.

9:30 a.m.—Vancouver, British Columbia

The sign on the door read MARINE INVESTIGATIONS. Inside, Ray Cunningham waited as Com. Billy Hemby and Squid were shown in. When a second plainclothes RCMP investigator was introduced as Cunningham's supervisor, the retired commander ignored him, took his seat, and spoke abruptly. "My time is limited. Just as I've repeatedly asked since 2002, where the hell is the *Sinner*?"

The supervisor, frowning at the display of rudeness, tossed a two-inch-thick file onto the desktop. "We have your queries. All thirty-nine of them. We also have our responses."

"You mean your excuses saying you're looking into the matter. My question remains." He raised his voice. "Where in God's name is my boat?"

The inspector leaned forward, smiling without humor. "To clarify a point, it has never been *your* boat, Commander. After your *removal* from the development project, the Maritime Command changed the craft to nonready status and declared it unsafe."

"It was never unsafe. I would never endanger my crew if it were. Now I am asking as a citizen of Canada, where is it?"

"It's very probably part of a reef somewhere in South America."

The commander looked stunned, and the supervisor's smile widened all too sweetly for Squid's liking. The two men disliked one another, but the supervisor's tone was insulting.

"Six months after the craft was declared unsafe, the MOD released the *CNR-2* to the Port of Vancouver for disposal, with the provision that it be disabled in such a manner that it could never be used again. What *happened*, Commander Hemby, was they cut a nasty hole in her bottom and sold the shebang, tender vessel included, as salvage to a maritime services company. Since then, we've heard that she was sold for scrap to a firm in Venezuela. I doubt very much that even terrorists have use for scrap metal."

Commander Billy looked miserable. "Why has it taken so bloody long to give me the courtesy of an answer?"

"In 1981," said the supervisor, "following the *Parti Quebecois* scandal, you may recall that heads rolled, and the RCMP was prohibited from domestic intelligence matters. Since I value my own head, and a Canadian firm was involved, I ordered Cunningham to wait." He looked at his watch and rose. "Sorry. Meetings, you know."

Cunningham rose dutifully as his supervisor departed.

Commander Billy shook his head sadly. "So the *CNR-2* was scuttled?"

"So it *appears*." The RCMP Inspector emphasized the last word. When Hemby did not take note, he turned to Squid, who gave an imperceptible nod, wondering.

"Well, damn!" said the retired naval officer, lost in his brooding.

Inspector Cunningham continued to regard Squid. "My reason for taking up the matter was that I'd served a tour in the Canadian Navy. Commander Billy was an icon for refusing to bend over for the military bashers, and we have a great number of those. I was damned upset yesterday when I saw him sucking from that bloody bottle."

Hemby was still tuned elsewhere.

"Same here," said Squid.

Cunningham went on. "The maritime services company that bought the *CNR-2* was Z-H Limited in North Vancouver. Since then she was sold for scrap to their parent company, Zerbini Holdings, in San Francisco, and then, on paper at least, to a firm in Venezuela."

The RCMP Inspector rose to his feet. "Thank you for coming, gentlemen."

Outside, Commander Billy remained unsteady and sour. He asked if Squid needed a ride to the airport, which was obvious since his clothes were in his backseat. Squid removed his bag and said he'd take a taxi.

He noted the names of the salvage companies involved. He would check out the local one, although he doubted it would lead anywhere, and then fly to San Francisco for a harder look at Zerbini Holdings, and perhaps their company records regarding the *CNR-2 Sinner*.

In the taxi he made a cell call to Mary Long. While he digested the terrible news about Dan Walsh's death, she said that Virginia Miller was about to complete her model of the dead tide. He asked her to make sure the data was sent to him, and not Commander Billy.

Laytonville, California

Link drove into the sawmill and ranching hamlet located on US 101, and ate at a restaurant located in a clapboard hotel. The food was marginally better than his mood.

He'd driven or run forty-five miles of off-road wilderness, and eliminated that red zone from contention. The search was slow going, and at this pace, the Weeping Tree would be found on the twentieth day, after Sajacento sent out his swarm. There were not enough hours in a day, so he decided to search through the nights, as well, and to catnap in the Yukon.

Night descended as he drove north toward the first hot zone, which was also the smallest, since he'd delayed inspecting the quaking grounds. In Garberville, he gassed up and bought more munchies, studied the map for references, replaced the batteries in the handheld

GPS, and selected Trip 1. Finally he pulled out the IR night-vision scope and illuminator.

As he drove to nearby Redway and continued past several resorts and RV parks, he was cast into inky darkness, the only illumination that of the headlamps. He continued past Briceland, then Whitethorn, and five miles farther slowed until the Yukon crept forward. He found an unimproved road shown only on the most detailed topographical map.

After half a mile, the road became clogged with pine branches. As he removed them, Link thought about the horror photos that had been sent to his cabin by someone who knew his address. The first, showing Sajacento and the beheaded men, had read, *Meet the Judge of Men*, and the second, *This is how I deal with your traitorous spies.*

What if there were two of them? Sajacento called himself the judge of men, but perhaps it was another who bragged about dealing with Link's spies. A Serpiente?

That message and all the rest were signed *S.* Erin and Frank had been branded with that initial, which they'd believed was for Sajacento. *How about "Serpiente"?*

That did not seem quite right either. The message sender was too egotistical to sign as a part of a group. It would be more like him to use his own initial, especially if it were the same.

Link could not come up with anyone whose name began with an *S*, and who would hate him so, except a few who were already dead.

Who was *S*, the slightly-built third person on the platform in Aozou? The one who was with Sajacento at the lakebed? Perhaps he had posed as the female driver of the automobile that Ahmed had climbed out of in New York?

All of those had triggered a sense of distinct familiarity.

He needed to talk it out with someone. Erin would be his first choice.

The next obstacle was a fallen pine tree. The detailed map showed nearby buildings, and the chain saw was loud, so he went slowly on by foot, for the forest was too dark to navigate using ambient light. He tried using an LED flashlight that Erin had included. All the while, his mind was busy with possibilities.

When he approached the first valley, he put away the light and changed to the IR illuminator and scope. The living things about him were displayed in bright green.

Farther ahead, a cougar stared inquisitively, as if wondering whether to try for a large dinner. The big cat decided he wasn't worth the trouble and padded off the path, soundless.

He stopped at the sound of a noise and peered through the night scope. A family of raccoons scampered across the path before him.

One thing was better about the night operation; he encountered no pot farmers toting weapons they did not know how to handle.

He came to the rim of the small valley and stood surveying for a while, thinking it was not quite right. There were no redwoods, only firs.

Link checked the GPS. He was at the north side of a valley, and although it was not promising, he decided to check it and not worry later that he'd missed something.

He'd found a game trail that made things easier, when he heard a metal-on-metal sound and froze. He'd been like that for more than a minute when he heard it again. *Click.*

Link could think of no natural explanation for what he'd heard, yet it seemed odd that he'd encounter a human in near-total darkness.

After a minute's wait, he eased the IR scope up and pressed the illuminator button.

The world came ablaze with infrared light, creating such a flood of bright green that he was momentarily blinded.

"FBI! Do not move!" came a booming voice. "And you make sure as hell you keep your hand away from your weapon."

Still looking through the scope, Link found himself confronted by six black-clad people wearing military night goggles.

Link raised his hands, which was the most prudent thing he could think of doing.

"How do you do?" he asked, and tried smiling.

23

Maggie was in the shower, well-lathered in outrageously expensive glycerine soap, her skin receiving the nourishment of two proteins that had been found in genetic studies to be critical to the development of the flawless skin of infants. The treatment involved sudsing up, turning off the water, and standing still with arms extended and foamy suds running down one's body for five minutes.

She had been at it for two minutes and had succeeded in hardly moving when the phone, which she had left in her bedroom, rang. From the tone of the warble, it was her official bureau line. During the fervor of a mad democratic moment—probably Flag Day or J. Edgar's birthday—she'd agreed to take her turn with her subordinate agents answering calls that were important enough to be booted up to human response level.

The phone warbled again.

The special soap had cost an extravagant amount of money, well beyond the reach of a career woman seriously trying to save for a fun-filled spinsterhood. The thought of her rhinolike epidermis and the way she could feel the tingling as it was transformed into baby skin made her pause longer.

After the fourth ring, the phone grew quiet. There was no answering machine on that line. If it was important, they'd start over and go through the seven steps that guarded her from receiving frivolous calls. She watched the second hand of the bathroom wall clock sweeping past three minutes. Two to go. The directions were emphatic about maintaining a five-minute timing.

She was the Assistant Special Agent In Charge of the Industrial Espionage Department, and had visions of foreigners invading one of their high-tech businesses to steal plans for the next generation of computer chips or robot vacuum cleaners. She was also on the softball team, and an augmentee on the special weapons and tactics team, and the call could be from either of those organizations.

She weighed it all carefully, thought at length of duty and honor, and decided that having the wonderful, poreless skin found on a baby's tummy was more important. *Just five frigging minutes. That's all.*

The telephone sounded again, shriller now, meaning it was her unlisted personal number, known to only six persons in the world, two of those being the Director in Charge of West Coast operations, and the SAC to whom she reported.

Three minutes and forty seconds had passed when she climbed out of the shower stall and stalked into the bedroom, dripping expensive suds on her new lilac-colored carpet, and answered. "Special Agent Tatro."

"I've got a slight problem."

She frowned. "Who is this?"

"Link. I've been picked up by the ATF."

"Good for them." She hung up and stalked back to her shower, arms held out like those of a scarecrow. While she was rinsing away the residue, her personal phone rang again. She shut off the water and was toweling off when the recorder picked up.

An unfamiliar man's voice: "ASAC Tatro? This is Special Agent In Charge Rogers with the ATF. Our special unit picked up a guy next to a weed patch about four hours ago. He had night-vision gear and a GPS, and he was packing a revolver. He's carrying ID as George Washington Andrews, and says you can clear it up. I'll try—"

She walked over and picked up the receiver, glaring at the mess on the floor, and introduced herself and said she'd never heard of anyone with the name of George Washington Andrews.

"I thought he might be a ringer, but it seemed odd that he'd have your name and phone numbers memorized."

Link has my phone numbers memorized? Despite herself, Maggie felt an old warmth rise.

"Let me talk with him again. Use a secure line, okay?"

"We're on a joint field operation, using space provided by the sheriff's department in Eureka, and I can't guarantee anything's secure."

"I'll talk with him anyway."

"Maggie?" Link's voice, this time not as sure of himself.

"Have I told you lately that you're a son of a bitch?" She went on, depleting her knowledge of descriptive curse words. Eventually she had to pause to catch her breath.

"I'm guilty of all of those. Just get me out of this mess. It's important."

"So was Stanley's career before I wrote the letter of reprimand." She pulled a khaki-colored microfiber blouse and matching slacks from the field uniform side of the closet.

"I won't do it again. Promise."

She liked the way he groveled. "I've been through all your promises. I trusted you again, and you took advantage." To the stack she added a pair of Levi's jeans, a Lee shirt with white snaps, a couple of cotton sports bras and lady's underwear, aiming for comfort.

"Maggie, would you please think about what I'm doing. Who I'm doing it for? I'm positive now that Gordon's wrong. They're here."

"Who's there?"

As he paused, then muttered excuses for not being able to say more, she pulled a gym bag from her closet, already packed with tactical gear that included a Kimber Custom III .45 auto.

Her weapon of choice was a diminutive H&K P-2000 .40-caliber automatic that she carried concealed, either in the small of her back or, if wearing a jacket, in an elastic pocket under her left arm. There was also a two-shot .32-caliber derringer in her purse.

Maggie pulled out the armored vest and in its place added her selection of clothing.

"Let me talk to Rogers."

A few seconds later: "Rogers here. You know this guy?"

"Have you got enough to charge him?"

"Naw. We've got nothing tying him to the weed patch except the fact that he was there, and in California who'd care? We might try obstruction since he almost walked away a couple of times, but it wouldn't work. Someone may want to prosecute for trespassing, but I doubt it."

Maggie was pleased that she didn't have to go toe to toe with the ATF. "How about a favor? Hold him and make sure he doesn't go anywhere until I can get there."

"With pleasure, but let me warn you. He's not cooperative."

"Tell me about it."

After contacting her boss and telling him she'd be out of the office for a few days, Maggie tried to phone ADIC Gordon Hightower but was unable to get through.

Gordon was getting to be big-time, working out of Washington, running his horde of agents and trying to locate the hostages, briefing people up to and including the president. His effort was integrated with those of the TTIC, Homeland Security, and the deputy director, who concentrated on ferreting out al Qaeda and the Hezbollah.

The public was aware of him. Gordon was the one at the press conferences looking grave but competent. He'd been present when the Secretary of Homeland Defense had raised the terrorism indicator from Elevated to High, and "urban large building security" to Extreme.

When Maggie had told him about Link's concern regarding sending another swarm of agents to muddle things up, he had said he was worried about Link's mental stability. He knew what Link thought was going on in California and told her some of it. She'd had to agree that it sounded goofy. His concern was that Link would interfere in Georgia, where the search was ever hotter, or make more headlines that confused the issue.

She agreed to help. If the disaster was averted, Hightower would likely be the next FBI director and take along his best agents.

Maggie talked with Gordon's voice mail, told him about the call from Link and how she intended to handle it. If Link made the slightest move toward Georgia, she'd stop him.

Maggie next called Special Agent Goldstein at the office and told him to request air travel to Eureka for them both, and pack his Boy Scout gear just in case. She had not officially reprimanded Stanley, just chewed his ass until he knew how fortunate he'd been to have it happen with Link and not some bad guy who would have *really* terminated his career.

Link was on a mission. His closest friends were in jeopardy. She sympathized.

Maggie washed her hair and blow-dried it as she pulled out hiking boots and a pair of comfortable shoes. She dressed casually, first pulling on a turquoise top and skirt, changing it for a yellow outfit, then nice chocolate brown skirt and lightweight forest green sweater that complemented her eyes. She added just enough highlight to show off her eyes.

Anger flickered. She stopped and looked at the mirror at what she was doing. Preparing like a harlot for a man she'd given up on five years ago, who had called her a total of six times during that entire time, three of those to ask for favors, such as to look up this person or that.

Maggie had phoned Link the same number of times, but that had been a matter of pride, so she wouldn't appear to be asking for another chance, which she would never do, when the fool should have been crawling back to her on hands and knees. Look at what had happened when she'd trusted him with just one small thing—he had humiliated poor Stanley on his first mission when he hadn't known his ass from his elbow.

Thanks a lot, Link Anderson. You can go straight to hell. With that she messed up her hair with both hands, working at getting it to fly this way and that.

Bastard. Link was on his way down the tubes, and she refused to help.

Maggie would fly up to Eureka and get him out of trouble with the ATF show him how easily that could be done by someone in her position—and when he asked her to dinner for her efforts, she'd tell him sorry, she had other things to do.

Tell him she had another date?

No, just something like, "Sorry, I'm busy and I have to go back."

She would make sure he didn't interfere in Gordon's effort.

Stanley Goldstein called. One of the Lears was available, already booked for a flight to Eureka by a Circuit Court judge. They would be traveling in style, not in tourist class in a cramped commuter. He offered to pick her up in front of her apartment in an hour, which would give them another hour to get to SFO General Aviation.

"I'll see you in front," she said.

As she waited, she pulled paperwork from her Coach briefcase, which she remembered had been a present from Link. Same with the pearl earrings she wore. Ditto the H&K in her shoulder holster, because he'd felt it was more reliable than the small revolver she'd carried.

A few minutes later, she put the paperwork away and placed the briefcase next to the bedside table, her mind jumbled with ugly thoughts about Link Anderson. She decided to keep a comb and brush and spray bottle of fritz out so she could redo her hair on the flight.

9:10 a.m. The Weeping Tree

Erin was coming around, despite spending the three days without water or sustenance, during which time she'd been forced to invade, compromise, and gut several of the largest, fastest, and most capable computer servers in the world.

Her final victim had been the three-terabyte server at Berkeley that had been used, among other important projects, to parallel and back up the restoration effort for Shepherd's Journal.

She and Frank had been drinking the condensation that ran in copious amounts off the big tree each morning, cupping their chained hands to capture the trickles of water. The redwoods were so immense that the morning fog gathered in the treetops and ran down the three-hundred-foot length of bark and branches in creeklets. They'd also caught insects and frogs and anything else that might be edible, and eaten them ravenously.

This morning was different. There were visitors. In this first shipment were four *jahid,* who would each be fitted with a bomb—at the safe houses they would join four other Hezbollah who would press the button at just the right moment, eliminating the problem they'd had with bin Polah. The martyrs spoke in Arabic, nervous chatterboxes who boasted and bolstered one another's courage for what would happen six days hence. They likely did not suspect that the miserable creatures peering from behind the maze of great roots with burning red eyes, understood their words. Likely none of them cared.

Kamil, the Hezbollah pilot, was there to receive the arrivals, greeting them in the name of the Party of God. He had returned from Montana, where he'd been sent to assist Damon Lee in bringing back Lincoln Anderson. By then, Anderson had disappeared.

Since then, Damon Lee had been relegated to minor tasks, such as acting as chauffeur.

Erin knew those things because the Serpientes had come to the Weeping Tree daily to prepare for their clients, and they spoke openly, as if Frank and Erin did not exist, or were already dead. Now all of them except for El Jefe were present for the arrival of the first *jahid.*

To continue to attempt to escape seemed futile. The previous day, Chief Welk had wrapped them more securely in the heavy logging chains and added a second sturdy padlock. He'd finally boarded up the cavern's entrance with two-by-sixes nailed securely in place.

In their presence, Peter Zerbini had asked Chief Welk what was to be done about the hostages if Sydney was unable to find Anderson for her revenge game. The chief had matter-of-factly answered that he'd let the sentinel shoot them.

After drinking the morning condensation and devouring a frog that they greedily tore apart, the captives whispered about the *jahid* bombers and where they would be sent "to destroy America's future." Frank believed they would attack western universities like Santa

Clara, Cal Berkeley, and Cal Tech, where great technical minds were gathered.

They were dismayed at how little time was left. The first of the *jahids* would be fitted with bombs and sent out on Aozou plus sixteen—just four more days. They'd be hidden in safe houses prepared by the Serpientes, located close to their individual targets, where they would remain until the morning of Aozou plus twenty, when Sajacento had promised death and destruction.

Only minutes before, as Frank had listened at the other side of the chamber, Erin had overheard the location of a safe house. Zerbini said he had visited the one in Menlo Park and found a lemon tree in the side yard that grew savory fruit. The *jahid* who would go there, a young woman, said she enjoyed ripened lemons. She spoke wistfully, as if sad, but it was not due to her deadly task, for she'd periodically spewed venomous hatred for Americans.

Erin repeated the location of the safe house to herself, and decided that Frank was correct. Menlo Park was adjacent to Stanford University, which was known for its openness to the public and for the colleges that had nurtured many of America's greatest minds. She told Frank what she'd heard.

"Memorize everything for when we escape," Frank repeated.

During the night they'd worked industriously, twisting the heavier chains and trying to break them, and straining in vain attempts to open the padlocks. Both finally determined that their best bet was to spend their energy on wearing down the most vulnerable links.

The chains were old and fashioned of iron, and while they were heavy and seemingly sturdy, they were pitted and scaled with rust. Some were worse than others. While there were few rocks in the cave, they discovered a few large flat stones embedded in the dirt floor. They dug them loose with sore and bloody fingers and deposited them in a meager pile that was hidden from the view of observers. Then they doggedly used them to work at the rustiest links.

One hundred and fifty years earlier, Augustus Shepherd had carved a key for his lock from ironwood, and during the confusion of a major earthquake had crept out of the Weeping Tree and escaped. There was no time to find ironwood and nothing to carve it with, but the rusted condition of the old chains might be the key to their survival.

There were the usual tremors, and each time the earth shook, the new arrivals looked about with wide, fearful eyes. One remarked that he would be pleased to get on with their task, and not be a victim of the earth opening to swallow them, or a giant branch falling on them.

As the Serpientes spoke about what they'd do next, Frank and Erin continued to listen and surreptitiously rub the rustiest links against flat stones, each stroke scraping away tiny portions of oxidized metal.

Erin repeated what she'd said the previous night. "When we escape, I'm not sure I can walk far. You should eat everything we find, Frank. Once we get free, you'll get farther." He answered in the same words as before. "We'll divide equally. If we escape, we stay together."

1:20 p.m.—Eureka Airport, North of Eureka, California

Judge Lyle S. Bull deplaned from the U.S. government–owned Learjet 35, appreciating the comfort of the ride. He preferred his private jet, a Cessna Citation, but much of that was because he enjoyed piloting it and making the decisions of flight.

He waited on the tarmac for the pilots to open the baggage compartment, periodically looking in the direction of the terminal for his ride.

The young man who had sat across the aisle from him during the flight—who had introduced himself as Special Agent Goldstein—waited also, as did a woman with hair the color of rust, who was several years senior to the young agent, yet pretty in a perky, energetic way. Bull and Goldstein had talked. At first Bull had learned only that he worked for the Justice Department—Goldstein had been careful not to be specific and Bull had not appeared overly inquisitive. The agent was here to pick up an offender who had eluded him once before, and said that as corny as it sounded, justice had prevailed. He could hardly wait to see the man's face when he showed up and snapped on the cuffs.

Likely a U.S. Marshal, Bull had assumed.

The young man had been impressed when Bull explained his position on the U.S. Court of Appeals. The agent said that he, too, was trained in law, although he had not used his degree in any fashion. He felt the bureau was wasteful of their human assets.

FBI, the judge had concluded. An idealistic young agent who would never believe anything deceitful about a judge of Bull's position and standing.

Judge Bull had not asked who the offender might be, and the agent had not offered the information, although he mentioned that the person had fallen into disgrace in only a single week.

Bull was moderately intrigued. He had close ties in the city and county where they landed, and had heard of nothing important going on. A Joint FBI–ATF exercise was under way, working out of the airport with the support of the county cops, but those were periodic events to be expected. They had a light fixed-wing aircraft to spot movement by day, and a helicopter to insert teams. Lennville's chief of police, the judge's fellow Serpiente, had asked the sheriff to let him know if there was more than an exercise on the Feds' minds. Thus far, there was apparently not. The Joint FBI–ATF team was checking out some new sort of night gear.

A white Town Car pulled onto the tarmac and stopped beside him. Damon Lee disembarked and retrieved Bull's heavy luggage planeside and carried them to the Town Car.

When Judge Bull took his seat in back, he noted that Goldstein and the rust-haired woman were lugging heavy gym bags into the airport van. He also noted that when the woman spoke the young agent nodded like an obedient pet.

"Pull up to the terminal and wait," Bull told Lee. "I want to see where those two are going." *And who they are going to see,* he thought.

*1:45 p.m.—Humboldt County Sheriff's Department,
Eureka*

Link was cooling his heels in a holding cell at the rear
of the station, where he'd been since six o'clock that
morning. There were two others in the cell, a youth who
was drunk and passed out, snoring and smelling like
vomit, and another who was forlornly shaking his head,
awaiting a lawyer he could not afford.

Link was grumpy about his own situation. Although
he doubted they'd keep him for long, it would be time
he couldn't afford to waste. Maggie's refusal to help
made him feel better about not working harder at their
relationship. She'd been unreasonable, and had droned
on like an endless record. Of course, there were other
times when she'd been sweet and caring, and those had
outweighed everything else. Those and the way she'd
look at him with those big hazel eyes as if she were
falling in love with him for the first time, again. Making
up had been their best times.

She hardly ever called, which was another stumbling
block whenever he'd contemplated ringing her up to find
out how San Francisco was treating her, how things were
going in the land of fruits and nuts, how they were faring
with their muscle-bound governor, how she was doing
without them coming home—or at least to one or the
other's home—and deciding to "stay in."

A couple of times, or perhaps more, he'd felt like
flying out or meeting her halfway at the cabin in Boudie
Springs, where she'd enchanted everyone—including
Jamie and Moira and Joseph—with her down-to-earth
humor and ability to laugh.

No more. This was the final straw. As soon as they
let him near a phone again, he'd call Mary Long and ask
her to please get him out of this mess. She would listen.

An overweight deputy came into the room. Then Special Agent Stanley Goldstein looked around the concrete
corner and found him in the cell.

Link shook his head. "You've got to be shitting me."

"I hear you want out," Stanley said cheerfully.

Link did not answer. Just wondered why the twerp was here.

"Is that right? You want out?"

"Yeah. I want out of here."

"How about asking me real nice?"

"Go play with yourself."

Stanley recoiled in mock astonishment. "Why, I was trying to help, and—"

"Would you two cut it out." Maggie Tatro walked around the corner and into view.

The deputy pointed. "That one's George Andrews. He's the one you're looking for."

"He looks pretty grubby. You're sure he's the one?"

The deputy nodded, brandished a key, and called out, "Cell one's coming open!"

Despite all that he'd been saying to himself, at that moment Link thought Maggie was drop-dead beautiful.

24

Special Agent in Charge Lacy Rogers got out of a meeting with local law enforcement officials just in time to accompany them to a late lunch. While not overly friendly with George Washington Andrews—who still wore the clothing that he'd been captured in and smelled of the earthy odors of the forest—the ATF agent was courteous to Maggie Tatro and tolerant of Stanley's inexperience.

While Maggie conversed with Rogers, Goldstein took it upon himself to observe Link closely, as if he might bolt and run at any moment.

A lull came to the conversation as a large man with chocolate skin and hair so closely cropped he appeared to be bald, came in and took a seat beside Rogers. He introduced himself as Jack Hammer, took the others in, smiled just a little at Stanley's intensity, then focused on Link and gave an imperceptible nod, which Link returned.

Rogers regarded Link, as well. "My associate thinks they were lucky to take you last night, that you were among them before they realized you were there."

Link eyed Hammer. "Your people are good."

"I'll pass it on."

"Grunt or jarhead?" Link asked, meaning Special Forces or Recon.

Hammer shrugged. "Let's just say we're on loan to the ATF from another agency. You're a graduate of Polk." A statement, not a question.

"Friends at Camp Swampy call me Black Wolf." His code name.

Link periodically attended training exercises at Fort Polk Swampy, but his real alma mater of stealth studies was Blackfoot U. He excelled at Polk partly because he had studied the old ways of Piegan warriors who could hide in plain view. The previous night he had not impressed himself by allowing himself to be captured. He put it down as either temporary insanity or lack of concentration and allowing his mind to dwell on other things. It would not happen again.

A new signal passed between Jack Hammer (whoever he was) and SAC Lacy Rogers. A nod that he had inspected Link, and Rogers could speak freely. Lacy Rogers observed Link with a new level of respect. "See anything out there?"

"The pot farmers carry VHFs and do a lot of BSing," Link said. He mused. "Some farmer named Augie's gone missing."

"We're not after druggies."

"A guy calling himself Craig gave regular warnings over the radio and said your guys would be someplace called Big Daddy's wearing night-vision gear."

Jack Hammer wrote it down; then he flashed teeth. "You must not have listened."

"I had a stupid moment. Anyway, I'm not who you're looking for."

"Who said we're looking for someone?" asked Rogers. "See anything else?"

"How about the locations of twenty pot farms?"

"Forget 'em," said Hammer. "We fill out paperwork and no one cares."

"Anything else we ought to know?" Rogers asked vaguely.

A recon op out looking for something, Link thought. Unusual, but he doubted it had anything to do with the Serpientes.

"Such as?"

Rogers received another nod from Hammer. "Some big weapons and explosives are being moved around up here, mostly going into the Bay Area. They may be coming out of Canada, but maybe not. You have any ideas?"

Link had heard about it from intelligence.

"No, but I'll be moving around, and I'll keep my eyes open."

Hammer wrote four figures onto a napkin and pushed it over. "In case you see something."

Link looked once, and nudged it back. "Any chance of hitching a ride in your chopper to pick up my vehicle?"

SAC Lacy Rogers looked at Maggie. "Okay with you?"

She nodded. "We'll come along."

Stanley looked upset that she would have anything to do with Link.

Rogers observed Link. "Who are you?"

Jack Hammer caught his attention and shook his head. Link answered anyway. "One of the good guys, I hope."

Maggie snorted derisively. Stanley looked baffled at the intercourse.

Link stood. "We'd better go. The man offered us a ride."

"Good," said Maggie. "We'll get a chance to talk, and I'll decide a few things."

As she got to her feet, Special Agent Stanley Goldstein did not appear happy. It looked suspiciously as if his boss was no longer calling all the shots.

4:30 p.m.—Forest, 20 Miles SSW of Garberville, California

The helicopter pilot waved once and was off, creating a rotor blast so fierce that the three hunched over and held on to themselves.

"Why am I here?" Maggie asked, and Stanley looked hopeful that she'd recall the helicopter.

Link snapped the holstered .357 magnum revolver onto his belt and used Velcro to strap it to his leg. Stanley regarded him with narrowed eyes, keeping his hand near his coat front and wearing a Wyatt Earp squint.

Link slung the packsack onto his back and lugged Maggie's heavy gym bag through the forest. She followed close behind, talking about the enchantment of the huge redwoods, and how they made humans feel insignificant in their presence. "Pines are individuals, they all look different. These are uniform. All of the big ones look precisely the same. Two minutes in the forest, and I don't have the vaguest idea where we are. How in the world do you find your way?"

"I've got a handheld GPS. I'll show you how it works. Most of the pot punks carry them."

"You don't have yours out now."

"I've been here. This is my world, remember?" Link had taken her camping in the mountains of Montana years before. She'd enjoyed it, so long as he was no farther than ten yards away.

"I get the idea that Agent Rogers is fighting a losing battle."

"Back at the building I was briefed about the heavy weapons he talked about. Someone's smuggling everything from new SA-17 shoulder-fired missiles to RPGs."

"Is Jack Hammer military?"

"Probably with one of the federal agencies, possibly the same one you work for. In the last five years, there've been a lot of new players in the special-ops world."

Stanley brought up the rear, carrying his gym bag in his left hand so he'd have access to his shoulder-holster with his right, memorizing the path they were taking in case Anderson ditched them again.

After ten minutes of negotiating fallen timber and obstacles, they had arrived at the road. The Yukon appeared to have been untouched. Link unlocked it, opened a rear door, and deposited Maggie's gym bag and his own backpack. He then unsnapped the revolver from his belt.

Stanley dropped his bag and pushed back his jacket.

Link gave him an odd look and tossed the still holstered—and unloaded, courtesy of the ATF— Smith & Wesson in beside the pack.

The young agent retrieved his bag without taking his eyes off Link as he walked around and checked for fresh tracks.

Maggie observed the Yukon. "Looks like it's nice under all the dirt."

"So far everything's worked," Link conceded. He preferred his familiar old Ramcharger.

As Stanley stowed his bag, Link said, "It's good seeing you again, Maggie."

She didn't answer.

"I need your help."

"We tried to help once, and you screwed Stanley." She did not sound forgiving.

"Name your terms."

It was the correct answer. "First I want to know everything that's going on, including what you know that Gordon and his people don't. Then I'll weigh it all and make up my mind."

"How about Stanley?"

Special Agent Goldstein spoke up. "If she goes, I'm part of the package."

Link almost wished he hadn't made him look foolish back in Reno.

"If things get hot, just stay out of the way," he told him.

Maggie glared. "Don't be such an ass, Link. He'll hold up his end."

He held his tongue, wishing Stanley Goldstein would butt out. He wanted Maggie along; he'd worked with her, and she was good in a crunch. She had a good head on her shoulders and might come up with something he had not. She also had her connections at the bureau in case they needed big-time support in a hurry. But Stanley had too much to learn.

Link dug into the backpack, found the leather folder that Erin had given him, and passed it to Maggie. "How about you read while I drive?"

She took the right front seat and Stanley the rear one behind the driver, which made Link uneasy. He told him to move over behind Maggie.

"I'll stay here."

"Then keep your hand away from your weapon. It makes me nervous."

Stanley looked pleased.

"If you shoot yourself, we'll have to drop you off at a hospital and waste more time."

The Yukon started on the first try.

"There are two documents here," said Maggie.

"Start with the executive summary."

Link turned around and was headed toward the main road when Maggie realized what she was reading. "You're sure I've got the right thing?"

"I'm sure. When you've finished, I'll go over everything that's happened in the past two weeks."

Maggie was a speed-reader, and she possessed good comprehension. By the time he turned north on US 101 at Garberville, she'd finished both the executive summary and the recovered portion of Shepherd's Journal, and was staring out the window. While it had obviously been thought provoking, she did not display the interest he had believed she might.

Stanley, who occupied the backseat, was still reading, periodically snorting as if it were all humbug.

Link addressed Maggie: "Keep what you just read in mind, and we'll jump forward in time. Two months ago, someone began slandering the Weyland Foundation. You saw it in the news. Ridiculous stuff, but it was damaging. After the fourth week, Frank Dubois was beside himself trying to find the source, so we came up with a plan."

Maggie periodically asked questions, listening intently as he explained the hospital project in Chad, and how Doc Pete had received the RFIs from the CIA. He told her about the Green Mullah's declaration of *jihad* against America.

"Sajacento timed everything from the announcement at Aozou. Six days, and Ahmed bin Polah was to attack as a warning. Twenty days, and Sajacento said he'll turn loose a swarm of suicide bombers."

He explained how Doc and his crew disappeared.

"Five days later, I was flying a refurbished bird to the Middle East. A Learjet 60 D."

By the time Link finished, they were not far from the turnoff for Lennville, Ferndale, and Rebecca's Resort.

"Erin and Frank are somewhere here."

Maggie held her tongue, thinking over everything he'd said.

"It's a scam," announced Stanley. "Either you or the terrorists are jerking us around about where the hostages are held and who's holding them. You say it's a bunch of pirates that existed in the 1800s, like we're supposed to believe in fairy tales."

Link lost patience and snapped, "I'm speaking to your boss."

"Let him talk," Maggie said. "He's got a good argument."

"Then he should try getting it right. The Serpientes were formed five hundred years ago. That was Shepherd's estimate, and he made a good case."

"According to the summary," said Stanley, "historians agreed that the Serpientes were a myth. You want us to believe they're *still* around? I don't think so. In fact I don't think they ever existed. You're twisting the truth to stop the search in Georgia and change the focus to California, like the Hezbollah would have us to do."

Maggie interrupted. "That's going too far, Stan. Whatever else he might be, Link is one of the most honest men I've ever known, and he's as patriotic as any man alive. He hates terrorists, and would never do anything to harm Americans."

Stanley backed off a step. "What if he's being given bad information? What if everything he told us was staged or fed to him by the Hezbollah. At least we know *they're* real. Our agents are chasing them all over Georgia. Yesterday they almost caught one of them."

She regarded Link. "Could that be the case? A lot of your assumptions are based on a journal that may or may not contain truth. It may be an elaborate forgery. The videos and the photos *could* have been staged or altered."

"As far as I can tell, only one of the videos was staged. Gwen wasn't thrown out of the Learjet like they showed. She was dropped from an airplane over Georgia, but not from that one."

"The Bureau already knows that. How about the others?"

"Frank's message was real. The message was intended for me," he explained.

"I saw the tape, and I remember him blinking, but I thought he had something in his eye."

"Now *that* sounds plausible," Stanley said doggedly. "The so-called code could be coincidence."

"Frank risked his life getting the message out."

"And the FBI are stumblebums who don't know what they're doing?"

"The Bureau's working with what they have, which is a missing Learjet, a body dropped onto a highway, and a number of people who say they saw an airplane flying under the clouds in Georgia that morning."

"Sounds convincing to me."

Link drove in silence. Time was dear, and he did not believe there was a way to win the argument. "I'm going to keep looking. I'll drop you off at the airport in Eureka."

"Why?" Maggie asked. "I suggest we find a place where we can discuss the next step. I'm anxious about Erin and Frank, and there's too little time to waste any more of it."

Stanley released a loud breath of disappointment.

"You believe?" Link asked Maggie.

"Enough that I'd hate myself if it turned out to be true and we hadn't looked."

"If you're staying, so am I," said Stanley Goldstein. "I'm not leaving you with him."

"Now that that's out of the way, where can we go to talk?" Maggie asked.

Link had passed the turnoff, so he slowed to find a place to turn around. "I know where you can get rooms, but neither of you are properly dressed."

"It's that nice?"

"It's . . . hard to describe."

They found a service station in Fortuna with clean restrooms. Link topped off the Yukon while the others took a change of clothing inside. Stanley emerged first, wearing jeans and a golf shirt, took his seat, and sarcastically said he was surprised to find Link was still there.

Link responded in a low voice. "Keep something in mind. Maggie's a friend, like Erin and Frank. If it comes to a matter of prioritizing between them and you, you're on your own."

25

The new tenants used bogus names. Maggie's room was adjacent to Link's, Stanley's on the opposite side of hers. Rebecca could barely contain her glee, which Link decided was because she had, for the first time ever, succeeded in renting all eight rooms.

They gathered in Link's room, where it was least likely their conversations could be overheard by others. "My God!" Stanley proclaimed. "What's that smell?"

"Cigar smoke and old sweat," said Maggie, nose periodically twitching at the odiferous amalgamation.

As Link set up the laptop, he told them how he'd arrived to learn that Dr. Walsh and Professor Shaw had been killed in the accident, and how he'd acquired the DVD.

He brought up the index and went through the maps and charts, explaining how he'd come up with the hot zones and walking routes.

Stanley asked him to stop at one of the charts, and he studied the massive area involved. "We couldn't walk the entire forest if we had an army. You heard Agent Rogers. They can't find the movements of large weapons right under their noses. Trying to find this Killing Tree—"

"Weeping Tree," Link corrected.

"Words don't matter. It doesn't exist."

Maggie returned from the window where she'd been checking out the parking lot below. "What are you arguing about?"

"Without a whole lot of luck, we'll never find anything that way. It's too big an area."

Maggie said, "I think I agree."

Link's patience was flagging. "We sure as hell won't find it if we don't look."

Maggie examined the map presently displayed on the screen. "What about looking for the hidden lagoon. Shepherd said it was the other half of their hideaway."

"I looked for it on the maps," said Link. Then he admitted that he had not treated bodies of water as primary landmarks.

Stanley was peering intently at the map on the screen: *Northern California Goldfields, Map of (1852)—S*

He examined six squiggle marks that appeared like the letter *S* toppled onto their sides. The words "Dangerous Outlaws" were engraved beside the squiggles. Those had been highlighted with yellow marker, and alongside were the initials.

Stanley moved closer, looking at the initials scrawled alongside each: D.W. and W.S. "These look like verifications. You said Dr. Shaw was a professor of history?"

"Yes. Both men held doctorates."

"Could I look at the other charts?"

"We don't have a lot of time."

"Please. It's important."

Link gave him control of the laptop. Stanley advanced through the maps and read the different notations. His expression altered as he pored over each map. "I'll be damned."

Maggie was sitting back, looking over Stanley's shoulder as if troubled.

The young agent was increasingly excited. "Have you tried making a composite?"

Link unfolded the medium-scale map with the arrows and red marks, laid it out on the bed, and stepped back so Stanley could compare it to the charts shown on the screen.

Finally the agent sat back. "Too much area to search," he said.

"That's why I prioritized, so I'd check the most promising ones first."

"There's still too much. I agree with Maggie. We

should start on the ocean side and *then* look inland. That may be why others always failed, because they were looking for the three trees in the middle of millions. There are fewer lagoons than valleys. We should also look for Angel Rock, which Shepherd said was an off-shore marker for the hidden lagoon. There's also a pair of towering rock faces, one on either side of the lagoon. Now, how about another look at the nautical chart?"

"Watch out. You might start to believe."

Stanley brought up the one titled *California, Shipping Losses, Unknown Causes, Map of (1840 to 1865)—?H*

He pored over every inscription. While there were numerous "hazards to shipping," none were inscribed as Angel Rock.

"We need a larger-scale nautical map."

Link pulled out the topographical charts. Stanley stood over the bed, switching between charts and moving his finger as he checked one and then the next. He then went from one computer map to the next, searching the coastline. Finding and marking dozens of lagoons and inlets. About a third of them looked promising enough for another look.

"Got any more up-to-date nauticals?"

"We can buy them in Eureka when the stores open," Link said, although he'd prefer not to waste another day.

Since they might change to a seaward approach, Link borrowed Maggie's cell phone to call Squid for advice, hoping he'd returned. Although it was late there, he tried the office.

Mary Long answered, sounding tired. "Two-seven-seven-five."

He told her "the boss" was calling.

"Your voiceprint matches," she said. "We've been busy. Everything's secure again, including the satellite systems. Our engineers are calling out for pizza and working double shifts, and Helga Two's halfway there. Three days, and we'll send you a new sat phone."

"I'd like to pass a message to Squid."

"Mr. Worsczejius still isn't back, but he's done with his Canada project, and he'll join you tomorrow. I've booked him at the hotel you called from the last time we talked."

"Not a good place, Mary. Is he using his own name?"

"Shouldn't he be?"

"Cancel the hotel, and have him wait for us at the airport. Tell him not to use anything connecting him with the Weyland Foundation, including company credit cards."

"Got it. This is getting spookier, Mr. Anderson."

"I'd rather you call me Link. What's Squid's ETA?"

She gave a time and flight number. "He'll be arriving from San Francisco."

Squid had said he was going "up north." San Francisco was not "up north." It was south of them.

Mary gave him Squid's new cell phone number, which Link ran around his mind a couple of times. He had a talent for memorizing numbers.

She'd been unable to reach ADIC Gordon Hightower to run the background check on Mr. Cerone. He had not returned her calls or messages.

Mary asked, "Is there anything else I can do?"

Link said he'd be back in touch after Squid's arrival. He switched off, and grumpily wondered what the hell was lodged crosswise in Gordon Hightower's craw.

Maggie heard engine sounds and walked to the window. "This one's familiar. Lights?"

Link switched off the lamps to cast the room in gloom. When he joined her, a white Town Car was passing from right to left on the road, moving at a crawl. While it was difficult to see into the vehicle from their overhead angle, an Asian driver leaned out to observe the parking lot.

"Damon Lee gets around," said Link. "Last time I saw him, he was carrying a cardboard box out of the hotel. He was the long-range shooter that wounded my mare."

Stanley said, "He used that same car to pick up the judge I sat next to on the airplane."

"Federal judge?" asked Maggie.

"U.S. Court of Appeals. His picture's on the wall at the Federal Building in San Francisco. His last name's Bull, and he told me he keeps a home in Lennville."

"How much did you tell him?"

"That we were going to pick up a suspect. Hey, if you can't trust a federal judge—"

"Do you think Bull's associated with the Sociedad?" Maggie asked Link.

"No way to tell, but he's associated with Lee. Can you run their backgrounds?"

"Oh, yeah."

The Town Car came to a halt. After backing up even with the driveway, Damon Lee jabbed a forefinger in the direction of the Yukon.

"Someone's in the passenger's seat, and it's not the judge," said Maggie as a second man leaned over to see where Lee was pointing. He had dark hair, penetrating eyes, and a guileless child's face. Link had seen either him or his photograph, but could not recall more.

Damon Lee turned into the parking lot.

"Good," said Stanley. "We'll get a closer look."

"Or maybe we should run like hell," Maggie said, only half-joking.

The two men dismounted to examine a heavily dusted beater pickup with maroon-colored out-of-state plates, parked two spaces from the Yukon.

"I've seen the second guy's face somewhere," Maggie said. "I'll get my camera." She hurried from the room.

A new man stepped out the back door of Rebecca's and into the lot. Calked boots and suspenders, potbelly, grizzled features, and gray hair, wearing an angry expression. He pointed and yelled for the two to get the hell away from his pickup.

Damon Lee popped a bird in the owner's direction as the two climbed into the Town Car.

"They're interested in Montana plates," said Link.

A minute after the Town Car left, Maggie came in with a Nikon fitted with a telephoto lens that was larger than the camera. She'd taken several shots from her window, which she displayed on the digital camera's screen. Damon Lee had been captured in four photos. Pretty boy had been ducking into the Town Car, his face invisible to the camera. A final photo had been taken of the Town Car leaving the lot, showing a third person seated in back.

Through the rear window Link noted shoulder-length hair that reminded him of Erin.

He had Maggie adjust the light level and could now see the woman more clearly. He was immediately reminded of someone else, but that was impossible. "Sydney?" he asked aloud, but the others did not hear, and he could not be sure.

Stanley went to his room for a potty break.

Link shook his head at Maggie. "He's too nervous."

"With good reason after what you did to him in Reno." She made a little laugh. He remembered and liked the sound, wondered if she wasn't beginning to open up.

She looked at him with a sparkle of humor. "Know who's the luckiest man in the world? You, my dear. Did I tell you what Stanley's called at the office?"

Link shook his head.

"Have you heard of ten-ex?"

"Sure." The ten circle was the smallest on a bull's-eye target. Within it was an even tinier, dotted circle with an *x*. Ten-ex meant the bullet hole was entirely in the innermost circle. All shooters aspired to score a ten-ex, especially at ranges beyond ten yards. A friend of Link's in Nevada owned a firearms dealership called Tenex. Link had scored a few ten-exes in his life.

"Stanley's nickname is Ten-Ex. He's a match shooter. You ever see anyone fire six ten-exes out of ten shots, offhand at twenty-five yards with a .45 Colt Commander?"

Link stared at the door. "You're kidding."

"That's one reason I keep him around," Maggie said impishly

One reason? Link quelled a small rush of jealousy.

When Stanley returned, they went back to planning. After studying the maps and the verifying initials of the two "experts," Stan had done a mental flip-flop. There were no more arguments about the Serpientes' existence. He also agreed that the hostages were somewhere in the redwood forests. Time was at a premium. They had to act.

Link was intrigued with their idea of approaching

from the sea. He'd rejected the thought of renting a light airplane and scrutinizing the forest from the air. Trying to peer through the redwood canopy would be in vain— but it made a lot more sense to fly the coastline and search for the lagoon and Angel Rock.

When Stanley Goldstein debated whether they should inform Gordon Hightower, Maggie became increasingly brooding and noncommittal.

"We can't wait much longer," said Stanley "Ten-Ex" Goldstein, who had grown a couple of inches in Link's mind. "We're at Aozou plus fourteen. That leaves only six days. The terrorists could be smuggled ashore at any time now. They've got to be stopped."

"Let's talk about calling Gordon after the flight," Link said.

When Stanley started to argue, Maggie stopped him. "Link's right. We have to wait until we know more."

When Link tried to meet her eyes, she avoided him, as she did when she was withholding information.

Stanley went on with his argument. "The suicide bombers may already be here."

Link was still regarding Maggie. No change.

Stanley cocked his head at his boss. "Is there something I'm missing? I'm on board. The Serpientes exist, and there's good reason to think they're here."

Link had been on the cusp of agreeing to the phone call, asking Gordon to be discreet in deploying his people. Telling him the Sociedad were ruthless. Erin and Frank would likely be killed.

Maggie continued to avoid his eyes.

"You know something," said Link. Not a question.

Maggie looked at the window. "I've been in touch with Gordon."

Stanley saw nothing wrong with that. "Then make the call."

"Gordon won't believe us," Maggie said. "And if he doesn't, neither will my bosses."

Stanley started to argue. "Please stop," she told him, and finally looked at Link, a sign that she had girded herself. Link had the feeling that he was about to hear bad news.

"Gordon knows everything you've told us. Erin sent

him a copy of Shepherd's Journal the morning of the attack on the Weyland Building, along with a memo that she thought the Serpientes were connected to foreign terrorism."

"He knows about the Serpientes?"

"Yeah, but Gordon thinks everything in Shepherd's Journal is a fairy tale. He asked how I'd feel trying to convince the president a gang of nineteenth-century pirates were behind the Weyland Building attack. He feels it's an attempt to obscure the truth."

"He didn't tell me any of that."

"He thinks you've gone off the deep end, that you're an obstacle to finding Frank and Erin. He has proof that the Hezbollah are holding Frank and Erin in Georgia, and thinks you're just after another media show, like when you went after bin Polah and didn't tell him."

"Jesus," whispered Stanley, staring at Link. "*You're* the cowboy in the video?"

"Gordon's being irrational," Link told Maggie.

"That's what he says about you. He thinks something snapped when Frank fired you."

Link did not argue about the firing. He'd been there too many times. "Why weren't you straight with me?" he asked.

She shook her head. "Oh, Link, there were so many things I couldn't tell you."

"Did the FBI code-breakers read Frank's eyeblinks?"

"Except for the confirmation that Alpha-Nine was involved, they were at a complete loss. Gordon didn't tell them about Shepherd's Journal. To him, it's all embarrassing nutcase stuff that you had Erin pass along."

"We could send a copy of the journal to Quantico," said Stanley, "along with a request that they take another look at the tape."

Maggie was dubious. "The gods look after one another. Gordon has a lot of the senior staff—and one of the handful at the foundation—convinced that Link's a loose cannon and should be muzzled."

Which explains why Mr. Scott Cerone was so hostile.

"What about us?" said Stan Goldstein. "They'd believe us."

"I doubt it. Guilt by association."

Link asked, "What do you believe about the Serpientes, Maggie?"

"They were once real, and they may still be around. It's obvious that Frank Dubois saw the entrance to the Weeping Tree, and he and Erin are here somewhere. We still need irrefutable proof before we can go to anyone."

The room grew quiet until Stanley broke the silence. "You didn't ask what I think."

Link looked at him.

"Everyone will believe us if we find the camp and free the hostages," said Ten-Ex Goldstein.

PART III

The *Sinner*

26

Link picked a Piper Cherokee 180, built in 1971, from a lineup of newer rentals. The 180 could carry the three of them with room and power to spare, had reasonably good visibility, and could be flown low and slow.

He'd filed a local VFR clearance, which meant they could more or less go anywhere they wished north of the restricted areas surrounding the Bay Area. Link did not wish to go nearly that far. They would observe the coastline and some of the inland area, from south of Point Arena, northward past Cape Mendocino. He'd hardly spoken to Maggie beyond the words necessary to take their things from the rooms and head to Eureka. Her mood matched the weather forecast: surly. She'd offered to stay behind and look after the Yukon and their bags. He had said fine. She'd changed her mind, saying she'd take pictures. He had not argued, just packed the bags into the Cherokee's baggage compartment, passed out intercom headsets, and explained their use.

Stanley had the best vision of the FBI agents, so he occupied the right seat, where the view was better than in back.

Takeoff was made without event, which was the way Link liked it.

They were provided with a full load of fifty gallons of avgas, giving them a maximum flight radius of 350 miles at cruising altitude. They'd be flying much lower. He planned to use forty gallons and marked off a 250-mile radius, so if there was a problem, he could make it to Arcata or a small airport at Lennville listed for EMERGENCY USE ONLY.

He flew to Lennville and made a flyover of the airport so he'd have it firmly in mind should a problem arise. A Citation executive jet was parked in front of one of the two medium-size hangars, both looking so sturdy, they could withstand a nuke or two, and reminding him of the community's obvious wealth. As they passed over, he glimpsed a portable instrument landing system set up at the end of the runway, which would be handy if Eureka was closed when they returned. He found it interesting that the ILS wasn't shown in the letdown and approach book. Neither was airfield lighting, although he'd seen blue light bubbles along the runway's length. The facilities booklet showed that Lennville offered NO SERVICES.

Link banked and asked Maggie to get photos of the airfield, then turned back and climbed to seven thousand feet. He flew on to Lisbon, then to Cape Mendocino, which was the westernmost point of the contiguous states. The western cloud banks were still distant.

They flew south along the coast to observe the large rocks that jutted from the water. Maggie took photos out the side, hoping to capture Angel Rock.

Flying south, with the coast sliding past on their port side, Link had the best view. He scanned carefully, trying to miss nothing. Most of the craggy rocks that rose from the ocean were within a mile of the coast, but there were a few farther out on Stanley's side. Periodically he would bank so the young agent could get a better look and Maggie could take photos. Stanley, with his good vision spotted birds and sea lions that were not obvious to the untrained eye.

Maggie made her first observation. "I'm not feeling well."

"Stop looking out the side so much," he told her. "I've seen fighter pilots get sick just staring out the side. Look straight ahead."

"I can't be much help *that* way," she said archly.

"Damn it, give the camera to Stanley and look straight ahead."

She handed the camera over. A minute or two later she said, "I can't see anything but water and the horizon," and went back to looking out the side.

He rummaged around in the side pocket and found a barf bag, which he handed back. Two minutes later, she was making awful sounds.

She asked how much farther they had to go.

"One hour forty-five. We've just started."

Twice on the southerly leg, Link pointed out their position on the aerial chart, then turned inland, into the highlighted "hot zones." Large swaths had been clearcut off two of the zones. Both had been replanted with young firs, one of them already thriving.

The pot farms he had seen the previous day were not obvious from above.

Back over the water, they noted formations of stone that rose dramatically from the water. Stanley took a picture of each of them.

As they approached Point Arena, the weather to their west began to build up, and visibility started to diminish. He made a lazy 180 turn back to the north, and descended to only two thousand feet above the water. There the visibility was fine.

He told Stanley, "If you want to see something from closer up, let me know."

Stan pointed at a rock formation. "That one's interesting."

Link slowed and banked, and flew a 360 around the formation as the agent took photos. The rock was a mile from shore, with currents running so strongly past that they looked like rivers in the sea.

"Got to be Angel Rock," said Stanley. He sounded excited.

Link extended the turn for another ninety degrees, then they rolled out and flew toward the shore, which was a marsh of reeds and a thin line of beach. Still going very slow, with the mountain ahead. He pushed up from eighty to a hundred miles per hour to climb just slightly.

They cleared the ridgeline by a hundred feet. He glanced over. Stanley wore a grin. He looked back. Maggie was staring down and to her right, looking more than a little green.

Link set up a slow weave. Lots of lush forest but no small valley.

"See anything?" he asked.

"Just trees," said Stanley.

"Maggie?"

"An ocean of treetops. It's hard to realize the ground is a hundred yards below them."

Both ahead and right were vast clearings where the forest had been logged. To their left were more trees, and little more to discern. He flew straight ahead for five miles, then turned seaward and crested the ridge again.

"Wrong one," he said.

"It still may be worth a look on foot," said Stanley Goldstein.

"There's no valley."

"True." Stanley looked out at the promising rock formation with disappointment.

For a minute they flew parallel to the beach, over another large marsh where coastal grasses protruded from the water, alternately flooded by ocean waves. They passed over rocky beach. Farther to sea were several rock formations.

Link turned, pushed up the throttle and flew toward the nearest one. It was even larger even than the one that Stanley originally believed was promising. "Looks right."

They flew inland and found several eroded crevices that had swallowed entire trees, and a few rugged mountains with redwood stands.

"Maybe." Stanley snapped more digital photos.

Out over the water again, they came to another jutting rock that looked like it had potential.

So did the next four they checked.

The currents that rushed on either side of the final one were turbulent, roaring past the looming rock formation and boiling whitewater on the back side. A granddaddy rip tide so powerful that no sane person would venture toward it.

"No way I'd go there," affirmed Stanley.

"Let me see it again," said Maggie. Her face had regained a modicum of color.

Link banked so they could get a closer look.

"It really does look like an angel," she said.

The map showed they were abeam the place shown on older charts as the "Quaking Ground," and nearby, "Liquid Earth." The triple confluence of seismic faults was beneath.

Link turned shoreward, and they were confronted with a pair of marshy beaches, a soaring rocky bluff behind each, and between them a shorter stone wall of a darker hue. The bluffs and the central formation formed the base of the largest mountain in the area. Interesting in appearance, but there was no trace of a lagoon.

He flew alongside the mountain, then gained sufficient altitude for a look at the other side. There they found a wild forest they'd not encountered, with jumbles of narrow canyons and vales, and broken rifts and fissures that traversed the mountain. The redwoods there were seldom straight and regal; too many had been bent and twisted by the seismic actions of the centuries. Some reached from yawning fissures like piteous beggars.

Eighteenth-century artists used gnarled cypresses as representatives of death. Here, where the giants cast the surface in eternal gloom, it was easy to understand why.

The quaking grounds were so hostile to human presence that Link's sensibilities warned him to stay away. An inner emotion told him to proceed, but with care. Yet another tugged fiercely, telling him he must hasten and proceed on.

Stanley stared in unabashed awe. "The terrain's awfully rugged. How could a human even walk there?"

"Maybe they picked it because no one goes there." Link turned the Cherokee and eased over the mountain, then descended toward the Pacific. There was more to search along the coast.

Maggie stared seaward, and pointed. "That's the fourth ship I've seen."

"I counted seven coastal freighters," said Link. "I think that one's a fish-processing ship. Then there are trawlers and smaller boats that make up the rest of the fleets."

"Out of San Francisco?"

"Most are foreign. The majority of ours have to go to Alaska to make a living. A lot of small outfits went broke and their boats were repoed. Squid can tell us more when he gets here."

9:55 a.m.—Eureka Airport

The others waited at the Cherokee while Link went into the rental company, settled with the talkative owner, and listed a couple of minor maintenance discrepancies.

"Good flight?"

"Best kind. We beat the weather and had a safe landing."

Outside it was beginning to rain.

"The fixed base operator got a call a couple of hours ago. Police chief at Lennville said someone was flying low over their town, and asked who was flying. He got all the pilots' names on the clearances, including yours."

"Is that legal, giving out names?"

"To cops, it is. Was it you?"

"Possibly. I checked out the Lennville airport in case I had to use it."

"I wouldn't do that again. The people who live there are accustomed to getting their way. Rich as hell with plenty of time to make trouble."

"I'll remember that."

Link went out to the Yukon and tossed his bag in back. He took his time checking it over, and drove out to the Cherokee where Maggie and Stanley sought refuge from the rain by crouching under a wing. He got out and helped them load their bags.

The rain fell in fierce droplets that made pinging sounds on the aluminum skin.

"We had visitors," he told them. "When we get inside, don't say anything."

They rode silently for five miles until they reached a crowded strip mall. Link pulled into the mass of vehicles parked in front of a Wal-Mart and climbed out despite the downpour.

When Stanley started to question, Link put a finger to his lips and popped the hood.

There was a tracking device, similar to the tattle-tale he'd found in the Ramcharger, but wired to the battery whenever the ignition was turned on. This model was called a "bird dog" by the cops who used them. With the engine shut off, he cut the electrical lead using his pocket knife, then yanked it loose and pulled the entire harness out through the front.

Link used the LED flashlight as he peered under the dashboard, and pulled out two audio bugs that were taped there. He left the tangle of wires in a grocery cart, and drove out of the lot.

"Watch to see who's following," he said. Two blocks further, Stanley said they were clear.

Link explained that the installer had used high-powered transmitters, and likely didn't think he had to follow closely. The question was, who had attached them? It should have been a no-brainer since the installer had left a tag on one of the audio bugs. The manufacturer was shown as Tel-All Security Corp. The addressee was Marin County Sheriff Dept.

"Believe that," Maggie said, "and I've got a really big bridge to sell you."

Marin County was three hundred miles distant.

"It's my fault they're on to us," said Link. He explained the call to the airport from the Lennville police chief.

"It takes time and effort to install a bird-dog," said Maggie. "Usually they like to pull the vehicle inside and put it on a rack."

"They may have done that," said Link. "They had to get into the vehicle to plant the audio bugs. We know they drove it because the pavement underneath was wet. No sign of anything being forced, so there was a key involved. Meaning cops were involved."

Automobile dealers use VINs to copy automobile keys for police departments.

Maggie said, "How about I drop by the cop shop and show my identification. Tell them to back off because I've got an operation in progress, and remind them that it takes a court order to hang a bird-dog on a vehicle."

"Not yet."

"You keep saying that," said Maggie.

Stanley spoke up. "I agree with Link. Let's say Judge Bull's a buddy of the police chief in Lennville. He told me he has a pilot's license, so maybe he complained about the airplane. He wouldn't have trouble calling on a lowly county judge to get a court order."

After a thoughtful moment Maggie asked Link, "Did you use your own name on the clearance?"

"Nope. Erin included a pilot's license for George Washington Andrews."

"Same name you used at Rebecca's Resort."

"Yeah. Damn!" If bad guys were involved, they were now looking for George Andrews and the Yukon. If they'd talked to Rebecca, they had descriptions of Maggie and Stanley, as well.

"Time for a new vehicle?" Maggie asked.

"Maybe so," said Link, wondering why the chief was so sensitive about the flyover at the Lennville airport.

"I'll rent one in my name," said Maggie. "Yours we'll ditch for the duration."

1:45 p.m.

The American Eagle flight from San Francisco landed five minutes early. Stanley Goldstein waited, looking for a man who fit the description Link had provided. Squid Worsczejius was easy to pick out: large, neatly dressed, and looking around as if he were expecting someone.

Stan introduced himself, grinned like he'd just told a joke that was meant for any observer, and said he was an acquaintance of the "cowboy."

Squid had to think for a moment, looking him over, then warily followed as they went to claim his bags.

"He didn't want to be recognized, so they're waiting at a coffee shop."

"Who's they?" Squid asked.

"Your boss and mine. I'm FBI," he said in a lowered voice.

Stan had left the not-so-new Suburban parked in the loading area. They stowed Squid's luggage with the chain saw and other bags. The ex-sailor bore a look of skepticism, and waited for Stanley to get in before he took the right seat and drew the door closed.

"Before we go, I'll tell you something. I lost a buddy a couple weeks ago, and I'd love to meet the guys who did it. If you're screwing with me and you're with them, I'll rip your fucking head off and piss in the hole."

"Very colorful, but I'm real." Stanley reached for his leather ID packet.

"Don't!" said Squid, and clamped down on his hand.

Stanley, who was not about to be humiliated twice, moved very quickly and pressed the muzzle of a double-action Beretta 9 mm to Squid's forehead.

"Damn it," he said, "I'm real! My ID's in my right jacket pocket."

Squid's jaw drooped. "Where the hell did you get the gun?"

"Go ahead. Check my ID."

"Don't need to, now. Where'd the gun come from?"

Stanley put the pistol away in the console. "I left it in the door panel."

"Not very trusting, are you?"

"About as trusting as you. I learned the hard way, asshole." He started the engine.

Squid laughed uproariously and clapped him on the back so hard that the smaller man collapsed against the wheel. "You're okay, bud. Now let's go put that kind of hurt on the fuckin' terrorists."

27

When Stan pulled up in front of the coffee shop, Maggie hurried out to climb into the second seat. Link slid in beside her.

"I was nervous in there," she said. "I kept thinking someone was going to recognize us."

Squid Worsczejius shoved his hand over the top of the seat and introduced himself. "I couldn't miss you, ma'am. Link called you the best-looking FBI agent on the planet."

She gave Link a look of approval.

They were in a ten-year-old, barn-size Suburban from Rent-a-Wreck. After receiving advice from Link *not* to rent a sensible midsize Toyota—which she still thought would do just as well off-road and use so little gasoline, they wouldn't need jerry cans—he'd admired the gas guzzler. Something near the automatic transmission klunked when changing gears, meaning anytime they sped up or slowed down, but that did not seem to concern the men. It rattled constantly from two locations, one fore and one aft, even when not in motion. When she mentioned that those things were not good, Stan, of all people, had said, "It's a *working* vehicle," as if that explained all clunks and rattles.

"Do not," she'd said firmly, "expect me to get out and push."

In front of the coffee shop, Link had to slam his door twice before it closed.

"Are you in counterterrorism?" asked Squid.

"Industrial espionage," she said.

Link broke in, "Squid, I started out searching on foot, but I've been outvoted. We've decided to look from the water side."

"That fits with what I'd like to do."

"We don't have time to spare, and we need to find a boat."

"You bet. A navy buddy in Oakland told me where to start. Stan, look for a place called Maritime Corner. It's on Second Street near the waterfront."

Stanley found the store and parked in front. As they went inside, Maggie remained close to Squid, listening as he spoke with the old salt who owned the shop. They were both ex-navy, a fact that warmed up the conversation.

A seaworthy boat? The owner had a list as long as his arm. When Squid asked if they were brokered by a certain large company named Zerbini Holdings, the owner scowled. "I wouldn't put a penny into their bloody big pockets."

Squid grinned. "That's what I wanted to hear."

The owner mentioned a variety of eligible boatyards and marinas. When Squid asked about a dockyard at the tiny town of Lisbon, the owner said it was as good as most, then rang the number and introduced him to the owner-manager, who was named Silva.

Maggie understood there were thirty-odd fishing boats of varied sizes and ages, most of them reclaimed by banks in Eureka or San Francisco or bought off failing commercial fishermen. Two decades ago, the independent guys had been forced out of the business when the fish were being hauled away by foreigners in international waters, while at the same time U.S. government regulations tightened. The boats at Lisbon were stored on dry dock, the best ones retrofitted by the owner and a helper, then taken upcoast to Portland or Seattle and sold. They'd been on the market for ten or fifteen years.

When Squid asked about their condition, Silva said some were better than others, but they all floated, and the engines were "pretty reliable."

After Squid hung up, the store owner said Lisbon was an old-style fishing village settled by Portuguese fish-

ermen who sold salmon and snapper to hungry miners
during the gold rush. The place was on a small river
near Cape Mendocino, protected by a mountain ridge
from the Pacific. The road there was ancient blacktop,
paved with potholes. Except for two or three families,
the town had dried up. Their traffic came not from the
road but from the ocean. The few inhabitants that were
left were closemouthed.

As Squid purchased an armful of maritime charts,
Maggie wondered what the people of Lisbon had to be
silent about.

Outside, Squid cornered Link and spoke quietly. Link
nodded in agreement and asked Stanley to find a Bank
of America. He was low on funds. When they parked in
the bank's lot, Link rummaged in the pack, found the
name he wanted from the highly irregular ID packet
Erin had made for him, and went inside.

Maggie hit the jackpot on an ATM and withdrew two
hundred dollars, then went over beside Link, who was
at a teller's post that was now attended by the bank
manager.

"We're together," said Link, who looked like a homeless derelict.

"Yes, sir," said the smiling manager.

Weyland Foundation employees were not restricted by
the parsimony of the government as Maggie was. Link
used the fictional name and driver's license, entered his
PIN to pass the computer test, and received twenty thousand dollars in bills, two negotiable cashier's checks for
five thousand each, and twenty thousand in traveler's
checks. Erin maintained fifty thousand in each ID ac-
count, along with instructions for banks to provide mini-
mal hassle for withdrawals. She'd felt that losing fifty
thou to a potential thief was preferable to having to wait
when one's life might depend on it.

While the bank manager placed it all into a plastic
packet, as if he did that sort of thing every day, Maggie
realized that she was witnessing a crime. *To what depths
was Lincoln Anderson going to drag her this time?*

Link directed them to a sporting-goods store he'd seen
on Fifth Street and showed yet another identification to

the manager, including an up-to-date firearms dealer's permit and a valid guide and outfitter's license.

The store had a good selection of weapons, accessories, navigational devices, and sports clothing. "It's your lucky day," Squid said to the clerk. "We're restocking the fort."

Link and Squid did most of the buying. In just thirty-five minutes, they'd spent thousands, and were stacking it all into the back of the Suburban. Stanley could hardly believe that in the past hour Link had impersonated three different people and spent a year's savings like a drunken sailor.

Squid said, "Would you stop blaming us poor sailors? You fibbers use fake IDs all the time. Same with agency guys. When you spend a penny, you're using the citizens' money."

They were going to Lisbon to look at fishing boats. Tomorrow they'd search for Angel Rock and the hidden lagoon. In between, they needed to find a place to lay their heads.

When they headed south out of Eureka, they finally had time to talk. Maggie, Stan, and Link tried to fill in one another's blanks. Squid, who had the most to explain, was quiet.

3:30 p.m.—US Highway 101

Squid seemed reticent to explain what he'd been up to before joining them. "Just chasing an idea," he said.

Link asked, "If Major Stradley could determine locations of e-mail senders, where was the fake message sent from?"

"Part of that was a head game to make the bad guys think twice, but she really did have a fix on some of the senders. Not that one, though. You've gotta remember, it was probably Erin on the other end. Even the major admits that no one's as good as Erin."

Link brought Squid up to date. He was well acquainted with Shepherd's Journal and eager to examine the images of the maps stored on the DVD.

"They're awesome," said Stanley. "One look, and I was convinced the Serpientes exist."

Link asked, "Did Gordon mention that he had a copy of Shepherd's Journal?"

"You're kidding. Jesus, every time I tried to tell him the kidnappers might be somewhere other than the South, he'd act like I was a turncoat. When I'd mention you, he'd say you were schizo, that you hadn't been able to handle it when Mr. Dubois fired you. I sent him a copy of Erin's note explaining what was going on. After that, he wouldn't take my calls, so I went around him to the deputy director for Terrorism, who agreed to go to Montana to talk with you. When you took off, Hightower said it proved you were nuts."

"Whose side is he on?" Stanley wondered.

Maggie spoke: "Gordon's no traitor."

"I think we're all being outmaneuvered," Link said, "by a woman I believed was dead."

Link knew of only one person who was that good at controlling human perception: Irene Baumgartner, who sometimes called herself Sydney. He was also convinced that she was the one they'd seen in the backseat of the Lincoln Town Car.

He related her background at the CIA. "When she puts her talents to work, truth becomes whatever illusion she wants you to see."

Link said he'd been thinking almost constantly about it since the day before, and explained what *might* have happened with Gordon.

Sydney could have opened a dialogue with someone in Hightower's office—easily done in these days of computer blogging and bounce-off-the-wall chat rooms—with some hardworking analyst who would never dream of letting themselves be manipulated. Sydney would press an innocuous point, such as "Those who wear Western clothing are racists and can't be trusted to be fair." She would harp, and the analyst would eventually listen because Sydney picked her targets well. Then that seed is planted in other offices, including those of important people who are vulnerable because of past acts of indiscretion, and conditioned to repeat what Sydney asks.

They praise Gordon for single-mindedly pursuing the terrorists in the South, question the ethics of the people at the Weyland Foundation, and reinforce that Gordon is on track for promotion.

Sydney would plant those same seeds in key government offices and newsrooms. Link knew of no one who was her equal at twisting perception and turning lies into truths.

"Why did Sajacento, whom I'd never met, pick out my men and Gwen for atrocity? Because she was there with him. Why did Damon Lee try to shoot me? She gave the order. Sydney's the only person who hates me that much."

"Why?"

"A few years ago, she was riding high. She'd stolen from the government, then blackmailed enough people until they no longer hunted her. She put her talent to work for organized crime and was making bundles. I brought all that into the open and exposed her for what she was. The only way she could escape was to fake her own death. This wasn't the first time she fooled Gordon Hightower. He was sure that she was murdered by the mob."

"Now she's after you?"

"I beat her at her game, and Sydney has an ego that can't accept failure."

Link didn't explain that like Sydney, he, too, understood revenge.

Maggie mulled all that over. "How can you be sure?"

He did not respond. It would be too difficult to explain his feelings when he'd seen the slight man in Aozou and then in the Libyan Desert. The woman at the wheel of the car that delivered bin Polah to the Federal Building in New York. Instead he explained his idea of a "smart person" who was directing the scenario while the Hezbollah claimed credit.

"Do you think she's a Serpiente?"

That, he did not know, but she was working with them.

While they were still in range of a cell tower, Maggie contacted her San Francisco office and asked for background on Irene Baumgartner and the Lennville Chief of Police, and took notes about the reports she'd previously requested.

She pressed OFF and read what she had. "Judge Lyle Bull's from this area. Like he told Stan, he has a place in Lennville. Also a town house in San Francisco and a six-thousand-square-foot cabin in Incline Village at Tahoe. Married to the same woman for twenty years, but no children. No record of any hanky-panky. He has a yacht and flies his own private jet, and he's on the boards of several large corporations. He makes major contributions to charities and candidates from both parties. Returns to Lennville monthly to attend homeowners' association meetings involving the restoration of the Victorian-style homes. A real hometown boy made good."

"Nothing shady?" asked Squid.

"A hundred and ten percent solid citizen. A strait-laced, conservative judge."

"How about Damon Lee?" Link asked.

"Also from here. Lives in Fortuna. Gun enthusiast, but he's no great marksman. On three occasions, he tried to qualify on long distance-shooting teams, but never made the cut. He threatened the Eureka team captain who'd rejected him. Guy was shot dead in his driveway getting the newspaper. The local cops looked at Lee, but he had an alibi and a new barrel for his favorite rifle. The case was never closed. There've been two other long-shooter killings in the area. One in Santa Rosa, another in Willits. Both times Lee had alibis, courtesy of Lennville Police Chief Wendell Welk, who uses him for odd jobs. Lee's only conviction was for assault, a revenge thing because he thought he was slighted by a woman."

"And?"

"The conviction was overturned because of legal errors by a court clerk. Lee walked." She looked up. "Any doubts that someone's protecting him?"

"And we knows someone who swings that kind of weight," said Squid. "Judge Bull."

"Also the Lennville Chief of Police," said Stanley. "Name of Wendell Welk."

Squid regarded Maggie. "My buddy was killed by

Mullah Sajacento. Link's closest friends are here somewhere, held by Serpientes, and may already be dead."

"And you'd like to know my reasons for being here."

"Yes, ma'am. From what I gather, your superiors
might wreck your career."

"Not might. If we're wrong, my career goes down the
tubes. But Erin Frechette and Frank Dubois are my
friends, as well." She regarded Link and formed a smile.
"I also have an interest in Mr. Anderson's well-being."

Good, thought Link.

"He wasn't doing that well alone."

Cheap shot.

Link regarded her. "Maggie, there'll be a point where
I'll want you to drop out."

"It's not your choice to make. I swore to guard my
country against all enemies, foreign and domestic. If
there's nothing here, I'll slither back to my office. If
there is—?" She shrugged.

"How about you?" Squid observed Stanley. "The bureau brass will rip off your hide."

"Only brass's opinion I'm interested in is my boss's.
It would be nice to be able to call in the cavalry, but
since we don't know of any to call, I'll stay for a while."

Link spoke to Squid. "Stanley's nickname is Ten-Ex.
Care to guess why?"

Squid chuckled from deep down. "Now you tell me."

No one had left anything of value at Rebecca's Resort.
Since it was likely that Rebecca's had been a source of
the Lennville Chief of Police's information, they decided
to suffer the loss of a few toothbrushes and take their
business elsewhere. As he drove on by, Stanley somberly
shook his head. "Just when I was beginning to appreciate the variety of odors."

Ten minutes later Squid drew in a breath. "The Pacific
smells *good.* A chief petty officer told me it reminded
him of stately Tahitian ladies. Naked, of course, and not
an ounce of shame in a dozen, because they know how
natural and fresh they look and want to show it off.
They carry babies on their hips and walk in the surf to
look out at the world that they know well, because their
old chants tell them what the distant lands were like.

Their ancestors were master boatmen and took hundreds of families out in flotillas that swarmed over the surface of the water as far as the eye could see. They sailed and paddled for many months, until they decided to make land. Years later, a few great-grandsons would make the return voyage and take back the chants of new worlds, so the ones who had stayed behind could know what their people had done."

"That's interesting," said Maggie. "Is it true?"

"Maybe. The legend of the South Pacific is repeated in a lot of Polynesian cultures. The old chants in Tahiti and Hawaii about the floating villages are too similar to be made up independently. Some of the words are even the same."

"Then I believe it."

"It was stories like that, mixed with some great fiction like *Moby Dick*, that made me go to sea. Then there were others that make you want to fight."

Squid pointed to the south. "The pirates in Shepherd's Journal were good shallow-water seamen. They had to know the sea and be able to memorize landmarks."

"Such as Angel's Rock," said Stanley.

"Yeah. They also knew the tides and currents. That's the only way they could have gotten from sea to shore and back." He pointed. "The Japanese Current is out there a few miles; it almost touches at Mendocino and again off Monterey. At places, there are shelves that lift the incoming currents to the surface. I'll explain better when we take the boat out."

They came upon the first view of the ocean. A different Pacific from the one they'd viewed from the air. Tomorrow they would gain yet another perspective.

Squid stared at the vastness. "Sailors have always hated pirates who bastardize the sea. We despise them and give no quarter, and they know it. They fight to the death. They've nothing to die for except their greed, and greed doesn't sustain a soul. Once it was the Moors and Libyans, and in the past century the Caribbeans and Southeast Asians have been the worst, but they all pick on the helpless and kill indiscriminately. The Serpientes were no better. Neither are their spawn, these new Serpientes. There are great legends like the story of the

Pacific I was told by the chief. Then there are dark legends about monstrous murderers, such as the ones we'll face."

Link had once believed that Squid talked too much, that he spoke to hear himself. Now he listened, for their lives would depend on Squid's competence.

"When we find them, we'll have to be ready to act, and we'll need proper weapons to destroy them. That's why I wanted all the extra firepower."

They'd come away from the store with four nickel-plated Remington marine magnum shotguns, each with a seven-round magazine tube. Stanley picked combination high-power flashlights and laser sights to be mounted on the shotguns for night duty, and Squid took along enough ammunition, mostly double-aught and number-two buckshot, to start a small war. Link had picked out a GPS that was ruggedized for marine use, and four UHF handheld radios (requiring a permit from the FCC, which Link also managed to produce). In addition, there was a profusion of items that "might come in handy."

The clerk had asked, "What are you going for?"

Squid gave him a serious look and whispered, "Sasquatch."

He received a serious look in return from the man, who was not about to lose a big sale.

Stanley hardly contained his laughter. There was a mutual respect between the men that Link did not quite understand. Squid was big and tough, intelligent and streetwise. Stanley was slightly built and methodical to a fault.

Link also wondered how long it would take for word of the shotgun purchases to find its way to the Lennville Chief of Police.

Squid asked Stanley to stop at the coast guard radar station, where he rang a buzzer on the gate and waited until a sailor came out to let them inside. "I'll be back shortly," he said when Stanley parked in front of the small headquarters building.

Forty-five minutes passed before Squid emerged, and they still had things to do.

Stanley pulled back onto the poorly paved road and turned left toward Lisbon.

"How did it go?" Link asked.

"A coastie lieutenant's in charge of the station. Nice guy, knows his stuff. There's also a couple of civilians working with the radars, and a three-man U.S. Navy team. They're NIS, but they don't announce it. A master chief runs that show. We have a mutual friend in the business."

"What business?" asked Stanley.

Squid nodded seaward. "Keeping track of the fishing fleets out there."

"Link said you'd be able to tell us more about those. Japanese?"

Squid had a list. "How about Chinese, French, Russian, Japanese, Canadian, North Korean, Vietnamese, Chilean, Peruvian, Brazilian, and Australian."

"What the hell are they doing here? Just fishing?"

"You can't guess?" asked Maggie. "It's why they have all those antennas."

Stanley formed an *oh yeah* expression. "The assholes are stealing our technical secrets."

Squid nodded. "Some are. They don't even put up a front, just openly use their surveillance gear and screw Uncle Sam. Most have a processing ship, a couple of trawlers, and eight or ten boats. I call the ships big mamas and all the others babies."

"They take a lot of fish?"

"If the North Koreans didn't have fishing operations, the other half of their population would starve. Problem is the majority of their big mama crew doesn't give a hoot about fish. They're too busy with their electronic eavesdropping."

"Who's located where?" asked Link.

"Considering only the big guys, going from north to south it's Russians, Canucks, Koreans, Chinese, and French. The big mamas stay on their assigned stations, never varying more than a hundred yards." He smiled. "I've got their coordinates."

"Are they armed?" asked Stanley.

"You bet. Same as our electronic surveillance ships have been armed and escorted since the Pueblo Incident in 1968, when the North Koreans boarded and took the crew prisoner."

"And we're going out there in an itty-bitty fishing boat?"

Squid laughed. "One that floats, with an engine that runs *pretty* good."

"Why didn't we look in Eureka? It's a lot bigger and probably has better boats for sale. You and the store owner talked about a company to avoid?"

Squid hesitated.

"The company you mentioned was Zerbini Holdings," said Maggie.

Squid seemed reluctant to proceed.

"Tell them," said Link. "They're trustworthy."

"I know, but if one is caught and put through what they did to Erin and Mr. Dubois, they'd give everything away." Squid shook his head. "It's best they don't know."

"What if the someone is you?" Stanley asked. "Then we'd be left up that well-known stream of flowing feces without a wooden device for manual conveyance."

"For starters, I know how the Serpientes are smuggling in the terrorists."

"Great!" said Stan. Maggie gave him a look that suggested he restrain himself.

"A few years ago, the eldest son of a rich San Francisco family formed a company called Zerbini Holdings and bought idle fishing boats around the Bay Area and Eureka for ten cents on the dollar. If he's Serpiente, like I think, I don't want him knowing we're buying a boat."

"Zerbini?" Maggie asked, showing surprise.

"Peter Zerbini. He runs the family holdings, which are considerable."

"They're one of the oldest, best respected families in San Francisco."

"Yeah," said Squid. "Those Zerbinis. They've run fishing-boat fleets, seafood restaurants, and controlled a whole lot of shipping since the gold rush. The family's forgotten more about the California coast than most ship's captains ever knew. Peter Zerbini lives in a mansion on Nob Hill, and the family bought a home in Lennville a long time back."

"We'll need facts if we want to convince anyone," said Link.

"I've got some, but we'll need more."

Maggie tried her cell phone. She was at the fringe of reception. Finally she was able to get through and held the instrument tightly to her ear as she asked that another name be run. "Peter Zerbini," she said. She frowned, asked the person on the other end to repeat. Then she said in monotone, "I understand," and disconnected.

She looked shaken. When her cell phone rang, she shut it off.

"What's wrong?" asked Link.

"The duty agent was ordered not to assist me, just tell me to return ASAP. They want me back today. Stanley, too. We're to bypass our SAC and report directly to the director in charge of West Coast Operations in Sacramento."

They were momentarily stunned into silence.

"That's the sort of thing I was worried about," said Squid. "The Zerbinis have clout, and they're on to you."

"So is Judge Bull. It seems all of the Serpientes have clout," Stanley observed unhappily.

•

28

Sydney had taken a bedroom in her half brother's spacious home, which had been constructed in 1859, under the supervision of an ancestor named Jack Bull, who according to the book had descended from a Russian-speaking Aleut named Boo. That she had another father and could not share that proud tradition had once outraged her.

The day her mother had been informed of her widowhood—her husband had been dashed against the Angel Rock and his body lost at sea—she'd turned her considerable wiles and marginal beauty to work snaring another Serpiente, choosing Emmett Baumgartner, since he was a malleable man, not a frequent trait to be found among the Sociedad. That he'd been married posed little problem. The day after Emmett expressed his concern that his wife was suspicious, the woman came down with a bout of flu that she could not rid herself of. One hour after her death, her body had been sent to the mortuary kiln and reduced to ashes. Her relatives had complained, but were soon consoled by a considerable settlement that Emmett did not contest.

Sydney had inherited her mother's practicality and refusal to allow anything to stand in the way of her ambition. She supposed she had also inherited her father's evasiveness, in that she could twist the truth to whatever she wished it to be, and had grown to look forward to acting the chameleon. She especially loved the challenge of posing as another, then placing herself in a situation to see if she could pass the test.

There were still two hours before her brother would leave his office downtown and return home for dinner, so she ran a hot bath, stripped, and as water filled the tub, observed herself and imagined new ways that she might be changed. She would indulge herself after a busy day of e-mailing and phoning her many contacts around the world, using various pseudonyms.

She stepped into the scalding water slowly; it would soon become bearable.

During her past, she'd been a dancer, a courtesan, a nun, a streetwalker, a housewife, an adventuress, an airline attendant, a grand lady—and men?—a Hezbollah courier, an Israeli agent for the Israelis, a Saudi businessman, Sajacento's wise adviser. Her roles, those and many more, were never questioned. It was not as if she had made herself up and acted like those people, she had *become* those people.

The few who had known about her abilities had found her odd, and few lovers, whether men or women, appreciated the amusement that she provided by changing herself to whatever they wished her to be. Only one had guessed that the person he sated himself with existed only in his mind.

One had listened to her secret and knew to sample the identities, defile, and humiliate them. She'd told him how she wafted, detached, like a flatliner viewing her own death. They'd ventured into fantasies as strangers, he stalking and she running, and when they'd emerged from the violence, they'd share wonder. Her lover had hurt the women she had brought for him. Ridiculed and belittled and defiled them, forced them to perform every disgusting act he could imagine. Used them with imagination. They'd cried and begged and screamed in terror and pain. But later, when she returned to being Sydney, he had been ever the gentleman, ever sharing.

Dead, dead, dead.

She was rudely torn from her reverie. Her lover's destruction had been administered by the man she despised more than any other. She wished she had Lincoln Anderson so she could torment him for all that he had taken from her. Sydney believed in balancing the books, keeping them in order. A workaholic Serpiente accountant had once taught her about such bookkeeping.

There was another individual aside from Anderson with whom she had not reckoned, who was closer at hand, and she was uncertain whether she should kill him. She'd once feared him so terribly that she might hesitate even now. It was not often that Sydney considered the option of failure.

Wendell Welk, now a policeman, had been her brother's closest comrade. Maybe still was, although El Jefe did not allow camaraderie to cloud his judgment. Once she'd secretly admired Welk's strength and athletic ability. She had also been deathly afraid of him, and he'd known it. When her brother was away in law school, Wendell had taken full advantage. He was eighteen and she fourteen, and he'd continued for the two years until she left. No way she'd have told on him. Other girls were afraid of him and did not know why. But Irene Baumgartner had known why to be afraid, and whenever the big, acne-plagued Indian kid told her to kneel or lie back, she didn't hesitate for a second.

Welk had been as terse about those sexual acts as he'd been about most things. When he finished with her, he'd hike up his pants and walk off, already thinking of something else. It mattered very little to Irene. By then the Serpientes had taught her how to lose herself in her own mind.

The previous year she'd been a homely, bashful, brainy child whom no one took notice of, who, save for her superb school grades, was unexceptional in every way. Then, to her embarrassment, she'd developed breasts so large for her stature that she could not possibly hide them.

The first one had later told others he'd gotten the idea when his wife was away for half an hour. "Just one half hour," he'd emphasize, although Irene remembered it as an endless period.

He'd seen Irene passing by and called her inside. "Randy little bitch didn't hesitate." None of his listeners cared that she'd been thirteen, and they knew he was one of the fattest and meanest Serpientes, a man far too frightening for a young girl to disobey. He'd led her to the dining room, sat on one of the chairs, and held her on his knee while feeling her, then unclothing her, later saying he knew she was ready because of the way she'd squirmed. Snorting with lust, he'd hauled her onto the handiest surface and had to apply himself with determination, since it was her first time. Irene remembered crystal shattering onto the floor, then him yelling for her to hurry and clean it all up and bring replacements for the glasses from the fucking cupboard and get the fucking table reset before his wife came home because they had fucking guests.

She'd been dazed and afraid and had stumbled behind him, straightening things until he'd shoved her out the door. Thereafter he'd picked other handy surfaces, so he could say he'd had the little bitch on the poker table or countertop. Shoulda seen her afterward, crawlin' around, an' pickin' up poker chips. Once his considerable weight had caused a heavy glass coffee table to collapse. He had finished nonetheless. Mean and uncaring, and she had been too frightened to try to stop it, learned to endure by realizing she was not there at all. In her mind, he was doing it to a bad girl she knew at school.

One afternoon the "first one" had bragged about it to the workaholic, the cruelest of the Serpientes, who had called her father and growled for him to send her over—he had a chore. Thereafter, the workaholic had called her home every Wednesday night when his wife played bridge, telling, not asking, her mother to send her over to help him with paperwork. "Of course, hon, you know Irene loves to help." He'd toil with the books half the night with her in the foot well. Now and then, he'd groan and pat her head. At two or three o'clock, he'd send her home, admonishing her to not awaken his wife, who had come home sometime in the evening.

The two old men felt that doing it to Irene was better than getting it from someone on the outside, like keeping a special handshake within their secret family. They were tough and mean as nails, while her father was weak in comparison, and it was the way of Serpientes to prey on the weak. Others soon knew what they were doing because they boasted about it. If one had her do something, the other wanted it done. Periodically they'd meet at one or the other's home and take turns.

She'd uttered not a word. Just imagined herself in another's body. Tarzan's Jane or Dale Evans. Alice in Wonderland, a high-flying aviatrix. An evil witch. Getting better and better at losing herself and becoming another person.

Shamed only when she heard them bragging about doing it to *her*, not noticing that she'd change her voice, her hair, her gestures, and the way she dressed. Never acknowledging that they had done nothing to her, but rather to the ones she'd become.

Irene hadn't complained to her father, because he would have been too frightened to stop them. Maybe he'd have killed her. Weak or not, he was a Serpiente. When her mother had found out, she'd thought it was funny. "More power to you." As if Irene should enjoy what they did to those other girls. More likely, she did not care.

Not her half brother, though. If Lyle had known, there was no telling what he would have done. Another reason Irene did not tell anyone was her fear that they might decide she was loose tongued and send her to the stone. It was better to become another person and let them do as they pleased. If only they'd not continued to brag about doing it to Irene Baumgartner.

Like Wendell Welk, the old men had continued until she'd left home. At age sixteen, Irene had gone off to Santa Clara University—unsure of herself, unnoticed by boys and disliked by girls, frightened and compliant, slipping into a fantasy whenever threatened by harsh reality. Her redemption had been that she'd had a high IQ and earned superb grades.

When she'd returned to Lennville at age nineteen, Irene had changed. Although still plain, she'd learned how to make herself presentable. Something seemed different about her, yet she had no close friends to note that the size of her breasts was no longer remarkable, and no one to suspect that the reduction had cost a considerable amount of money.

Irene was more determined, knew what she wanted, and had learned that careful planning and bold execution were the ways to get there. While she had not interrupted her studies to attend her parents' funeral—they'd died in a questionable light airplane crash—she had been concerned about another matter, and returned home for the summer before transferring to Georgetown.

Her half brother had become a Serpiente at age twenty-two after another member had become a victim of the dead tide. When Irene returned, Lyle was twenty-five and believed himself too young to vie for the vacated Jefe's chair. He remained in San Francisco working at a reputable law firm while the other Serpientes connived.

The morning she'd arrived home, Welk had entered her room while she was unpacking, snapped his fingers, and pointed—and like Pavlov's dog, she complied. As he'd labored over a harlot from her imagination, she had asked pointed questions about Lyle, and realized that she wanted the Jefe's chair. Two minutes after he'd zippered and left, cold as a chilly wind, she'd been on the phone with her half brother, encouraging him to return and seek to become the new Jefe.

She'd launched her plan, starting by pleasuring the "first one." The harlot from her imagination had given him a night to remember, as Irene detailed how the workaholic was stealing from him and the others by cooking the books. She'd also whispered it to Wendell Welk, then to her half-brother.

Things fester when left like that. She'd been good at such things even then.

Within the week, those three had conspired to send the workaholic Serpiente to the stone, and had exuberantly beaten his head off with their clubs. Sydney had been overjoyed, for the workaholic accountant had been the most dangerous of the Serpientes.

Without him, the rest of it was less difficult.

The "first one," whose name was Philip Zerbini, grandfather of Peter Zerbini, was next. He and his visiting children were returning home from a movie in Eureka when they were killed by a hit-and-run truck driver. Neither truck nor driver were ever identified or found.

Hard to plan. Easy to do. She'd figured the timing and parked in a pickup at the highway intersection well ahead of the dump truck, waiting to signal her half brother. Twice it had failed to come off because of traffic on the back road. Finally she'd signaled, and her brother had driven head-on into the slower-moving Cadillac.

Heart pounding, feeling a sweet throb between her thighs, she'd followed Lyle on a remote logging road and helped push the dump truck off a cliff.

The first one's wife had been skeptical until she had come down with a bad case of flu. Irene had found the poisonous concoction written on a note in a cookbook left to her by her dear mother, who had once used it to handle another situation. Like wife one, Philip Zerbini's widow had still been warm when she had been hurried to the crematorium.

The remaining Serpientes, Welk and Julius Lilac, had no longer opposed her half brother, Lyle Bull, who took over as El Jefe, thinking how much he owed Irene. He'd never learned what the two old men had done to his half-sister, or that their deaths had not been about him at all.

She had not considered killing Wendell Welk. He had done to the girls she'd become what was expected of Serpientes, and was close mouthed about it.

There was another she despised far more than Welk. Lincoln Anderson had exposed her, and shamed her, and taken her happiness.

Sydney was dressing when the front doorbell rang its stately chime. She heard the maid responding, then rapping on her bedroom door and announcing the visitor.

She'd not been expecting Chief Wendell Welk, and felt an instinctive pang of apprehension, so she hurried. When she emerged, he regarded her with his steady, unfriendly stare, as he would give a worm—or perhaps a corpse.

Sydney almost felt the old fear, a warning to prepare to slip into a role, but she was able to quell it. If he touched her, El Jefe would kill him. *If El Jefe found out. Would I tell him?*

Welk brusquely motioned at the sofa, sat, and sprawled. Sydney told the maid to leave, brought him a Budweiser—knowing it was his preference—and poured herself a tonic water on ice. She took her seat on the sofa and waited. Primly, like a lady.

"Yesterday El Jefe flew back from Frisco with a couple of FBI agents on their way to Eureka to pick up some troublemaker. He had Damon Lee follow them to the county sheriff's office, which made sense if they were picking up a suspect, so he went on."

Sydney listened closely, and while she already knew those things, she let him continue, nonetheless. Welk's task was to guard the Weeping Tree and the Serpientes. He did so with arrogance, fearlessness, and professionalism. He knew everything that was going on in the area, and nipped problems in the bud. During his tenure, no one had gotten close. A few too-curious tourists and locals had suffered lethal accidents, although none had been found near Lennville.

He sipped beer, reflected, and continued. "I spoke with my informer at the sheriff's office. The FBI agents showed up and pulled out a guy named George Andrews, who they were holding as a favor to a team of feds here on some kind of exercise to check out new night-vision equipment. Still no alarm bells, except they didn't treat Andrews like a prisoner."

So far it was all explainable, but the way he regarded her with his dead eyes, Sydney knew El Jefe had sent him to brief her, since Welk would not willingly share anything with a woman he'd once had with a snap of his fingers.

"This morning an airplane flew low over the airport. That got my attention, so I called around and found that it was a rental plane and the pilot was named George Andrews. Same Andrews? I didn't know, but the coincidences were growing. He had two passengers, a man and a woman. Since the airplane would be up for another hour and a half, I had my plant and some others locate Andrews's vehicle at the airport, pull it into a hangar, and hang a bird-dog tracker and a couple of bugs. Then

I took a look at our list of visitors to the local area, and guess who matched?"

"George Andrews." He was a pilot? Sydney felt a tingling of anticipation.

Welk took a swallow of beer. "Two days ago, he paid for a week's stay at a trashy dive near Ferndale. A man and a woman checked in there last night. The descriptions matched those of the agents. More coincidences? I don't think so. Ferndale's too damned close. Now they're looking at our airport, and it would be nice to know where they were flying.

"I dispatched four of my cops to join the informant deputy with orders to follow Andrews using the bird dog. If they separate, keep following Andrews. I'd make up my mind if and when they should take them."

"We can't get into a pissing contest with the FBI."

He stared, hard. "No one would know what happened to them."

"Where are they?"

"Listen to the rest of it," he snapped. He was defensive. She decided there'd been a screwup.

"Go on." She was excited by a possibility.

"Andrews landed before my guys got there, so the deputy went after them alone. He'd tracked them into a shopping center when all the signals went dead. Half hour later, he found a wad of wires in a Wal-Mart shopping cart."

"They got away?"

"For now."

Sydney remembered how quickly Lincoln Anderson had found the tracking device on his pickup in Montana. How he'd eluded Damon Lee. Could it be?

"Did they get a mug shot of Andrews?"

"He was never charged, just held until the agents showed up. The deputy said he was tall and dark haired. Unkempt, like some homeless wino."

She wondered. That last part did not fit at all.

"He hardly talked until the agents got there. Then he told the male agent to go play with himself and turned his back on him, which my guy thought was funny."

"How about the agents?"

"Both short. Woman's in her thirties, a little overweight and stacked, auburn hair, about five-two. The man looks like a kid, with brown hair in a military cut. Maybe five-six or -seven. When I told El Jefe about it all, he phoned people he knows in Sacramento. Told the West Coast FBI honcho that he'd met the agents on the airplane, and they were drunk and insulting. The honcho said he'd recall them both. He didn't know why they were here, only that they're assigned to corporate espionage. Like I told El Jefe, that's bullshit."

"What do you think?"

"Maybe looking for drugs. Maybe looking for the heavy weapons we've been smuggling."

She rolled it around in her mind. It didn't sound right.

"Worst case, they're after the hostages at the Weeping Tree. Maybe the rag-head bombers?"

"If they knew about either of those, there'd be hundreds of agents."

"True." Welk finished his beer, put the mug onto the coffee table.

Sydney looked for a possible hole in her master plan. She found none, but wondered if the FBI might be investigating the double murder. Fuentes had insisted on the staged accident for the history professor from Berkeley and Dr. Walsh from the Weyland Foundation, saying they were getting too close in their search for the Weeping Tree, and were talking about the Sociedad too much. El Jefe had finally agreed and allowed it.

Lincoln Anderson had worked for the Weyland Foundation. Perhaps the act of killing another of his employees had drawn him.

"El Jefe said you could find out more using your connections."

She went to the built-in bar, doused the tonic water and poured a whopping Wild Turkey over ice, and thought about it all. She felt like celebrating. *He's here!*

Regardless of *why* he had come, Lincoln Anderson was falling into her trap.

"Tell us what you come up with," said Welk, and he stood up to leave.

"Wait." Sydney took a drink of whiskey, admired the taste, and gave him a look that was as harsh as any

he had cast. She was no longer concerned about what
Wendell Welk had done in the past to silly make-
believe girls. Regardless of the Sociedad, he was only
a corrupt country cop, while she was a world citizen,
about to mastermind the biggest disaster since 9/11
and Madrid.

He remained standing, not liking her attitude.

"Did your informant say anything about a scar on Andrews's forehead?" she asked.

He made an expression. "Ycah?"

"You should have told me," she admonished. "Now I
know who he is."

He glared back. "Tell me."

"We'll speak with El Jefe."

She exulted, feeling wonderful about the development.

5:35 p.m.

"It's an unofficial operation," Sydney told El Jefe.
"Even if the two agents refuse the recall order, there
are only the three of them, and they have no one to
turn to."

They were in an office in the building adjacent to the
old IOOF Hall, where El Jefe often worked in solitude.
Earlier he had hosted an eleven-way telephone conversation with his fellow U.S. justices. The court would not
meet for another two weeks, but there were considera-
tions regarding an important review.

What Sydney brought El Jefe was important enough
to warrant the imposition. Lincoln Anderson was obviously here, as she had warned them he might be.

Welk suggested they kill Dubois and Frechette and
transport their bodies to another place to be discovered,
far from Lennville and the old encampment, perhaps to
Georgia or Florida, where a massive FBI search was
taking place. It made sense, for that would take some of
the pressure off the search to find the hostages while
they were alive.

Sydney argued against it, but it was no easy thing, to
deny a Serpiente like Welk when he gave a suggestion
regarding their security.

His half sister was firm. "It's happening just as I wanted. Anderson's isolated and vulnerable. Capture him for me. I live for that moment. We can wait to kill the hostages for that long."

El Jefe had told Sydney she could have Anderson and the two hostages, and none of the Serpientes had argued. If it were a simple matter of honoring a promise, he could change his mind and no one would argue. Serpiente promises meant nothing. In the past, they'd honored no truces, given no quarter, slain messengers who brought terms of capitulation or begged for the return of prisoners who had likely already been executed. When ransoms were offered, they'd taken them and killed both captives and messenger.

El Jefe vacillated, first leaned toward killing the hostages and letting them be found elsewhere, then remembered how much he owed his talented half sister, and how Welk had screwed up by allowing Lincoln Anderson to get so close.

Neither Damon Lee nor the Hezbollah soldier, Kamil, had been able to track him. The man was elusive, and Sydney had warned them that he was dangerous.

He made up his mind. First he regarded Sydney. "There are five days until the *jahid* attack. Tomorrow we take the first four to their safe houses. The day after, we'll bring in the rest of the bombers. The hostages will be kept alive for that long. Then they'll be killed and their bodies taken to Georgia as Wendell suggested."

She knitted her brow, likely wondering if it would be enough time.

El Jefe looked at Chief Welk. "If you find Anderson in time, wait until she kills him and the hostages, and *then* take their bodies away to be found."

"Fair enough."

El Jefe stared with intensity. "I'm not happy with you, Wendell. Anderson should not have been allowed to get this close. If you can't find him in two more days, I'll announce that I've lost faith in you."

Welk took a step back as if he'd been struck. If he did not succeed in finding Anderson, he would be taken to the stone.

"Use every means at your disposal, Wendell. Work with Sydney. You're both after the same thing."

Welk left the room, obviously shaken. Sydney had outmaneuvered him, and he knew her connivery would be the reason for his death—if he allowed it.

29

They arrived at the small town before sunset. The homes were weather-beaten and empty, the businesses abandoned. To their right was the dry-dock boatyard, announced by a homemade sign promoting ANTHONY SILVA'S USED BOAT SALES AND LEASE. To the left, a sign showed that the Mateole Bridge was three miles distant.

Maggie was first out. She stretched to get the kinks out of her legs, then followed Squid and Stanley. Link hung back, leaving the selection of the boat to Squid.

There was no one to greet them when they walked down to the utilitarian fishing craft that looked as if they had not been afloat for a long while. They were arranged in two rows, the smaller ones farthest from the water were on pallets, the larger ones rested on four-by-fours with wooden rollers only a few feet from the river's edge.

Squid observed the large boats with a critical eye. All had trawling arms that extended high in the air with pulley assemblies to raise or lower them, and eye hooks for rigging and fishing lines. The wheelhouses were uniformly boxlike. Few had flying bridges. Some of the hulls were damaged here and there, and only two sported new coats of paint.

"It's a better selection than I thought they'd have."

"They all look tired," observed Maggie.

"Nothing to make them stand out," Squid said. He pointed at the far end, toward the smallest of the larger craft. "Twenty-two footer down there looks like the sort of thing we're after. Good vee bottom for rough water. But the cabin's too small, and the red trim makes it noticeable."

A rattletrap Jeep pulled in beside the Suburban. A rotund man emerged.

"I like this one," Stanley said.

"Too big," said Squid. "Thirty-four or thirty-six feet, and probably not maneuverable."

He stopped at what Maggie felt was the ugliest boat of the bunch, with mottled patches of white, gray, and black, and walked its length, running his hand over its side.

"It's hideous," said Maggie.

"Good choice," called out the fat man who approached them, listing on a gimpy leg. "Best one in the yard. Just inspected, scraped, and caulked. We'll have it painted by the end of next week if my help shows up. It'll look like new."

"Thirty feet?"

"Twenty-eight. Sleeps ten if you stack 'em, four if you're shy. Small quarters for the captain—or the lady. Has a refurbished big four-banger marine diesel. Disassembled it and put in new cylinders and electrical myself. Fast enough and reliable as you can get."

"I'd want a kicker."

"I've got a nice Evinrude twenty. Also a Merc."

"The others have names," observed Maggie, frowning at the patchwork.

"That's because the paint's been chipped off and we're just starting on the base coat. She's the *Lady Rosalie*, out of Seattle."

"We'd have to change the name," said Maggie. "My roommate in college was a Rosalie, and she ended up with a football player I had the hots for. How about the *Lady Margaret*?"

"Bad luck to change a boat's name," said Squid. He pointed at an aerodynamic antenna with a faded Raytheon logo. "Does the radar work?"

"Last I checked. Same as the Loran and backup radio. She's a real sleeper. Like I said, it's the best of the lot."

"Depth finder?"

"Sure. Just don't operate it in the extended range

modes in the areas I've marked on the chart in the wheel room. It's mating season for the whales."

"We also have the new GPS," Link reminded Squid.

Squid took another long look at the boat. "Can we get it into the water for a trial run?"

As promised, the boat was watertight, and the engine ran without coughing. Squid bargained, and Link forked over one of the cashier's checks and two thousand dollars in cash. Rigging ropes, an extra bank of batteries, a twenty-five-gallon bottle of propane, and a portable generator cost another thousand. The inflatable dinghy was another five hundred, the fuel three hundred. The mottled camouflage look and a decrepit Evinrude kicker were tossed in for free.

Silva did not comment when they passed on buying fishing gear. They had enough heavy line and weights that they could *appear* to be trolling the waters.

It was dark, and the boat was tied fore and aft to the dock, illuminated by lighting mounted on poles when Silva topped off the diesel and potable water tanks and the jerry cans from the Suburban with gasoline for the kicker.

They were transferring bags and gear from the Suburban when Silva commented, "Our friend at the maritime store said you were ex-navy."

"Seven years, four months. I was a petty officer first in submarines." Squid nodded at Link. "My boss here was a zoomie. Flew fighters in Desert Storm."

"Retired Chief Bosun's Mate Tony Silva."

The three shook hands all over again.

Chief Silva gave them a somber look. "I'm not asking what you're doing or where you're going, but watch yourselves. The seas here are as temperamental and dangerous as you'll find. Punta Gorda, where the river runs into the ocean, can be treacherous. You've got to listen to the weather band and heed their warnings."

"We'll keep a good watch," said Squid.

"I take it from what was said that you've had some kind of run-in with the Zerbinis?"

"I've heard things," said Squid. "Never met any of them."

"Best to keep it that way. They think the entire coast belongs to them."

"Do they come by?"

"Only Peter Zerbini. Doesn't like it when I buy another fisher from someone who went bust. He's tried to buy me out a couple of times. He wants my holdings: a few fallen-in houses; a couple of old stores, and this boatyard. He makes big offers—four, five times what it's worth."

"But you're not selling."

"I'm not ready to give up yet. My family's been here for a long time, and not one of them's sold to a Zerbini. There used to be a lot of net-cutting and stealing crab pots."

"But not anymore?"

Silva shrugged. "There'll be some of that as long as there's fishermen, but except for Zerbini, most are fighting to stay even. I'm okay. I keep ten boats working in Alaska while others have three or four. Zerbini's got sixty up and down the coast, and a few are kept busy stealing other people's catches. No, it's my location that he wants." Chief Silva regarded them, light from the posts playing on his aging features. "I gather you're not here for a pleasure cruise or to catch a big salmon."

Squid let it ride. An answer in itself.

Chief Silva lowered his voice. "There's something going on out there that Zerbini doesn't want me knowing, and since it doesn't concern me, I'm not sure I want to find out. A few days ago, I was out in one of the boats, running the coast about three miles from shore and concentrating on peaking the engine, when a forty-footer came up real fast. Peter went up on deck with two guys looked like they picked their teeth with crowbars, and eyed me over like I was somewhere I shouldn't be. Zerbini had a mean look, like he was mad as hell and would kill me for a dime. Since I was alone, I turned the boat around and headed back."

"Where were you when it happened?"

Silva looked away. "Ten, fifteen miles south of the river's mouth. I wasn't watching."

"Thanks for the heads-up. Okay if we remain tied up here for the night?"

Silva took his time answering. Finally he pointed up-stream. "The river up there's not affected by the tide. There's a safe anchorage up close to the bridge. Might think about shutting off your lights while it's dark and leaving at first light."

"Safer there than here?" Squid asked, surprised.

"Like I said, Pete Zerbini would like me gone. Wood burns, know what I mean? It's a dark one tonight, with the overcast and all. Being the cautious type, I'll sleep in the office with a shotgun. If his men found you here, there'd be questions, and we may all have health problems."

Squid didn't argue. "We'll pack the boat and clear out."

They finished transferring their belongings from the Suburban. When Squid asked Silva if there was a local 7-Eleven where they could buy a few groceries, he laughed. He did, however, confess to owning the small, local market a mile down the road. They could swing by, and he'd open up and sell him what they needed. He could leave the Suburban in any of the vacant garages. Silva had paid the back taxes on most of the abandoned homes.

The others stayed at the boat, stowing things until Squid and Silva returned in the Jeep. They lugged the purchased groceries into the *Lady Rosalie*'s galley, untied, and set off.

The boat's lights were not bright enough to navigate the river, so they used flashlights and called out obstacles. Squid was pleased when they made it to the bridge without running aground. There he made a tight 180-degree turn, backed up so they were headed downstream, let it drift for a hundred feet, and dropped fore and aft anchors.

11:45 p.m.—Aboard the Lady Rosalie, Mateole Bridge

They'd doused the exterior lights and were gathered around the table when a pickup rattled across the river bridge. There was no more traffic.

The galley was equipped with an assortment of appliances, including some that worked. Fortunately the range top and freezer were among those. Stanley thought he could repair the propane oven by cleaning the burners, but the refrigerator posed a challenge.

They ate hot dogs and chili prepared by Chef Maggie, listened to the weather forecast on the marine radio (there would be storms), tried and failed to get a cell phone signal, and talked about Tony Silva.

"I wish he'd paid attention to his location when Zerbini stopped him," groused Stanley. "Hopefully he got the direction right."

"He knows precisely where he was," said Squid. "He also knows he's vulnerable."

"That forty-footer will be a problem," said Stanley. "From the way our engine sounds, I doubt we could outrun a rowboat."

Squid disagreed. "She's sound, and she's faster than you think. We got a great deal. Good wood and a rugged design. Ten years ago, the *Lady* would have brought forty thousand."

Maggie snorted. "The Rosalie I knew was no lady." Like Link she poured chili onto her hot dog. The others ate chili and dogs separately, using plastic spoons and disposable bowls.

Squid continued: "I doubt we have to worry about Zerbini. The coastal radar's keeping track of things, and if what I think's going on is real, he doesn't want attention right now."

"Ready to tell us the rest?" Link asked.

"Yeah. We're in it together." Squid dug out a nautical chart.

Maggie took a small bite. Link decided she was the only person alive who could look feminine eating a hot dog doused with chili.

Squid leaned back in the weather-cracked cushion, belched with his hand over his mouth, and looked around the table. "Did anyone bring antacid?"

Maggie searched her purse and held up a roll of Tums. "Start talking, and you'll get one."

Squid munched a tablet. "After reading Shepherd's Journal I figured there were two big questions for a sailor. The first is how did they go back and forth from sea to shore in the days before internal combustion engines."

"The *marea muerta*," said Stan. "Shepherd said they used tides and currents."

"Yeah. The dead tide, but how does it work?" Squid took them through a quick tutorial about chasms, trenches, and great undersea mountains lying just off the coast. The Pacific here was deeper, and seismically and volcanically active.

"Then there's a thing called the Mendocino Triple Junction." As Squid brushed over the faults and plates, and the fact that they were overdue for an eight- or nine-point earthquake, he captured their attention. Then he went back to the dead tide.

He had a stack of faxes from Dr. Virginia Miller, of the Habitat Earth division, that concluded that the phenomenon could be explained only by a perfect combination of tides, currents, and underwater terrain.

"There's a couple basic things you gotta understand. Start with two major sea currents running side by side on the Northern California coast. They started as one down in the tropics near the Philippines, headed north to Japan, and crossed the Pacific in a clockwise arc like a river in the ocean, then split into two, one of which made a sharper turn and never got close to a glacier or ice floe. That one's comparably warm, but the other one detoured to Alaska and Canada, and it's cold as hell, like fifty-two degrees all the way down in Monterey Bay."

Link agreed. "Aircrews are briefed that if they go down within twenty-five miles of the coast without an antiexposure suit, they'll survive for only fifteen minutes."

"How fast are the currents?" asked Stanley.

"Three to four knots. They're slow, but they have massive volumes. Even the subcurrents are tremendously powerful."

"Aren't we looking for something a lot faster?"

"You bet, and that was Dr. Miller's challenge, to convert volume to rapidity. What was going on at Angel Rock to drive a craft ashore—or back—at high speed. In fact, in one newspaper report, Shepherd said the dead tide flowed shoreward on one side of Angel Rock, and seaward on the other! Her computer model considered variations in terrain, current volume, shelves and ledges, and tidal variations, even water salinity, and she ran thousands of combinations before she found three that showed promise. This morning, before I left SFO, she faxed me a condensed version of the winner."

Squid grinned. "I present the *marea muerta*." He pulled an inch-thick sheaf of papers from his carry-on bag and plopped it onto the table.

"We're supposed to understand all that?" asked Stanley.

"Dr. Miller made it easy for us. All we have to do is find a place with the following—" He showed them the summary:

1. Proximity to a pass-over of the Japanese and Canadian currents.
2. Surface water temperature between 56 and 61 degrees F.
3. A chasm wall sloped at a forty-five- to forty-nine-degree angle, rising from 2,100 feet to 3,100 feet up to a shelf at 220 to 280 feet.
4. A second wall, preferably sheer or convex, reaching up to a shelf depth of 15 to 40 feet.
5. Tidal flow negligible or within four feet of low tide.

"We're looking for deep water and a warm subcurrent that's drawn shoreward, passes beneath the colder Canadian current, then picks up speed as it's compressed into a channel worn into a massive stone wall."

"Like a river shooting through a gorge," said Stan.

"That's it. Then there's the second barrier, with a wall so steep that the subcurrent curls back on itself and rushes out to rejoin the mother current. The flow constantly changes according to tidal flow and water temperature, but for three hours every twenty-two-hour tidal cycle, the subcurrents flow almost side by side." He smiled. "That's the secret of the dead tide. According to Dr. Miller, that's the only way it could happen."

Maggie looked dubious. "Catch it on the north side of Angel Rock, and you're carried shoreward; to return to sea you go down the coast a short way and catch it going out."

"So we look for a place like that on the maritime charts," said Link.

"That's next. The Serpientes probably found it by chance, and from then on used Angel Rock for a visual reference. The turbulence had to be tremendous. Enough so that if they steered for the north side of the rock, they'd be swept around it, and accelerate like a snowboarder in a chute or a surfer riding a curl. We know they lost people because of all the bodies found by passing ships as recently as four years ago. Some were likely Serpientes."

Maggie finished her chili. "It would be better if they'd all died."

"Amen," said Squid, holding in another belch as the Tums went to work.

Squid displayed a chart showing underwater terrain and ocean depths. There were nine matches between San Francisco and Eureka. Two were north of the mouth of the Mateole River, on which they were presently anchored. The remainder were to the south, the southernmost was thirty miles north of Bodega Bay.

"I'd like to start checking them out in the morning. It's going to be dangerous as hell."

"We can drop off Maggie and Stanley," said Link.

Maggie shook her head; she was coming.

"If the Serpientes did it, so can I," said Stanley.

"I think they got tired of dying," said Squid, "and found a way to smuggle in people without killing half of them, something much more efficient."

"What draws you to that conclusion?" asked Stanley.

"For the last few years, there've been no bodies found."

Link thought of something. "We flew over at high tide, when there's no dead tide. Would anything look different?"

Maggie took the rest of the chili that she'd been eyeing. Link remembered her cast-iron stomach—when she wasn't flying.

"Maybe," said Squid. "Especially if the hidden lagoon's a tidal pond."

It made sense. Perhaps there'd been no lagoon because it was filled in. Link wished he could take the airplane up again, this time at low tide.

"We can look for it tomorrow," said Stanley.

"It'll be difficult to see a lagoon where we're going unless we get close," said Squid. "We're better off searching for Angel Rock. The lagoon may have washed away, but not a big granite formation that took a couple million years to form."

Maggie delicately licked the last of the chili from her spoon. "Now the other question. How did the Serpientes become more efficient?"

"Because Mr. Peter Zerbini owns more than a fleet of fishing boats and fancy San Francisco restaurants. I believe he's got his hands on an incredible submarine."

Suddenly, the sound of an explosion came booming up the river.

"Oh, my God!" cried Maggie.

Downriver the sky glowed bright orange. There were the *bam, bam, bam* sounds of a shotgun. The rattle of an automatic weapon. Two pops from a handgun. The noises continued.

"Sounds like a firefight," said Link.

"The boatyard," said Squid. "I'm weighing the anchors."

"I agree," said Link. "The chief may need some help."

"We don't have to go anywhere," said Maggie. "Listen."

Guttural sounds of an engine echoed off the river, ever louder, coming toward them.

30

They scrambled below, where the weapons were stored. Link snapped on his holstered revolver, hefted a pump shotgun loaded with double-aught buckshot, and went back up on deck, kneeling behind the railing, the others following and looking into near-total darkness.

The only illumination was from the flames at the boat-yard three miles distant.

"The water's deep here," said Squid. "If you have to get off, go to the starboard side, where it shallows out."

"What the hell's a starboard?" Stanley asked.

"To our right. What are you carrying?"

"A shotgun, .45 Colt auto, and a hideaway Glock on my right leg."

"Know how to use them all?"

"You bet."

"He means it," said Maggie.

"I've never fired a shotgun. I was waiting to pop off a few rounds when we got to sea."

"Just point and shoot, and anticipate the kick. We're using three-inch magnum rounds."

"Boat's getting closer. Sounds like an outboard."

Dim running lights appeared on the river downstream. In the distance beyond, there was another explosion, this one powerful. Debris could be seen blasting skyward, floating down, illuminated by bright flames. The boat before them became visible—a twenty-foot runabout that had been tied up to the dock at the boatyard.

A man was hunched over an outboard motor at the rear.

"Identify yourself," Link called out.

No one answered. The boat continued its course.

"He's going to hit us," said Maggie.

The open boat continued until twenty feet away; then the power was chopped to idle and the nose veered slightly leftward. Momentum kept the boat coming.

Link went to the side of the *Rosalie*, reached out and grasped the tie-up rope on the prow and secured it, then climbed down and went aft. He shone the flashlight on the boat's operator.

"It's Tony Silva," Link called out. "He's taken a round."

"I'm okay," whispered Silva. "Chest hurts like hell. Hard to talk."

Maggie joined them in the runabout. "Flash your light on the wound," she told Link.

There was no wound, only a gouge in the Vietnam-vintage flak vest that he wore.

"I told you I'm okay," said Silva in his pained voice. "Knocked the shit out of me, but it didn't penetrate."

"What happened?"

"I was sleeping in the office when I was awakened by engine sounds. When I turned on the pole lights, Pete Zerbini's fancy forty-footer was there, cut back to idle so it'd hold its position in the river. Four or five guys were on deck. One was filling Molotov cocktails, and a skinny guy was lighting one up."

"Was Peter Zerbini there?"

"I didn't see him, but they were his guys. I recognized the two big bastards."

"They fired first?"

"Hell no." Chief Silva gave him a look like he was crazy. "I was outgunned, and you're suggesting I make it a fair fight? The skinny guy lit the first cocktail, so I shotgunned the sucker. He was yelling and jumping around when he realized what he was carrying and tried to toss it over the side. Didn't make it. *Whoof*, right on the deck beside him. Then another cocktail caught fire, and that one lit another. A few seconds, and flames were everywhere."

Silva caught his wind for a few huffs, holding his chest. "They were all shooting or jumping off, every one of 'em mad as hell. Two headed for the office, and one shot my Jeep like a fool, because I was running for this boat. I started up, turned around for a last look, and wham, got knocked on my fat can."

"What were the explosions?"

"First one was the can filled with gas the guy was using to make the cocktails. Second was the boat's fuel tank. Also gasoline. That's why I prefer diesel. Won't burn as fast and doesn't blow. Half the old fishermen here have gone through a bad explosion."

"Did they have time for a radio call?"

"I doubt it. It went up fast, and the real big guy came running like hell out of the cabin."

"Where are they now?"

"Dumb shits shot the Jeep up so they're on foot." His eyes widened. "Aw, shit. They'll head for my house, and my wife's there alone. I've got to go."

"Forget it," said Link. "You can't even walk. Where's your house from here?"

3:00 a.m.—Lisbon, California

Link went alone. The others would slow him, and might be reluctant to do whatever had to be done. He was not sure what that would entail, but an FBI agent might hesitate.

Squid thought Zerbini was a Serpiente. Silva had recognized the attackers as being Zerbini's men. One of them might have the information that Link wanted.

The Serpientes were holding Link's closest friends. This was no time to consider scruples or waste time. Some of the attackers would go down. Since that desire would be mutual, Link would have to watch his own back, check his own six o'clock.

He jogged along the road in a trot and had already traveled a mile from the bridge, where Squid had taken him ashore in the dinghy. He'd shunned taking a radio and briefed the others to wait for him until daybreak, then take every weapon they possessed to check on Mrs. Silva, and then head for Eureka in the Suburban.

It was very dark, a state that Link preferred whether

he was hunter or prey. He carried the illuminator and nightscope, although he had not yet used them.

He saw a flashlight beam, then the shadows behind it. After stepping behind an abandoned shed as they passed, he fell in behind the five men, trailing six feet behind. In step. Quiet as the night itself. Listening.

He learned their names and what they were doing here. They'd been sent to burn the boatyard and scare the hell out of Silva and his wife. Since there was no way to tell Zerbini they'd been ambushed, they were improvising. They'd shut down the town's telephone service by turning off the equipment located at the boatyard, where they'd left the man Silva had sprayed with number two buckshot.

They knew where Silva lived and were going to drop in on his wife. There they'd leave one or two men to watch over the wife and make sure her husband didn't sneak back. The rest would take the Silva pickup and cruise the riverbank. One was certain that he'd hit Silva, so it was unlikely he'd made it far. When they'd decided what to do with the couple, they'd drive to the boatyard and finish what they'd started there.

The two large men that Chief Silva had told them about were the loudest. He called them Bigfoot and Dumbo, dominant alpha males who were walking in front, swaggering. Dumbo complained that they still hadn't found a car in the stupid town. Bigfoot told him if he hadn't shot Silva's "fucking Jeep" they'd be riding. Dumbo hoped Silva's old lady hadn't seen the fire and taken off in the pickup.

The rearmost one trailed behind the others, trying to work a stone out of his shoe. He stopped and bent down.

A short while later, another member of the group called back for him. When he got no answer, he told the others the rearmost one was gone. The ones in front ignored him and went on as he and his buddy went back to look. "Catch up," snapped Bigfoot.

The two large men did not notice when Link returned and fell into step. They talked about the house ahead, illuminated by the same kinds of pole lights Silva used at the boatyard, and decided to split up in the event that something more than Silva's wife was waiting there.

Maybe Silva had gone there to die. Dogs did that, one said, dragged themselves home to die.

They separated.

Link took Dumbo, who was closest, thumped him with the revolver barrel behind the ear as he'd done to the others. Dumbo went down like a sack of potatoes. He hogtied him with a length of the cord that he'd brought from the *Lady Rosalie*, cut it off with a Kershaw skinning knife he'd bought at the sporting-goods store, and went on to deal with the final one.

Bigfoot was almost difficult. He turned at some imagined sound and stared directly at Link, whose face was cast in the shadows of the pole lights. The bigger man jumped, startled, and started to raise the barrel of his pint-size Uzi.

Link held the muzzle of the revolver to Bigfoot's head and slowly cocked the hammer, an ominous sound in the still night. "Betcha can't make it," said Link, half-hoping that he'd try.

He took away the Uzi, and then marched Bigfoot down the road to find a place where no one would hear the big man's screaming.

6:05 a.m.—Mouth of Mateole River

Squid piloted the *Lady Rosalie* into the rolling waters of the open Pacific, leaving the relative calm of the river. Maggie watched closely, too filled with adrenaline to sleep. Stanley questioned Squid often. The two men got along famously.

Maggie was thankful. Link had returned two hours after leaving them, driving Chief Silva's pickup, with five men stacked in back like cordwood. All were hogtied and unconscious, with major lumps behind their ears. None were dead, but they'd suffered concussions or fractures and bled from nostrils and ears. There was another at the boatyard, the one Silva had shot when he'd tried to throw the Molotov cocktail. Link had not gone there and did not know his condition except Bigfoot had told him that he'd been peppered with buckshot and bled a lot.

The FBI agents surprised Link by showing not a hint of a problem with the battered condition of Zerbini's boatmen.

Silva said he'd haul them into the sheriff's office in Eureka and not mention Link or his crew. He was grateful, although not hopeful that the attackers would be convicted of anything more than trespass. Peter Zerbini kept a team of San Francisco lawyers on retainer, and they had a record of intimidating local prosecutors regardless of what Zerbini's miscreants had done.

Despite his gratitude, Tony Silva had still been unable to recall where he'd encountered Zerbini in his fast forty-footer.

"He's bullshitting us," Squid had said as they'd pulled anchor and proceeded downriver, on past the boatyard and the charred remains of Zerbini's forty-footer.

Link had told them it didn't matter. He'd talked with one of Zerbini's goons he called Bigfoot. They'd become buddies and traded secrets.

Squid had exploded with laughter. "What did he say?"

"Stay off the radio. They monitor everything." Link had yawned, said he'd tell him the rest later, and headed below to pick himself a bunk.

Sleep? The others were wide-eyed with excitement. *Who could sleep?*

"Which way do I turn when we get to the open water?" Squid called after him.

"South."

"How far?"

"Stay three miles offshore until you get to Angel Rock. Bigfoot thinks it's one of the three that'll be to your left. There'll be a big boat off to your right."

"The Canadian big mama?"

No response. Maggie went down to check and found Link in the tiny captain's quarters. The door was ajar, and he was sleeping like the dead.

She considered snuggling up against him to see what his reaction would be. Just as a joke, of course. She knew precisely what he would have done a few years ago, tired or not. She felt warmth creeping into forbidden areas.

"Away with thee, Satan."

Or was it, *"Later, alligator?"* She smiled to herself.

7:00 a.m.—The Weeping Tree

El Jefe stood in back, beside the blood stone, scanning the four Hezbollah and their sturdy cotton vests. Each vest was tailored specifically to their measurements, and held eleven two-kilo units of pliable RDX explosives in mesh pockets. None of the bombers, including the female, were notably large or small. The males were clean shaved, with neatly shorn hair. Each wore a school blazer, appropriate for collegiate wear at graduation ceremonies, which fit neatly over the vest.

The four, as well as those to follow, had been picked by Hezbollah cell leaders in Palestine for their fervent hatred of America, and for their families' dire need. Sajacento would deposit impressive sums into their survivors' bank accounts.

Kamil walked among the martyrs, congratulating them, but their attentions were on the one standing before them, whose blazing-hot eyes penetrated into their souls. Mullah Sajacento wore a turban and robes cut from fine linen, dyed the bright shade of green that was the trademark of the Judge of Men.

El Jefe, Peter Zerbini, and Mayor Harry Deaton observed the ceremony without expression. None said what they thought, that the bombers were fools and the man in green was a pompous idiot who believed his own pronouncements of greatness.

Sydney stood beside and behind Sajacento in a shapeless dark dress and a white modesty scarf. More often, the Green Mullah dealt with a slightly built pious man who constantly wore the traditional Muslim headdress called a *kaffiyeh*. He believed that Sydney was the pious man's courier, and never guessed that she was both of those persons.

They would drive the bombers to the airport in the big four-wheelers, and Kamil would fly them to airports nearest their safe houses. There they would be joined by the second Hezbollah on their teams, who would operate the remote controls.

The Hezbollah leaders had sent word. There must be *absolutely* no room for error. The second man would have control. From a proper distance, he would press the buttons in order. One for arming, the other for detonation.

Peter Zerbini whispered that everyone should hurry. He had brought Mullah Sajacento ashore two hours earlier to speak with El Jefe—with Sydney interpreting—and observe his bombers. As soon as the bombers were on their way, Zerbini would take Sajacento back to the safety of the processing vessel that lay offshore.

Zerbini said the currents would become dangerous in an hour.

He also had to look into an operation at Lisbon, where El Jefe had approved the encouragement of the town's proprietor to sell out and leave. Zerbini had not heard from his crew of "persuaders." He was not concerned that they'd fail so much as he was about the new gas-turbine forty-footer that ran like a hurricane and had cost an arm and a leg.

"It shouldn't be much longer," El Jefe told him.

The fifth Serpiente, Police Chief Wendell Welk, had been unable to attend; he was checking every available source about the locations of Anderson and the FBI agents. El Jefe wished him success. He did not want to eliminate any of his Serpientes quite yet. They were already one person short, and he was not confident of Damon Lee's abilities. But Welk had been complacent, letting Anderson snoop around right under his nose and ignoring Sydney's warnings. When El Jefe chose to act, he would have to be quick and ruthless about taking Welk to the stone. Otherwise, there might be a messy power struggle.

Before them, Sajacento's eyes blazed as he raised his arms before the bombers. He reached high as if something were there, and spoke in his high and strange voice. Sydney interpreted: "I know you will not fail me. Go and take their future."

The terror bombers cried out, unable to contain their enthusiasm.

31

Link came topside looking rested, much cleaner and close shaved. When he asked for their position, Squid showed him the chart, then went out on deck to put the boat into order and tie down a trawling arm more securely.

While Link had slept, Maggie had listened to Squid's explanations about how to take the boat to sea and establish a course. She'd spent little time on the ocean and soaked it all up eagerly, such as the way you must head into waves and swells, and as fast as you can brew coffee, the crew will ask for more. Happily, she'd felt no ill effects of mal de mer.

"Need a cuppa?" she asked Link. Thinking it was nice to be with him, even if she'd flushed a relatively promising career down the toilet.

"I got one on my way up," he told her, displaying a steaming mug.

Squid came into the wheelhouse and applied a friction clamp to steady the helm.

"It's time to share the rest of it with us," Link told Squid.

"Aye, aye," said Squid, which he had explained in salty talk meant, "I'll jump right to it." A single *aye* meant just plain old "yes," or—in their case—maybe an affirmative vote when the crew decided to mutiny because the admiral had slept and they had not.

Link ushered Maggie into a bosun's chair, and Stanley, who was drooping, into the other.

He nodded to Squid. "Tell us more about this special submarine. Also why you went to Canada then San Francisco."

Maggie listened raptly as Squid explained the American deep submergence craft used for underwater exploration and research that had been called the *NR-1*. Only one had been built, and it was now in mothballs.

But there had been a copy.

Stanley interrupted. "The Serpientes built one?"

"Even if they're as rich as we think, they couldn't afford it."

Stanley looked puzzled, as if wondering, *Then what's this about?*

"In 1995, I was sent to Nanaimo, British Columbia, on an exchange program to help the Canadians build a scaled-down version of the *NR-1*."

He told about the brilliant Commander Hemby and the *CNR-2 Sinner*, and how it had succeeded in its own right, using a titanium tether/lifeline. How after the craft was proved to work beyond all expectations, the project was canceled when a mysterious and powerful lobbyist had convinced the politicians in Ottawa that the *Sinner* was unsafe.

At the Weyland Foundation, Squid found himself thinking that the *CNR-2* would be perfect for smuggling people—not just the idea of a submarine because there were a lot of those on the civilian market, but one that could handle the heaviest seas, large enough to haul several people.

An RCMP investigator in Vancouver had learned that the *Sinner* had been disabled and sold, tender vessel included, as salvage to a maritime services company in North Vancouver. "Z-H Limited, immediately transferred it to Zerbini Holdings, in San Francisco."

"I'll be damned," said Maggie, spellbound.

"So you think—," Stanley started, his eyelids drooping precariously.

Squid continued. "I flew down to the City, but I couldn't get squat out of Zerbini's office. They had paper showing it was sold for scrap metal, but the Venezuelan company they sold to had gone bankrupt."

"End of story?" Link asked.

"Almost," said Squid. "I tried looking into who got the tender vessel, because of the special instrumentation required for the *Sinner*. Also a twenty-mile reel of titanium-enforced tether/conduit. Same story as before. The vessel had been resold intact to a company in South America, where it was gutted and sold again."

Stanley began to snore.

"Next I came here."

Maggie put on more coffee and visited the "head." When she returned to the wheelhouse, Stanley was still snoring and Link and Squid were deep in their own minds.

Squid made a minor correction of heading. Link was staring blankly, but his eyes were fixed on Maggie's breasts.

"Don't do that," she snapped.

Link came around and took the coffee that she offered. "Don't do what?"

"You were staring," she said.

Stanley was sleeping, Squid had not noticed, and she wished she'd not mentioned it. Link muttered something apologetic, and she felt foolish.

Stan was sliding off the chair, so she nudged him upright.

"Okay, Boss. It's your turn to tell secrets," Squid told Link.

"First go back to Z-H Limited. You said they bid on Canadian government contracts."

"Sure. Both federal and provincial. Most have to do with marine operations and services. Like they have an ice-cutter used to keep passages open in places like Prudhoe Bay."

"Go on."

"The British Columbian government isn't exactly pro-American when it comes to their interests. They're unhappy with Ottawa's agreement about fishing rights and access to ports. U.S. Customs won't allow their fishing crews ashore unless they go through the inspection and identification routine. Now Z-H provides two big jet-assisted, long-range De Havilland Flying Boats, like the Brits use between their smaller islands, to fly the crews back and forth between their trawlers and a moorage north of Vancouver. Customs isn't involved, and passengers come and go as they wish."

"Including terrorists fresh in from the Middle East."

"I don't have proof, but that's what I think."

"How would the terrorists get into Canada?"

Squid laughed. "Who *can't* get into Canada? Their immigration rules are a joke."

Link was aglow with excitement, and again his eyes wandered to Maggie's breasts. This time she tightened her tummy, looked as if she didn't notice, and shivered at a memory.

Stop that!

She spoke quickly to show she'd been listening. "Is Z-H involved in Canadian fishing?"

"Big fleets here, South America, and the Atlantic, all flying the maple leaf."

"Including the big mama here?"

"Yeah. Ottawa gives them a free hand and rakes off revenue."

Maggie exulted. "It's coming together."

Link realized where he'd been staring and without repentance moved his gaze to her face. "If we told Gordon our pirates had a submarine, he'd think we were crazier than before."

Squid went to his notes taken during his visit to the coast guard station. "The Canadian fleet came on station in the 1990s. One big mama processing vessel, three large trawlers, and eight fishing boats. The *Sinner* was sent to the scrap yard in 2001, and disappeared within three months. The flying boat operation started the following spring, when De Havilland hardly had the design off the drawing boards."

"Then everything fits," said Maggie, propping up Stanley again.

Squid cocked his head. "I figure the *Sinner's* released from the big mama with a full battery charge. That's only twelve miles out, so they can use the power cable. Since the *Sinner* can only hobble along at four knots, it descends into the inbound ocean river and accelerates to twenty knots or more as it rises with the current. It whistles past Angel Rock picking up steam."

Maggie listened intently.

Squid sighed. "Then things get fuzzy, because when it emerges, an observer could see it as it crawls ashore. There's got to be a way to hide it."

"Submerged in the lagoon?" Maggie asked.

"Doesn't work. It's too heavy. There has to be some kind of concrete runway and resting pad, and it would have to remain there until they're ready for the return trip."

"They'd have a blind."

"Probably, and since the *Sinner* spends most of its time berthed on the mama ship, they'd have to hide it there, too. That presents another problem. Where? The coast guard keeps its eyes on the operation, and now and then the big mama's captain, presently a Newfie with an accent you can cut with a knife, invites the coasties from the cutter aboard for lunch and a tour. The coasties say everything's shipshape, like an efficient fishing ship should be. If there was instrumentation like the tender vessel carried, they'd notice. And they'd sure as hell notice a hundred-and-thirty-foot submarine."

"Maybe they're tied up to one of the trawlers."

"I doubt any of those are large enough."

Maggie mused. "What if the Serpientes are working with someone else. The North Koreans or French, for instance? I'll bet *they* don't allow inspections."

"With Zerbini involved, the Canadian connection makes the most sense," said Link, "so that's where we'll concentrate our energy. We have to find Frank and Erin quickly."

"No way we'll forget about them," Squid said with passion.

Maggie was not so sure. The loss of two lives paled when measured against those that would be incurred by suicide bombers. Gordon Hightower was sure the Hezbollah were trapped in Georgia and would have to call off the attacks. But if they were launching them from here—

"By nightfall we have to be in port," said Squid. "The weather service is forecasting a storm before morning."

"We'll return to Lisbon for the night," Link decided.

"When are you going to tell us about Bigfoot? I'm surprised you got him to talk."

Link was deadpan. "I couldn't shut him up."

"What does he do for Zerbini?"

"Nothing requiring an IQ over fifteen. Mostly goon work, like stealing nets and crab pots, and scaring the hell out of any fisherman who strays into their area."

"What does he consider their area?"

"Everything twenty miles south of Cape Mendocino."

"The Canadian zone," Squid said.

"If anyone came within a mile of the ship, he was to sink them. No exceptions."

Squid wasn't shocked. "Fishing is serious business. No one wants their competition to know what they're catching and where. Some fishermen make bogus radio calls. If they can cause others to run aground, so much the better. They're competition. They carry rifles and automatic weapons to protect themselves with, and I don't mean from sharks. There are feuds and shoot-outs that aren't shown on news programs. The bodies are lost at sea."

"Zerbini's guys in one of the trawlers listen to the traffic on ship-to-shore and any other frequencies they can pick up on scanners. They have jammers they can use, but Zerbini has to authorize it. We'll just stay off the radios unless there's an emergency."

"What did Bigfoot know about the *Sinner*?"

"Nothing. He's been on the big mama ship and mentioned extra cabins that are set off by themselves, but every foot of extra space is taken up by storage freezers. There's no place to hide a submarine or anything else."

Link had learned two more things from Bigfoot. "When a trawler pulls up to big mama to transfer its catch, a large screen tarp is raised so no one can see what they're doing."

"That's one I've never heard of, but it makes sense. They're *really* paranoid."

"The last thing Bigfoot discussed was a damn big seaplane that lands and taxis over beside the big mama. The last one was two days ago."

"The De Havilland. Did he see who came off?"

"They pull up the shield. It could have been anyone."

"Then so far," said Squid, "there's no evidence that they're using the *Sinner*."

Maggie felt as discouraged as the men looked. Stanley sagged again, and she caught him. He came awake and tried to clear his head.

Link was trying to mask his disappointment that they'd more or less disproved Squid's theory. "Something I learned while flying combat and spooking around. Being tired makes you vulnerable. I want to start a watch schedule. Four on, four off. If you're not on watch, rest. I've had enough to take the edge off, and Maggie requires less than most people."

At least he remembers that much about me, she thought.

Link nodded at Squid and Stanley. "Find a bunk, and we'll see you in four hours."

Squid called out to Stanley, who was already on his way. "Make sure you strap in. We're leaving a fighter pilot in charge."

"He's not kidding," said Maggie. "The berths have seat belts."

"Where will you be going?" Squid asked Link.

"Searching the twenty-mile stretch for anything suspicious."

"Keep an eye out." Squid nodded northward, toward the big mama. "They'll have us on radar, and may send someone for a closer look."

10:00 a.m.—The Weeping Tree

Erin held her stomach and knelt so her face almost touched the ground. She was hurting again. Sydney had her beaten when Erin had first refused to destroy Helga—she had a hulking man strike her repeatedly in the stomach with his fists until her organs turned to jelly. That had been before she'd shown Erin photos of her son Johnny, and told her what could be. *Would* be if she didn't cooperate. Imagine him with a bright red necklace.

She'd been sliding the rustiest chain link back and

forth on the flat rock, not with vigor for there was no more of that, but slowly and leaning against it with some weight.

Sydney had told her that her idiot offspring was being flown to Arizona to stay with her parents near Flagstaff. They could get to him whenever they wished. If she refused again, Sydney would return with photos of Johnny after they cut his scrawny throat, and show her photos of her parents and son all laid in a row, all with the same red necklace. Did she doubt her?

She did not.

To get at the rusty link, she lifted a section of the chain. It was impossibly heavy.

Sydney had dosed her with drugs to make her compliant, left her, then returned, and the man had beaten her again. Erin had held up her arms in defense, screaming that she'd do it. Sydney had taken her secrets and her dignity. Clipped off her hair, left her with a stubble and laughed at the spectacle. Came back and flaunted her new blond tresses, and had her continue to commit treason. Gaining her country's secrets and giving them to the enemy. She had never balked, the vision of her son too vivid, but she had not exposed the most sensitive of her nation's plans, especially those to do with counterterrorism.

Erin leaned down and continued to scrape the chain link on the stone.

Frank was in a bad way. He insisted that she eat the same amount as he did, although she'd repeated that she was smaller and required less. Still he'd shared, and became steadily weaker. Erin was now the stronger of the two.

She'd caught two frogs that morning and they'd eaten them. What mattered was not whether a morsel was disgusting, but whether it was edible.

Sometimes there were grating noises when they worked the chain links against a stone. Once Chief Welk had been drawn and peered through the boards nailed in place over the entrance. She'd rocked back and forth and wept, and her chains had made similar noises. He'd gone on.

No one was out there now. The sentinel was in his

hut. Sajacento had left with Peter Zerbini after the departure of the young terrorists, with their vests of high explosives fashioned by the chemists. The master and his assistant were in the bungalow, doing what they did often when left alone. The assistant cried out with pleasure as the older man grunted.

The Weeping Tree was adjacent to the bungalow, and they heard their conversations and other utterances. They'd learned many of the terrorists' secrets during the past hours.

They had to get away, take the secrets to someone who could stop them.

She heard Frank make a small cry. "Are you—okay?" she asked.

"I—broke the—chain link."

"That's—wonderful." With so little to drink, and that only early in the morning, they'd become parsimonious with words, often uttering a single syllable at a time.

"I've—taken—it off."

She was pleased for him.

"Then I will look—at the boards."

The wooden barrier would be just as difficult to get through without tools as it had been to file through an iron chain with a stone.

There were things they knew. They must get the word out soon.

Six more young terrorists were about to arrive. She had seen the determined face of Sajacento. If he succeeded, they would send more, and then more.

Where are you, Link?

Erin loved Link dearly, despite his complexities. Friends were so essential. If it was at all possible, he would come for them, yet they must not sit back and wait. They must get out.

Sydney had planted lies to convince the FBI to concentrate its search in Georgia. The Hezbollah had sacrificed two zealots who had died fighting as they were discovered fleeing. One had carried papers in his shoes giving locations of other terrorists, and those places had been set up to look as if others had just fled. Hezbollah leaders had made false statements on cell phones in

Syria that were monitored by the NSA. Everything pointed to Georgia.

Erin knew that her own rusty link would soon give. Then all they had left to do was remove the two-by-sixes barring the entrance, get past the sentinel, and somehow not be heard by the chemists, who were presently whispering endearments and vows of eternal love. Finally they must find the energy to walk out to wherever they had to go.

Frank pressed his frail weight against the two-by-sixes. Nothing moved.

Erin started to tell him to wait, that she would soon be done with her own chain and join him, but another severe pain jolted through her abdomen, and she curled up to wait it out.

32

Maggie was doing her job as helmsman while Link stared through binoculars at the shore. So far, he'd seen no more than he had from the air, although the craggy stone formations were more foreboding from close up.

There were three candidates for Angel Rock within the twenty-mile zone that Bigfoot had protected. The northernmost one was the terror they'd noted from the air. That craggy rock soared higher than the others, and the sea about it was achurn. Seawater boiled, and great plumes spouted at either side. That one was located six miles behind them. The other candidates were three and five miles beyond it.

"Turn back for another run," Link told her.

"Aye, aye, Captain," she said with a serious face, but she did not maneuver. Link had mounted the new nautical GPS. The device was secured—brackets had been included—on the instrument panel. A line ran to a twelve-volt outlet, another to an antenna mounted on top of the wheelhouse. The screen showed that they were being observed by sixteen satellites, meaning the position reading was precise. They were 3.2 miles from shore.

Maggie grease-marked the location on the Plexiglas protected nautical chart, then announced, "I've marked the northern waypoint. We're coming about."

She made the turn gently so the men below wouldn't be thrown about.

"Since I'm in the market for a job, maybe I'll become a ship's pilot or fisherwoman."

"You're a great first mate." He glanced over and noted that she blushed. He smiled, feeling easy in her presence.

The seas were moderate. The depth meter showed the bottom at seven hundred feet.

They listened to a weather band broadcast. A storm warning was in effect from Point Arena to Eureka, forecast to come ashore near Cape Mendocino with thirty-five-knot winds at two o'clock in the morning. A period of calmness would prevail before a second storm front with high seas and gale-force winds arrived tomorrow. Small craft—such as the *Lady Rosalie*—were advised to find shelter for the duration of both storms.

Rain was misting the windshield. The wiper was operated manually by a lever, which Link periodically moved back and forth.

"It's a lousy time for a damned storm," Link said.

"There's time to finish our tour and for Squid to make a few runs."

He observed the depth finder. "The bottom's now at fourteen hundred feet. It's like a mountain range down there."

"We're in the whale area Tony Silva told us about, so turn the finder to low power."

Link made the adjustment.

"Can you imagine a big male humpback trying to climb on *Lady Rosalie*?"

"I'd rather not."

She paused. "I don't think you should walk tonight. The weather's going to be bad."

"Three nights are all we have. I can't waste one of them."

"I'm coming. Two heads are better than one."

She peered closer to the windshield, then at the GPS, then at the nautical chart. Satisfied that nothing was there, she said, "Why didn't you call more often?"

He told the truth. "I was waiting for you to call first."

"Me, too." She laughed. "What a pair we are. Both of us so egotistical, we think the other should phone first."

He made a stern face. "I don't consider myself egotistical."

"Yeah, right. Like I suppose you're not going to make a move when we go below as you so neatly arranged."

"Of course I won't make a move on you."

"What's that supposed to be? Another confidence builder?"

"Does that mean you'd like me to make a move?"

"Five years ago, you blew your chance. Now you expect me to roll over and smile?"

"I do not."

She cast him a grin. "Do too."

He chuckled.

"Kinda like the old days."

"We knew how to end arguments."

She glanced over. "You think we forgot?"

"Yeah. We're too serious." He pointed. The largest of the rock formations was ahead and only slightly left.

"I've had it on the GPS all the way." She turned to avoid it. "What do you think?"

"I hope it's not this one. The others are scary enough."

"We're in the low-tide window. If Squid's right, there's a lagoon forming somewhere."

Maggie gave the rock a healthy berth as she started around its right side. The seas before them appeared choppy and mean, and worsened by the second.

He started to ask what she was doing, but held his tongue.

"Feels like I'm fighting a heavy current."

Maggie continued to angle leftward around the rock, proceeded with the wide turn—until suddenly the boat veered sharply left and rolled, threatening to turn broadside.

"Damn thing's fighting me!" she said, shoving the throttle full forward and cranking in more right helm until they were on the north side of the rock, now being swept toward the distant shore. She corrected more, until the *Lady Rosalie* slowly straightened.

"Keep the pointy end forward."

"You're a lot of help."

"Want me to take it?"

"I would rather die." She held on fiercely, working with the throttle, now pulling it full back. They were being drawn ever faster.

"The current was against us—now it's dragging us forward."

Ahead were two beaches separated by a huge gray stone that appeared indistinct, moving yet stationary. He blamed the phenomenon on the rain-spattered windshield until she pointed.

"I can't make that out. It looks all fuzzy."

She saw it, too. Seawater seemed to flow into the fuzzy area with hardly a ripple. An optical illusion?

"How far are we from shore?" she asked as he used the lever to clear the windshield.

He switched GPS modes. They were traveling at twenty-eight miles per hour, although the throttle was back and it seemed they were hardly moving. Then Link realized that the two beaches were much closer.

He changed to map mode. They were one mile from shore and closing fast.

"Turn starboard," he said.

They slowed, the water suddenly manageable, and she was back in control. They'd passed over the second ledge that Squid had described. The vicious current had curled back on itself and was left behind. She continued the turn, and the boat responded nicely.

He peered back at their eight o'clock. The twin beaches were clear. Not so the fuzzy area between. *Camouflage net?* That didn't seem right. He'd seen camouflage netting in Iraq covering SAM sites and bunkers. This was different. Something was not right.

Maggie headed to sea. At first slowly, then steadily picking up speed. The GPS showed that they sped along at fifteen, then twenty miles per hour. It settled on twenty-eight mph.

"Would you believe I've got it in idle again?" she asked.

"Right now I'd believe anything."

"Is that where you're going tonight? Back there?"

"Yeah. Shepherd wrote about hand- and toeholds dug by slaves on the north face. If they're not there, I'll try something else, but I think this is the place."

"I'm tagging along," she said. "My curiosity bells are ringing."

As they continued past the rock, the current diminished. Neither of them doubted that they had found Angel Rock.

She turned and resumed the southeasterly heading down the coast. Several minutes passed, and they were approaching the next big rock when Link pointed starboard. A deep-hull fisher was paralleling their course, too distant to make out fine details.

They watched on radar as the boat altered course to intercept them.

Link checked the shotgun that he'd brought up. With the tubular magazine extension installed, he had ten rounds of double-aught buckshot available.

"Do you feel like guests?" Maggie asked.

"Not especially."

She pushed up the throttle. "Me neither. I'm not properly dressed."

"You don't have a thing to wear, right?" It was one of their old litanies.

"I'll head for Nordstrom first thing in the morning."

They were doing twenty-eight, then thirty miles per hour. He checked the radar. The other boat was at two miles and steadily falling behind."

"I like the *Lady Rosalie*," said Maggie.

It was one o'clock. Another hour remained before Squid and Stan would relieve them. Despite their maneuvering, Maggie had obviously not awakened them. Link stood close at her side, wondered what would be in store when they went below.

1:30 p.m.—Lennville

A day had passed, yet Chief Welk was no closer to finding Anderson and the two agents. The possibility of failure before tomorrow's deadline was distinct on his mind. It would be difficult for anyone to disregard the thought of imminent death, and he was no exception.

He'd scoured every inn, hotel, and motel from Eureka to Garberville and found no one who recalled a person fitting Anderson's description. There'd been several possibilities that ended in dead ends, but nothing more. He had received a phone call from the chief of police in nearby Fortuna incensed that Welk's policemen had strong-armed one of their citizens, Gerard Andrews, and Welk had halfheartedly apologized. The daytime deputy from Eureka whom he paid off regularly reported that four people had purchased a large number of weapons the previous day. A telephone check showed that the sale was to a properly licensed firearms dealer.

Welk had begun to think of an alternative plan that might keep him alive. No way was he going to let El Jefe haul him to the stone without a fight.

He was looking at the doorway when Sydney arrived, still wearing the blond wig she'd had on the previous day when they'd gone to see El Jefe.

She was not the same person he'd known when they were young. That Irene had been easily dismissed, a convenience for his horniness.

He was not friendly. "Help you?"

"Actually El Jefe told me to help *you*." She formed a laconic smile and remained standing, a game some people employed. Welk was irritated by it. Real power was not a game of looking down or up; it was knowing you could squash someone like a bug if you wanted.

Welk teepeed his hands. *You are insignificant,* he said with his eyes. "Do you know where I can find Anderson?" he asked.

"No."

"Then I don't need you, so get your scrawny ass out."

He waited for outrage. Perhaps fright as she remembered how it had once been. Instead there was not a flicker of emotion.

"Have you ever been to Lisbon?"

"Sure." The Serpientes sometimes talked about Lisbon, which was situated too close to the old encampment. The town was even mentioned in the book. The Portagees there had always been stubborn about moving. If they'd eliminated the fifty-odd people, they would draw attention from relatives, and a flock of lawmen would undoubtedly descend on the area.

What the Serpientes had been unable to do, the lack

of salmon had done. When no one could any longer make a living, the citizens of Lisbon had moved on. All but one stinking family—and one family they could handle.

"Last night Zerbini sent six tough guys to Lisbon to encourage the Silvas to leave."

It was old news. "El Jefe gave him permission to run them off."

She held up a hand to gain his attention. "Tony Silva shot one when they arrived, and then took off. They shut off the phones and went to visit him and his wife in the dark."

Sydney paused, which irritated him. "And?"

"Two are too badly injured to talk, and all the other four know is they woke up in the back of a pickup, headed for Eureka."

Welk stared in disbelief. "Tony Silva did all that?"

"He said he did. Peter Zerbini says he's too old and fat. The sheriff escorted Silva to the hospital to drop off the boatmen and told his deputies to keep quiet about it until he finds out more. Now they're keeping the Silvas' location quiet. He's protecting them."

The county sheriff was new to office, trying to clean up a county filled with pot farms and little industry, and a history rife with lawlessness. Welk was paying off two of his deputies, one on night shift, the other on days. Why hadn't they called?

"How did you learn all that?" he asked.

"El Jefe has friends at the courthouse. Zerbini's lawyers are on the way from San Francisco to tell the boatmen to keep their mouths shut. Actually it doesn't matter. The four with concussions don't know what hit them. Just something in the dark. The one who was shot lost a lot of blood and may not pull through. Same with a big guy who has compound skull fractures."

"Silva couldn't have done all that."

"I know who could have. If Anderson was in Lisbon last night, he was awfully close to the valley."

Welk was very aware of that. "El Jefe?"

"He's in his office, steaming about it. I told him I'd come over and lend you a hand."

Welk was concerned. If it was another major fuckup,

he wondered how long he had before El Jefe sent someone to take him to the stone.

Sydney studied him with an amused expression.

"So what do you think we should do?" he asked.

"As I recall, you told me to get my scrawny ass out of here."

"Forget that shit. I was out of line."

She cocked her head cutely. "And . . ."

He knew what she wanted, and hated saying it. "And I need your help."

Sydney smiled, as if that were much better. "Yes, you do, and I still want to find Lincoln Anderson to settle an old score."

He brought up a subject he'd never broached with anyone. "I didn't treat you so good when you were a kid. Maybe I—"

She stared, her body tense, and hissed, "You did nothing to *me*."

Who was she shitting? Welk had trouble keeping a stone-face expression as he muttered, "Musta been someone else."

"Yes." Her face relaxed. "Now, what do you propose to do about the situation?"

"For openers, send a couple men to Lisbon for a look."

"That would be pointless." She settled into the open chair. "Lincoln Anderson is never predictable. If he was in Lisbon last night, be assured he won't be there today."

He listened quietly.

"What you should do is find out more about Anderson. What weapons does he possess? How much food? What's he driving? Where's he staying? Are the FBI agents with him?"

"How the hell would I—?"

"Tony Silva."

Welk stopped.

"The Silvas should be first on your list. Find them, and encourage them to talk." She went on. "Anderson was close to the Weeping Tree last night, but did he know it? I doubt it. He would have been unable to resist the urge to try to save his friends."

"He may call in more Feds?"

"I doubt he's able to. My sources in Washington tell me that the seeds I planted are bearing fruit. He's out of favor with his former friends, including Hightower at the FBI. He can't call on them or anyone until he's got something to show them." She looked at Welk. "He's looking for the Weeping Tree."

"There's a storm tonight. A second one tomorrow. They'll buy us time."

"Storms won't stop Lincoln Anderson, and they mustn't stop us. I want you to use every available person, including Kamil, Damon Lee, and more boatmen on loan from Peter Zerbini. Have them guard every possible approach to the Weeping Tree and shoot anyone who comes close. I want Anderson alive, but dead is almost as good."

For the next half hour they came up with the remainder of a plan.

33

They were moored a hundred yards from the bridge, precisely as they had been the previous night. Maggie decided it was another of Link's insights, that the Serpientes would not think he would go there twice. Call it gut feeling or premonition, when he was this sure, something within him had urged him to make the choice, and the something was seldom wrong.

Link had been a good fighter pilot, and the best of those honed their situational awareness to track and predict the positions of multiple bogies and determine enemies from friendlies in the sky. He was also a Piegan Blackfoot, and his ancestors had used intuitive visions to guide their lives. While he did not try to explain the phenomena of his perception, in emergencies he lived by them. Maggie knew those things about him.

Her fighter pilot. Her Blackfoot.

She felt languid and happy, and loved. Not ecstatic with it as she had once been with Link. This time she felt a warmth that she had always known was out there but was never before achievable. She felt complete, as a dove instinctively knew when it was with precisely the right mate. Her place was at his side, and she would feel that same way tomorrow, that she *should* be with him and support him and provide the companionship that a fulfilled woman knew her man needed.

She smiled, not at him or the others but at something within her that said here was her man, and if she cherished him enough, she would never lose him again.

When he'd told them he would walk to the hidden lagoon—by now transformed to two marshy beaches overshadowed by the twin granite rock faces—she'd not had to argue to be included. He knew that she could not be far away from him, not yet. He had told her that she must wait somewhere as he forayed. That, too, was her agreement, to not hinder him.

They had come together on all the spiritual and intellectual planes, but oh God, the physical loving they'd given one another in the tiny captain's quarters had been utterly perfect. Both of them weary but moist and hot and ready and knowing what to do without the other having to say a word. It had not taken long the first time, and they'd drifted off still joined, pressed together but not clinging, fitting into one another perfectly, then a single microsecond later coming alive, at first slowly and magically and feeling the sweetness, ever faster and harder until they'd pounded together, huffing and yearning and straining—relaxing and letting themselves flow along with the coming—sleeping intertwined again, as familiar as if the five years had been a single day.

Link laid out a shotgun and the AR-15 carbine from her kit bag and let her decide. Of course she'd carry the H&K .40. Although she had never yet aimed it at another human being, after five years of hauling it under her arm and in her bag and qualifying with it, going into harm's way without it would be unthinkable. He wanted her to choose a long arm, as well. When he deposited her and went on, he wanted her to have more firepower available than the handgun could provide.

Magnum twelve-gauges recoiled too much for a woman who had been called runt all her life. She selected the AR-15 that kicked hardly at all.

Stanley mounted a laser sight on her H&K, then collimated it, an aligning process that entailed sliding an expandable rod down the barrel and superimposing two ruby laser dots. Finally he modified her holster to allow for the device, and complained about being left behind.

Link did not rise to his defense. Someone had to protect the boat, and the previous night they'd all heard Squid's announcement that he was a lousy shot. Stanley

"Ten-Ex" Goldstein was not a lousy shot. He had the trophies to prove it. He taught gun safety courses to kids in Eddie Eagle programs. He knew guns, and had changed to openly wearing the .45 Colt high on his hip. He could draw and fire eight rounds in an incredibly short time. He had trophies for that, as well.

Stanley never mentioned that Link had once disarmed him. Neither did Link or Maggie.

It began to rain harder, and was so dark that the late afternoon appeared as night.

Squid and Stanley drew on rubberized rain gear and left. They'd take the dinghy to the riverbank and go after the Suburban so Link and Maggie would have its shelter for their first leg. That the two were once again lovers had been obvious since they'd come topside on the *Lady Rosalie* grinning foolishly and trying to act innocent. Aside from a few snickers and nudges, the others had taken it in stride. It was no earthshaking development. That Link and Maggie would reconvene their love affair had been obvious from their jousting and petty arguments.

Things were better now that the tension of the chase was over.

Link gave her a pat on her derriere, and Maggie pecked a kiss that triggered a bodily response.

"How much time do we have?" she whispered.

"Just enough."

They hurried below hand in hand. She leading and he following with a smile.

They used up every second, and were interrupted by the sound of a vehicle at the bridge. He peered out to make sure it was theirs as he scrambled to find strewn clothing.

"Where are my socks?" she asked, but he was having trouble finding his shorts.

Maggie brushed against his stiffness and laughed. "Hold that thought, dear."

The men came inside and gathered in the galley, where Maggie was now serenely working a comb through her hair. "We should get ready to go," she said, still floating from the sex.

"Tony Silva and his wife still aren't back," said Squid, pulling back his hood and avoiding an urge to stare. "It didn't look like anyone's messed with the Suburban."

Stanley held out the two black rain suits he'd customized for their use. Maggie pulled on rain pants, then a hooded jacket with vents cut at strategic points for access to her handgun. Last came black running shoes from the sporting-goods store. He wrapped black duct tape around their arms and legs to keep it all from flapping.

Stanley had modified two of the shotguns, as well. He was a believer in laser sights for night work, also the firepower provided by the marine magnums.

"You're sure you don't want to take one?" he asked Link for the umpteenth time.

"I'm sure." Link checked that the revolver's grips were accessible. Maggie checked hers as well, then the laser; a small rectangular box that would affect the handgun's balance. Something to remember and adjust for.

Link doled out UHF radios and reminded them they were for emergencies. "If you have to, use channel three."

Like the others, Maggie preset her radio to STANDBY, CHANNEL 3.

Link would leave his radio in the vehicle. He didn't want to bump a switch and have the thing announce him.

They took a final look at the topographical map, and the two beaches he had drawn in—since they'd not been shown. He'd also sketched what might be a camouflage net.

He went out. Maggie followed, then Squid, who would row them to the bank.

Link drove through the ghost town, looking for a turn-off that on the chart appeared to be no more than a trail. According to the map, it followed the twisting Mateole River for three miles.

There he would leave Maggie with the vehicle, and somehow proceed around the rock face to the camouflage net, or whatever it was in their center. Shepherd had indicated that a hand and toe path had been gouged into the northern face. Even if it existed, a portion of the climb would be made hanging over the churning Pacific.

Just over the mountain were the tangles of underbrush and soaring redwoods once called the "Quaking Ground," and "Liquid Earth."

He found the turnoff. The gusting rain became heavier, and the tires began to slip on red clay. He changed to four-wheel drive, but was forced to stop when the rain pounded so furiously that the wipers could not keep up and the world was obscured.

After five minutes, the flood from heaven slacked off, and he continued. To their left was the river, on their right massive redwoods. Ten more minutes, and Maggie held the handheld GPS to the windshield so it could "see" the satellites, and announced that they'd come two miles. Shortly afterwards, the path left the river, and they became mired. He picked low range, rocked the vehicle a couple of times, and they slithered on.

At seven o'clock, they were firmly stuck. He waited for the sheets of rain to subside, and climbed out. Maggie held the flashlight as he attached clip-on chains to the rear tires. Those on one side were immediately thrown off, but the ones on the other side did the job, and they proceeded for another hundred yards.

The road ahead was an impossible mire. Beyond was the base of a cliff.

He told her to remain with the vehicle, and Maggie did not argue.

"It's seven thirty. If I haven't shown by morning's light, head back."

"Be careful," she said quietly as he got out.

Link stopped then and did something unexpected— that he had not done before on a mission. He went to her side of the Suburban, opened the door, leaned down and kissed her.

He left then, masked by rain and darkness.

Link had surprised himself with the maudlin moment, and forced himself to refocus on the mountain. Wondering, if they were really so close to the Serpientes, why some citizen of Lisbon had not discovered them.

Within minutes, he knew the answer. The mountain-side was so steep and so cluttered with fractured, shale-like rock—not the solid granite he'd anticipated—that it seemed ludicrous to even attempt to climb it.

For the next half hour he tried to at least get a start, moving here and there along the sheer mountainside, trying and slipping back each time. Making more noise than he preferred and showing no progress. After a while of it, he chose the most impossibly steep place, made it for a half dozen feet, and was forced by the darkness and downpour to gauge the stability of the rock solely by sense of feel. Moving left or right as was necessary, remembering what he could of the few times he'd tried his hand at free climbing, he slowly and precariously proceeded.

At 8:40 he had progressed to yet another particularly steep section of mountainside, yet his task was somehow becoming easier. He'd discovered a series of firm hand- and toeholds that were becoming increasingly predictable. When he came to a rightward trend in the firm holds, he followed them. Another half hour, and he paused at a ledge and a bush that had somehow found nourishment, and was temped to stop to rest. He was about to pull himself onto it when a bout of pounding rain and whistling wind threatened to dislodge him—and he dug in and clung fast to his previous fingerholds.

If he'd rested on the ledge, he would have been blown off.

When the rain relented, he avoided the ledge altogether since it had been the gouged holds that had saved him. The handholds continued to take him to the right, and he was increasingly sure they'd been created by humans. Not recently, though. If Shepherd had been right, they'd been devised as an escape route for the Serpientes.

He heard the sounds of ocean waves crashing against the rocks directly below in the inky darkness. The hand-holds began to lead him on a descending path, and rather than proceeding, he tried alternative routes. After trying three of those and discovering they were infirm, he went back to the ancient indentations that had been laboriously chiseled out and were evenly placed.

Time passed, and he doggedly continued around the massive formation, climbing past more patches of shattered rock, thinking of inconsequentials instead of focusing on the danger of the precipice. Link recalled what he had seen earlier, how the two stone faces rose to a thousand feet above the ocean, yet the green mountain soared two thousand feet higher. Thus the rock formations rose only a third of the total height, and he was not near the top of it. More likely, he was only two hundred feet in the air.

Somehow that thought made him feel better, although if he fell, the trip would be just as lethal. Not the fall. Just the landing. Water or rocks—take your pick.

He went on, steadily descending. During a break in the sometimes pounding rain, he could see shadows below. He discerned the beach, marshy and only a hundred feet away—straight down. From somewhere he heard the sound of radio feedback, and someone speaking.

On his next foothold, he kicked loose a small avalanche of fractured stone.

He waited for a minute, and continued. Abruptly the face ended, and just ahead was a jumble of very large rocks. He started to climb over the first of them, and looked up in time to see something very large swinging through the air toward him.

11:00 p.m.—Hidden Lagoon

Damon Lee wrapped himself and his new rifle carefully in an oversize black plastic poncho, tucking in corners and pulling the hood forward, huddling, assured that there was nothing to threaten him in the darkness and wet.

He was miserable. Not only was it raining toads and lizards, but he had also been told not to go near the freaking warehouse behind the canvas sails, which was the only place he knew of where he might dry off. But there were people in the windowless warehouse, and if he joined them, they might rat on him to Chief Welk or Mr. Peter Zerbini.

He'd tried staying behind the sails, but the rainwater fell in concentrations like a hundred waterfalls competing to see which could get you wettest. It was no better.

Since his return from the freaking Wild West empty-handed because Anderson had disappeared, El Jefe no longer mentioned his membership in the Serpientes. Which made him wonder why he was out here being miserable if they weren't going to make him rich.

They called this place Hidden Lagoon, but from what he'd seen, it was a cruddy marsh with a few sandy areas, cut in half by a big slab of concrete that disappeared under the old canvas sails. He guessed the name "Hidden Lagoon" was some holdover from the past.

He wanted to get back to practicing his long-distance shooting, since he'd bought a new rifle to replace the one Anderson had thrown off the mountain.

As a replacement he first wanted a .50-caliber BMG that used a single big machine gun bullet and was accurate at a mile. Problem was, he'd been told that if it malfunctioned the blowback could just possibly break your arm. He half believed the guy was bullshitting him. Maybe not.

He'd gone the other way. Moved way down in caliber to a Savage Arms .223 varmint rifle with cool-looking black fragmenting bullets and a 6X–25X B&L scope that could take out a gnat's right testicle at half a mile. It wouldn't tear down a house like the BMG, but he could afford the lower payments, and it would do the job on a human. Frags everywhere!

He was getting so sick of being miserable at the marshy swamp called the Hidden Lagoon that he was looking forward to going up to the lookout, where the road was scary and the freaking wind would do its best to blow him over the side.

Behind the warehouse was the trail to the Weeping Tree, guarded by one of Peter Zerbini's ex-con boatmen, with confusing forks, one branch winding back and forth and around to a shelf a thousand feet up the mountain. From the lookout, when it was clear he could observe the crummy old ghost town called Lisbon. He'd been told by Chief Welk to go up there every four hours, meaning the next trip would be in an hour. He would take the Jeep they kept at the road fork, and not think about negotiating the slick-as-snot road with a storm blowing. But things were relative and he was even more frightened of Chief Welk than a scary drive. Perhaps there'd be a break in the weather. Maybe he'd see something to shoot with his new rifle.

Damon had heard sounds of falling rocks from the north side. Now there came more from behind one of the sails that had come loose and was flapping in the heavy wind. He slogged past the hanging sails, wended through them, then used the flashlight. Moved the beam around like he was interested, in case it was Welk who had dropped in to check him out.

Falling rock in the middle of a freaking storm? So what? He didn't want to radio and get Chief Welk upset unless there was something suspicious, and the only suspicious thing he'd seen was the freaking warehouse with tire tracks leading up to it from the freaking water.

11:05 p.m.

When he'd seen the monstrous thing swinging toward him, Link had dropped onto the rock pile, creating another racket of falling stones, crouched and reached into the rain jacket for the pistol.

It took a moment to realize that the monster consisted of dozens of tattered canvas sails hanging from a ledge far above and anchored at the lower corners. One had come loose and flapped in the strong gusts, accounting for the ever-changing fuzzy area he'd seen from the boat. Some of the sails had weathered well. Most were rotted and ancient. The sails were of varied sizes, and collectively covered an opening in the mountainside that was forty feet vertical and seventy-five feet wide. He could not see the back of the depression to estimate the cavern's depth.

Inside the sails, he saw a guard huddled in a plastic poncho, using a flashlight to check out the rockslide. Although the guard was no dynamo, Link was surprised that they had him here at all. No sane person would approach from the sea, or circumnavigate the fractured rock had he not known about the ancient handholds.

The guard halfheartedly flashed the beam about the enclosure, creating enough light for Link to discern a long, large, gray-painted warehouse.

When the guard left, Link quietly walked forward. The exterior of the warehouse was dimly illuminated by a glow that seeped out from around poorly aligned doors. He went around it, and found it was electrified by one of a pair of generators in back of the building. The other was much larger and smelled of diesel. Link wondered what could require that much electrical current. As he circled the building, he stopped every few feet to listen, and approached the garage-style door.

It was high tide, so there was water in the heavy-walled concrete channel that led to the door. He noted vehicle tracks of something wide and so heavy, it had worn ruts in concrete.

The warehouse's closed overhead door measured twenty feet square. He'd paced off a 145-foot length. It was just large enough to hold the *Sinner*. According to Squid, the *Sinner* was attached to its support vessel, although they'd all but ruled out the big mama processing ship. Perhaps there was something inside the warehouse to tell him. The only way he knew to find out was to go there. He could hear three voices inside. Two men and a woman playing stud poker, the woman shrilly complaining about the men. They were obviously drinking. Others might be sleeping inside, but if so, he had not heard them.

There were three standard-size doors in the warehouse, two along the building length and another at the back end. *Will there be an alarm?* It was likely, although with people moving around inside, it would be dearmed.

Link found an almost dry place, stripped down to his jeans, and left the rest of his clothing and the revolver behind. The more vulnerable one was, the more alert, or so Joseph Spotted Horse had told him. He believed that portion of the old man's wisdom.

He went to the door at the rear of the building, and thought: *Be invisible.*

That one was locked. He went to the next one, and

found it the same. The final door was only twenty feet from where he'd heard the voices. It was unlocked.

He eased it slightly ajar, ran his fingers down the frame, and found a magnetic switch. The installer had used double-sided tape. Link pulled the magnet off and placed it against the one on the alarm side to complete the circuit. He pushed the door open a few more inches. There was a mat. He checked underneath for a pressure switch, found two, and knew where not to step.

He could hear all three of them talking as he slowly eased his way past the door and made first visual contact. They were in the adjacent room, a living quarters with bunks, a table and chairs. All were seated. He could see the woman clearly, but very little of the two male players.

It was darker in the hall than in the room. *Be invisible.* He went in.

"Pete Zerbini's a sexy bastard," the woman was saying, slurring her words.

"Two drinks, and you'd back up to a billy goat," said one of the men.

She snorted. "You'll never get close enough for a sniff."

The second man leaned back in his chair, giving him a view of Link as he drank amber liquid. Link noted that he held three deuces.

"I'll raise ten bucks," he said.

"Damn you!" muttered the woman.

A handheld UHF radio was on the table, periodically squawking, as he'd heard from the one carried by the guard. The radios were obviously scrambled, making it sound as if they were all talking into a bucket. He heard several guards, manning Post One, Post Two, and so on.

The woman turned so she had Link in her view. "I want another drink," she said.

"First you've got to either call him or fold."

She focused on her cards with some difficulty. "Call."

Link moved out of her view, silently closing the outer door as he went.

There were a number of small rooms along the length of the warehouse. Opposite them, taking up the length of the warehouse, was the *CNR-2 Sinner*.

Link took his time, trying to observe everything. There were several video cameras located inside and out—but those were useless, since no one was manning the console room. He found the recorder, rewound the tape for a full minute, and turned the function switch to ERASE.

A charger cradle held two Motorola radios, both of them with scrambler circuits like the ones he'd heard. He took one. After their night of carousing, he doubted the crew members would tell anyone that they'd lost it.

Next was a control room with gauges and scopes and tomorrow's schedule shown in columns under: DEPT TIME, SHIP TIME, and ARR TIME. He memorized them.

Forty minutes after his arrival, Link left the same way he'd come in.

One of the men was sleeping in his chair as the woman argued vehemently with the other. Complaining about hauling seasick Arabs and about the second trip added on for tomorrow, which was cutting it too close. Finally pouring another drink to take to bed.

From outside, he pulled the door until it was cracked, replaced the magnetic switches in their original positions, and silently closed it.

34

12:01 a.m.—Hidden Lagoon

Damon Lee heard another rockslide from up on the side of the mountain, and methodically focused his Maglite where he thought the racket had come from. He prepared to see nothing, and noticed only a dark smudge on the cracked gray stone.

While he had not seen it before, Damon Lee was trying to think up an excuse for not making the drive up to the lookout. Then there was yet another noise on the north face, and again he shone the light. *Odd.* The dark smudge was not there. At first he decided his eyes had played a trick. It was improbable that he'd see anything on the side of a big mountain, in the middle of the night, in a lull in a rainstorm.

Or had he seen something like a big bird and was missing his chance to let off a shot?

Since there was a pause in the downpour, Damon removed his new rifle from under the black poncho, then awkwardly held the flashlight between his knees while he reassured himself that it was loaded and ready. Since he had no low-light compensation he'd take "sound shots"—hold the weapon ready and listen, and when he heard a noise, adjust and aim—as he sometimes did when he was deer hunting.

He focused the beam, tried for the dark smudge again, and once again saw nothing. He began to doubt it had ever existed, and moved the beam both laterally and vertically. He saw movement. He steadied the beam and saw nothing.

You got the rifle out, take a shot.

He dropped the flashlight, raised the rifle, and aimed in the general direction of where he thought he had seen the smudge. Waited until he thought he heard something again

Bam!

The rifle shot was loud in the night. He worked the bolt and chambered a new round.

Bam!

"Who's firing?" came a voice over the radio.

Damon Lee leaned the rifle on his hip and fished the radio from the poncho pocket.

"Post Three," he said. "Thought I saw something on the mountain."

"Warn us next time, okay?"

"Yeah, sure."

Damon examined the places where the bullets had hit, splintered, and gouged good-size holes. The new rifle had hardly kicked at all, compared with the .300 Mag that Anderson had tossed down the hill. *Bastard!* He wished he had another chance at him so he could shoot his eyes out. He took the cloth from his pocket and wiped the rifle down, admiring the feel of it.

Whatever had been there was gone. It was time to drive up to the lookout and observe the world from above. If the lull continued, he'd use the rifle's bipod. Surely there'd be *something* to shoot. *Gotta remember windage*, he reminded himself, *since the bullet's so light.* He grinned in anticipation.

12:03 a.m.

At the back of the enclosure, Link had found a pathway and, mostly by feel, an ancient M-151 military jeep. He'd also heard a distant sound of laughter and considered scouting ahead, then decided that would be foolish. He had gotten more than he'd hoped, and needed to inform Squid and the others, and come up with a plan.

He returned to the rock face, noted the guard was in the same position outside the curtain of sails, and struck out the way he had come. He went quickly, partly because he knew what to look for, and partly because he was eager to share his discovery.

The rain paused, yet the rock was as slippery and fragile as before. He continued to methodically climb, recalling the placement of good hand- and toeholds. Still in view from the beach and the guard there, he slipped and created a clattering rockslide.

Link flattened himself and froze in the illumination of the guard's flashlight. When the beam was moved, he hurried again, farther around the face. Stopped long enough to look back and see the guard illuminating a long rifle with a synthetic stock and pistol grip—a Varminter, with a bipod on the forestock folded back. A small-diameter bullet, but it would be accurate. No sound suppressor, so it would announce itself.

He hurried, and slipped again when transferring weight from his right foot. There was another skittering of stones, but he continued, although the beam was momentarily cast again.

Bam!

The impact was a few feet to his right—the bullet splintered and fragments slapped the rubberized rain suit. He felt no pain and would not stop if he did.

He thought he heard the bolt action being thrown over the sound of the surf.

Bam!

Rock chips shattered just overhead.

The guard's radio sounded. Link froze, trying to hear what was said over the sound of the surf. The guard answered, and he recognized the wise-guy voice of Damon Lee.

The long-range shooter was back in his life.

Another few seconds, and Link was out of Lee's line of sight, thankful that it was not easy to hold a flashlight and fire a long weapon.

He wished he'd heard what had been said. There had been no excitement in Damon Lee's tone, so he had not realized that an intruder was actually there. Shooting at shadows?

Link reached behind himself and found the holes in the rain suit made by the bullet fragments. His stepfather was nicknamed Lucky, and some of that luck had rubbed

off. He continued, pleased with the discoveries he'd
made, thinking that Squid had not been wrong about the
Sinner, just about the way they operated it. The *CNR-2*
was berthed in the warehouse at the Hidden Lagoon,
not tethered to a support vessel.

He was getting used to shifting his weight and making
sure of his foot- and handholds. Trying to concentrate
on what he was doing while he remembered what he
had seen. He discerned a vehicle's sounds, revving its
engine and changing gears, crawling up some difficult
road on the mountain. The little four-banger military
jeep. The mountain road and the vehicle would be things
to be watchful for when they returned.

The climb in had taken more than three hours. Link
was back down, stepping onto the dirt road, now a quag-
mire of mud, in less than two, a much shorter period
than he'd anticipated.

He could not dispel an uneasy feeling as he flashed
the single LED light twice in the direction of the Suburban, then twice again, their prearranged signal that he
was coming in. For the last two hours there had been
little rain, and he wondered if the storm wasn't past.

Link could make out the dark hulk of the Suburban
fifty yards distant. Maggie opened the passenger's door,
and the dome and entry lights illuminated, a beacon
shattering the darkness. Her hood was down, and he
admired the rusty glints of her shoulder-length hair.

She'd heard the gunshots and was concerned about
him.

He remembered the engine sounds from up on the
mountain. Damon Lee might not be a great marksman,
but he had the Varminter—

In the vehicle, Maggie leaned across from the passenger's seat.

Do not turn on the lights, he thought, not knowing if
he spoke aloud.

Maggie was looking toward him as the headlights
came on.

"Turn the lights off!" he shouted, and began to run.

"Now you can see," she called out.

Link slipped and almost fell, caught himself as a bullet

whipped past. The gunshot report was not nearly so loud from here as it had been on the rock face.

He waved his arms. "Turn off the lights!"

Maggie had heard the gunshot and realized the danger. She dived toward the switch. The headlights shut off.

Link was no longer visible. She was. The dome and entry lights remained on.

A round thumped into the windshield, and he heard her cry out.

He ran the final few yards, opened the driver's door, and found her slumped, holding her stomach, one leg still hanging out the open passenger's door.

Her voice was pained. "Aw shit, Link. I screwed up."

He started the engine and pulled her the rest of the way inside. Threw the shifter into reverse and swung the vehicle back and around.

Whang! The round had hit metal. He scrambled over Maggie and grabbed the passenger's door. *Whack!* The side window spiderwebbed. His shoulder stung.

He slammed the door, and the interior lights shut off. The night was inky, and he couldn't see as he drove straight ahead. The vehicle went off the road, and he wheeled it back on. The tires caught and held. While he'd been away, she'd put on the other chain.

"Hold on, Maggie."

She remained slumped in her seat. "I missed you," she said.

After a while, when they were well beyond Damon Lee's range, he switched the headlights on so he could see the road. "Hold on."

2:12 a.m.—Mateole Bridge

The bullet had splintered as advertised. Maggie's wound was bleeding profusely, and the shock factor was causing her to slip back and forth into unconsciousness.

"Link," she said once. "Gotta tell you about Gordon. Jack Hammer . . ."

She went under again.

Link stopped at the bridge, blowing the horn and yelling to the men in the boat. "Maggie's hit," he told them.

"I'm coming," said Stanley.

"Yeah, and bring your bag. Squid, you stay and hold it down. I'll be back."

Stanley brought both his own and Maggie's kit bags. As soon as he was in the Suburban, Link accelerated. He took the only corner in town at fifty, and never thereafter allowed the speedometer to drop below seventy despite the treacherous road. Stan leaned over the front seat and tried to stanch Maggie's bleeding.

Twenty-five minutes had passed when he slid up to the closed gate of the coast guard station and leaned on the horn.

There were lights on in the operations building. The coasties were working around the clock because of the storm. He hurried to the gate and pressed the buzzer as Squid had done. A voice came over a speaker.

"I've got a wounded FBI agent with me. She needs immediate help."

The gate swung open. Link drove inside; then they waited as two men in white utilities came out. One was the station's officer in charge.

Link showed him Maggie's bloodstained leather ID wallet he'd taken from her jacket pocket. The lieutenant tried to make it out in the dim light.

"She needs help *now*!"

The station was too small to have a doctor, but there was a medic on duty. A uniformed enlisted man was leaning into the Suburban. Link and Stanley helped him lift Maggie out.

There were two other emergencies in progress. A helicopter was only five minutes away and would transport her to a hospital in Eureka.

When the station commander started to talk about a second storm that was headed toward them—much larger than the current one—Link pushed past him to the gurney that Maggie was being loaded upon.

She'd tried to tell him something about Jack Hammer, but she was no longer conscious.

Link spoke quietly to Stanley about what he and Squid would do. "Are you carrying?" he asked.

"Always."

"Stay with Maggie no matter where they take her. We're too damned close to the bad guys. If anyone looks at her cross-eyed, shoot the fucker."

Link gave him a few further instructions, then watched as they went inside.

2:25 a.m.—Lennville

Chief of Police Wendell Welk was awakened by a call from the office, asking him to get on the scrambler radio. One of the guards had shot someone. He picked up. "Welk here," he said.

Damon Lee was on the other end of the conversation, sounding excited. "I'm up at the lookout. Fifteen minutes ago, I saw a guy climbing off the mountain below."

In a storm? "Could he have gotten anywhere near the lagoon?"

"Impossible. I'd just come from there, and I would've known."

"Go on."

"It was a long shot, like four hundred yards. There was a woman waiting in a van or something big, and she switched on the headlights, so I started shooting. The woman went down and I hit the guy. Then I shot the shit out of the van. Two magazines. They gotta be holier than the pope." Lee laughed at his joke.

"And they got away?"

Lee became defensive. "Maybe, but they're hurting and couldn't have gone far."

Welk was unsure of how to take the report. He had slept little. Most of the evening he had spent setting up the traps he'd planned with Sydney, all the time knowing that unless he caught Lincoln Anderson, he might as well strap a bomb to himself. Blowing yourself up was no worse than getting your head beaten to pulp.

He doubted that El Jefe would send him to the stone with everything that was happening, but it would be stupid not to be prepared.

He drove to the PD despite the early hour, ate a few meth pills, and felt the wires in his brain jangling to life and a harsh *thump-thump* in his chest. His sleepiness drained away.

As he sat at his desk in his back office, the senior night cop, whose first name was Elbert, walked past the door and Welk jumped and grabbed at his pistol. He sat back in his chair, breathing hard, thinking again that he was not about to go easily, but on the other hand he should do nothing prematurely. El Jefe might call it off. Welk might find Anderson.

He called Elbert in and told him to send a cruiser to Lisbon. Look for the Silva husband and wife and also for a couple in a van that was decorated with a few bullet holes.

"I'm out of people," said the senior night cop. He looked tired. "They're all either out manning posts or resting for the six-o'clock shift change."

"I'll take the desk while you go. Call me with what you find."

Welk had nineteen men available to set the "traps," which included a number of Peter Zerbini's boatmen, and he would use them in twelve-hour shifts. Only seven were presently posted because of the unlikelihood that Anderson would do anything in the storm. The remaining twelve would go on duty at six o'clock, which was only two hours away. He was parsimonious with radios because only eight were outfitted with scramblers so no outsiders could listen in. Zerbini's people had four more, but were not charitable enough to lend them.

A big day was coming. Peter Zerbini's shuttle would get a workout. Going out to get Sajacento and his six new Hezbollah bombers and six fighters to set them off would take two round trips—scheduled for nine thirty and eleven o'clock departures.

Welk's mind was churning with methamphetamine.

He phoned the sheriff's office in Eureka and asked for the night deputy he was paying. He was away, likely screwing off, Welk thought. He was on probation and would soon be terminated, meaning Welk would have to find *two* new informants. The crusading sheriff was trying to change things. The daytime deputy that Welk paid had been caught asking for information about the Silva husband and wife, and was relieved on the spot.

Speaking of the Silvas, he still did not have a clue where they were staying.

He left his cell phone number for the night deputy. Five minutes later, his call was returned. The night deputy had not heard about any shootings near Lisbon.

"You will," Welk told him. "Keep your ears open, and let me know what you hear. Also find out where the Silvas are holed up."

"That one I know. They left for home twenty minutes ago. The sheriff offered to send a cruiser along, but Tony Silva said they'd just pack and head up to Seattle for a while."

Welk felt better. If Silva knew something, he'd find out.

He punched the cell phone OFF, then called a local number, thinking it was time for Kamil to earn the big bucks he was making.

Welk told him to awaken three of the guys who were scheduled for guard duty at six, and gave directions to Lisbon and the Silva home. They shouldn't have trouble finding it in a town with two streets. He told him what he wanted from the couple.

Kamil listened, said okay, and hung up.

Welk almost recalled Elbert from Lisbon, but decided to wait because that seemed to be where the action was taking place.

Chief Welk waited, listening to sleepy radio calls from the guards he'd posted. Feeling anxious and suspicious, remembering how Sydney had told him he'd be wasting his time sending anyone to Lisbon because Anderson wouldn't be there two nights in a row. Well *someone* had gone there and climbed around on the mountain in the rain and wind and darkness, and lately it had been Anderson who had been causing him grief.

Welk wondered if Damon Lee might already have taken out Lincoln Anderson, or was it just some dumb-shit drunked-up kids out for a night of thrills.

He walked around his office, nervously running a hand through his hair, thinking of all the wrong things, then went out to the night dispatcher and asked if there'd been any calls.

Nothing.

He was standing there when his cell phone buzzed. The informant deputy was excited.

"A female FBI agent was shot somewhere near the coast guard station. She was brought in with another agent by a chopper. They landed here at Saint Elmo's Hospital fifteen minutes ago. The sheriff said to send two deputies to guard the operating room."

Wendell Welk smiled so hard, he almost split his face, hardly daring to believe the change in his fortune. "How bad off is she?"

"Life threatening. Lots of internal bleeding."

"See if you can get yourself assigned at the hospital."

"It's already done. They were tired of me hanging around here."

"You can expect company."

"That's what I figured. Make sure they beat us both up. I'll put up a fight but not really, know what I mean?"

Chief Welk looked at his watch. It was 3:20. "At a quarter after four, go out back for a smoke break. I'll be there so you can tell me the layout. What rooms the agents are in, is the woman coherent, who's armed and who's not—also anything else you think of."

Welk disconnected. He was on a roll.

He called Kamil, told him there was a change of plans, and asked where he was. Kamil said they were already inside the Silva home.

"Did you get anything from them."

"I just started."

"Finish them, and head for Saint Elmo's Hospital in Eureka. The guys with you know where it is. I'll meet you in back of the place in half an hour."

He shut off the cell phone, used the radio to tell Elbert to return to Lennville, and thought again of his good fortune.

Eureka was twenty-five minutes away, a little longer for Kamil. The terrorist had more than enough gunmen with him to overpower the doctors and nurses, the second deputy, and the male FBI agent El Jefe had described as a lightweight.

Welk would go along to make sure there'd be no screwups. There could be no witnesses. Welk would return in the same vehicle with the two agents—the wounded woman and the male—and gain every ounce of information they possessed about Lincoln Anderson before dumping their bodies on the north side of the town. Up past Arcata, near McKinleyville.

Both Eureka and McKinleyville would be placed on the national map tomorrow when Kamil and his Hezbollah took credit for the slayings of the policemen and FBI agents—not close enough to Lennville or the old encampment to concern El Jefe.

He was still wired, still elated. Tomorrow he would take Anderson prisoner for Sydney's pleasure, and dispose of the hostages' bodies when she finished cutting them up.

Everything was back on track.

Welk considered awaking El Jefe with the good news but decided it would be better to tell him about his success after they were done.

35

Link was in the galley, explaining to Squid what he'd seen at the lagoon: the concrete channel with the ruts made by something very heavy, the control console, gauges and readouts that he'd memorized. The big diesel generator in back of the warehouse. The reel of titanium-sheathed conduit that took up the back end of the warehouse and was firmly connected to the *CNR-2 Sinner*. And finally, the schedule.

The radio he'd taken from the warehouse lay on the table, turned low so no one could hear it from the river bridge. They listened to the needless chatter of poorly disciplined guards.

Squid was excited, yet unable to smile because of what had happened to Maggie.

Link's emotions had been in combat mode since he'd climbed the rock face. The wound that puckered the skin of his shoulder went without notice. Later he would come back to earth and get the news about Maggie's condition, and that might destroy him. He'd never accepted the death of his fiancée, Marie, and it would be no different if Maggie died.

"I'll have to make new guesses about their operation," Squid said, looking up from his notes. "I couldn't get past the idea of using a control vessel."

Link tuned to Squid's words, shutting out thoughts of Maggie, Frank, and Erin.

"It's easier using a land base. The pilot lets the current carry the *Sinner* out and keeps back pressure on the cable, steering so he'll cross over to the other side of Angel Rock or the tether would be tangled on the return trip. Then he dives and lets it run with the current, using the maneuvering planes to keep the boat steady. At the right time, he ascends; they slow down to approach the big mama, and surface under the blind. Then he just holds it steady. The big mama has an extra large docking cradle for repairing the fishing boats, which they'll use to hold the *Sinner* in place while they load or unload passengers."

"The return trip?"

"Same as going out, but reversed. They ride the incoming current, winding in the cable like crazy to keep tension." He paused. "The schedule tells us the trips take only half an hour each way. That's fast!"

"What's their most vulnerable moment?"

"If they're beyond the Angel Rock in a nose-down attitude and the restraint cable were to break, they wouldn't be able to surface in time and would instead sink."

Squid wanted to leave early so he could watch the *Sinner* in operation and make his "modifications" before the second trip. "I want it to go down with Sajacento aboard."

Link used a fine-scale map for a look at where he'd be going while Squid did his task. There were several small valleys shown, but none appeared to be connected to the lagoon.

Their attention was captured by the sound of a vehicle's engine. Both men went topside into the dark wheelhouse. There were bright headlights, and although it was still dark, they could make out the light bar of a police cruiser as it proceeded very slowly onto the bridge.

"Make you a five-dollar bet it's got 'Lennville Police' painted on the side," said Squid. "Where did you park the Suburban?"

Link kicked himself. "At a pullout on the opposite side of the bridge."

"They'll find it."

"I agree," said Link. He pulled off his boots, snapped the holstered revolver in place on his belt, and started over the side.

"You can't make it in time," Squid said.

The cruiser stopped in the middle of the bridge, fifty yards distant. A spotlight came on and swiveled to illuminate the upriver side.

"*Damn* it!" Squid whispered.

The cruiser's radio crackled with an incoming message. "Elbert, this is Chief Welk. I'll be out of the office for a couple of hours. You'd better come back and handle the desk."

"On my way, Chief," said Elbert.

The spotlight was switched off, and the cruiser backed up across the bridge, swung around, and headed toward Lennville.

They heard a series of gunshots coming from the direction of the Silva home.

Although they hurried, they were not there in time to see the vehicle speeding off. Link burst through the open door of the Silva home with his revolver drawn.

Tony was bound with his eyelids duct-taped open, slumped where he'd been made to watch as his wife had been tortured, her corpse dropped aside like bloody trash. Other obscenities had been carried out as her husband was forced to look on.

Both had been executed, shot in their foreheads from close up.

"If I hadn't been convinced that the Serpientes needed to be exterminated," said Squid, "I would be now."

Link looked on, face calm but rage pounding in his heart.

4:20 a.m.—Saint Elmo's Hospital, Eureka

There were six people in two vehicles. The minivan was driven by one of Peter Zerbini's boatmen. Chief Welk was in the passenger's seat. They'd been waiting for twelve minutes.

Finally the sedan with Kamil and three others arrived.

Only one thing remained. The informant deputy was late for his smoke break. As long as he didn't take too long, Welk was unconcerned. He did, however, want to talk the situation over with someone who knew what was happening inside. He could just see a bunch of hooded gunmen asking a desk clerk how to find the operating room—and oh yeah, a couple of FBI agents.

They were parked at the side near the emergency entrance where two ambulances waited. The helipad situated at the middle of the lawn was empty, so the chopper that had brought the female agent had obviously already left.

Welk could take no more inactivity, so he got out and walked around. After a moment, he approached the sedan and was looking inside when one of them got the message and rolled down the window. They wore knitted face masks pulled onto their foreheads. His cops were all ex-cons who had been in similar situations. All were overpaid, married with kids, and had a stake in staying in his town and in his good graces. Not so Kamil, whose eyes were as cold as any he'd seen. Welk wondered what the American-hating terrorist thought about being in the land of the Big Satan, making big bucks and about to take a few nonbelievers' lives.

"Remember," he told them. "Leave your identification behind. When you're inside, make it cool and sweet. Take both agents and kill the cops and anyone who sees too much. Any of our people get hurt, we bring them back with us. You wanna die, do it somewhere else."

"What if the FBI asshole takes a shot?"

"Then figure it out. I want them both alive. Period. That's what this is about, learning what they know so we can find Lincoln Anderson. If you take out the woman and the guy's alive—no big deal. If you take out the guy, and the woman's able to talk—okay. But you don't know those things, so don't kill either one."

" I will make them talk about Anderson," said Kamil.

A uniform walked around the corner and toward them. Welk recognized the night deputy who was his informant, and waved him over.

The informant said the female agent was out of the operating room, now in recovery, room 202. The male agent was a chocolate milk–drinking kid. Except when she'd been operated on, he'd stuck with the woman agent like ugly on a two-dollar whore. He did not know what weapons, if any, the kid carried. The woman was in no shape to shoot anything. The other deputy carried a 9 mm and might be trouble. He was known for being tough and honest.

He checked his watch. "I'd better go back in before they think something's wrong."

"Anything else we should know?"

"The hospital's new and still half-empty. Should be a piece of cake."

"Good." Welk pulled his hand from his pocket like he was going to place it around the deputy's shoulder and—*phut!*—shot him in the back of the neck with a silenced .22.

He nodded at the shooters. "You guys heard him. Room two-oh-two."

They were getting out of the sedan, pulling down ski masks. Before Kamil led them inside, Chief Welk had them drag the deputy's body behind a hedge. Then he pulled on his own mask and followed. Curious and still very wired.

4:23 a.m.—Mateole Bridge

They were as ready as they would be, and the plan—considering how little they knew about the place they were going—was as good as it would get.

"I'll be a few minutes," Link told Squid. He walked to the prow—the *Lady Rosalie* had been turned about to face downstream—and in a low monotone began to recite an old chant learned from Joseph Spotted Horse.

Squid asked, but Link did not elaborate about the old Blackfoot ritual regarding honoring, avenging, and covering. Squid could not be expected to understand.

When he asked again, Link said, "It's a private time." Squid got the message and held his tongue as his friend stripped to nakedness and dived from the boat into the dark water. Link emerged a dozen yards downstream and quietly waded for a while. Finally he stopped at an appropriate place and remained quiet, trying to cleanse his mind of impurity.

Joseph Spotted Horse might have told him that a better Blackfoot warrior would have found the time to construct a spirit house and build a fire to endure the heat and steam and sing out his mind to helper spirits. That was the old way and may have been the reason that in the history of the nation before treaties no enemy had been able to invade their land by force or stand in their way. Not the white man's army or the Sioux or the Crow or any other had defeated them in a single major battle.

Those warriors had seldom allowed themselves to be rushed, but with so little time, Link would make do with what he had, which was only himself and one other. He must not dwell on hatred, even toward his worst enemies. It was the nature of men that while few have true friends all have enemies, and a warrior must know them both. Friends because they made life better, enemies because they presented the opportunities that brought success or failure.

He concentrated on his fallen friends and those now in mortal danger, and each time he thought of one he cried out the word, "Ha-ai!" Included were long-dead childhood friends, military comrades, his beloved fiancée, his Blackfoot mother, Frank, Erin, Maggie, Stanley, Squid, Doc Pete and his employees, and all the others. In the old society, their names were not spoken after their deaths, so he used "Ha-ai!" as he had been taught, and vowed to always remember them. "Ha-ai! Ha-ai! Ha-ai!" he cried out, clearly so the sounds echoed down the river and to the ocean. On and on, his voice mournful and occasionally cracking with emotion.

When finished, he stopped and raised his head, "I honor you!"

He walked farther down the dark streambed, stopped, and recalled the valiant ones he had faced, those who deserved to be remembered because they had fought well. Some military, others not. Some of them members of his family. A few who should be honored more than others. "Na-ai! Na-ai! Na-ai!"

He spoke more quietly then. "I honor you, as well."

Link halted and spat and offered a curse in the Blackfoot tongue, refusing to think of the unmentionables, the monsters, the cowards, the torturers, those he had seen slink off in defeat. He thought of those who had harmed his friends and how they must pay.

He offered a challenge in the Blackfoot language that reverberated along the river.

"Old Man, tell my enemies that I will dishonor them and take their lives and the lives of others who threaten or have harmed my people. I will touch them with my coup stick, for their puny weapons cannot hurt me. I am stronger. My friend I bring with me is also stronger. Tell them it is a good time for them to die and be forgotten. Tell them all of that, Old Man, and let them know that we are coming, and that they should run and hide and be afraid."

He stood silently for a moment, decided that there was no time to do things more properly, and turned and slogged back.

Squid said nothing as Link's dark shape climbed aboard and walked by. "Prepare to go," Link said as he started down to his bunk to retrieve his gear.

"All that you were doing out there. It sounded like some sort of death ritual. You don't think we have a chance of coming out of this alive?"

"You've got it all wrong, Squid. That was for the poor bastards we'll face."

4:38 a.m.—Saint Elmo's Hospital, Room 212

FBI Special Agent Stanley Goldstein waited for the operating room nurses to come for his boss again. The remaining deputy sheriff—the other one had gone outside for a cigarette—wanted to talk about how he could attend the FBI academy's shooting course for law officers, but Stan ignored him, too drained to remain alert and enter a discussion, as well.

Sounds of footsteps came from down the hallway beyond the surgical unit nurse station.

The surgeon and his OR team of nurses and techs?

No. They wear paper booties. These are louder, more like leather soles and heels.

How many of them?

Upon their arrival, Maggie had been wheeled into the pre-op room, where they presently were, to endure a battery of tests. She was taken to the operating room and opened up. She'd received a transfusion as excess blood was suctioned away. Splinters from the bullet were removed, her spleen and stomach sutured where they'd been damaged, and she'd been closed.

All that time, Stanley had stood outside the OR's double doors, observing everyone in the area, hardly speaking to anyone, including the two deputies.

Forty minutes ago, they'd wheeled Maggie out to the recovery room—room 202, which was down the hall—and they'd all thought it was over. He'd asked for chocolate milk from a recovery room nurse who offered beverages, and the deputies had exchanged grins.

One had gone for a smoke.

Fifteen minutes ago, the surgeon told him that Maggie was bleeding internally again, and that the damaged spleen was the culprit. They'd have to go back in and perform a splenectomy.

Maggie was sufficiently aware to complain that she did not wish to lose her spleen. The doctor said it was necessary.

The nurses had moved Maggie back into pre-op, room 212, and hooked her up again.

The clicking of footsteps grew closer. They went into a room down the hall.

"They're not here," announced a man with a heavy accent and unpleasant tone.

The surgeon was a Pakistani with an impossible name and accent, but this voice was very different.

"My purse," whispered Maggie.

"Not yet, hon," said the pre-op nurse. "After the procedure."

Stanley pushed the nurse aside, grabbed Maggie's purse, and shoved it under the sheet.

"What are you doing?" asked both the nurse and the deputy sheriff, as Stanley "Ten-Ex" Goldstein pulled his Colt automatic from his belt holster and switched off the overhead light.

4:40 a.m.—Mateole River

Link and Squid wore gray sweats with hoods pulled up and black running shoes. The cache of weapons they'd amassed was mostly left behind.

Link wore his too-old, too-heavy but familiar Smith & Wesson .357, offset by a pouch with fifty rounds of ammunition, alternately steel tipped for penetration, and Federal Hydra-Shok hollow points for stopping power. At the back of the pouch, he'd placed six phosphorous tracer rounds. Those were issued to fighter pilots on combat missions. If they were shot down, their comrades would see the bright red lines to determine their position, and would call for rescue.

On his left calf, Link carried a Kershaw hunting knife with a five-inch blade. In his pocket was one of the UHF radios they'd purchased. No GPSs, long arms, or laser sights.

He had, however, taken the 1.5-inch diameter, four-foot wooden pole from the captain's closet.

"What's that for?" Squid had asked when he'd seen it.

Link had shrugged. "Just a stick."

Squid carried one of the shotguns, with a magazine tube that provided seven extra rounds. The nickel-plated finish had been dulled by spray-painting it with swirls of green and black, and it was alternately loaded with double-aught buck and Number 2 shot shells. The previous afternoon, he'd practiced from the deck of the *Lady Rosalie* until his shoulder had been raw and his aim so improved that Stan had been pleased. The sound might have bothered Link and Maggie if they'd not been occupied in the cabin below.

He also carried the pilfered UHF radio with scrambler, and would be able to hear either Link or the decoded conversations. On his belt he carried a custom-made Randall fighting knife with a seven-inch blade. Unlike his inexperience with firearms, this he knew how to use.

They moved efficiently—rowed the dinghy ashore, relocated the Suburban into an empty garage, and hurried through the early morning.

"Let's get a final weather check," said Link. They slowed as Link tuned to WB-1.

The forecast called for calm seas until noon, then a drop in atmospheric pressure and increasingly heavy waves. A storm surge was predicted at 1400, followed by gale-force winds.

When they picked up the pace. Squid went over his final guess at a timetable.

9:00—Seaplane lands and unloads passengers.
9:30—*Sinner* departs Hidden Lagoon for big mama.
10:00—*Sinner* loads half the passengers.
10:30—*Sinner* at Hidden Lagoon. Purge air and recharge batteries as necessary.
11:00—*Sinner* departs Hidden Lagoon for big mama.
11:30—*Sinner* loads remainder of passengers, including Sajacento.
12:00—Seaplane picks up passengers from big mama and takes off.

The pieces fit. No other schedule would work.

"Bad weather won't matter to the *Sinner,* just the tidal flow that restricts them to between nine thirty and twelve thirty."

"Yeah, but if they're bringing in people, they'll have to land the seaplane and dock with the big mama. I wouldn't like to do that in rough water. My bet is that they won't stick around for long."

Link went over the radio procedure for the operation, making it simple:

- *One click on the radio means yes, two clicks mean no.*
- *If they're about to capture you, speak the word "three" over the radio.*
- *Say the word "ten" and I'll create a diversion, but give me a minute or two.*
- *Keep the volume low, transmit only when necessary, and do so over the Serpientes' frequency so it can't be jammed without screwing them up.*

They'd make the climb while the rock face was shadowed in morning gloom. Link would lead—he'd already been there. Squid was an experienced climber, although he was leery of the fractured rock. They'd continue until they were above the first marshy beach, and then split up.

After they separated, the plan was "according to the situation." There were few specifics, mostly common-sense directives. "If I do this, you do that."

Link would take the same path as before: behind the sails and the rear of the warehouse to the pathway where he'd found the jeep. From there he would find the Weeping Tree. The matter of a three-thousand-foot mountain being in the way presented a challenge. He assumed there was a chasm or a tunnel of some sort. Since they'd arrive early, he should have time to find it, and find a way past the guards.

Squid would climb to the ledge from which the sails were suspended and eyeball the operation as the *Sinner* went to sea and returned with the first load of terrorists. At eleven, it was scheduled to set out again. Before that time, Squid would call "ten." If Link responded with a single click, he would create a diversion to draw attention while Squid sabotaged the *Sinner*.

Link lifted his UHF radio. "Jack Hammer, this is Black Wolf. Request assistance." There was no response. He observed his Rolex, and twice more tried to raise Jack Hammer. As they turned onto the muddy road he'd taken with Maggie, Link broadcast: "Jack Hammer, Black Wolf has the information you were looking for. Request—"

A hissing sound emerged from the radio's speaker.

"Jamming," Squid said without surprise.

Bigfoot had told Link about their capability to scan for radio signals, estimate the direction, and jam that sector.

They'd never before been authorized to use jamming.

"Today's special for them," said Link, "or they wouldn't show off their secrets."

"It's seventeen days after Aozou," said Squid. "Everything's coming together for them."

"For us, too," said Link.

"It feels good to finally be doing something."

There was new chatter over the scrambled radio, Post One telling the guards to be alert for someone calling himself Black Wolf who might be out there.

"You've got them rattled," said Squid.

"Worried people make mistakes."

"When will you change to Hammer's frequency."

"Later," said Link as they continued. "When I've found the Weeping Tree." Link had picked the previous frequency at random. From Maggie's utterance, he believed Jack Hammer might be intercsted. If they were listening on scanners and things went badly for Link and Squid, at least they'd know where to look.

They'd also just learned that it took the Sociedad ninety-five seconds to find a signal, listen to it, and put a jammer on frequency.

Who was their enemy? That one was easy. Except for the possibility that Frank or Erin might be alive, there were no good guys where they were going.

36

Before Stan turned off the light and stood in the middle of the room with the big Colt in his hand, Maggie drifted in and out of lucidity, each period of consciousness just a little longer than the last. When she was with it, as she was *not* right now, she was aware that something bad was going down. With the jumble of leads and hoses connected, there was no way that she'd escape.

Stanley thought all of that as the heavy footsteps continued down the hall, and whoever it was checked the rooms.

"Not in here," he heard from a couple of doors down—the unpleasant, accented voice.

Visitors would have paused to read the room assignments board at the nurses' station. The guys in the hall had gone breezing by as if they'd known where to look—which meant not very much since hospital staff, police—*or* terrorists—all might do that.

Answer: He had to get a look before he acted, regardless of his gut feeling.

The deputy sheriff had drawn his own handgun and was looking back and forth in the gloomy room like he was trying to figure out why anyone would be coming to bother them, not putting two and two together that Maggie had already been shot once by someone in the area. The good news was that he looked competent.

The pre-op room nurse knew something bad was happening, and had backed over next to a door. Likely the toilet. Stan motioned for her to go inside, which she did—one less person to keep track of and worry about.

The people in the hall obviously heard the bathroom door close because they stopped, and the one with the accent called out: "Is anyone in room two-twelve?"

"Announce yourself," said Stan, which any cop in the world would understand but seemed to momentarily baffle all bad guys.

No one responded, but he heard heavier breathing.

How many? Stan wondered. From their footsteps and utterances, he guessed there were at least four. That did not mean they were four times as dangerous. He would have freedom of motion. They'd be worried about getting in one another's way.

Remember the tactical course. Do not shoot good guys.

An arm appeared, the hand holding an automatic pistol. Still Stanley held his fire until a head darted around for a look, wearing a ski mask and looking precisely like the bad guy posters on the tactical range.

Bam!

The man went down hard, drilled in the middle of his nose. The head jerked only once. The body dropped like a sack of sand, and the dead man's autoloader clattered on the tile. Someone in the hall yelled, and they started scrambling for cover.

Stan stepped out, keeping a low center of gravity, looking down the hall. More masks.

Bam! Bam! . . . Bam! . . . Bam!

The nearest one he'd shot twice and was down for good. The next one he'd hit in the leg, and he was also down, blood squirting with his heartbeats, mouth open and going into shock as anyone should after taking a .45 hollow-point. The third one he'd hit as he'd scrambled into a room. Mortally wounded? He thought not. More of a graze.

Two shooters were down hard. Make it three, because leg shot wasn't getting up. Another was hit, but the severity of his wound was unknown. Likely he was still a player. Stan had seen two other flickers down the hall, so there were more. Three down, three still upright.

Two of the uprights were close. The other one was farther, nearer the nurses' station.

The accent, who was the one hit but not down, spoke to a buddy in the opposing room.

Stan had no desire to wait for trouble to become organized. He stood from his crouch, still staring hard, shook out the kinks in his shoulders, and started forward.

A woman's voice at the nurses' station was phoning for help, saying there was shooting on the second floor of the hospital. Probably a 911 call. *Phut!* She dropped heavily. The telephone clattered. She'd been shot by a silenced weapon.

Hopefully the 911 computer was providing the source address of the call.

The closest two were muttering, getting up their courage by talking to one another. Including the one at the nurses' station, there were definitely three left.

A man's voice sounded behind Stan. One had somehow gotten past him!

He whirled and almost shot the deputy, whose face was chalky. "Are there others?" the deputy asked.

Awful timing.

Stan heard feet scrambling into the hall, turned and fired, and hit one of them in the neck, and took a round in the chest himself. He grunted loud. *Damn, oh damn!* Another round thumped into his stomach, and he dropped the .45, staggered, and fell into the room beside him.

His life did not flash before his eyes, and there was no tunnel as Stanley Goldstein descended into pain and darkness.

5:05 a.m.

Chief Welk had killed the chief nurse making the 911 call, then stayed at the station. He was trying to figure his next move when a new roar of gunfire erupted in the hallway.

Being no fool, he waited, wondering if there was a way out of the building without exposing himself to the youthful FBI agent that El Jefe had so underestimated, wishing to hell that he'd brought something bigger than the stupid .22 pistol.

He heard Kamil speak in Arabic, then say in English, "I shot them both!"

Relief flooded over Welk as he cautiously emerged from the nurses' station.

Two of his men sprawled in death poses. Two others were unconscious and bleeding out, one neck shot, the other hit in the leg, both pumping blood so profusely that neither could last long. Kamil stood in the middle of the hallway with a bloody arm, wearing a triumphant look as he loomed over the wounded deputy, who was defiantly staring back.

Bam!

"Where's the agent?" Welk asked Kamil.

"I killed him."

"The woman?"

Kamil pointed. "In there."

"Get her."

Kamil turned a hate-filled stare on Welk, as if deciding whether to kill him, as well. Finally he walked down the hall to the room, reached in, and turned on the light.

Welk followed, trying and failing to avoid stepping in the still-collecting pool of blood, then looked inside to see Kamil going to the occupied bed.

The female agent remained immobile, her face pale.

Welk snapped, "See if she's alive."

Kamil gave him the look again, then pointed his weapon at the monitors. "She's alive."

A siren hee-hawed in the distance, coming from downtown. As Welk moved forward to help move her, Kamil leaned down and swept the sheet off the female agent, whose midriff was wrapped with gauze soaked with fresh blood.

She raised herself up slightly, holding a derringer in Kamil's face.

Bam!

Kamil wilted, his eye bloody where she'd shot him.

The woman turned toward Welk with a determined look, and he fled, slipped in the thick pool of blood, and fell headlong down the hall. He scrambled to his feet and ran toward the stairwell, favoring his knee and hearing the sirens coming ever closer.

5:15 a.m.—The Weeping Tree

Aside from the sentinel and the two chemists of Alpha-Nine, Frank and Erin were alone in the old encampment. They'd worked for half the night trying to loosen one of the two-by-sixes that Chief Welk had nailed in place, and labored still, fingers bloody and raw from the effort.

If they'd had a pry bar or claw hammer to gain leverage, it would be different, but nothing like that was available. They'd tried digging with their fingernails, and when those were gone, pressed their fingers against the infinitesimal seams between board and tree roots, even pounded with the heels of the other hands until their joints were cracked and swollen.

They were without answers, although they knew they must get free. Not for themselves—they were beyond hunger and no longer wasted energy chasing grubs and beetles and other things that did not nourish them and only made them ill. They partook only of the water from the rivulets that coursed down the Weeping Tree each morning.

"Do not give up hope," Frank had periodically told Erin throughout their captivity.

Erin whispered the words in her mind. *Do. Not. Give. Up. Hope.*

This was the final day of their lives. They'd been told that by Sydney during yesterday's visit. One way or another, with Link Anderson's presence or without it, they would be killed, and their mutilated bodies taken far away. The Hezbollah would take credit.

Too bad. So sad. Sydney had winked and called them her darlings and explained how they would be recognizable as humans because of the wonders of science. *It was amazing what could be learned from DNA analysis, even from small bits of flesh.*

She'd thanked Frank for telling her that Lincoln Anderson was nearby, searching for them. So valiant of Anderson. So utterly *stupid.*

She knew precisely how to honey the trap.

Hello, honey. She'd laughed gaily and gone about her task of stationing the guards. Two here, one there, some on the approaches to the clearing so they would have a shot if Anderson came for his friends.

The sentinel had been up all night, staring about as if confused by the hidden guards. Since there were not enough shiny symbols to protect them all, they'd taken his rifle and told him not to make trouble or he would never be fed again. He stared back with a troubled expression, wondering—if he was capable of thought—why he was not allowed to earn more food.

Erin looked out at him, sitting on his haunches in front of his lonely hut. Since her arrival, she'd tried to befriend him as Frank had done, speaking pleasantly and cajoling him to utter words in response. Not once had he acknowledged her. Chief Welk had beaten and starved him into submission, and somehow had taken his mind.

There must be *something* she could do to help in their escape.

Erin whispered the words again. *Do. Not. Give. Up. Hope.*

6:30 a.m.—Hidden Lagoon

Damon Lee was burning mad. His replacement had arrived a half hour late.

The dipshit looked about slyly. "Three hours ago, Chief Welk pulled five guys out of bed to go to Eureka. When he showed back up, no one was with him. There's talk of a shoot-out."

"Anyone ever tell you it's not smart to talk about Serpientes?" ·

The replacement snorted. "I never mentioned the word, dumb fuck. *You* did."

Lee was retrieving his rifle case from inside the sails when the knowledge came to him that Anderson was coming for him. That thought had periodically recurred all morning, popping out of the blue for no reason, like the words were being planted in his head—and he heard faint chanting in some language he couldn't understand.

Lee felt a chill, stopped and looked around, and found no one there.

Come ahead, asshole. I need more practice with my rifle.

With the thought, he felt tougher. He walked past the warehouse, where it was dark enough that he had to switch on his Maglite, toward the Jeep he'd parked at the path. Beyond it, where the tunnel began, there were guards, and he'd have to use the password. Most of the guards he knew, but others were Peter Zerbini's boatmen.

Something grabbed his shoulder, and he let out a squeak. The hand tightened until he dropped the rifle case and wanted to pass out from pain, and still all he could manage was the small, frightened mouse's eeking.

A voice whispered, "I owe you again, Damon Lee. You shot my lady."

Damon wanted to offer something in his defense, but all he did was squeak. Then something smacked him in the temple, and he did not even remember falling.

"Please," he managed as they skidded around a turn, but Anderson would not answer.

Damon was untied, free to reach forward and wrestle with the driver, but at the moment, looking out over a thousand feet of nothing but empty space, it did not seem the wisest thing to do.

The realization hit him. "You're going to kill me!"

"That's what I should have done before."

Damon Lee was filled with terror.

They came to the lookout abruptly. Anderson locked the brakes. They slid forward until the bumper extended over the precipice. "Oh God!" Damon cried, mortally afraid.

Anderson thumped Lee's leg with a four-foot pole, and he squealed and scrambled out of the Jeep. He must escape—or he'd be killed.

The false dawn painted the sky with reds and pinks, but Damon Lee saw no beauty through his veil of foreboding. He was prodded forth until he stood wavering at the precipice, whimpering as he stared down. A single nudge or misstep, and he would fall.

"Are you going to push me?"

"I ask questions, you give answers. What is your mother's name?"

Thump! The pole smacked the side of his head. Damon Lee wailed not only in pain but also because he dared not answer. If the Serpientes learned he'd cooperated, he would die horribly!

Thump! His arm felt as if it was broken.

Thump! His leg! He squealed again, and Anderson did not care that he almost toppled over the side. *Thump!*

After the fourth strike, each harsher than the previous one, Lee dropped onto his stomach and grasped the earth so he couldn't fall, and he began to cry.

Lincoln Anderson thumped his head. "Be quiet."

He abruptly stopped crying.

Thump! He dared not whimper.

"Get up." Lee took to his feet with great care.

"This is your last chance. What is your mother's name?"

Damon Lee told him, sniffing and wiping his nose with the back of his hand.

"Your sister's name?"

Anderson posed innocuous questions that gave nothing away, although some made Lee think—What was your dog's name? Where did you go to the fourth grade?— When he hesitated, the pole thumped him so hard, he knew that bones must be breaking, so he answered more quickly.

"How many guards are posted?"

"Nineteen."

Thump! "How many?" he asked more sternly.

Lee remembered what the replacement had told him and cried out: "Fourteen. Welk took five away, and they didn't come back!"

Blood bubbled from his nose, although Anderson had not hit him there.

"What kind of weapons are the guards carrying?" Lee recited the ones he'd seen, rushing his answers, anxious to avoid the edge and being thumped with the pole.

Anderson nudged him just slightly toward the precipice. "Where's the Weeping Tree from here?"

Lee told him.

"Who are the Serpientes?"

"They'll kill me!" he wailed.

Thump! As he named them, a ringing noise sounded in his head and would not go away.

"Where do they live?" He told him. "Where does Sydney stay?"

"In El Jefe's home in Lennville. She's his half sister."

"Where are the hostages?" Damon Lee's head rang and hurt fiercely, yet from somewhere within he found a glimmer of courage.

"I don't know," he said with an almost bold ring.

Thump! Thump! Anderson nudged him to the cliff's edge.

Lee sobbed, holding his head. He felt blood running from both ears and smelled the pungent odor of feces from his loosened bowels.

"Who do you fear the most? Me or them?" he was asked quietly.

"They're in the Weeping Tree!" Damon Lee wailed, and the final vestige of rebellion fell away. "Sydney's going to kill them. She wanted to capture you and make you watch, but they're out of time, so she'll do them after the rag-heads arrive. Watch for the sentinel. If you don't have a star badge, he'll kill you." He spoke faster, to please Anderson. "Welk made him crazy, and he can't think and has to kill people so he'll be fed. The two rag-head chemists build their bombs in the bungalow next to the Weeping Tree, but they're sissy faggots and won't be trouble."

Lee looked fearfully at him, wondering if Link wanted him to say more. Bruises appeared wherever he'd been struck. His head was a mass of knots and lumps.

"You shot my lady," said Anderson.

"I'm sorry," he whimpered. Oh God, was he sorry.

Anderson stared with deadly eyes and tore the star badge from his shirt. "Forget this. Only I can protect you. Now come," he said, and walked to the Jeep.

Damon Lee edged away from the precipice and hurried after him. "There's a password." He was more afraid of Lincoln Anderson than he'd been of anyone or anything in his life.

The shame of his cowardice had not yet come to Damon Lee.

37

Squid waited on the ledge above the cavern from which the collection of sails—undoubtedly from the ships of Serpiente victims—were hung, observing the warehouse and the lagoon that was forming as water drained out. For a while, at least, the only other human presence was the guard. Finally the two men and woman of the *Sinner*'s crew emerged sleepily from the warehouse and trudged down the vaguely lit pathway that Link had noted.

Deciding that his time could be better spent, Squid climbed down early. The descent was easy enough; the third sail from the outermost one was the sturdiest of the lot, so he rode it like a child on a slide. Under other conditions, he would have enjoyed it.

Knife in hand, he observed beyond the sails. The guard slept on a sandy spot he'd found, head propped on driftwood, Uzi cradled in his chest. Squid resisted the temptation to use the Randall. Instead he went back inside and took his time looking over the cavern, thinking he'd like to take a look inside the *Sinner* and see if anything had been added. He doubted that he'd be caught. Despite what they'd read of their fierceness, the Serpientes were not infallible. They were members of a rich man's club, out to make a profit off the terror and blood of others. Their secret to success was similar to Napoleon's: audacity and more audacity.

Squid tried the end door that had been used by the crew and found it unlocked. He crept inside and went first to the surveillance room, to observe for sign of human presence in the cavern. The room was as Link had left it, except now the last of the three radios was missing as well as the one Link had pilfered, and Squid now carried.

After the *Sinner*'s first voyage, Squid would call for the diversion. Then the fun would begin. *It won't be long,* he whispered to an imaginary Tanker.

The recording system's function switch was still turned to ERASE, which meant nothing was being recorded. The crew was sloppy, and perhaps hungover.

Otherwise they'd know about the large guy in a sweatsuit carrying a mean-looking shotgun who had been nosing around.

He observed the control console, where one of them would monitor the progress of the *Sinner.* There were fewer gauges and controls than had been in the support vessel.

A pang of apprehension niggled at him to hurry, although there was plenty of time before the nine thirty launch.

He went to the submarine, observed it as he walked its length, and reflected on the fact that the once-proud submergence vessel was reduced to ferrying terrorists. What a terrible way to use such a superb scientific achievement.

At the back of the warehouse, he examined the huge roll of titanium-sheathed electrical cable, and the union where it connected to the *Sinner,* as well, and again decided that it was the "vulnerable node." The *Sinner* would be reeled out on its seaward journey, and back in during the return. But not if it were sheared.

Just once before he ended the *Sinner*'s life he wanted to see her interior again, and almost went there until he reminded himself he was here to destroy, not admire her.

He went through the large toolbox beside the cable reel until he found the set of large, heavy-duty bolt-cutters. These were provided in the event the cable had to be spliced. As the *Sinner* was on the second return trip, with Sajacento aboard, Squid would sever the cable and the *CNR-2* would be dragged to the bottom by the cable's weight.

Hurry, repeated the voice of caution, and he stepped inside the surveillance room to see if he had company. The video system was set to an exterior camera—and his heart sank. On the monitor the threesome ambled back, walking directly toward the warehouse's rear entrance.

Regardless of which door he used, he would be in their view when he exited.

Shit. Go to plan two! He rummaged through his brain but could not recall thinking of this circumstance. He could always kill the crew and the guard, then disable the submarine. Dumb! The Serpientes would be alerted, Frank and Erin killed, he and Link would likely be pursued, and the ones who deserved killing would escape.

As the crew approached, he wondered about a place to hide.

7:30 a.m.—Saint Elmo's Hospital, Eureka, Room 310

A doctor had told Stanley that his ribs would not heal for "six weeks or a month and a half, whichever was longest." *Ha, ha.*

Not funny, but it certainly could be worse.

He'd had a Kevlar vest in his kit bag, and had taken a lesson from Tony Silva, whose life had been saved by an older model. Since Stan had never before been shot while wearing a vest—or without one, come to think of it—he had always wondered if the old pro agents had been truthful when they'd said it felt like being kicked by a large Brahman bull. Instead he had been kicked twice, once in the chest and again in the stomach, from close up. He'd been unconscious for half an hour, and spent as long getting his breath back.

Two ribs were broken, and they hurt like hell, but he had things to do. Such as get into street clothing from the kit bag that did not look like something worn by an FBI agent.

Pandemonium reigned at the hospital. State troopers and local police were everywhere, and incoming patients were being sent to the old General Hospital.

Thus far, Stanley had kept his responses simple, answering questions and completing forms with vague but accurate statements. At eight o'clock they'd transport him to the station for another friendly interrogation, since they were confused as to where Maggie had been shot and the identity of the gunmen who had tried to kill, kidnap, or whatever, her at the hospital.

He had better things to do than spend hours at a police station giving evasive answers, and thus had carefully handwritten two letters to help straighten things up.

The room telephone buzzed, and he picked up, answering hello in a low voice that wouldn't disturb his boss, who had been brought here following her second surgery since the pre-op and recovery rooms on floor two were part of the crime scene.

"Special Agent Goldstein?" someone asked on the phone line. When Stan acknowledged, he was asked to stand by for Assistant Director In Charge Gordon Hightower.

Stanley had not met him, only remembered him from conversations with Maggie, Squid, and Link. "Good morning, sir."

"Congratulations for saving ASAC Tatro's life. She's an old, dear friend."

"Thank you, sir."

"So is Link Anderson. In fact, I'd like to speak with him about a matter, and I've been made to believe you may know where he is."

"Not really."

Hightower became less pleasant. "You don't know, or you don't want to tell me?"

"This is a nonsecure line, sir. My supervisor advised me to never discuss an ongoing sensitive operation over an open line unless I use a bureau-approved encoding device."

"Aw, for God's sake. I've verified the line's clean. Also, you're not on an ongoing official operation. That's part of what I want to talk with Link Anderson about."

"If I recall my supervisor was referring to FBI directive number . . ."

As he spoke in bureaucratese, Stan remembered Link's concern about swarms of agents getting the hostages killed. It might have been difficult to determine where his duty lay if Maggie had not been shot, and if the attack on the hospital had not occurred. But those things had happened, and it was no longer a question of whether the Serpientes existed. Now it was a matter of rescuing any living hostages and stopping the terrorist attacks.

At the coast guard station, Link had told him what to do about contacting the federal authorities and trying to gain their support, and when. Since it was still too early, he went on about the regulations and how he could not tell anyone outside his chain of command.

Hightower swore, then said, "Let's go at this from another direction, *Special Agent Goldstein*. Have you met ATF Agent In Charge Rogers and his chief of operations who goes by the name Jack Hammer?"

"Yes, sir." Link had said to contact Jack Hammer first.

"Hammer happens to be a senior FBI supervisory agent. As we speak, he is flying to the hospital to see you. If you refuse to cooperate, I will order him to arrest you for impeding justice."

"Sir, I—"

"We've had complaints about you lodged by a Circuit Court of Appeals Judge, as well as a subordination charge for ignoring a direct order to withdraw. Now if you'll just explain what the hell's going on, perhaps you can avoid suspension and we can include you in our operation."

Stan Goldstein did not try to explain that Judge Lyle Bull and the prominent citizens were members of the terrorist organization that Hightower did not believe existed. Instead he hung up.

He placed, on his supervisor's bedside table, two envelopes. Printed on both were the words: *Official Use Only*. One he addressed to *Supervisory Special Agent Jack Hammer*, the other to the *Sheriff, Humboldt County*. He then walked out past the troopers in the hall.

Stan found the taxi he had called parked in front, and
directed the driver to the storage company where they'd
garaged Link Anderson's GMC Yukon.

His ribs were sore, and every slight jolt and breath
were painful, and he was reminded of the journey he
still faced. There was no alternative. His friends were
in danger.

8:30 a.m.—Pathway to the Weeping Tree

During the mile-long walk with Damon Lee, Link made
discovery after discovery of interesting places that had
not been in the excerpt from Shepherd's Journal. Parts
of the path were at the bottom of a crevice in the mountain, other portions wended through dark tunnels.

Twice they passed others on the path, but it was dark,
and except for their muttered password, they ignored
one another's presence.

Damon Lee carried his rifle case as Link had told him,
and periodically halted to vomit or just groan in self-
pity. Each time Link rapped his calf or shin, urging him
to walk faster. When he tried to speak, Link would give
his head a harsh thump.

Now and then he asked Lee if he always smelled of
shit.

All those demeaning acts had a purpose.

The paths through the tunnels had once begun as
something smaller, a cave, perhaps a fissure in the stone
mountain, but the smooth surface of the walkways that
wound past dark stalactites and underground ponds and
small chambers bore marks of picks and chisels, and he
decided the improvements had been made by long-dead
Sociedad slaves.

There was no beauty to any of it, only gloom and an
occasional oily lamp, which Damon Lee had explained
were lit when important arrivals were on the way.

Important like Sajacento and his Hezbollah?

Lee said that no one liked to be in the tunnels because
of falling stones. To confirm his words, in the middle of
their trek, a tremor caused two boulders to rattle
ominously.

The next guard was positioned unseen near the end
of the tunnel. He challenged, Link spoke the password,
and they went on. Finally they emerged and followed a
well-beaten trail through the forest. Lee slowed, received
another rap, and continued ahead.

As they passed a redwood that was half-sunken into
a raw crevice in the earth, Lee nervously called the password. The response came, and Lee motioned for Link
to follow closely.

Link's senses were tuned. The course would take them
close to the guard, in open view, and he decided that
this was the trap that he'd been expecting.

He started in a lateral direction.

"*This* way," Lee hissed, but when he looked back, he
found himself alone.

Link circled around to Lee's other side, then proceeded parallel to their direction of travel, listening to
the sounds of Damon Lee pulling his rifle from its
metal case.

The two guards were forward and right of Damon
Lee, whose ego was fast returning and would be his
downfall. He smelled bad, sported a hundred lumps and
bruises, and wanted to shoot Link Anderson in the
worst way.

If Lee so wished, all he had to do was call out for
assistance and raise the hue and cry to find Link. Instead
he seethed inside, craving a more personal revenge.

Link remained low as he positioned himself between
Damon Lee and the guards, and abruptly stepped into
the open a dozen yards in front of Lee.

It took Damon Lee a moment to realize that Anderson was standing before him, staring in another direction. A sitting duck.

Lee hastily drew up the rifle and fired—*bam!*—and
heard an outcry.

The rifle was unwieldy, and by the time of the shot
Link had disappeared and was moving in a new direction. From behind, Link heard a guard cursing and then
the *brrrr* sound of an Uzi. Lee firing again. *Bam!* There
was a longer *brrrrrr* sound, then more cursing and movement, and finally the surprised and angry mention of
Damon Lee's name.

Lee had wounded one guard and had been shot by the other. If he lived, no one would believe him about being tricked into it by a man with a stick.

Link crept on. He came on two more guards, these talking low between themselves, wondering what was going on. The radio they shared announced that there'd been two accidental shootings. Post One announced for the guards to continue watching for Anderson. "But don't shoot unless you're damned sure."

Link was moving slowly through a thicket past another guard when he caught a whiff of pungent, rotten meat. It would not diminish, and he was wondering what it could be when he came face-to-face with a filthy creature in rags who hardly appeared to be human.

9:20 a.m.—The Weeping Tree

Frank Dubois had heard the shooting, and later the sounds of someone being brought into the bungalow. A few minutes later, the man died. An accident they said, and Frank hoped they would suffer many more. He and Erin listened to everything that went on in the camp, but they no longer struggled with the impossible two-by-sixes. The damn things had won.

Periodically he looked out to keep track of the guards whom Sydney had called the jaws of her trap. Some were well hidden, others almost obvious, but all had a view of the Weeping Tree and its approaches. If Link came to save them, he would run a gauntlet of guns. Frank had become bitter and even resigned to his fate, although he still vowed not to go easily.

It was Erin, who was so terribly battered, who refused to give up hope.

"Frank! He's—here!" she whispered, looking out the side nearest the bungalow.

Frank went along. "I'm happy for us, Erin."

"He's in—bungalow—looking over—the explosives."

He made an agreeable sound. "Mmm-hmm." Thinking how wonderful it would be to have this place blown up with the terrorists' own explosives.

Frank went slowly to join her where she peered out. "Don't use—so much energy."

A shadow appeared at the window, gazed in for a look and a wink, and went away.

"See?" she said. "He's really—*here*." Her tone was lilting and joyous.

Frank had seen him, a convincing illusion down to the new scar on his forehead.

Link's voice whispered, "Can you both walk?"

Frank's heart pounded as he realized that it was truly happening! Link was here to rescue them. Yet after a moment filled with joy, he realized that he would be unable to take more than a few steps. He started to say so when Erin interrupted.

"Yes!" she hissed anxiously. "We'll walk!"

Link handed them both something to wear.

9:25 a.m.—*The* Sinner

When the crew returned to the warehouse, Squid had hidden in the place he knew best, the submarine. When all three had immediately followed him through the hatch, noisily discussing the tight schedule, he'd taken the bolt-cutters and the shotgun and hastily packed himself into the aft equipment bay.

The electronics controlling the object recovery claw had been removed along with other unnecessary gear. While the entrance was a tight squeeze, the space was five feet long and three and a half in diameter and not cramped. He had closed the hatch behind himself, switched on a dim electrical lamp he'd remembered, and listened and waited for a chance to sneak out.

The three had mopped and cleaned around the crew console and passenger compartments, and the woman constantly complained. As their departure time approached, one of the men left for the control room in the warehouse, and the remaining two prepared for departure.

Squid was increasingly concerned that he might not get out and past them in time. He considered new options, and liked none of them.

Wait until they were under way and take over the vessel? He could bring the *Sinner* to the surface and broadcast to Link that he'd been forced to blow the entire plan. Scuttle the *Sinner* in the deep water and try to swim to the shore? He'd die of hypothermia, but who'd want to live knowing he'd let Sajacento and his Hezbollah get away.

There had to be a better way.

He heard the big diesel generator roaring to life right on schedule. From the crew console just four feet forward from where Squid lay, the woman began reading the launch checklist.

"Main Power—on." The instrumentation and lighting were switched to internal.

"Scrubbers—on." Up forward, fresh air hissed from vents.

To hell with waiting. Squid pulled the shotgun up and prepared to go out.

"Hatches—locked." *Bzzzz—clack.*

Oh, damn! The hatch to the aft equipment bay, and all others, had been electrically closed. There was no way for him to get out until they were reopened from the crew compartment. The only air Squid would get was that which was ambient and trapped in the compartment with him. Unless they reopened the hatch soon, he would suffocate.

Squid shallowed his breathing to use as little air as possible. He felt the sub's motions as it rolled forward on its wheels into the concrete channel and submerged, then proceeded out into the current, straining against the tether line to go faster. Ballast tanks on either side of him, like others up forward, filled or were blown to adjust their depth, but he could not be sure where they were at any time—only study his watch for approximations, knowing that they were speeding through the water, carried by the swift current.

After twenty-six minutes, he felt the submersible rock with the waves as it bobbed to the surface. From his time and distance calculation, the average speed had been almost thirty miles per hour, faster than he had believed. There were metallic clangs, and the *Sinner* ceased bobbing.

They were at the big mama, hidden by the shield and held fast in the cradle.

Little time was wasted. He heard the terrorists come aboard speaking Arabic as they went forward into the passenger compartment. He counted eight of them. Then the top hatch was secured.

As soon as they were released, the craft dived for the swifter current and the return trip.

The air in the equipment bay was stale and thin. Squid wondered how long he would last before losing consciousness, and then how long for his brain's oxygen-starved cells to die.

10:40 a.m.—The Weeping Tree

Sydney, El Jefe, and the other Serpientes had come to observe the arrival of the second wave of Sajacento's swarm. Just as the first four had been, the new *jahid* were young and filled with excitement. Sydney doubted that any had ever been in an airplane or a seaplane or a ship or submarine before. Now they were worldly adventurers with experiences that would amaze everyone at home, and none would live to brag to friends or relatives.

The remainder of the terrorists would arrive on the next underwater shuttle, and all would debark for their destinies with martyrdom. Sajacento would remain on the processing ship, awaiting word of their success. It was a jubilant time for the Hezbollah, so close to triumph.

The Serpientes were not nearly so pleased. Peter Zerbini's lawyers were pouring in from San Francisco to ensure that none of the ex-cons killed at the hospital in Eureka would be linked to them. Too bad about Kamil, but at least his fingerprints and DNA were unknown to Washington. Now Damon Lee had gone berserk, killed a guard and wounded another before he had been stopped. All those things pointed to the shortcomings of one person.

El Jefe could hardly believe that Welk had become so incompetent, regardless that Sydney told him that Lincoln Anderson's presence tended to make people look inept. Sydney was herself somewhat nervous, despite the fact that Welk would keep all the guards on duty until they caught him, and Zerbini promised even more reinforcements.

The two Serpientes—the chief of police and the judge—stood apart, periodically eyeing one another. Welk was sure that El Jefe would send him to the stone at the first opportunity. El Jefe wanted to do just that, but Sydney had convinced him to wait at least until they'd disposed of the hostages and Sajacento's *jahids* were on their way to their targets. There was big money at risk.

Sydney idly walked over and looked into the cavern under the Weeping Tree, then stared in growing disbelief. One of the boards was ajar. The captives were gone!

"They've escaped!" she shrieked in a voice filled with rage. It was impossible! Eight guards had been assigned to watch over the hostages and any sign of rescuers.

El Jefe cursed bitterly and glared at Welk, who warily kept his eyes on El Jefe as he radioed for an immediate search. All guards were called in from their posts and ordered to search along the way. They could not possibly have gone far in their weakened conditions.

Four Hezbollah martyrs were enlisted in the hunt when Peter Zerbini drew his pistol and led them to search the pathway to the Hidden Lagoon. Other *jahids* stood staring at the bedlam with confused looks.

When precious minutes passed without sign of Frank Dubois or Erin Frechette, Sydney tried to reason it out. As she continued to come up without answers, a nearby guard's radio came to life with two short transmissions. First the word "ten." Then a single *click*, as if in response.

Sydney frowned. The calls had not been made by the undisciplined guards, but seemed more like the pre-briefed procedures of police or government agencies, transmitted over their enemy's radio frequency so they would not be jammed.

It had been an important message or it would not have been transmitted, yet it was as if she was the only one who had noticed. She looked slowly about, still wondering as three streaks of red lightning shot across the clearing.

Bam! Bam! Bam! The gunshots coming so quickly they sounded as one.

At the sound, Chief Welk turned to El Jefe, crouching as he drew his pistol.

"No," she cried out, but by then El Jefe had pulled his own automatic.

Bam! Bam! Welk was deadly accurate. El Jefe's bulk shuddered as the bullets struck. He stumbled once and fell.

"Dead, dead, dead!" she whispered. Sydney felt no particular pity—her half brother had allowed himself to be vulnerable—but the shooting must stop or they all might be destroyed.

Joe Fuentes had also drawn his pistol, and was looking at Chief Welk, who turned to face him. Welk was a crack shot and would kill him.

"No!" Sydney called again, and pointed. "The shots came from the forest."

Red phosphorus rounds. She'd once taught agents the uses of the special rounds: either as a signal, or to light fires. Phosphorus-ignited material burned at high temperature, such as the crackling fire that blazed in the room of the bungalow where the chemists kept their explosives.

Sydney's heart pounded wildly, but not from fear. Rather it was from the anticipation that rushed through her veins as she realized there was only one person who could free the hostages and create such havoc.

"Lincoln Anderson is here!" she shouted, which only seemed to confuse them more.

Fools! Must I do everything myself? She walked deliberately across the clearing, determined to end it here. When she reached the body of her half brother, she stooped to pick up his silenced pistol, studied it for a moment, then continued ahead.

From behind she heard a frantic voice. "We can't stop the fire! The bungalow is about to blow!"

38

Upon the *Sinner's* arrival at the warehouse, when the Hezbollah *jahid*s had disembarked for the Weeping Tree, the *Sinner's* captain electrically unlocked the airtight hatches, switched on fans to vent the accumulated foul air, and left the submarine.

Squid was unaware of those things, for he'd gone too long without breathable oxygen. His life was spared only because he had passed out with his weight against the hatch, and when unlocked, it opened for just a crack. He returned to consciousness slowly, his skin sallow, his fingernails turned blue. For another few moments, his thoughts were jumbled and difficult. Finally he pushed the equipment bay hatch farther open, waited as his lungs were purged and replenished, and climbed out, taking the heavy bolt-cutters, shotgun, and radio with him.

He made his way to the still-open top hatch and looked out, noting how the submarine had been drawn up the concrete channel and halfway into the warehouse by the sturdy cable.

None of the crew were in sight. Even the guard was missing.

Squid switched the handheld radio to the *Serpiente's* frequency channel.

"Ten," he said into the mic, telling Link to go ahead with the diversion.

He heard Link's immediate response, a single click, meaning he would comply.

Squid's watch read 10:50. In ten minutes, the *Sinner* crew was to depart on their second round trip. He hoped Link's diversion would be a good one, for he wanted them to be shaken.

He lifted the heavy-duty bolt-cutters and climbed out the open hatch. As he went, he heard the clip-clopping of a dozen helicopters' blades to the north, headed inland.

Ignoring them, and as well the distant gunfire that erupted from beyond the cavern, he set to work on the tether cable with the bolt-cutters, careful to weaken only the outer titanium sheath and not cut the conduit.

10:55 a.m.—The Weeping Tree

Link stayed on the move and continued to evade the searchers. A guard carrying an Uzi passed several feet distant, and he let him go. Another came closer and was not so lucky, and went down hard when Link whacked him in the face with the heavy pole. He bent and retrieved a prize.

The bungalow was burning brighter. It would not be long.

He'd poleaxed the master chemist and his assistant, and piled hundreds of pounds of RDX and Semtex over their bodies.

At four minutes before eleven, he heard sounds of distant helicopters. They were early. He switched frequencies on the radio, quickly gave out a four-number coordinate for the LZ east of the clearing, and another for the clearing itself. He added, "Jack Hammer, this is Black Wolf. The LZ is hot. Hold for five." The buzzing of the comm jammers prohibited further conversation. Peter Zerbini's radio people were reacting faster at their task.

Crack! The sound of the explosion was earsplitting. Link dropped toward the ground, but he'd not yet landed when the concussive wave threw him several feet into a redwood. He hit hard, then shielded himself as debris and giant branches fell from far overhead.

Finally he rose, ears ringing from the overpressure,

and staggered into the clearing. Some of the terrorists, Serpientes and Hezbollah, had run, but those who had dawdled were scattered around in bloody pieces and death sprawls.

A man wearing a disheveled gray suit tried to stagger past. A Serpiente, Link guessed. He swung the pole hard and heard a *crack!* as it impacted the man's head. Another prize.

The Weeping Tree, born during the time of Hannibal, had slipped a dozen feet, and for a while it shuddered as the huge roots that had moored it strained. As if in response, the earth trembled with a violent seismic shudder. The entire forest swayed, and the already taut roots of the Weeping Tree began to snap like strings. The Goliath twisted grotesquely, paused ominously, and then fell, shattering lesser trees as it crashed to earth, spraying its giant branches about like great missiles. The remaining brethren trees trembled for several more seconds, then as the earthquake subsided, settled to grow for another millennium.

Link stood in time to deal a harsh blow to another fleeing *jahid* killer and only too late noticed that Chief Welk had risen a dozen yards away. The Serpiente stared at him with a hate-filled look, still weilding the pearl-handled .45 automatic.

"Anderson!" he rumbled, aiming the .45. "You are a dead man, you son of a bitch."

Welk had displayed his accuracy when he'd killed the judge. Link Anderson returned his stare. It was too late to act, and he realized it was his time to die. He had faced the dark specter of death before, but the reckoning had never been more sure.

An animal's outraged scream reverberated in the clearing.

Welk turned in surprise toward the source—the ragged scarecrow that Link had encountered earlier stood at the door of his hut, carrying a rifle taken from a guard.

Bam! Bam! Welk fired before the ragged man could react, and hit his target precisely—striking the sentinel in his neck and torso. He immediately swung the muzzle back to Anderson, who had dropped away in desperation and was reaching for the big revolver.

Welk shot first. *Bam!*

Link felt fire in his left arm and was spun half about as he hit the ground and rolled, almost losing the revolver. He hastily acquired his target and squeezed the trigger. *Bang!*

The tracer struck the Serpiente in the stomach, creating a smoldering fire that sizzled in flesh. Welk screamed as he stumbled against the blood stone.

Bang! A second red phosphorus round impacted Welk's chest and burned into his heart.

11:01 a.m.—Hidden Lagoon

The passengers burst from the pathway behind the warehouse just after the explosion—which Squid thought was a damned good diversion—including four Hezbollah terrorists and a handsome man in a dark suit over whom the two crewmates fawned like serfs.

Squid waited as they scrambled into the open hatch, and became the sixth passenger to board, making no secret of the shotgun he carried. All the guards and boatmen were armed, and no one paid him notice as he followed their lead and strapped himself into a passenger's seat.

The dark-suited man holstered his pistol into a shoulder rig that bulged at his armpit. The four nervous, would-be bombers were unarmed.

"No more passengers," the pilot said, and secured the top hatch. The explosion had rattled him, and he hardly checked the craft over. The female crew member who had complained so much spoke not at all. Squid noted that neither she nor the pilot appeared to be armed.

Hatches were closed and locked, and electric motors whined as the craft crept forward on its wheels, slowly then faster. Within seconds they were submerged and on their way. The *Sinner*'s metal skin groaned and shuddered as if it were alive. Periodically the craft would roll some as they maneuvered, making it feel like an airliner.

The man in the suit made an acidic comment to the pilot, who responded in an apologetic rush of words. Squid had not met him, but he knew his identity.

Four Hezbollah bombers and a Serpiente. Not a bad catch.

As they continued and entered the strong outbound current, Squid remembered his friend. *These are for you, Tanker.* He checked his watch. Six and a half minutes since they'd launched. They were approaching Angel Rock, and the underwater ledge and immense canyon beyond.

As Squid had guessed, they momentarily turned into the other current to keep the tether on the north side of Angel Rock, and slowed dramatically. The second they were past, the pilot turned back and pushed the *Sinner*'s nose down to take advantage of the swift current.

It's time. Squid released his seat belt, and used built-in handgrips to steady himself as he made his way to the pilot's console.

His movement caught them by surprise. The pilot frantically pointed for him to return to his seat. Squid grasped his shoulder with a heavy hand, slung him hard toward the passengers, and set the friction lock on the plane controls to keep them steady for what was next.

The man in the dark suit scowled as he reached into his suit jacket.

Squid had seen his photograph on his company's wall in San Francisco.

Peter Zerbini pulled his pistol.

Boom! The sound of the shotgun's blast in the enclosure was deafening.

A bloody hole gaped in Zerbini's chest. He hung over his seat belt, muscles contracting in spasms as he died. The woman crew member screamed.

Squid ratcheted in a new round. Stanley would have been proud of his marksmanship.

He'd anticipated the next problem—he could not manage the hand-operated controls without releasing the shotgun, and must free himself of further problems.

"Open the aft compartment," he told the female crewmate.

The death of her employer had been motivating. She flipped the electrical switch releasing the lock, then ran back and opened the hatch.

"Get in," he told the four Hezbollah. "If you hesitate, I'll shoot you."

He wondered if they understood English. It would not matter.

Boom! He shot the dead man again for effect and ratcheted another round. The four live ones scrambled and shoved their way into the equipment bay that Squid had previously occupied.

"Lock it," he told the female crew member. She did.

"What about me?" asked the pilot.

"Both of you grab a Mae West, then strap in and hold on."

The nose was slightly down, and there was too much left yaw. They were at 350 feet depth, riding the current and making twenty-seven knots. The big mama was four nautical miles distant. Squid was proud he'd remembered how to tell all that. *Like riding a bicycle.*

When the crew were secured in their seats, Squid wedged the shotgun in place on the console and took the controls. It took a few seconds to correct the yaw and heading and bring up the bow.

A light flickered, telling him the man in the console at the warehouse had noted a problem and was trying to take control.

The *Sinner* began to slow. Squid applied full power ahead, and the *Sinner* strained, but only for a moment. When the titanium tether snapped, they shot forward as if fired from a slingshot. A new light illuminated. Contact with the warehouse was lost—forever.

Squid hastily corrected both roll and yaw.

They were freed from all constraints. When their momentum and electrical power were lost, they would sink into the abyss.

The boat rolled slightly and began to slow some as Squid went for the surface. Twenty-one, then twenty knots, slowing gradually but still hurtling along at a good clip.

From behind, he heard thumping sounds as the prisoners began to kick the hatch. The paralyzing moments of

their fear had passed, and they knew they must escape
or die.

At forty feet of depth, ascending, Squid raised the
periscope with its high-definition television camera,
which was chancy going this fast. Fortunately everything
stayed together.

He tuned the image to dead ahead and observed that
the big mama was five hundred meters away, and they
were closing.

Thump! Thump! The prisoners began kicking the
hatch in unison.

Eighteen knots and slowing. The *Sinner* broached the
surface, then nosed back down and up again. He held
the controls and made slight inputs until they were
steady.

The woman was wide-eyed and afraid.

"Open the top hatch," he told her.

She unbuckled and did as she was told. Fresh air
gusted in from the outside.

Thump! Thump! Thump!

Four hundred meters and closing on big mama, at
fourteen knots and slowing. The water temperature
showed fifty-five degrees. Fifteen minutes in the water
could bring death by hypothermia.

"Both of you climb out and jump off."

Neither crewmate argued. The man beat the woman
out of the hatch. They wore heavy clothing under the
lifejackets and had a chance of survival, if slight.

Squid pulled on a Mae West and went up to stand in
the open hatch and operate the secondary controls there.

Thump! Thump! The kicking noises became louder;
they'd succeeded in warping the hatch enough that it no
longer muffled the sounds. He could hear them speaking
in Arabic.

The big mama loomed larger as the *Sinner* closed.
Someone had seen the impending disaster, and figures
appeared on deck. He noted the flash-flash-flash of automatic weapons as they tried to shoot the deadly fish out
of the water before impact. They were too late. He'd
set the friction locks to keep the controls steady if he
was disabled.

Eighty meters directly before him, a figure in green

turban and robes stood staring at the *Sinner*, hands raised as if he could stop the submarine with willpower alone. *Wrong!*

Spang! Spang! Ricochets. Eleven knots and slowing.

The big mama was finally getting under way, slowly moving off its spot.

The *Sinner* was only thirty meters out and closing, headed directly for the two lifeboats on the port side of the ship—it was unlikely that even the two on the opposite side would survive the impact of the sturdy submarine.

They were no longer taking gunfire; the shooters were fleeing.

Squid heard the prisoners breaking through the hatch below, then the sounds of them scrambling out of the equipment bay.

"Take the con, Tanker," he said as he climbed over the *Sinner*'s rail, took a last look at the Green Mullah running from the point of impact, and dived over the side.

11:32 a.m.—The Weeping Tree

One by one, Link picked them off with the "coup stick." Some tried to use firearms, but the forest made it difficult to aim and fire before he'd dart behind a tree only to reappear behind them or before them or beside them.

Although his left arm was bloody and useless—Welk's last shot had been as accurate as all his others—he'd strapped it in place with a belt taken from a guard's body and wielded the pole with his right. Their last images of life were of a dark, avenging angel swinging a club.

The Sociedad had begun as Indian criminals and renegades. Death by coup stick was apropos; the demise of an evil society using an honorable tradition of others.

When he'd hunted down the last of them near the clearing, Link returned and looked for any who might remain. He would not have long to search, for he could hear the Black Hawks setting down at the eastern edge of the valley, half a mile away.

He called to his friends, and Frank and Erin painfully emerged from the sentinel's hut, both wearing the star badges he'd provided them. Link had worn one, as well, all taken from those he'd killed. Welk's had been lost in the tumult—to the sentinel's tortured mind, his master had become prey.

Link and his friends had been spared. He sensed that none of the Serpientes or their men, or Hezbollah terrorists, remained alive about the clearing, and slowly began to relax his guard.

At the sight of his friends, emotion so filled and warmed him that he could not speak.

Link felt his adrenaline high shutting down, replaced by waves of pain and weariness.

Frank Dubois felt for the sentinel's pulse, and shook his head.

The ruined man had looked on without emotion as Link had led them behind the bungalow and brethren trees to the safety of his home. When the Serpientes had searched for Frank and Erin, they'd been repelled by the stench. The crude hut had been protected from the blast's concussive waves by the Weeping Tree.

Link heard sounds of people approaching in the forest.

"Get back inside until we're sure," he told Erin and Frank, and although he suspected they were friendlies, he leaned the pole against a tree, drew the revolver, and warily waited.

No one would harm his friends again.

A voice suddenly rang out. "FBI! Drop your weapons."

Link holstered his revolver and raised his hands as figures in black uniforms and SWAT protective gear came from three sides, aiming M-16s and Squad Automatic Weapons. Their jackets were stenciled HRT. The pros were in town.

"Down on your stomach," one commanded, and Link complied.

A two-place Scout helicopter made a flyby, then pirouetted and landed in the much-expanded clearing. The rotors were still turning when a black uniform dismounted and strode over, dropped onto his haunches, and observed Link.

"Every time I see you, you're dirtier," said Jack Hammer.

"I figured you were FBI. There goes the neighborhood," said Link.

Hammer pulled him to his feet by his good hand and couldn't suppress a smile as Frank and Erin emerged from the filthy hut.

"Ma'am, Mr. Dubois. All of America's been praying to see you safely home."

"Frank needs medical help," snapped Erin, and Link decided she hadn't changed.

Hammer called for medics, then for an EMT chopper that was holding out of the hostile fire zone.

"Link, too," Erin managed. "He was wounded in the arm. Also minimum—publicity for all of us, please," said Erin, getting back into the swing of running things.

"Yes ma'am," said Jack Hammer as medics began to examine the wraith-thin hostages. He pointed at a body and turned to Link. "Local?"

"From Syria, I'd guess. Maybe Palestine. Hezbollah. The worst of the scum."

Then a new wave of apprehension came over Link, and he shuddered involuntarily, and wondered if the evil would ever be destroyed from this place.

"Is something wrong?"

Sydney adjusted the trousers to compensate for the small difference in height, then looked herself over for a final time. She'd picked a female agent, and there was not too much adjustment to make. She'd smeared on the camo paint found in the dead agent's shirt pocket, and knew she was utterly unrecognizable.

She hefted the M-16, held it up and ready, and walked back toward the clearing, passing agents who were making sweeps of the forest. She observed them and emulated them more closely, pulling her helmet down just a little and shortening her stride, thinking how superb it felt to be fooling people again.

Sydney paused at the edge of the clearing. Twenty

feet distant, Lincoln was listening to a large black man. Beyond those two, her unappreciative guests, Erin and Frank, were being pampered and checked by corpsmen. *Don't bother,* she said to herself. *They're as good as dead.*

They would be first so Lincoln could look on.

See, Lincoln. This time you lose, no matter how hard you try. It's the way it had to be.

Dead, dead, dead.

She edged closer.

The big black man was speaking. "ADIC Hightower is starting to realize he's been scammed and doesn't have anyone cornered in Georgia. When he finds out about the hostages, he'll go into orbit. He knew something might be wrong after this morning's shoot-out in Eureka—"

"What shoot-out?"

Jack Hammer gave him a synopsis. Between them, Agents Tatro and Goldstein had killed five attackers in the hospital. Link voiced concern about Maggie.

"Goldstein disappeared after leaving your message for me to have my team ready, and monitor the frequency I'd given you. When Maggie Tatro came around and told us what was happening here, every FBI agent in the state volunteered to go in."

One of the medics came over and said that Mr. Dubois had something important.

So far so good, Sydney told herself. *They have absolutely no idea I'm here.* I'm invisible.

She lifted the muzzle just slightly, preparing to swing it around to shoot Erin.

Link had sensed the danger before he saw the rifle barrel begin to pivot. The uniformed agent should not be in the already-pacified clearing with the raised weapon, and her finger sure as hell shouldn't be on the trigger. He'd started to move before she did, and when she continued to bring the weapon to bear, he knew precisely whom he was confronting.

She was going for Erin! Finger already curling in the trigger guard.

"Sydney," was all he had time to cry, but the two agents wearing the rags of the hostages were already dropping for cover, and four HRT agents were preparing to shoot. They delayed then, confronted with one of their own.

Brr-aaat!

The woman in the subdued FBI SWAT uniform fired, sweeping the flow of bullets about the group.

Link had no time to think, just raised the revolver and hastily fired the last remaining bullet at her most vulnerable area. The muzzle flashed, and the phosphorus round created a new fiery path. At first he thought he'd missed, for Sydney staggered just once, then slowly turned the rifle's muzzle toward him.

Λ gurgling noise issued from her throat, and they could see the smoldering flesh there.

The HRT agents began to fire in full-automatic volleys of three rounds. *Bap-bap-bap! Bap-bap-bap! Bap-bap-bap! Bap-bap-bap!* Bullets pocking the armored padding of her uniform, tearing away more flesh at vulnerable places. The hail of bullets continued until the carbine slipped from her grasp and she staggered about.

She fell and writhed, and her throat pumped more blood.

Link went closer, slowly knelt by her and removed her helmet.

The last words he heard were spoken in a gurgle as she died.

"Not me," Sydney whispered. "It wasn't me."

Sydney's face relaxed, and despite her awful killing wounds, she looked as she must have once appeared— like a frightened and innocent girl.

The evil had passed.

In a protected area beyond the giant trees, Frank Dubois and Erin Frechette were held upright by two agents as they'd both insisted— swigging fresh water and Gatorade, and eating nutrient bars.

Frank spoke carefully, periodically interrupted by Erin. Four terrorist teams were already positioned at safe houses near the campuses of large universities, waiting to set off their explosives during graduation exercises in three days.

When Frank's energy ran out and he was near collapse, the medics helped him onto a litter. Erin took over. Despite her physical condition, she was determined to speak.

She explained that the Serpientes and Hezbollah had spoken freely in their presence, and she and Frank had memorized everything about the plan. Targets, addresses, frequencies, how the bombs were made and how they'd be employed—all of it.

"Then we can stop them," said Jack Hammer.

"Only if you act quickly. The Hezbollah have alternative plans. If there's the slightest hint that they've been compromised, they'll move the bombers to new safe houses and switch to backup targets. They're here to kill Americans."

Hammer used a satellite phone to call his superior's boss, the deputy director for terrorism in Washington, and told him what he'd learned. There was little time.

Erin placed a grimy hand onto that of Jack Hammer. "They'll need my information. Before I give it, I'd like to make a condition."

It sounded very much as if Erin Frechette were committing blackmail.

The Scout was flown out of the way to make room for a Black Hawk with red crosses on both sides and its belly. Link stood with Jack Hammer, watching the medics prepare Frank and Erin for evacuation.

"We've found only one person alive so far, and he gave up without a fight. Nine others have been clubbed. None of those are alive."

"That's too bad."

As Link climbed onto the med-evac helicopter, Hammer took a radio call. The coast guard was reporting that a Canadian fish-processing ship had sunk at the international limit. The distress call had been delayed because of electronic jamming.

39

The twenty-eight-foot fishing boat eased its way through the debris. Much of it had gone to the bottom, but there were crates, millions of frozen fish, and a handful of life-jacketed survivors whose cries the boat's pilot callously ignored.

Periodically, the *Lady Rosalie*'s pilot sounded the air-horn to attract the attention of the person he was look-ing for. A few sharks circled at the outer edges of the flotsam, and more dorsal fins cut their way through the abundance of dead fish. Thus far, the boat's pilot had not seen them attacking humans. Except for the one he was searching for, he did not care. *Bon appétit* to you, Sir Shark.

He noted a man beyond the debris, swimming toward the unseen shore in deft, efficient strokes, and steered in that direction. When he pulled alongside, the swim-mer turned onto his back, stared up at the boat's pilot, and upon recognition, formed a wide grin.

"Permission to come aboard, sir?"

"I've always wondered why you navy guys say that?"

"It means to get your butt down here and give me a hand—please."

"Can't. You'll have to get aboard by yourself."

"It's cold as hell, and there are sharks," said the man in the water.

"I wasn't joking. I have two broken ribs, and I can't help you, but you're right about the sharks. There are two headed this way now."

Squid clambered over the transom and lay catching his breath. "Guess who I saw on the big mama ship just before we collided."

"Sajacento?"

"How did you guess?"

"I saw a guy dressed in a green robe a few minutes ago, holding on to a wooden crate."

Squid's face clouded as he stood and went into the wheelhouse. "Where?"

Stanley squinted, and nodded. "Somewhere there."

"I'll take the helm." Squid said woodenly.

"No," Stanley said. He rode out a swell as he turned the *Lady Rosalie* about, then nudged up the throttle as they went back into the flotsam and survivors calling out to be saved.

"There's the seaplane," said Stanley, motioning at the large aircraft two hundred yards distant, taxiing precariously over the swells. A man stood in the open side hatch, calling out for survivors. Under other circumstances, he might have appeared heroic.

"He'll be unable to take off if he waits much longer," said Stanley.

"Terrible thought," said Squid. "Now give me the helm."

"No," Stanley steered past a terrorist who was turning blue from the cold.

"Remember I told you about my buddy? God what a great guy the Tanker was. Always laughing and ready to do the right thing."

They saw Sajacento at the same time. He wore no life jacket. Instead he had a green-clad arm wrapped around a flimsy crate and waved frantically at them with the other.

"Sounds like your friend was a good guy," said Stan Goldstein.

Squid kept his face hard as Stan made a lazy turn through a patch of frozen fish. "Sajacento didn't have to kill him—he just wanted to show how much he hated us."

"I understand."

The *Rosalie* idled as Stan finished the turn. The man in green was dead ahead, twenty yards distant. He looked miserable and cold, and pleaded in broken syllables of Arabic.

"Run over the son of a bitch."

"No."

"I *need* to kill him, Stan."

"You already have."

The Green Mullah began to lose his grip on the crate. His movements diminished until there was only the reflexive chattering of teeth.

They waited for another minute, until the mullah's eyes glazed and went dead and he drifted away from the crate, sinking slowly in a blossom of green.

"You've got the helm," Stanley said quietly.

Squid watched the dark water for another moment, then took the wheel, thoughtful as he slowly backed away. He turned and pushed the throttle up, leaving behind the bright green robes that swirled and billowed in the water as they descended out of sight.

Stan watched the big De Havilland seaplane crew take on two bodies. There were no more survivors in the icy water. He wondered how many they'd rescued.

A while later, they passed a coast guard helicopter, then a cutter headed for the disaster.

"Better push it up," said Stanley, eyeing the ominous clouds.

The seaplane flew past, climbing.

8:15 p.m.—Menlo Park, California

The white house with brown trim was small, less than a thousand square feet, a single floor with a single bedroom, kitchen and living room—a holdover from the days when citrus groves had lined the roads and highways. This particular home had belonged to the foreman at a ten-acre lemon grove, and now was one of the final grandfathered holdouts in the path of the urban sprawl that reached from Santa Rosa to Gilroy.

It was a particularly desirable location, since it was within walking distance of Stanford University.

A K-7 satellite, controlled from a blue cubelike facility

in Sunnyvale at what had been Moffett Naval Air Station and was now operated by NASA, had been periodically focused upon the small home for the past three hours. This particular satellite was equipped with highly classified radar and IR detectors that observed through the walls of structures. The request to do so at this location, and at three other specific addresses near other western universities, had been approved under the auspices of the PATRIOT Act. Since no one was taking chances regarding political condemnations, authorization had been granted by a Justice of the Supreme Court.

Two black Ford Excursions were parked on the secluded street only four doors away from the small home. The first was manned by FBI agents in charge from the San Francisco office. They monitored the cell phone inside the house—issued by Kamil to the two *jahid*—and were also in contact with members of Jack Hammer's West Coast HRT, forty-three of whom were manning strategic points around the neighborhood. The house was stoppered.

In the second vehicle were an agent-driver and three senior personnel, including the FBI's deputy director for West Coast operations, the Department of Homeland Security's officer-in-charge for the state of California, and the chief of police for the City of Menlo Park.

In the middle seat were Erin Frechette, who was fulfilling a promise to herself and Frank, and Link Anderson, who was there to ensure her safety. Both had received emergency medical treatment at Stanford Hospital, and were to return as soon as possible.

One hour earlier, they'd received confirmation that there were two persons in the small home. Neighboring residents were quietly removed to a radius of one-half mile and asked not to contact anyone, including the media. It was not a drill, they were told. Americans were at risk.

The same had been done at the other three safe houses. No one had argued.

Erin had revealed the HF frequencies for the remote detonating devices—two each: one for arming, another for detonation—at all the locations except this small house. The driver-agent waited with transmitter in hand to set in the numbers for the Menlo Park house.

When told of the operation, some officials had expressed concern at the summary justice. *What if innocents are harmed?*

They were told that was improbable. If there were no bombs, nothing would happen.

The president had taken no time at all with his go-ahead.

"Ten minutes to go," said the DHS officer in charge. The teams at all the safe houses were in continuous contact. The plan was to set them off concurrently, so none of the terrorists would be alerted if they were watching the news.

He looked back at Erin, since she alone had the frequencies.

They received a radio transmission from the other vehicle. "They're getting a cell phone call!"

As they waited for the message, tension mounted.

Erin leaned forward. "The remote, please." The driver-agent hesitated.

"Give it to her," said the FBI deputy director. It was a part of Erin's deal.

The voice on the radio announced: "The *jahid*s were just told that they've been compromised, and to get ready to move."

"Damn!" exclaimed the DHS officer.

Calls began to come through from other locations. The other *jahid*s were getting similar calls.

Erin set in and double-checked the frequencies: 67.12 and 71.55. She pressed the status button, found the battery was fully charged.

"Link?" she asked.

"This one's yours."

She remembered what had been done to Frank Dubois and herself.

The explosion blasted a gaping hole in the side of the small home.

One minute later, they were advised that the last of the safe houses had been destroyed, along with the terrorists in each.

Epilogue

July 4, Boudie Springs

Link got up to put more firewood in the potbelly stove.

Maggie hmphed and turned away. "Now I remember why I left you last time. All you think of is yourself."

They'd been arguing about his cavalier approach to her career. When Link had picked her up in Kalispell that morning, they'd not seen one another for more than a month. After the confrontation at the Weeping Tree, he had maintained his anonymity, but everyone knew about Maggie Tatro and how she'd stopped the terrorist attacks and uncovered the Serpientes. There were film offers and book deals, although she would not take them because they'd be lies if she omitted Link.

"You could be *Time*'s Man of the Year if you weren't so pigheaded."

"Frank insists on no publicity."

"Baloney." Maggie wiggled herself deeper under the down comforter. "If someone offered you a million dollars, you wouldn't take it if it meant getting your face on television. Look at what Gordon did to you, and you haven't mentioned a word about him to anyone."

"Gordon thought he was right."

She dripped a little sarcasm. "He's your friend, right?"

Five weeks had passed since her surgery, and she had recovered well. Only a small amount of residual soreness reminded her of the loss of her spleen. Link had also been fortunate. The .45 round from Chief Welk's automatic had severed the bone above his elbow. He'd spent a week at Massachusetts General, where the surgeons had inserted a titanium rod that extended most of the length of the humerus.

Link had cajoled her by telephone—had even made the first call—to meet at the cabin, knowing they both needed it.

Maggie Tatro had done her job in outstanding fashion, and she deserved the FBI's offer of promotion and a position in the Washington office, which she was still considering. Stanley "Ten-Ex" Goldstein would be in nearby Quantico, ASAC of the tactical firearms courses.

There was another deserving heroine, who also called Link often. Erin was getting her face repaired, and was pleased that so far she'd been able to keep off some of the weight she had lost. With her figure, he could not understand. Nor could he understand the way Maggie grumbled whenever he talked about Erin.

"Happy birthday," Maggie said in a sweeter voice, reminding him that he had turned forty-one years of age an hour before.

It was not a pleasant thought, to be forty-one.

"I think we should make up again," she added.

"You're a sex maniac," Link said happily.

Maggie turned to him and was revealed in the flicker of the fire, showing off the cute little twist to her mouth as well as the other features that endeared her to him.

In the background, Willie Nelson sang "Georgia on My Mind."

Life was good again.

About the Author

TOM "BEAR" WILSON was a career United States Air Force officer with three thousand hours of flying time, mostly in fighters. During his five hundred hours of combat flying he was highly decorated. Since leaving the military Mr. Wilson has worked as a private investigator, newspaper publisher, and program manager for a high-tech company in Silicon Valley. He has published eight novels and recently appeared on the History Channel's *Suicide Missions, The Wild Weasel Story*. When he is not visiting locations to obtain background material for his books, Mr. Wilson resides in the Big Thicket country of East Texas.

ACCLAIMED AUTHOR
TOM WILSON

"WILSON JOINS THE RANKS OF TOP
MILITARY NOVELISTS."
—W.E.B. GRIFFIN

BLACK SKY

WHEN A RESPECTED US SENATOR IS FOUND
DEAD—KILLED BY HIS OWN PEOPLE, THE
MANIDO-OJIBWE TRIBE—A TREATY PREVENTS
THE FBI FROM INVESTIGATING THE CRIME.
ENTER NATIVE AMERICAN COVERT OPERATIVE
LINK ANDERSON.

"TOM WILSON IS EVERY BIT AS GOOD AS
COONTS, BROWN, AND CLANCY."
—USAF COLONEL GLENN DAVIS

0-451-19556-6

AVAILABLE WHEREVER BOOKS ARE SOLD OR AT
WWW.PENGUIN.COM